OMOO.

THIS map is intended to show the relative position of the Marquesas and Tahiti.

The black line described, inland, about the N.W. peninsula of Tahiti, is intended to represent the course of the "Broom Road."

The lines drawn round about Tahiti and Eimeo represent the course of the encircling reefs.

OMOO:

A NARRATIVE OF ADVENTURES
IN THE SOUTH SEAS

HERMAN MELVILLE

Edited by
Harrison Hayford
and
Walter Blair

HENDRICKS HOUSE, INC.

NEW YORK   1969

PS
2384
B5
1969

Manufactured in Italy by
Tipografia Luigi Parma s.p.a. - Bologna

TO

HERMAN GANSEVOORT,

OF GANSEVOORT, SARATOGA COUNTY, NEW YORK,

THIS WORK

Is cordially Inscribed

BY HIS NEPHEW,

THE AUTHOR.

CONTENTS.

CONTENTS. xi

EDITORS' PREFACE

The text of this edition of *Omoo* follows that of the first American edition, published by Harper and Brothers in New York, about 1 May 1847. A few errors have been corrected. A collation with the first English edition, published by John Murray in London, about 1 April 1847, has revealed only unimportant variations. The English edition was based upon the American proof-sheets, and is therefore a later text; but Melville does not seem to have been responsible for the numerous minor alterations in it, most of which simply bring it into conformity with English conventions of spelling and punctuation. The author never revised the book.

The 1892 edition, published in New York by the United States Book Company, was based upon the first English edition, and contained a few alterations and corrections by Arthur Stedman, the editor. The text in Constable's Standard Edition of Melville's *Works*, London, 1922-1924, drew upon both first editions but adhered to neither. The plates of Stedman's edition were used in the *Omoo* published by L. C. Page and Company, Boston. Among other editions recently in print, that in Everyman's Library follows the first American edition; also that in *Romances of Herman Melville* (Pickwick Publishers, 1929; Tudor Publishing Company, 1931) follows the first American edition. In none of these are found such important variations as those in some currently available texts of *Typee* and *Moby-Dick*.

This edition was prepared in the years 1947-1951, and during that time we were in friendly communication with scholars who were studying other aspects of Melville's life and works for books some of which have since been published with generous acknowledgment of our assistance. Now it is our personal as well as professional pleasure to give public thanks for their help to Jay Leyda, Merrell R. Davis, Leon Howard, Gordon Roper, Merton M. Sealts, Jr., John H. Birss, and J. L. Earnshaw. Special gratitude is due to Wilson L. Heflin who exchanged information and shared his discoveries with us while preparing his study of Melville's whaling years; by his painstaking and cautionary criticism he tried to make our work as accurate and thorough as his own—it is not his fault if he did not succeed. Thanks for criticism and encouragement of other sorts are offered to Josephine W. Hayford, Wallace W. Douglas, Walter B. Scott, Jr., and Dr. Charles F. Wishart.

In our Explanatory Notes we are most heavily indebted to Charles R. Anderson for the indispensable use of his *Melville in the South Seas* (1939). This was the first book to reveal Melville's method of patching the fabric of his own experiences with cloth from other bolts. Anderson's search for source books was so exhaustive that we have been unable to discover any used by Melville which he did not find. With only *Omoo* to account for, however, we have been able to study Melville's use of these books much more closely than the scope of Anderson's work permitted him to do, and we believe this closer study has justified us in modifying some of his conclusions about *Omoo*. We make full acknowledgment here of our continuous use of his *Melville in the South Seas*; to mention our debt to it upon each occasion would be hopelessly repetitious.

We have been privileged to use resources of the libraries of Northwestern University and the University of Chicago; the Newberry Library; the New York Public Library; the Mitchell Library, Sydney, Australia; the Houghton Library, Harvard University; and the Library of Congress. We have received research funds from the Graduate School, Northwestern University.

Finally, we confess with pleasure our debt to our genial General Editor, Howard P. Vincent.

HARRISON HAYFORD
WALTER BLAIR

Evanston and Chicago, Illinois
1951

Circumstances have conspired to delay publication of this volume for some years. The Editors' Introduction and Explanatory Notes have been revised somewhat and certain sections have been omitted, mostly to take account of books published since they were first written. Our detailed account of the circumstances of composition and publication was made unnecessary by the excellent treatment of these, in context, by Merrell R. Davis in *Melville's* MARDI: *A Chartless Voyage* (1952). Unfortunately his examination and bibliography of the reviews, the most thorough to date, remain unpublished in his Yale dissertation (1947). Jay Leyda's *The Melville Log* (1951) and Leon Howard's *Herman Melville* (1951) fill in the account of the years 1846-1847 when *Omoo* was written, published, and reviewed, as well as the year 1842 when the events it relates took place. In our comments on the reviews we had remarked that " The fact is that both the hostile and the favorable reviews of *Omoo*, as well as of Melville's other books, especially in the New York press, were motivated to an as yet undetermined extent by the personal, political, commercial, and critical affiliations of a clique-ridden little literary world which historians of American literary activity have not yet mapped."

Now that world has been opened up wide by John Stafford's *The Literary Criticism of ' Young America.' A Study in the Relation of Politics and Literature, 1837-1850* (1953), and brilliantly explored by Perry Miller's *The Raven and the Whale. The War of Words and Wits in the Era of Poe and Melville* (1956). One valuable study has not been cited: that is Edwin H. Rosenberry's *Melville and the Comic Spirit* (1953), which not only places *Omoo* in the tradition indicated in our Introduction, but views Melville's work as a whole from the perspective of its comic rather than its tragic qualities. The broad significance of Melville's Polynesian experiences and ' primitivism ' is examined in James Baird's *Ishmael* (1956). In preparation for the press at the same time as this edition is Wilson Heflin's book on Melville's whaling years.

One work we have now made extensive use of is the French translation, *Omoo, ou le Vagabond du Pacifique,* by Jacqueline Foulque (Gallimard: Paris, 1951). Its unique value lies in the translator's knowledge of Polynesian languages and the care she has taken to 'correct' Melville's erratic forms. We have cited her readings in the Explanatory Notes (see note on 2.28). Full acknowledgment is here made of our debt to the scholarship of her excellent translation.

A word as to the division of editorial labors. The Explanatory Notes, likewise the determination of the text, with the Textual Notes, and the Appendix, are the work of Mr. Hayford, as criticized and revised by Mr. Blair. The Editors' Introduction was a joint undertaking: some parts were written by Mr. Blair (xvii to xix, paragraph 3; xxxiv to xlix), others by Mr. Hayford (xix, paragraph 3, to end of xxxiii; xlix, paragraph 2, to lii); sections written by each have now been jettisoned; and all of it as it stands has been several times revised by both editors. Mr. Hayford undertook to see the edition through the press.

A further great obligation has been incurred, to a most gracious gentleman and friend, Mario Casalini, of La Nuova Italia Editrice, Firenze, whose generous assistance was indispensable among the circumstances that at last made possible the publication of this edition.

HARRISON HAYFORD

Fiesole
May, 1957

For various reasons this volume has remained in page proofs since 1957; it is now published without revision and without reference to scholarly works that have appeared in the meantime.

Fiesole, 1969.

EDITORS' INTRODUCTION

In *Typee* (1846), his first book, the pattern of Melville's experiences had enabled him to tell a fairly unified story. The beginning had been his escape from a ship; the bulk of the narrative, his life ashore among the natives; and the end, his escape from them to another ship. His single subject, as he himself stated it, had been " Polynesian life in its primitive state." The contrasts offered by " civilized " life as represented by the American whaleship and the French warships had helped highlight the felicities of the Happy Valley. To be sure, some friction between his " plot " and his theme had presented a problem: after all he was a captive of cannibals, and his fears of being tattooed or eaten by them, which motivated his escape, obviously contradicted his case for their simple goodness. But by managing his emphases he had made use of both points, one for suspense, the other for theme; and moreover the contradiction embodied paradoxes of thought and feeling that were to prove fruitfully troubling through his whole literary career.

The success of *Typee* called for a second book, and the composition of this book, *Omoo,* presented tougher problems. One was the problem of just what segment of his experiences to take up, where to begin and end, and what to develop as his subject. Another was how to spin out and build up his actual experiences, none of which had the inherent richness of those he had used in *Typee.* And still another problem was that of reconciling his characterization of himself, his attitude toward himself and his experiences, with the development of a serious theme.

For this second book much material was left from Melville's Pacific experiences; he could draw upon his two years of wanderings from the time when he left the Typee valley to the time when he got back to the United States. During these years his rovings had taken him on the Australian whaleship *Lucy Ann* from the Marquesas to Tahiti (August-September, 1842), where the crew had revolted; to the native jail ashore; thence for a few days' stroll around the islands; thence aboard another whaleship for a six-months' cruise (November, 1842—April, 1843); to Hawaii, where he lived for three months (May-August, 1843); and thence on an American frigate, by a devious route, home to the United States (October, 1844). But if he were to tell all these wanderings in one book, he would merely produce an episodic sea narrative or a journal of travels such as many others had written. He had already gone beyond such shapeless summaries in *Typee*, where his originality in the genre had shown in his developing one action and one theme. Its form and technique brought that book closer to the novel than to the travel narrative or journal—so much so that it was at once suspected of being fictitious and is still usually classified and criticized as a romance or novel.

What Melville chose to do when he wrote *Omoo*, during 1846, was to deal with his life from the time when he was rescued from the Typees by his second whaleship to the time when he boarded his third, which carried him away from Tahiti. Therefore, *Omoo*, as he indicated in his preface, dealt with at least three matters: the wild kind of shipboard life led by Pacific whaling crews; " the present condition of the converted Polynesians as affected by their promiscuous intercourse with foreigners, and the teachings of the missionaries combined; " and his experiences as " a roving sailor " about the islands. The last matter gave its title (" Omoo "—a rover) to the book.

One can speculate about Melville's reasons for adopting such a scheme. He evidently felt impelled, somehow, to tie *Omoo* up to his earlier book: his preface remarks that the present narrative "necessarily" begins where *Typee* concludes. This feeling, and the narrative value of the unruly crew and their revolt, brought in the story of his weeks on the Australian whaleship *Lucy Ann*. Further, *Omoo*, like *Typee*, was designed for John Murray's informative travel series, and so it had to include plenty of factual material. This brought in his "observations" of the condition of the natives, of flora, fauna, buildings, customs, and so on. At the same time, he recognized the appeal of a racy narrative of comic and titillating scenes. Finally, as *Mardi* was shortly to prove, he was not fully aware of the disadvantages of a sprawling structure. All of these and probably less obvious considerations made integration of the sort he had achieved in *Typee* impossible and led him to write an episodic book which hardly could be expected to have unity of either action or theme.

But even though he allowed himself so wide a range, Melville had trouble spinning his actual experiences and observations out of his own head to the desired length. In his preface, all the same, he disingenuously presented *Omoo* to the public as "a circumstantial history of the adventures befalling the author" during "about three months" at Tahiti and Imeeo. His claim was that, though unfortunately he could not draw upon a journal for dates, his frequent recounting of his adventures had kept his memory of them accurate. He insisted that for the most part he had "merely described what he has seen."

A number of contemporary readers found support for his claims of veracity. They traced his footsteps through Tahiti and Imeeo and had no trouble authenticating the revolt on the Sydney whaler and confirming the veritable existence of Consul Wilson and Dr. Johnstone (who displayed Melville's name in his dose book and uttered threats to sue the publisher of *Omoo*). They saw the Calabooza Beretanee and got word of Long Ghost, Father Murphy, Mr. Bell the sugar-planter, and of Shorty and Zeke with their potatoes. One of them even ran into poor carpenter Willie, who had meanwhile won his little Lullee. Still, most readers at the time and through the years were happy to take *Omoo* simply as good reading and wasted no worry over its authenticity. Three-quarters of a century after the book appeared Melville's first biographers transcribed it as dependable autobiography, with scarcely a suspicion that in writing it he had recorded anything more than he had experienced. He had, it was assumed, only given heightened expression to his simple observations and recollections.

Some of Melville's contemporaries, however, sensed that his claims about the truth of *Omoo* were by no means candid. Some of them scouted his experiences as romance, others branded the "observations" as libel, and a few pounced upon errors in particular passages. And Melville himself in his own preface indicated that he had made use of some printed sources; upon several points connected with history and local customs, he had, he said, gathered "collateral information" from "the oldest books of South Sea voyages and also from the 'Polynesian Researches' of Ellis." He had also at times "deemed it advisable to quote previous voyages, in corroboration of what is offered as the fruit of the author's own observation."

In the 1930's, scholars prying into Melville's life and works found that he had greatly understated his indebtedness to other writers. Robert S. Forsythe, in several articles, and notably Charles R. Anderson, in his book *Melville in the South Seas* (1939), told what they had found when they had dug into obscure records and forgotten books. They found, indeed, that the history they had pieced together corroborated the general narrative outlines of *Typee, Omoo,* and *White-Jacket.* But they also found that Melville was not always accurate, or even truthful, within the bounds of "simple recollection." In sum, Anderson revealed that, far more than anyone had ever suspected, Melville had compounded autobiography with fictional techniques. He had altered facts and dates, elaborated events, assimilated foreign materials, invented episodes, and dramatized the printed experiences of others as his own. He had not plagiarized, merely, for he had always rewritten and nearly always improved the passages he appropriated.

Yet he had composed his books in a way he had not really acknowledged, and in a way that even his most suspicious contemporary critics had never dreamed.

But we believe that even Anderson understated the pervasiveness of these fictional procedures in *Omoo*. From the biographical facts and literary sources Anderson had assembled, it appeared true of *Omoo* that "most of these adventures were drawn almost literally from actual experiences, in this most strictly autobiographical of all Melville's works.... In spite of some embellishments here and there, always obviously motivated, the entire fabric seems to be remarkably veracious...." [pp. 109, 309.] Forsythe's conclusion was similar. Now, however, we believe that such a description of the book must be modified. For we have found that one can distinguish throughout *Omoo* the same procedures that Anderson uncovered most fully in *White-Jacket*.

New evidence since the publication of Anderson's book throws another light on the experiences and observations behind *Omoo*. Most important, Consul Wilson's official records of the *Lucy Ann* revolt have come to light, wormholed but wonderfully complete. They disclose full particulars of that serio-comic affair and sharply contradict details of the account Melville gave, particularly of his role in it. The identity of his "Vineyard whaler" has also been ferreted out, and thereby the term of his stay at the islands and the date of his farewell have been fixed. More of the borrowings from other books that fattened *Omoo* have proved identifiable. Putting together the known facts and identified borrowings, we can gauge the surprising extent to which Melville modified strictly autobiographical elements by the fictional procedures already defined by Anderson. In the Explanatory Notes, at the back of this volume, all these matters are set forth in documentary detail.

When Melville wrote his "autobiographical" South-Sea books he drew not only upon his memory and invention but also upon other books. Still he was by no means a scholar of South-Sea literature—even for *Moby-Dick* he

was not to "swim through libraries." It has now become
clear that usually, while first writing his manuscripts, he
had no more than two or three books close at hand. From
them he freely drew fact and suggestion whenever memory
ran thin or invention flagged. These might be called his
prompt-books. From a few others—to adopt a cavalier figure
he applied to his labors on *Moby-Dick*—he shook various
seasonings over the whole manuscript while it was cooking,
or already cooked.

In writing *Typee* Melville was prompted again and
again by Stewart's *Visit to the South Seas* and less frequently by Langsdorff's *Voyages and Travels.* Later he added
further "observations" from Stewart's *Visit* and David
Porter's *Journal.* Although he acknowledged using Ellis's
Polynesian Researches in *Typee,* he found it actually of
only slight assistance. In writing *Omoo,* by contrast, this
work became his major prompt-book.

Embarking early in 1846 on the composition of *Omoo,*
with lively memories of the *Lucy Ann* affair and a free-
working imagination to expand them, Melville had pretty
clear narrative sailing all the way to Tahiti. From the outset,
however, he invented expansively. He did so, doubtless,
because he realized that his memories were not abundant
enough to fill out a book, and also because his instincts
were spontaneously those of the born story-teller, who im-
proves the facts without being exactly a liar, because he is
true to what ought to have happened. Such properly dilated
versions of his real adventures were doubtless what Melville's frequent forecastle and fireside retelling of them had
stamped on his memory. By the time he sat down to write,
in his own mind fiction was no doubt already inextricably
fused with the facts.

In writing this second book, moreover, Melville had his
Library readers in mind from the start. As he assured
Murray, "a little experience in this art of book craft" had
"done wonders" for him. To entertain and inform his
readers, and lengthen his manuscript for two-volume publication, he prolonged the Australian whaleship's stay in the
Marquesas by several weeks. Because he needed help in

detaining her, for Chapters 6, 7, 8, he took another look into his recent prompt-books. From Stewart probably he drew a short sermon (Ch. 6) upon the wanton cruelty of sea-captains to the natives, and, on the basis of this, invented an exemplum which improbably dressed meek Captain Guy in cutlass, boarding-belt, and pistols, and sent him filibustering ashore to pot a poor native in the rear with a pistol-shot. From Langsdorff he took the tattooers of La Dominica (Ch. 8), inventing a character, Lem Hardy, to tell him about them. Later something about this group of chapters bothered Melville, and after the manuscript was completed he decided to cut out the two originally numbered V and VII. One possibility is that the borrowed materials from Stewart and Langsdorff, and the cancelled chapters (if indeed they were both finally cancelled) may have been leftovers from *Typee* which he was economically trying to salvage. (Captain Guy's exploit certainly seems more appropriate to " Captain Vangs " of the *Dolly*, who shot albatross off Cape Horn and tabu birds in the Vale of Tior.)

After verbally quitting the Marquesas, Melville sailed merrily along toward Tahiti with his narrative, filling up sprightly chapters (8-17) with personalities and antics, real and imaginary, aboard the old whaler. He had an eye all the time to their representative quality, and an ear to Dana and possibly to more obscure printed " voices from the forecastle." Sighting the Coral Islands (Ch. 17), he could give them in his first draft, it appears, only a few fanciful remarks, but later he evidently inserted nine or ten supplementary paragraphs about their topography, geology, history, and commerce. This sound information he gleaned from Ellis's *Researches*, Wilkes's *Exploring Expedition*, and Russell's *Polynesia*. With the peaks of Tahiti in narrative view (Ch. 18) Melville evoked the famous island's magic associations by quoting the words of Bougainville and summoning the shades of other illustrious navigators—from his little summary compendium of voyages, *Circumnavigation of the Globe*. Ellis and Stewart were also of use in his remarks on the island.

Memory and liberal imagination were, for the most part, sufficient to the demands of twenty more chapters (19-38) about the revolt and the ensuing consular, constabulary, and medical affairs afloat and ashore. Melville interrupted his recital of this comic history only with Chapter 32, on the "Proceedings of the French at Tahiti," which he patched together from memory and journalistic accounts. But he did in time draw upon his authorities for some details. To show Jermin's foolhardiness and skill in bringing the ship into port unaided (Ch. 26), he took from Wilkes some facts about the harbor. Very likely, also, he took from Wilkes some suggestions for his comical scene with old Jim the native pilot. He reminded himself of the Broom Road and the picturesque scenery of the island (Ch. 30) by glances at Wilkes and Stewart. He may have been reminded by Olmsted's *Incidents of a Whaling Voyage* of an old whale-ship from the port of Hudson, New York, which lay bilged on the beach. All of these passages, as well as a few footnotes and some slight passages from Ellis, bear the mark of proba-ble later insertion.

Thus the affair of the *Lucy Ann*, from Melville's signing aboard in the first chapter, to her sailing from Tahiti in the thirty-eighth, gave him substantially the first half of his materials for *Omoo*. Although he dramatized and in-vented as he pleased, he needed no prompt-book in order to create any organic part of his early narrative, excepting for the two chapters in the Marquesas (adapted from *Typee* leftovers?) and perhaps the half-chapter on Jim the pilot. From the internal evidence it seems likely, therefore, that he took little from open books in the original process of telling the *Lucy Ann* story. Evidently he worked most of the expository borrowings into the manuscript later as insertions designed primarily to load it with solid in-formation.

But the second half of his materials, that is his ensuing experiences on the two islands, obviously put demands upon Melville which drove him to open a book. After all, his whole stay on the two islands had lasted scarcely over a month. He needed not only heavier drafts of information for expository padding but suggestions for the creation of organic episodes in the action.

As soon as he had written the passage in which the Australian whaleship sailed, Melville's memories struck a shoal. Sure token of this is the heavy proportion of borrowed material in the chapters (39-49) dealing with his life and observations while he was residing in the Calabooza and before he decamped for Imeeo. Although he had only slight experiences to tell, he was faced with the task of supplying his Library readers with some solid information about the condition of Tahiti. For this he turned to Ellis's *Polynesian Researches.*

Through the rest of his account of the islands, Melville fastened upon the pages of Ellis, and Ellis proved to be a bounteous guide, if not philosopher and friend. Not once did Melville cite Ellis as his authority: he simply set down Ellis's information without credit, or claimed it as his own observation, or credited it to a native informant— to " Captain Bob," or " Tonoi," for example. Little reverence as Melville paid him, Ellis was his historian, geographer, botanist, anthropologist, dictionary of native words common and proper, and even his eyes and ears. Although Melville claimed that in the Calabooza (Ch. 33) he had " a fine opportunity of making observations " on the condition of the natives, it was Ellis who observed for him their diseases, physique, size, color, and preference of dark skin to sickly European white. Melville inserted such details in a lump as his own "observations"; but similar information in the pages of Ellis soon suggested whole chapters of *Omoo* with only a slight infusion of memories. So, when Melville told of going church, Ellis furnished the entire chapter (44): first his account of the Royal Mission Chapel twenty years earlier, and then his " eyewitness " description of the interior of the contemporary "Church of the Cocoa-nuts " which he was attending—an interior from another church on another island, also twenty years earlier. At church, it was Ellis who enabled Melville to point out the ingenious substitutes for church-bells, to sound off Old Hundred, and to comment on the singing.

And the chances are that it was Ellis who supplied the
hints for Melville's most brilliant invention, the wonderful
missionary sermon. But Melville declared with a straight
face that he heard this impossible travesty delivered in
Tahitian by " a good old missionary " and translated into
pidgin English on the spot by " a Hawaiian sailor " named
Jack. After church, Ellis explained the filiation between
old heathen taboo-day and Christian Sabbath, enabling
Melville to draw an ironic reflection from it. Ellis was
fashion-book for the whole chapter (47) on " How They
Dress in Tahiti." With a smile he pointed out native
women in horrid straw hats and related how his own wife
and other missionary ladies had taught them to make these
monstrosities. But Melville said he heard this " report " and
piously " trusted " it was " nothing but scandal." Ellis told
about native men shoehorned into odds and ends of European dress, and described the dignified costumes of their
ancestors; Melville (who doubtless had seen similar sights)
borrowed the queer outfits for " Kooloo " and " a bachelor
friend of Captain Bob."

While Melville took over what he pleased from Ellis,
he read his pages carelessly, or deliberately rejected his
statements. For example, Ellis deplored the old custom of
a week's binge on breadfruit baked in a community oven.
Melville misunderstood, taking *opio* to be the festive-
gathering rather than the breadfruit itself. And he credited
the misinformation to " Captain Bob " whom he furthermore caused to deny that the week-long orgies had any
" immoral tendencies." When Ellis told about all the ancient games and pastimes of the island—and patiently explained their inextricable connection with the " abomi-
nations " of idolatry—Melville deliberately refused to credit his report: they were, so he said, " pleasant and
seemingly innocent." When Ellis gave the history of missionary attempts to introduce cotton and sugar as native in-
dustries and attributed their failure to the cupidity of interfering white traders, Melville disregarded this reason and
blamed inherent native laziness. And so on.

Information, in short, Melville was obliged and evi-

dently quite willing to take wholesale from Ellis, as a
neutral commodity. But not attitudes. He was sure that
his own month of familiar intercourse with the natives, as
a beachcomber, had shown him " more of their real dispositions and habits " than the missionaries, as men in spiritual authority, could discover in years—or at least more
than they would usually admit. He wanted to inform
his Library readers that missionary reports were giving
them a sentimentalized, Sunday-school picture of Tahiti.
What he had honestly seen, and honestly wanted to say,
he had put in what was evidently his conclusion to his
argument as originally written: " so far as mere temporal
felicity is concerned, the Tahitians are far worse off now
than formerly; and although their circumstances, upon
the whole, are bettered by the presence of the missionaries,
the benefits conferred by the latter become utterly insignificant when confronted with the vast preponderance
of evil brought about by other means." In this, no doubt,
he was on pretty solid ground, and no objective modern
reader is likely to quarrel with this conclusion. But as he
later elaborated his argument his honest intentions were
subverted, more than he probably realized, by the temp-
tations of forensics and rhetoric. They were marked too,
one must conclude, by some real hostility to the missionaries and their kind of religion. He confused, for himself
and his readers, what the missionaries had misguidedly
done or impotently failed to do, their sins of omission, with
the sins of commission of the white traders, sailors, invaders, as a whole.

For the abounding information, then, Ellis was Melville's major source in the group probably of four chapters
(45, 46, 47, 49), which he originally worked up on the
condition of Tahiti under the missionaries. But for in-
terpretation Ellis was of no help. For that, on second
thought, Melville went to other books; and if his " reflections " were at first, as he asserted, " spontaneous," they
were in his later additions bolstered by some " philosophic
research," though he disclaimed " pretensions " to such.
In Chapter 48, at least, when he "paused to bestow some-

thing more than a cursory glance" upon "Tahiti As It Is," he
followed the philosophic reservations, and even more closely
the topics, quotations, and footnotes, of the unevangelical
Reverend Michael Russell's *Polynesia*. This chapter, spill-
ing over into the first two paragraphs of Chapter 49, he
evidently added as an afterthought to the original ones
based on Ellis. For secondary assistance in the whole group
Melville plundered Lieutenant Wilkes's chapters on Tahiti
in the third volume of his *Exploring Expedition*. And,
probably in a last-minute nervous ballasting of the whole
group of chapters, just before he showed the manuscript
to his friend Evert Duyckinck in December, 1846, he
"deemed it advisable to quote previous voyages in corroboration of what is offered as the fruit of the author's
own observations." These were the volumes of Kotzebue
and Beechey to which Russell's footnotes and quotations
had directed his attention; those of Daniel Wheeler and
W. S. Ruschenberger (or a source quoting his book); and
probably those of "the oldest voyagers," Captains Cook
and Vancouver, and the *Duff* missionaries. From each of
these voyagers Melville quoted in a way that can only be
described as unscrupulous. Elsewere in *Omoo* he used
their volumes not at all, or only slightly, in scattered
passages that are probably late insertions.

With these expository-argumentative chapters, Melville's
most troublesome job of composition was out of the way,
though he probably set them aside for intermittent tinker-
ing while he was turning out his chapters on Imeeo. Still,
his troubles were not over. His real Imeeo experiences,
occupying only about two weeks in late October and early
November, 1842, rather than the ten or eleven weeks he
allows, provided a narrative skeleton but not enough flesh.
His remaining narrative fell into three sequences, corresponding in general to his experiences: potato-grubbing
and bullock-hunting (Ch. 51-60), with a side-excursion to
Tamai (Ch. 61-65); then journeying round the beach (Ch.
66-72); and, finally, visiting the Queen and signing aboard
the American whaleship at Partoowye (Ch. 73-82). To
fill out each sequence he was forced to invent and to borrow

more and more heavily for fact and suggestion from Ellis.

For the first sequence (Ch. 51-60), Melville had usable memories of farming and loafing, and probably of hunting, with Shorty and Zeke. He had no difficulty in writing eight or nine chapters from his memories. Even here, however, he wrote with an eye on Ellis, and later he added a chapter mostly from Wilkes. Consulting Ellis's pages about this neighborhood, he learned or was reminded of three of its features—its luxuriant groves of trees, its vestiges of former inhabitants, and the nearby mission-station at Afrehitoo. So he spliced in "observations" (credited to Zeke and " Tonoi ") on the trees and the depopulation (in Ch. 55), and probably took a hint for " Musquitoes " (Ch. 56) and a Sunday visit to the church at Afrehitoo (Ch. 58). For all three topics he drew details from other pages of Ellis, and he managed to wring from each a symbol of Christian failure or white depredation. In Wilkes's chapters on Hawaii Melville found many details about hunting wild cattle there. Some of these he dramatized as a story about Tonoi's brother's being gored and carried for hours on a wild bullock's horns; some he tossed together with other information about Hawaii, its volcanoes, and its cattle industry. He inserted the resulting paragraphs as "Some Account of the Wild Cattle in Polynesia " (Ch. 54).

A few pages further along in Ellis's volume, Melville's eye fell on a description of the sequestered lake and village of Tamai, part of the account of Ellis's own journeys across and around the island from Afrehitoo to Partoowye. Stimulated by this, he invented rather than remembered a week's side-excursion to an unspoiled native village. We can be sure it is invention because he confessed to Murray that he had salvaged its vital core, the dance or " old-fashioned hevar," from a rejected chapter of *Typee,* and furthermore because he confused its geography, placing it in the heart of the island to the west of Martair rather than in its true location between the mountain and the sea on the northeast coastal plain. (Melville's notion and account, as well as the map he supplied, of the geography of Imeeo were all cockeyed.) But he doubtless included some real memo-

ries in his story of this excursion, memories perhaps of the
preparations for departure and of the mysterious native
with musty old sailor-trousers for sale.

For the second sequence (Ch. 66-72), the journey round
the beach, Melville dipped even more deeply into Ellis.
He had memories mostly, apparently, of exhilarating
weather, beautiful landscape, and painful passage for ill-
shod feet over sharp rocks and burning sands. Actually
his journey can have taken up only one or two days of his
probable two weeks or so in Imeeo. In *Omoo* he stretched
it out to ten, punctuating it by three leisurely stopovers
with hospitable natives along the way. In telling of all three
of these visits he moulded slight memories around the
printed suggestions of Ellis. At the first stop, with old Darby
and Joan (Ch. 67), he sounded Ellis's theme of Polynesian
hospitality. At the second he developed it fully. Three
native maidens (with romantic names right out of Ellis)
welcomed him and the Long Doctor to "Loohooloo,"
where a white-bearded native host heaped before them (Ch.
68) an "old-fashioned Tahitian banquet" (exactly the same
served thereabouts to Ellis twenty years earlier—supplemented by dishes described elsewhere by Ellis). After
dinner he found food for reflection (Ch. 69) in a landscape
cursed by foreign guava bushes and blessed by native
cocoa-palms—both supplied by Ellis. He enjoyed "Life at
Loohooloo" (Ch. 70), spearing fish on the reefs by torch-
light at midnight, just as Ellis directed, and swinging
"over land and sea by the hour" on a native swing, as both
Ellis and Wilkes suggested. Bidding farewell to Ellis's
maidens, banquet, and sports, he and the Doctor took to
the beach again, admiring the picturesque reef and its
thunder of spray, with Ellis's, not his own, eyes and ears, and
perceiving its utility with Ellis's practical mind. Their
third host, "a dealer in the contraband," was likely enough
an old native they really encountered somewhere, but it
was certainly in the pages of Ellis that Melville encountered
the dealer's name and his *aoa* tree as well as his home-made
distilling apparatus and powerful brew of *ava*.

In the third and final sequence (Ch. 73-82), Melville

made his most daring and sustained raid upon Ellis. It is clear that he remembered very well meeting Mrs. Bell and her sunburned planter husband at Partoowye, also an English carpenter sighing for a native maid, and a rollicking band of beachcombers. The chances are good that, at Partoowye also, he really had seen Queen Pomare; we know he had signed aboard the *Charles & Henry* there. But his visual memories of the place must have been pretty dim indeed, and his other experiences very few, for he modelled his description of the village all too closely upon Ellis's description of the village of Fa-re, on the altogether different island of Huahine, as it had appeared to Ellis twenty years earlier. He followed closely the topics of Ellis's chapters. (Since they were the same chapters from which he had already taken his church scenes at Tahiti it is amusing to note that he thereby introduced a curious reduplication of the topics he had discussed in the Tahiti chapters.) In Ellis he found the native house of Eree-mear Po-Po (Ch. 74), whose Christian name and the reasons for it he also found, in another passage. Thanks to Ellis he saw the floor of dried ferns, the cocoa-nut-oil lamps, and the communal sleeping arrangements, including, it seems, even the brother's sailor-hammock. Through the courtesy of Ellis he viewed the village with its bamboo-picketed houses peeping into sight at odd angles to the serpentine avenue, and noticed their solitary panes of glass and strange-looking doors on clumsy wooden hinges. And through Ellis's helpful eyes, too, we suspect, he saw the half-finished European houses. He may even have dared to go so far as to metamorphose poor Ellis himself into the Yankee carpenter who built them. For like Ellis the carpenter was " a sober, steady man " who first " obtained the confidence of the several chiefs, and soon filled them with all sorts of ideas about the want of public spirit... and the humiliating fact of their living in paltry huts of bamboo, when magnificent palaces of boards might be so easily morticed together." This is precisely what Ellis did at Fa-re, as he proudly relates in the very paragraphs from which Melville was borrowing. The carpenter's fiasco, in this characteristic private joke of Melville's (if this is indeed what it is, as we suspect), was only what Melville had been attributing all along to the missionary efforts.

As for Queen Pomare, Melville may really have seen her, if not under quite the circumstances he relates, for she was indeed in residence at Partoowye at the time, a fugitive from the French. But he found in the same pages of Ellis the palace set on a coral pier, the rickety schoolhouse, and the octagonal Taloo chapel which he erroneously places also on a pier. He may have attended a native court, here or elsewhere, but his comic treatment of the laws and penalties was set off by Ellis's Code of Huahine. Marbonna may have been drawn from some noble Marquesan Melville recalled, but his presence at Pomare's court, carrying the two royal princes, was probably suggested by Ellis's discussion of this old custom of the chiefs, which Melville used at the end of the previous chapter. For that chapter (80) he took from Ellis the historical account of the Pomare dynasty, adding more recent developments from Stewart and Wilkes. With these final borrowings, Melville closed his invaluable volumes of Ellis.

Composition of *Omoo* was completed in late November, 1846, but during December Melville made last-minute revisions, and submitted the manuscript to Evert Duyckinck for his opinion and " hints." Three early chapters, he told Duyckinck, he had " rejected altogether," but their omission did not "break the continuity of the book." These were the ones " listed as Nos. V, VII, & XVII in the table of contents." He asked Duyckinck to pay particular attention to chapters " *33, 34*—& *45, 46, 47, 48, 49, 50.*" " They all," he wrote, " refer more or less to the missions & the condition of the natives." Since Melville may not have permanently rejected V, VII, and XVII, and may have cancelled or rearranged other chapters, we cannot be sure which published chapters are referred to in the second group. Chapters V and VII would have fallen on either side of the present Chapter 5 (which is a postdated version of ship's affairs that had taken place in the southern Marquesas prior to his coming aboard), and just before the present Chapters 6, 7, 8, which are fictitious. Chapter XVII would have followed the present Chapter 14, where there is no obvious gap. Melville's "*33, 34*" may have been the present Chapters 32 and (less probably) 33, and his "*45, 46, 47, 48, 49, 50*" were certainly the present Chapters 44-49, the heart of his exposure of conditions at Tahiti under missionaries. [For the quoted letters, see *Log*, I, 229; Davis, p. 29; Anderson, pp. 238-239.] Since *Typee*, published nine months before, had so offended some proper and evangelical-minded readers as to require expurgation both before and after publication, Melville's concern about the second book is understandable.

What is harder to understand, in view of such concern, is the fact that Melville renewed his attack upon the missionaries in *Omoo*, not only renewed it, but re-enforced it. Perhaps he returned to the attack because he was stung to perversity by the imputations of pious reviewers. Whatever the reason, he was not necessarily inconsistent in deleting the hostile passages from *Typee* and then immediately making similar charges, more fully developed, though far more carefully couched, in *Omoo*. For in *Typee*, as his letter of 15 July 1846 pointed out to John Murray, "Such passages are altogether foreign to the adventure," [Davis, pp. 202-203] while in *Omoo* he must rightly have considered them organic parts of his subject. In the Marquesas, after all, there were no missionaries; in Tahiti everything he saw seemed to be conditioned by their presence. Duyckinck thought he knew how to account for Melville's attitude and attack: "He owes a sailor's grudge to the Missionaries and pays it off at Tahiti. His account of the church building there is very much in the spirit of Dickens' humorous handling of sacred things in Italy." [Davis, p. 30.] Yet Duyckinck, a devout Episcopalian, was more amused than disturbed by these chapters—indeed he chose Chapter 44, on the Church of the Cocoa-nuts, as a sample extract to reprint in his weekly *Literary World*.

The book thus composed—from memories of his experiences, on the ill-regulated *Lucy Ann*, in and out of jail at Tahiti, and round about Imeeo; from other books; and from invention working upon all these—was unavoidably and undisguisedly episodic. But it was pulled together to some extent by Melville's portrayal of himself in it as " Omoo," the first person narrator. The scenes, characters, and attitudes expressed were, to a degree at least, inter-related because they were refracted through the senses and the mind of this rather striking personality. More-over, a pattern which the episodes repeatedly followed through the book was given its shape by his character.

The narrator, as he ordinarily pictures himself, is a *picaro* in the original sense of the word, a young rogue on the loose. He is a sailor before the mast or a beachcomber, easy-going and ingratiatingly frank. Despite the fact that he is writing for a Victorian audience, he is surprisingly shameless about his laziness, his irresponsibility, his joy in good food and even bad liquor, his eye for beautiful native girls. (He records his embarrassment on only three occasions, and each time it results from a woman's laugh-ing at him or snubbing him.) His talk often has the horsy openness of one male talking with other males—such open-ness in fact that he puts off criticism and charms us even as he charmed a good share of his purportedly prudish readers. He offends none but the virtuous.

Often his way of viewing and portraying places and personalities goes well with such a character. His zest for experience, his pleasure in the sights and scenes of the islands, his amusement at the ways of the islanders are reflected in detailed and humorous descriptions. His lively interest in personalities shows itself in characterizations far more vividly achieved than all but two or three which Melville had managed in *Typee*. The finicking captain and bullock-hearted drunken mate of the *Julia*, shipmates such as the pathetic Ropey and swashbuckling Flash Jack, islanders such as portly Captain Bob and meagre Varvy the hermit, and an impressive array of other characters (more than twenty) are neatly discriminated. Best drawn of all, of course, is Doctor Long Ghost, an even more ingratiating rogue than the narrator.

The Doctor is remarkably like an exaggerated version of the narrator, more irresponsible and shiftless, and with similar but more outright carnal urges which he manages from time to time to satisfy in a way the narrator obviously envies. Omoo vastly delights in Long Ghost's fantastic raffishness, and his attitude is important in conveying the man's quality. Similarly with the other characters: so colored is their depiction by the narrator's attitudes towards them that they seem of a kind. His attitudes classify them. Enemies of irresponsibility are portrayed as villains, while the relaxed, the lazy, and the fun-loving are affectionately sketched. Few of the more respectable characters are tolerated; some are shown to be in certain ways disreputable— incompetent, drunken, or greedy; and a large share of the others are exposed as downright rascals and clowns. None are wholly worthy of respect. If the rebellious sailors are reckless and uncivilized, their sins are venial—larkish excesses of high animal spirits or hot-hearted reprisals for injustices heaped upon them.

The message of the book and the way it is conveyed also often reflect the personality of the narrator. Although Omoo is attacking the work of the missionaries, he is temperate enough to admit that " they have striven hard to mitigate the evils resulting from the commerce with the whites in general " and that " the morality of the islanders is, upon the whole, improved by their presence." His stories illustrating the wickedness of the natives show amusement rather than distress. When he gibes at the missionaries, often it is because they are Malvolian spoil-sports and hypocrites. And as a rule he is humorous rather than indignant in making his criticism of them and the other Sunday citizens.

The qualities of the narrator's personality which thus show themselves in the descriptions, the characterizations, and the preachments also initiate an oft-repeated pattern of happenings. Both the " I " of the narrative and his good friend the Doctor have simple wants which they are trying throughout to satisfy. They have a fair amount of curiosity about life on the islands. More important, they would like a job which entails no work, and they would give up even an easy job for other more important felicities such as exotic scenery, satisfactory shelter, good food, hard liquor, and girls who are both beautiful and hospitable.

A passage in Chapter 61 shows their wants. They have just decided that they can no longer stay in Martair, since, pampered though they have been by Zeke and Shorty, they have had to work there. Says the narrator:

> The doctor was all eagerness to visit Tamai, a solitary inland village, standing upon the banks of a considerable lake... and embosomed among groves. From Afrehitoo you went to this place by a lonely pathway, leading through the wildest scenery in the world. Much, too, had we heard concerning the lake itself, which abounded in... delicious fish....
>
> Upon its banks, moreover, grew the finest fruit of the islands, and in their greatest perfection....
>
> Besides all this, in Tamai dwelt the most beautiful and unsophisticated women in the entire Society group....

The prospect is irresistible, and accordingly the next day they go to Tamai. There they enjoy the hospitable reception given them; they watch the voluptuous dance of the backsliding girls. They even contemplate staying in so fine a place. But natives from a more civilized island appear; there is danger that the two sailors will be apprehended as runaways; so they move along.

In general outline, this is the simple pattern which relates, so far as they are related, a large share of the incidents of the book. The narrator, having left some unsatisfactory scene, moves to another place. At first he has, perhaps, high hopes of being contented in the new surroundings. Then for one reason or another the new spot proves unsatisfactory, and a new departure follows. So the hero escapes from the Typees, but is unhappy aboard the *Julia*. Hopefully, he leaves the *Julia* for the French frigate. There, too, his expectations are shortly dashed. The

Calabooza Beretanee is the next stop. " Though extremely romantic in appearance," says Omoo, " on a near approach, it proved but ill adapted to domestic comfort." Still, it has its good points, and the writer and Long Ghost stay there until their condition begins to be " a little precarious ": the food supply is uncertain, ships come in less often, and the natives are no longer to be exploited. So they sign up with the planters of Martair, only to learn that, to their horror, work is required of them there. They begin extended wanderings, with the vague notion of eventually " being promoted to some office of high trust and emolument, about the person of her majesty, the queen." This last hope is dashed when the two bedraggled beachcombers finally stand before Queen Pomare and, " surprised and offended," she promptly waves the ragamuffins out of her presence. So the narrator begins his last chapter, " Disappointed in going to court, we determined on going to sea." And the book ends as it begins, with Omoo aboard ship and the wide Pacific all before him.

As a result, though a fair share of the happenings recounted were either invented or purloined by Melville, their very similarity and their common motivation give the book a certain cohesiveness, perhaps a kind of unity. The episodes constantly underline qualities of the narrator and his like-minded companion the Doctor. Furthermore, the characterizations, the motivations, and the frustrations harmonize well with the tone of the book—a comic tone. *Omoo* has something like the pattern of Melville's next book, *Mardi*, but here, since the comfort-loving characters lazily pursue not the idealized Yillah but low creature pleasures, their defeats are laughable rather than tragic. And the " I " of the narrative joins the reader in perceiving the comedy involved.

One who reads the book carefully, however, will see that the characterization of the narrator is not handled as simply as the consideration of it so far has implied. At times, he is given traits and attitudes which seem to clash with those of the irresponsible roving sailor, his head and heart against captains, shipowners, consuls, missionaries,

and those having authority. These qualities and feelings
are those of a more conventional young man, a more
dispassionate observer, than Omoo as a rule makes himself
out to be.

For if this assumed character is a common sailor and a
beachcomber, he is so only because of circumstances: by
birth and upbringing he is a gentleman. In this respect
as in others, he resembles his closest companion, of whom
he says, "from whatever high estate Doctor Long Ghost
had fallen, he had certainly at some time or other spent
money, drunk Burgundy, and associated with gentlemen."
The narrator not only gives evidence of a similar
background; he also has in common with the Doctor an
appreciation of learning and a love of reading: "His books,
though sadly torn and battered, were an invaluable re-
source. I read them again and again...."

While American readers of the time knew it was common
enough for young men of good family and education to
choose or be forced to go a-whaling, to the more stable
Briton the idea seemed most dubious. The reviewer of
Omoo for *Blackwood's* declared that though the author had
doubtless visited the country he describes, it could not
have been in the capacity he states. "His tone is refined
and well-bred, he writes like one accustomed to good
European society, who has read books and collected stores
of information, other than could be perused or gathered
in the places and amongst the rude associates he describes."
[June, 1847.] The critic for the *Dublin Review* repeated
and extended this line of criticism: "We wonder how
such a book came to be written by one 'before the mast,'
as he describes himself to be; or how one capable of so
thinking, reflecting, recollecting, and inditing, could have
gone before the mast. And in a whaler, too, of all ships in
the world." [December, 1847.]

The critics have a point: the narrator, as charged, does
not always think, reflect, and recollect in a manner befitting
the picaresque role he usually assumes. Although he
pictures himself as irresponsible, he is somehow, he indicates, not really unprincipled. He relaxes in the free and

easy life and morals of the natives, yes; but at intervals he is qualified to get righteous about the hypocritical claims of the missionaries or about their highhanded procedures. He thinks Long Ghost is a capital rogue when he strolls off "to pick flowers" with native girls, and he hints that he would like to collect a few himself. But in another chapter, he is indignant about the diseases spread by "unprincipled foreigners." Hence he is both a beachcomber and a gentleman, both a rogue and one competent to rebuke roguery. Criticizing the preachers, he goes to church every Sunday.

And the narrator, as charged, does not consistently "indite" in a fashion probable for a whaleman. *Blackwood's* reviewer declared, "His speech betrayeth him." In a typical passage, taken at random, one finds an allusion to Damon and Pythias, to narratives of old voyages, a high proportion of Latinate words, and elaborately suspended sentence patterns, none of which, one feels certain, were typical of talk in the forecastles of most whaleships.

So, often, the style offers support for Omoo's implied claims about his background and learning. A small sampling of the moderately learned allusions which dot the pages of the book will show references to "the genealogy of Odin," "Tempe," "Trenck's mouse," "Lacedemonian," "Friar Tuck," "Titus Oates," "Rizzio," "the Hegira," and "King Charles's beauties"—none extraordinarily erudite but all, one imagines, somewhat beyond the ken of most common sailors. The number of recognizable literary allusions is fairly impressive: to Butler, Smollett, Milton, Virgil, Pope, and Hobbes. There are echoes of at least six plays of Shakespeare—*Richard III, Julius Caesar, Lear, Henry IV, Henry VIII*, and *Hamlet*. The author's religious training is attested to by dozens of quotations, paraphrases, or allusions the source of which is the Bible. On occasion, in other words, the inkhorn terms, the fairly complex and sometimes studied sentences, and the rapid associations and far-fetched allusions are prophetic of the ornate and highly allusive style of *Mardi*.

Yet a good share of *Omoo*, by contrast, is written in

relatively informal language. Put alongside *Typee,* this book shows conspicuous tendencies toward the use of colloquial speech. At times, the style has something like the informality of oral discourse. And often when the author reports the conversations of his shipmates—for instance, the exchange between Ropey and the others in Chapter 14—the language is as lifelike as can be. Thus the narrator's way of writing, like his picture of himself, has two aspects.

One reason for these clashes is to be found in the fact that Melville is, consciously or unconsciously, attempting to justify Omoo's appearance in two somewhat different roles. He is, so the preface avers, an "unbiased observer," retailing information about the islands and islanders, impelled to rebuke the missionaries for their shortcomings. But he is, in addition, " a roving sailor in the Pacific." The conservative critics, therefore, found some basis in the book for discrediting Omoo as a witness. Who could credit a licentious and irresponsible beachcomber, they asked, when he criticized morals and civilization? And how could a rascally fellow who mutinied against law and order, despised the rights of property, and cohabited with savages claim to be unbiased? The better he was as an unprejudiced observer, the less convincing he was as a rogue, and *vice versa.* So, in *Omoo* as in *Typee,* there was friction between the development of Melville's theme and the motivation of his happenings.

There was friction. But fortunately Melville discovered or happened to fall into a way of writing which somewhat alleviated the friction. The inception of the book, the humorous tradition with which it was associated, and Melville's actual relationship to the events he reported quite possibly helped him toward this way of writing.

Apparently it was Melville's skill as an oral storyteller that first led his family to urge him to transfer his talk to writing. The preface to *Typee* notes that " notwithstanding the familiarity of sailors with all sorts of curious adventure, the incidents recorded in the following pages have often served, when ' spun as a yarn,' not only to

relieve the weariness of many a night-watch at sea, but to
excite the warmest sympathies of the author's shipmates."
The preface to *Omoo* states that "The frequency... with
which these incidents have been verbally related, has tended
to stamp them upon the memory." At least parts of both
Typee and *Omoo* were rehearsed in oral form before they
were written down, and some of the qualities of oral pres-
entation were echoed in the written narrative.

Nathaniel P. Willis, a contemporary, so testified. This
gossiping columnist, in 1849, started a review with a
comment upon a current literary trend which he felt was
illustrated by Melville. Wrote Willis:

> *Conversational literature,* or books written as agree-
> able people talk, is the present fashion with authors and
> passion with readers. Herman Melville, with his cigar
> and his Spanish eyes, *talks* Typee and Omoo, just as
> you find the flow of his delightful mind on paper. Those
> who have only read his books know the man—those who
> have only seen the man have a fair idea of his books.

Willis cited as works representing the trend toward conversational literature Thackeray's novels, *Two Years Before
the Mast, Kaloolah,* and the book which he was reviewing,
Wise's *Los Gringos.* He might have associated it with the
long-established traditions of picaresque fiction, or such
spinners of seafaring yarns as Marryat and the author of
Tom Cringle's Log, men who wrote in a salty, conversational
style. Or, nearer at hand, he might well have cited a
number of books of a rather different class—the humorous
books of the period.

For the decade just ending when *Omoo* appeared was
one in which a sizeable group of American humorists had
found how useful the imitation of talk might be for their
purposes. Such Eastern characters as Whitcher's Widow
Bedott, Shillaber's Mrs. Partington, and Lowell's Hosea
Biglow and Birdofredum Sawin had recently talked themselves into fairly wide fame. Also, such Western characters
as Thompson's Major Jones, Thorpe's Jim Doggett, and a
host of yarnspinners for *The Spirit of the Times,* in the

greatest decade of that great magazine, had become known widely through dialogues in the vernacular.

Since Melville's narrator was (a good share of the time, at least) a raffish and irresponsible fellow who tended to see characters and events in a comic light, his role was moderately close to that of some of these humorous characters. Melville, an intimate of the editors of the comic magazine *Yankee Doodle,* and a contributor to that periodical, doubtless knew at least some of the humor of the day. Whether he deliberately wrote as a humorist or not, his style and his attitudes resembled styles and attitudes to be found in the humor. And his handling of both elements caused disparities between elements in the book to be less damaging than they might have been.

The disparity between the learned diction and the vulgar diction in *Omoo,* for instance, was not unlike that to be found in much of the humor of the time. In the 1840's most humorists imitating common speech did not bother to weed out all the relatively learned words or to use markedly idiomatic expressions. In the days of mannered prose such as Irving, Cooper, Poe, and Hawthorne were writing, a few touches of dialect went a long way. There was not, therefore, so great a disparity between the learned diction and the vernacular diction used in humor as there might have been. Similarly, Omoo's learned words were not as far above his unlearned phrases as they might have been. Even his echoes of Biblical passages (also typical of much humor of the period) did not clash unduly with the humble expressions he used.

Again, the narrator's attitudes in *Omoo,* like those of several humorists of the time, alleviated some disparities between the speaker and his preachments. It was conventional for certain humorous writers (especially in the Down East group) to use the humor of self-disparagement—to paint themselves as more naive, or less upright, than they were. Omoo humorously pictures himself as worse than he is, exaggerating his laziness, his lechery, his love of liquor. (Perhaps Melville recalled oral rehearsals before sailor audiences.) His faults therefore are discounted. Similarly, though like many humorists of the 1840's he preaches, and at times harangues as if the reader were a meeting or a jury, he does so with a smile: his criticisms of the missionaries are often couched in comic, or mock-serious, tone. The preachments and arguments thus lose some of their qualities of self-righteousness and serious-ness. It is therefore helpful to have both the narrator's self-characterization and his attacks discounted by the aura of humor which surrounds them.

Finally, it was the habit of popular humorists of the period (particularly in the old Southwest) to combine attitudes of superiority and sympathy in their portrayal of characters. The humorists were presenting humble characters, their ways, behavior, and outlook with sympathy and relish; but at the same time they were observers, half-participants, in a way implying some condescension. Their writings gained in humor because they were not a tran-script of the unselfconscious lowlife character, but of such a character refracted—seen by a sympathetic, amused, but nevertheless half-aloof observer conscious of the morals, manners, and mode of speech of the more sophisticated class to which the humorist himself really belonged and for which he wrote. Once more, Melville belongs to the tradition. The frequency with which he places colloquial expressions in quotation marks reflects this pair of atti-tudes: his using the expressions shows his knowledge of colloquial speech, but the quotation marks show that he views the expressions with indulgent superiority as amusing and quaint rather than as admirable or natural. Like the humorous writers of the day, Omoo is simultaneously sympa-thetic and aloof, and his two aspects are drawn together by the fact that their incongruity is mirth-provoking.

The seemingly incongruous aspects of Omoo's character underlined by the humor were, after all, drawn from life. Although one cannot be sure of the degrees, it is quite certain that on the spot, in the midst of the events upon which *Omoo* is based, Melville himself was in some ways allied with both sides and in some ways aloof from them. This gentleman's son never was wholly and heartily with the mutineers, for the official documents show that he did not, as he claims, join with them at once. This sailor before the mast was never wholly, we also know, on the side of respectability and law, for in the end he cast his lot with the others and went to jail with them. Thus the humorous tone of the book, in juxtaposing incongruities, was, in accordance with doctrines Melville was later to lay down for the representation of characters in fiction, "not false but faithful to the facts" of human nature. [*The Confidence-Man,* Ch. 14.]

Whether or not *Omoo* is, as we have suggested, untrue in detail but true in general outline and spirit, readers of this minor book by a major writer will find that it has its interest and even its virtues. Those who consider the author's use of his sources will be impressed by the reckless ingenuity with which he expanded and developed his actual experiences. If they are less concerned about historical fact than fictional truth they may greet this as an admirable display of artistic skill. As H. T. Craven remarked in 1919, "Happily, the impression that Melville wrote from his own fresh and vigorously individual point of view is indelible. That, of course, is one of the reasons why *Omoo* has lived."

Most readers will probably agree that the characterization and style of the book, if not its " plot," show advances beyond *Typee* towards Melville's major achievements. The characterization of the narrator, in particular, does much to give the book its coherence and its peculiar flavor. It motivates the repeated pattern of his movements from place to place. It accounts for his detailed observations, a large share of his attitudes, and his generally humorous tone. His manner, said F. L. Lucas, "recalls the deposition of an intelligent witness with a sense of humor." This humorous tone may cause readers to discount somewhat the discrepancies in the narrator's character which, otherwise presented, might be disturbing. The humor also colors the scenes visited and the characters encountered by the wandering sailor. The comic vignettes of priests, planters,

government officials, seafaring men, down-and-outers, and
natives—converted and unconverted—against a brilliantly
lighted background, give a vivid sense of visiting faroff
islands with an amusing companion.

Readers common and uncommon, from its first publication, have felt the charm of *Omoo*, as both their delighted
comments and its printing history through the years testify.
Omoo was published in London by John Murray between
27 March and 3 April 1847, and in New York by Harper
& Brothers about 1 May. [For details, see Davis, pp. 30 ff.]
The book was widely reviewed, and a great majority of
the reviewers were highly laudatory. The most recent
student of its reception, Merrell R. Davis, has examined
forty-five notices, reviews, reprints of reviews, or excerpts
from the book which were published in 1847-1848.
Twenty-six reviews not among these supplied com-
plimentary cullings for the advertisements in the Harpers'
1849 edition of *Typee*. Reviews were published in many
kinds of newspapers and magazines in England, Scotland,
and the United States. Their number and wide distri-
bution are evidence of the efficiency of Murray's and the
Harpers' promotion methods. But their predominantly
enthusiastic tone both encouraged and echoed the popular
verdict registered at the booksellers' counters.

What pleased most frequently were the book's " living,
moving, wide-awake characters," its " vivid descriptions
of nature," its " glowing pencillings " of exotic scenes, and
its " romantic and all absorbing interest." Another element
frequently praised was Melville's style, " its clearness and
simplicity, and the utter absence of all approach to pro-
lixity." Many reviews specifically complimented the book
because it held the reader. Frequently Melville's ability
as a story-teller was ranked with that of DeFoe, and his
book was repeatedly and favorably compared with those
of other travellers and literary figures.

The question of the book's autobiographical authenticity was raised by some of the favorable reviewers, such

as the reviewer for *Blackwood's* [June, 1847], who doubted that it was a veracious account but did not feel that it greatly mattered. "*Omoo* is of the order composite, a skilfully concocted Robinsonade, where fictitious incident is ingeniously blended with genuine information." Even the name Herman Melville sounded to this reviewer like "the harmonious and carefully selected appellation of an imaginary hero of romance." (Writing to Murray, Melville himself was amused rather than displeased by the way "old Maga [*Blackwood's*]—bless his cocked hat, shakes his venerable head sagaciously, notwithstanding his relish for the humours.") Most of the British reviewers approving *Omoo* were similarly unconcerned about its historicity or had no doubts. In America, too, a majority of the favorable critics did not doubt that *Omoo* was a dependable account. Reviewers might have a variety of attitudes toward the book as autobiography and still praise it as entertaining literature.

A relatively small number of critics were hostile to *Omoo*. Such critics chiefly concerned themselves with Melville's veracity, and one other matter—his morality. Indeed, his veracity and his morality were not considered to be unrelated topics. Some critics held that by the very fact of misrepresenting the results of missionary labors Melville proved himself an immoral fellow.

Naturally enough, the most ferocious attacks on Melville's truthfulness were made by the religious reviewers. William O. Bourne, in the New York *Daily Tribune* [2 October 1847] declared that Melville's "caricatures of the Missionaries" and his own portrayal of himself as a mutineer, a lover of low society, a drunkard, and a rake "all entitle him to rank as a man, where his absurdities and mis-statements place him as a writer—the shameless herald of his own wantonness, and the pertinacious traducer of loftier and better men...." Melville's friends on the New York *Weekly Mirror* [6 October 1847] retorted with a defense against this "ill-natured and bigoted notice." Thereupon Bourne redoubled his attack, in the *New Englander* [January, 1848], with sixteen pages of refutation of Melville's charges against the religious folk in Polynesia, ending up by calling him not only a liar but " our modern Boccaccio." Similar attacks in religious organs were printed on both sides of the Atlantic. One curious byplay was the defense of Melville's charges against the Protestant missionaries by the reviewer for the *United States Catholic Magazine and Monthly Review* [November, 1847], a defense which may be supposed as biased as that of the *Eclectic Review* [October, 1850], organ of English Dissenters, which found Melville so "prejudiced, incompetent, and truthless" that the question arose whether he were not a Catholic.

A further cause of bias in the reviews was more political and personal than religious, though religion and morality were the openly declared grounds of complaint. This motivated the review by George Washington Peck of both *Typee* and *Omoo* for the (Whig) *American Review* [July, 1847]. Peck declared himself shocked equally by Melville's attack on the missionaries and by his obvious " immorality." Melville was a deliberate fabricator who did not " seem to care to be true." Peck was offended by " the reckless spirit " of the author, " the cool, sneering wit, and the perfect want of *heart* " apparent in *Typee*, and the offense was only augmented by what he found in *Omoo*. Melville's friend Evert Duyckinck noted this attack in his diary as " grossly abusive," and their common friend J. B. Auld rushed to the defense with a stinging rejoinder to Peck in the *American Literary Gazette and New York Mirror* [21 July 1847]. " *Omoo*," he declared, " is free from the guilt of pandering to a depraved taste "—it is the reviewer himself who is guilty: " in the pleasant disguise of a moralist and conservative, he launches forth as much disgusting loathsomeness and personal blackguardism as could be crammed in the compass of his few pages." This exchange of shot was only one burst in a continuing guerrilla warfare among the politico-literary cliques of New York City, in which *Omoo* drew fire at least as much because its author had become associated with Duyckinck's clique of " Young Americans "—known as nationalist and Democratic—as because of any of its own qualities.

Still, the qualities that Peck and the religious reviewers caught hold of were more or less there to be held against the book by anyone who insisted on reading it with a serious eye. Such a reader was Horace Greeley, who had high praise for the literary qualities of *Omoo* and for Melville as " a born genius, with few superiors either as a narrator, a describer, or a humorist." [New York *Weekly Tribune*, 26 June 1847.] But Greeley was a temperance advocate, with strong prejudices against sexual laxity of any sort, and so he had to conclude that *Typee* and *Omoo* were immoral books. " Not that you can put your finger on a passage positively offensive; but the *tone* is bad.... A *penchant* for bad liquors is everywhere boldly proclaimed, while a hankering after loose company, not always of the masculine order, is but thinly disguised." Praise for high literary genius and blame for low moral tone were weighed in the minds of such reviewers, and Greeley concluded, reluctantly, that both *Typee* and *Omoo* " will very fairly be condemned as dangerous reading for those of immature intellect and unsettled principles."

Doubtless, as Davis argues, some of the printed attacks on Melville's veracity helped to shape his future literary development. *Mardi*, which followed *Omoo*, was prefaced by the declaration that since his first two books had been received in many quarters with incredulity the thought had occurred to him of " indeed writing a romance of Polynesian adventure and publishing it as such; to see whether the fiction might not, possibly, be received for a verity...." But other important facts were influencing him to write this kind of book. (After all he *had* " romanced it "!)

Study of the reviews, in any case, shows that in this preface Melville was recalling the exceptional criticisms rather than the typical ones. The number of critics who scolded him for being a romancer in *Omoo* or in *Typee* actually was pretty small. So was the number who had been distressed by his " immorality." *Omoo* had a critical reception, upon its appearance, both in the United States and Great Britain, such as must have delighted any but a hypersensitive author. The indications are that Melville was indeed hypersensitive to criticism; on the other hand, he was sensitive also to the verdict implied by sales of the book, and here he was sufficiently encouraged by the results to take a wife and embark upon another, and more ambitious, book.

In America *Omoo* was an immediate commercial success, "selling rapidly and carrying with it large quantities of *Typee*." [*Log*, I, 245.] Within a week the first printing of 3000 copies was sold out and by 25 June the third printing was exhausted; in all, five printings were called for by the end of the year. Thereafter the demand subsided; Harpers reprinted it in 1855, 1863, and 1868. In London, Murray's hope for a similar rapid success, which might stimulate sales of *Typee* there, was disappointed. Nevertheless, he assured Melville, he expected not to lose in the end. [Davis, pp. 60-61.] In fact, the sales were steady though not rapid, and Murray reprinted it in 1848, 1849, 1859, 1861, 1866, 1877, and 1893. In the meantime Routledge had injured Murray's sales but increased the book's circulation by large pirated editions (based on the American text) in 1850 and 1855. Upon Melville's death in 1891, his friend and admirer Arthur Stedman, with Mrs. Melville's devoted assistance, carefully prepared a new edition along with uniform editions of *Typee*, *White-Jacket*, and *Moby-Dick*, which were published both in England and the United States (1892). From the plates of this Stedman edition numerous reprints by various publishers have been issued, one of which is even currently in print. In 1904 W. Clark Russell, who had for years indefatigably praised Melville's writings, in public and in private, edited *Omoo* for Lane's New Pocket Library. That Melville was far from forgotten, if equally far from valued at today's rate, is demonstrated by the inclusion of *Omoo* (1908) with *Typee* and *Moby-Dick* (1907) in Everyman's Library.

Translations of *Omoo* into foreign languages have been noted by the editors: in Germany, 1847 (by Friederich

Gerstäcker, Leipzig), 1939, 1952, 1955; in Italy, 1945 (by Giovanni Manaco, Rome); in France, 1946-1947, 1951 (by Jacqueline Foulque); in Austria, 1947; in Yugoslavia, 1952.

Up to the time of Melville's "revival" about 1920, *Omoo* was second in popularity and number of reprintings only to *Typee*. It was regarded, indeed, as more or less a continuous piece with that book, and together these two provided the basis for the quiet but sound reputation Melville held between the Civil War and the first World War. While occasional admirers placed *Moby-Dick* or another of the later books above both, it was these first two that so many people had read, remembered fondly, and taken for granted as classics. Some had even re-enacted them—Charles Warren Stoddard, Pierre Loti, Henry Adams, John La Farge, and Robert Louis Stevenson, among others. (Stevenson's copy of *Omoo*, Murray's 1861 edition, with his autograph notes and markings, now in the Houghton Library of Harvard University, was inscribed by Isobel Field [1929]: "The book that took Louis Stevenson to the S. Seas—given to him in San Francisco by Charles Warren Stoddard.")

Since the Melville revival, the center of interest in his work has shifted steadily away from the earlier books to *Moby-Dick*, with increasing emphasis on the writings following it. In the 1920's Julian Hawthorne, who claimed childhood memories of Melville as "Mr. Omoo," declared in bewilderment that he never could understand him "in the new light." In several reviews of books that placed him in that light, Julian reiterated that *Typee* and *Omoo* were his best work: "Melville's era appraised him justly enough. As long as he did good and sane work, he was widely read and extolled; when he fell into metaphysical rubbish, his audience turned to more agreeable books." [*Literary Digest International Book Review*, August, 1926, p. 561.] Few of the post-Victorian generation of critics were inclined to assent. Busy admiring *Moby-Dick* more, they automatically spoke of *Typee* and *Omoo* less, so that by 1929 Lewis Mumford felt it necessary to call attention to *Omoo* as "perhaps the most underrated of Melville's books..., treated

as if it were but the rinsings of the heady Typeean jug."
[*Herman Melville*, p. 82.] Ludwig Lewisohn, to be sure,
found in 1932 that " In no other book is Melville so tolerable a companion, so free from fretfulness and spleen." But
this was largely because Lewisohn believed the whole re-
estimate of Melville had " overshot the mark "; Melville
was a " regressive neurotic," " not even a minor master,"
and even *Typee* and *Omoo* are " somehow morose books."
[*Expression in America*, pp. 190-193.] Critical currents were
running strongly against this view, however, and against
that of another forthright champion of the South Sea
romances as such, Charles Roberts Anderson, who as late
as 1938 declared, " the popular judgment seems today to
be a sound one. The survival value of Melville's reputation
lies in the fact that he was the literary discoverer of the
South Seas. *Typee*, *Omoo*, *White-Jacket*, and *Moby-Dick*
(as a romance of the sea rather than as a ' hideous and intolerable allegory') have all along been his most popular
books; and, as literature, they are beyond question his
best. " [*Melville in the South Seas*, pp. 4-5.] In 1923
D. H. Lawrence had found that " *Omoo* is a fascinating
book: picaresque, rascally, roving.... Perhaps Melville is at
his best, his happiest, in *Omoo*. For once he is really reckless. For once he takes life as it comes." The book, said
Lawrence, is " good reading." Yet it was Lawrence, too,
who declared that " Melville at his best invariably wrote
from a sort of dream-self, so that the events which he relates
as actual fact have indeed a far deeper reference to his
own soul, his own inner life." [*Studies in Classic American
Literature*, pp. 193-213.] And the course of Melville criticism since the thirties has on the whole passed over *Omoo*
not content, with Julian Hawthorne's generation—as Lawrence himself was not at all content—that it is good reading
or that it takes life as it comes. Its companion volume,
Typee, on the other hand, has remained interesting to
critics because they can easily enough find in it that
" far deeper reference to his own soul " which Lawrence
discerned—" the struggle, as we struggle in a dream, or in

the act of birth, to emerge in the green Eden of the Golden Age, a bit of birth-myth, or re-birth myth." But since *Omoo* has not seemed to open such reference to the dream-life little has been found to say of it lately aside from this very fact, as by Arvin: in this book there is no such "inner drama and no such stylistic musicality" as in *Typee*. [*Herman Melville*, p. 85.]

Far stranger indeed than the turn of critical taste that has made *Moby-Dick* and the later works so absorbing for the complex passion they reflect, would be any conceivable re-birth into a new Golden Age where again *Omoo* might find favor simply as good reading. Meanwhile, barnacled by our editorial annotations, here it is, to show what scholars (who must not take it merely so) can make of it.

PREFACE.

Nowhere, perhaps, are the proverbial characteristics of sailors shown under wilder aspects, than in the South Seas. For the most part, the vessels navigating those remote waters, are engaged in the Sperm Whale Fishery; a business, which is not only peculiarly fitted to attract the most reckless seamen of all nations, but in various ways, is calculated to foster in them a spirit of the utmost license. These voyages, also, are unusually long and perilous; the only harbors accessible are among the barbarous or semi-civilized islands of Polynesia, or along the lawless western coast of South America. Hence, scenes the most novel, and not directly connected with the business of whaling, frequently occur among the crews of ships in the Pacific.

Without pretending to give any account of the whale-fishery (for the scope of the narrative does not embrace the subject), it is, partly, the object of this work to convey some idea of the kind of life to which allusion is made, by means of a circumstantial history of adventures befalling the author.

Another object proposed, is to give a *familiar* account of the present condition of the converted Polynesians, as affected by their promiscuous intercourse with foreigners, and the teachings of the missionaries, combined.

As a roving sailor, the author spent about three months in various parts of the islands of Tahiti and Imeeo, and under circumstances most favorable for correct observations on the social condition of the natives.

In every statement connected with missionary operations,

1

a strict adherence to facts has, of course, been scrupulously observed; and in some instances, it has even been deemed advisable to quote previous voyagers, in corroboration of what is offered as the fruit of the author's own observations. Nothing but an earnest desire for truth and good has led him to touch upon this subject at all. And if he refrains from offering hints as to the best mode of remedying the evils which are pointed out, it is only because he thinks, that after being made acquainted with the facts, others are better qualified to do so.

Should a little jocoseness be shown upon some curious traits of the Tahitians, it proceeds from no intention to ridicule: things are merely described as, from their entire novelty, they first struck an unbiased observer.

The present narrative necessarily begins where "Typee" concludes, but has no further connection with the latter work. All, therefore, necessary for the reader to understand, who has not read "Typee," is given in a brief introduction.

No journal was kept by the author during his wanderings in the South Seas; so that, in preparing the ensuing chapters for the press, precision with respect to dates would have been impossible; and every occurrence has been put down from simple recollection. The frequency, however. with which these incidents have been verbally related, has tended to stamp them upon the memory.

Although it is believed that one or two imperfect Polynesian vocabularies have been published, none of the Tahitian dialect has as yet appeared. At any rate, the author has had access to none whatever. In the use of the native words, therefore, he has been mostly governed by the bare recollection of sounds.

Upon several points connected with the history and ancient customs of Tahiti, collateral information has been obtained from the oldest books of South Sea voyages, and also from the "Polynesian Researches" of Ellis.

The title of the work—Omoo—is borrowed from the dialect of the Marquesas Islands, where, among other uses, the word signifies a rover, or rather, a person wandering from one island to another, like some of the natives, known among their countrymen as " Taboo kannakers."

In no respect does the author make pretensions to philosophic research. In a familiar way, he has merely described what he has seen; and if reflections are occasionally indulged in, they are spontaneous, and such as would, very probably, suggest themselves to the most casual observer.

ADVENTURES IN THE SOUTH SEAS.

INTRODUCTION.

In the summer of 1842, the author of this narrative, as a
sailor before the mast, visited the Marquesas Islands in an
American South Seaman. At the island of Nukuheva he left
his vessel, which afterward sailed without him. Wandering
in the interior, he came upon the valley of Typee, inhabited by a primitive tribe of savages, from which valley a fellow-
sailor who accompanied him soon afterward effected his
escape. The author, however, was detained in an indulgent
captivity for about the space of four months; at the end of
which period, he escaped in a boat which visited the bay.

This boat belonged to a vessel in need of men, which
had recently touched at a neighboring harbor of the same
island, where the captain had been informed of the author's
detention in Typee. Desirous of adding to his crew, he
sailed round thither, and " hove to " off the mouth of the
bay. As the Typees were considered hostile, the boat, manned by " Taboo " natives from the other harbor, was then
sent in, with an interpreter at their head, to procure the
author's release. This was finally accomplished, though
not without peril to all concerned. At the time of his
escape, the author was suffering severely from lameness.

The boat having gained the open sea, the ship appeared
in the distance. Here the present narrative opens.

CHAPTER I.

MY RECEPTION ABOARD.

It was in the middle of a bright tropical afternoon that we made good our escape from the bay. The vessel we sought lay with her main-topsail aback about a league from the land, and was the only object that broke the broad expanse of the ocean.

On approaching, she turned out to be a small, slatternly looking craft, her hull and spars a dingy black, rigging all slack and bleached nearly white, and every thing denoting an ill state of affairs aboard. The four boats hanging from her sides proclaimed her a whaler. Leaning carelessly over the bulwarks were the sailors, wild, haggard-looking fellows in Scotch caps and faded blue frocks; some of them with cheeks of a mottled bronze, to which sickness soon changes the rich berry-brown of a seaman's complexion in the tropics.

On the quarter-deck was one whom I took for the chief mate. He wore a broad-brimmed Panama hat, and his spy-glass was leveled as we advanced.

When we came alongside, a low cry ran fore and aft the deck, and every body gazed at us with inquiring eyes. And well they might. To say nothing of the savage boat's crew, panting with excitement, all gesture and vociferation, my own appearance was calculated to excite curiosity. A robe of the native cloth was thrown over my shoulders, my hair and beard were uncut, and I betrayed other evidences of my recent adventure. Immediately on gaining the deck, they beset me on all sides with questions, the half of which I could not answer, so incessantly were they put.

As an instance of the curious coincidences which often befall the sailor, I must here mention, that two counte-nances before me were familiar. One was that of an old man-of-war's-man, whose acquaintance I had made in Rio de Janeiro, at which place touched the ship in which I sailed from home. The other was a young man, whom, four years previous, I had frequently met in a sailor boarding-house in Liverpool. I remembered parting with him at Prince's Dock Gates, in the midst of a swarm of police-officers, truckmen, stevedores, beggars, and the like. And here we were again:—years had rolled by, many a league of ocean had been traversed, and we were thrown together under circumstances which almost made me doubt my own existence.

But a few moments passed ere I was sent for into the cabin by the captain.

He was quite a young man, pale and slender, more like a sickly counting-house clerk than a bluff sea-captain. Bidding me be seated, he ordered the steward to hand me a glass of Pisco.* In the state I was, this stimulus almost made me delirious; so that of all I then went on to relate concerning my residence on the island I can scarcely remember a word. After this I was asked whether I desired to " ship; " of course I said yes; that is, if he would allow me to enter for one cruise, engaging to discharge me, if I so desired, at the next port. In this way men are frequently shipped on board whalemen in the South Seas. My stipulation was acceded to, and the ship's articles handed me to sign.

The mate was now called below, and charged to make a " well man " of me; not, let it be borne in mind, that the captain felt any great compassion for me, he only desired to have the benefit of my services as soon as possible.

Helping me on deck, the mate stretched me out on the windlass and commenced examining my limb; and then

---

* This spirituous liquor derives its name from a considerable town in Peru, where it is manufactured in large quantities. It is well known along the whole western coast of South America, whence some of it has been exported to Australia. It is very cheap.

doctoring it after a fashion with something from the medicine-chest, rolled it up in a piece of an old sail, making so big a bundle, that with my feet resting on the windlass, I might have been taken for a sailor with the gout. While this was going on, some one removing my tappa cloak slipped on a blue frock in its place; and another, actuated by the same desire to make a civilized mortal of me, flourished about my head a great pair of sheep-shears, to the imminent jeopardy of both ears, and the certain destruction of hair and beard.

The day was now drawing to a close, and, as the land faded from my sight, I was all alive to the change in my condition. But how far short of our expectations is oftentimes the fulfillment of the most ardent hopes. Safe aboard of a ship—so long my earnest prayer—with home and friends once more in prospect, I nevertheless felt weighed down by a melancholy that could not be shaken off. It was the thought of never more seeing those, who, notwithstanding their desire to retain me a captive, had, upon the whole, treated me so kindly. I was leaving them forever.

So unforeseen and sudden had been my escape, so excited had I been through it all, and so great the contrast between the luxurious repose of the valley, and the wild noise and motion of a ship at sea, that at times my recent adventures had all the strangeness of a dream; and I could scarcely believe that the same sun now setting over a waste of waters, had that very morning risen above the mountains and peered in upon me as I lay on my mat in Typee.

Going below into the forecastle just after dark, I was inducted into a wretched " bunk " or sleeping-box built over another. The rickety bottoms of both were spread with several pieces of a blanket. A battered tin can was then handed me, containing about half a pint of " tea "—so called by courtesy, though whether the juice of such stalks as one finds floating therein deserves that title, is a matter all ship-owners must settle with their consciences. A cube of salt beef, on a hard round biscuit by way of platter, was also handed up; and without more ado, I made a meal, the salt flavor of which, after the Nebuchadnezzar fare of the valley, was positively delicious.

While thus engaged, an old sailor on a chest just under me was puffing out volumes of tobacco smoke. My supper finished, he brushed the stem of his sooty pipe against the sleeve of his frock, and politely waved it toward me. The attention was sailor-like; as for the nicety of the thing, no man who has lived in forecastles is at all fastidious; and so, after a few vigorous whiffs to induce repose, I turned over and tried my best to forget myself. But in vain. My crib, instead of extending fore and aft, as it should have done, was placed athwartships, that is, at right angles to the keel; and the vessel going before the wind, rolled to such a degree, that every time my heels went up and my head went down, I thought I was on the point of turning a somerset. Beside this, there were still more annoying causes of inquietude; and, every once in a while, a splash of water came down the open scuttle, and flung the spray in my face.

At last, after a sleepless night, broken twice by the merciless call of the watch, a peep of daylight struggled into view from above, and some one came below. It was my old friend with the pipe.

" Here, shipmate," said I, " help me out of this place, and let me go on deck."

" Halloa, who's that croaking? " was the rejoinder, as he peered into the obscurity where I lay. " Ay, Typee, my king of the cannibals, is it you! But I say, my lad, how's that spar of your'n? the mate says it's in a devil of a way; and last night set the steward to sharpening the handsaw: hope he won't have the carving of ye."

Long before daylight we arrived off the bay of Nukuheva, and making short tacks until morning, we then ran in, and sent a boat ashore with the natives who had brought me to the ship. Upon its return, we made sail again, and stood off from the land. There was a fine breeze; and, notwithstanding my bad night's rest, the cool, fresh air of a morning at sea was so bracing, that, as soon as I breathed it, my spirits rose at once.

Seated upon the windlass the greater portion of the day,

and chatting freely with the men, I learned the history of the voyage thus far, and every thing respecting the ship and its present condition.

These matters I will now throw together in the next chapter.

CHAPTER II.

SOME ACCOUNT OF THE SHIP.

FIRST and foremost, I must give some account of the Julia herself; or " Little Jule," as the sailors familiarly styled her.

She was a small barque of a beautiful model, something more than two hundred tons, Yankee-built and very old. Fitted for a privateer out of a New England port during the war of 1812, she had been captured at sea by a British cruiser, and, after seeing all sorts of service, was at last employed as a government packet in the Australian seas. Being condemned, however, about two years previous, she was purchased at auction by a house in Sydney, who, after some slight repairs, dispatched her on the present voyage.

Notwithstanding the repairs, she was still in a miserable plight. The lower masts were said to be unsound; the standing rigging was much worn; and, in some places, even the bulwarks were quite rotten. Still, she was tolerably tight, and but little more than the ordinary pumping of a morning served to keep her free.

But all this had nothing to do with her sailing; at that, brave Little Jule, plump Little Jule, was a witch. Blow high, or blow low, she was always ready for the breeze; and when she dashed the waves from her prow, and pranced, and pawed the sea, you never thought of her patched sails and blistered hull. How the fleet creature would fly before the wind! rolling, now and then, to be sure, but in very playfulness. Sailing to windward, no gale could bow her over: with spars erect, she looked right up into the wind's eye, and so she went.

But after all, Little Jule was not to be confided in. Lively enough, and playful she was, but on that very account the more to be distrusted. Who knew, but that like some vivacious old mortal all at once sinking into a decline, she might, some dark night, spring a leak and carry us all to the bottom. However, she played us no such ugly trick, and therefore, I wrong Little Jule in supposing it.

She had a free, roving commission. According to her papers she might go whither she pleased—whaling, sealing, or any thing else. Sperm whaling, however, was what she relied upon; though, as yet, only two fish had been brought alongside.

The day they sailed out of Sydney Heads, the ship's company, all told, numbered some thirty-two souls; now, they mustered about twenty; the rest had deserted. Even the three junior mates who had headed the whale boats were gone; and of the four harpooners, only one was left, a wild New Zealander, or "*Mowree*," as his countrymen are more commonly called in the Pacific. But this was not all. More than half the seamen remaining were more or less unwell from a long sojourn in a dissipated port; some of them wholly unfit for duty, one or two dangerously ill, and the rest managing to stand their watch though they could do but little.

The captain was a young cockney, who, a few years before, had emigrated to Australia, and, by some favoritism or other, had procured the command of the vessel, though in no wise competent. He was essentially a landsman, and though a man of education, no more meant for the sea than a hair-dresser. Hence every body made fun of him. They called him "The Cabin Boy," "Paper Jack," and half a dozen other undignified names. In truth, the men made no secret of the derision in which they held him; and as for the slender gentleman himself, he knew it all very well, and bore himself with becoming meekness. Holding as little intercourse with them as possible, he left every thing to the chief mate, who, as the story went, had been given his captain in charge. Yet, despite his apparent unobtrusiveness, the silent captain had more to do with the men than they thought. In short, although one of your sheepish-looking fellows, he had a sort of still, timid cunning, which no one would have suspected, and which, for that very reason, was all the more active. So the bluff mate, who always thought he did what he pleased, was occasionally made a tool of; and some obnoxious measures which he carried out, in spite of all growlings, were little thought to originate with the dapper little fellow in nankeen jacket and white canvas pumps. But, to all appearance, at least, the mate had every thing his own way; indeed, in most things this was actually the case; and it was quite plain that the captain stood in awe of him.

So far as courage, seamanship, and a natural aptitude for keeping riotous spirits in subjection were concerned, no man was better qualified for his vocation than John Jermin. He was the very beau-ideal of the efficient race of short, thick-set men. His hair curled in little rings of iron gray all over his round, bullet head. As for his countenance, it was strongly marked, deeply pitted with the small-pox. For the rest, there was a fierce little squint out of one eye; the nose had a rakish twist to one side; while his large mouth, and great white teeth, looked absolutely sharkish when he laughed. In a word, no one, after getting a fair look at him, would ever think of improving the shape of his nose, wanting in symmetry if it was. Notwithstanding his pugnacious looks, however, Jermin had a heart as big as a bullock's; that you saw at a glance.

Such was our mate; but he had one failing: he abhorred all weak infusions, and cleaved manfully to strong drink. At all times he was more or less under the influence of it. Taken in moderate quantities, I believe, in my soul, it did a man like him good; brightened his eyes, swept the cobwebs out of his brain, and regulated his pulse. But the worst of it was, that sometimes he drank too much, and a more obstreperous fellow than Jermin in his cups, you seldom came across. He was always for having a fight; but the very men he flogged loved him as a brother, for he had such an irresistibly good-natured way of knocking them down, that no one could find it in his heart to bear malice against him. So much for stout little Jermin.

All English whalemen are bound by law to carry a physician, who, of course, is rated a gentleman, and lives in the cabin, with nothing but his professional duties to attend to; but incidentally he drinks " flip " and plays cards with the captain. There was such a worthy aboard of the Julia; but, curious to tell, he lived in the forecastle with the men. And this was the way it happened.

In the early part of the voyage the doctor and the captain lived together as pleasantly as could be. To say nothing of many a can they drank over the cabin transom, both of them had read books, and one of them had traveled; so their stories never flagged. But once on a time they got into a dispute about politics, and the doctor, moreover, getting into a rage, drove home an argument with his fist, and left the captain on the floor literally silenced. This was carrying it with a high hand; so he was shut up in his state-room for ten days, and left to meditate on bread and water, and the impropriety of flying into a passion. Smarting under his disgrace, he undertook, a short time after his liberation, to leave the vessel clandestinely at one of the islands, but was brought back ignominiously, and again shut up. Being set at large for the second time, he vowed he would not live any longer with the captain, and went forward with his chests among the sailors, where he was received with open arms, as a good fellow and an injured man.

I must give some further account of him, for he figures largely in the narrative. His early history, like that of many other heroes, was enveloped in the profoundest obscurity; though he threw out hints of a patrimonial estate, a nabob uncle, and an unfortunate affair which sent him a-roving. All that was known, however, was this. He had gone out to Sydney as assistant-surgeon of an emigrant ship. On his arrival there, he went back into the country, and after a few months' wanderings, returned to Sydney penniless, and entered as doctor aboard of the Julia.

His personal appearance was remarkable. He was over six feet high — a tower of bones, with a complexion absolutely colorless, fair hair, and a light, unscrupulous gray eye, twinkling occasionally with the very devil of mischief. Among the crew, he went by the name of the Long Doctor, or, more frequently still, Doctor Long Ghost. And from whatever high estate Doctor Long Ghost might have fallen, he had certainly at some time or other spent money, drunk Burgundy, and associated with gentlemen.

As for his learning, he quoted Virgil, and talked of Hobbes of Malmsbury, beside repeating poetry by the canto, especially Hudibras. He was, moreover, a man who had seen the world. In the easiest way imaginable, he could refer to an amour he had in Palermo, his lion hunting before breakfast among the Caffres, and the quality of the coffee to be drunk in Muscat; and about these places, and a hundred others, he had more anecdotes than I can tell of. Then such mellow old songs as he sang, in a voice so round and racy, the real juice of sound. How such notes came forth from his lank body was a constant marvel.

Upon the whole, Long Ghost was as entertaining a companion as one could wish; and to me in the Julia, an absolute godsend.

CHAPTER III.

FURTHER ACCOUNT OF THE JULIA.

OWING to the absence of any thing like regular discipline, the vessel was in a state of the greatest uproar. The captain, having for some time past been more or less confined to the cabin from sickness, was seldom seen. The mate, however, was as hearty as a young lion, and ran about the decks making himself heard at all hours. Bembo, the New Zealand harpooner, held little intercourse with any body but the mate, who could talk to him freely in his own lingo. Part of his time he spent out on the bowsprit, fishing for albicores with a bone hook; and occasionally he waked all hands up of a dark night dancing some cannibal fandango all by himself on the forecastle. But, upon the whole, he was remarkably quiet, though something in his eye showed he was far from being harmless.

Doctor Long Ghost, having sent in a written resignation as the ship's doctor, gave himself out as a passenger for Sydney, and took the world quite easy. As for the crew, those who were sick seemed marvelously contented for men in their condition; and the rest, not displeased with the general license, gave themselves little thought of the morrow.

The Julia's provisions were very poor. When opened, the barrels of pork looked as if preserved in iron rust, and diffused an odor like a stale ragout. The beef was worse yet; a mahogany-colored fibrous substance, so tough and tasteless, that I almost believed the cook's story of a horse's hoof with the shoe on having been fished up out of the pickle of one of the casks. Nor was the biscuit much better; nearly all of it was broken into hard, little gunflints, honeycombed through and through, as if the worms usually infesting this article in long tropical voyages, had, in boring after nutriment, come out at the antipodes without finding any thing.

Of what sailors call "small stores," we had but little. "Tea," however, we had in abundance; though, I dare say, the Hong merchants never had the shipping of it. Beside this, every other day we had what English seamen call "shot soup"—great round peas, polishing themselves like pebbles by rolling about in tepid water.

It was afterward told me, that all our provisions had been purchased by the owners at an auction sale of condemned navy stores in Sydney.

But notwithstanding the wateriness of the first course of soup, and the saline flavor of the beef and pork, a sailor might have made a satisfactory meal aboard of the Julia had there been any side dishes—a potato or two, a yam, or a plantain. But there was nothing of the kind. Still, there was something else, which, in the estimation of the men, made up for all deficiencies; and that was the regular allowance of Pisco.

It may seem strange, that in such a state of affairs the captain should be willing to keep the sea with his ship. But the truth was, that by lying in harbor, he ran the risk of losing the remainder of his men by desertion; and as it was, he still feared that, in some outlandish bay or other, he might one day find his anchor down, and no crew to weigh it.

With judicious officers the most unruly seamen can at sea be kept in some sort of subjection; but once get them within a cable's length of the land, and it is hard restraining them. It is for this reason, that many South Sea whalemen do not come to an anchor for eighteen or twenty months on a stretch. When fresh provisions are needed, they run for the nearest land—heave to eight or ten miles off, and send a boat ashore to trade. The crews manning vessels like these are for the most part villains of all nations and dyes; picked up in the lawless ports of the Spanish Main, and among the savages of the islands. Like galley-slaves, they are only to be governed by scourges and chains. Their officers go among them with dirk and pistol—concealed, but ready at a grasp.

Not a few of our own crew were men of this stamp; but, riotous at times as they were, the bluff, drunken energies of Jermin were just the thing to hold them in some sort of noisy subjection. Upon an emergency, he flew in among them, showering his kicks and cuffs right and left, and " creating a sensation " in every direction. And as hinted before, they bore this knock-down authority with great good-humor. A sober, discreet, dignified officer could have done nothing with them; such a set would have thrown him and his dignity overboard.

Matters being thus, there was nothing for the ship but to keep the sea. Nor was the captain without hope that the invalid portion of his crew, as well as himself, would soon recover; and then there was no telling what luck in the fishery might yet be in store for us. At any rate, at the time of my coming aboard, the report was, that Captain Guy was resolved upon retrieving the past, and filling the vessel with oil in the shortest space possible.

With this intention, we were now shaping our course for Hytyhoo, a village on the island of St. Christina—one of the Marquesas, and so named by Mendaña—for the purpose of obtaining eight seamen, who, some weeks before, had stepped ashore there from the Julia. It was supposed that, by this time, they must have recreated themselves sufficiently, and would be glad to return to their duty.

So to Hytyhoo, with all our canvas spread, and coquetting with the warm, breezy Trades we bowled along; gliding up and down the long, slow swells, the bonettas and albicores frolicking round us.

CHAPTER IV.

A SCENE IN THE FORECASTLE.

I HAD scarcely been aboard of the ship twenty-four hours, when a circumstance occurred, which, although noways picturesque, is so significant of the state of affairs, that I can not forbear relating it.

In the first place, however, it must be known, that among the crew was a man so excessively ugly, that he went by the ironical appellation of " Beauty." He was the ship's carpenter; and for that reason was sometimes known by his nautical cognomen of " Chips." There was no absolute deformity about the man; he was symmetrically ugly. But ill favored as he was in person, Beauty was none the less ugly in temper; but no one could blame him; his countenance had soured his heart. Now Jermin and Beauty were always at sword's points. The truth was, the latter was the only man in the ship whom the mate had never decidedly got the better of; and hence the grudge he bore him. As

2

for Beauty, he prided himself upon talking up to the mate, as we shall soon see.

Toward evening there was something to be done on deck and the carpenter who belonged to the watch was missing. "Where's that skulk, Chips?" shouted Jermin down the forecastle scuttle.

"Taking his ease, d'ye see, down here on a chest, if you want to know," replied that worthy himself, quietly withdrawing his pipe from his mouth. This insolence flung the fiery little mate into a mighty rage; but Beauty said nothing, puffing away with all the tranquillity imaginable. Here it must be remembered that, never mind what may be the provocation, no prudent officer ever dreams of entering a ship's forecastle on a hostile visit. If he wants to see any body who happens to be there, and refuses to come up, why he must wait patiently until the sailor is willing. The reason is this. The place is very dark; and nothing is easier than to knock one descending on the head, before he knows where he is, and a very long while before he ever finds out who did it.

Nobody knew this better than Jermin, and so he contented himself with looking down the scuttle and storming. At last Beauty made some cool observation which set him half wild.

"Tumble on deck," he then bellowed—"come, up with you, or I'll jump down and make you." The carpenter begged him to go about it at once.

No sooner said than done: prudence forgotten, Jermin was there; and by a sort of instinct, had his man by the throat before he could well see him. One of the men now made a rush at him, but the rest dragged him off, protesting that they should have fair play.

"Now, come on deck," shouted the mate, struggling like a good fellow to hold the carpenter fast.

"Take me there," was the dogged answer, and Beauty wriggled about in the nervous grasp of the other like a couple of yards of boa-constrictor.

His assailant now undertook to make him up into a compact bundle, the more easily to transport him. While thus occupied, Beauty got his arms loose, and threw him over backward. But Jermin quickly recovered himself, when for a time they had it every way, dragging each other about, bumping their heads against the projecting beams, and returning each other's blows the first favorable opportunity that offered. Unfortunately, Jermin at last slipped and fell; his foe seating himself on his chest, and keeping him down. Now this was one of those situations in which the voice of counsel, or reproof, comes with peculiar unction. Nor did Beauty let the opportunity slip. But the mate said nothing in reply, only foaming at the mouth and struggling to rise.

Just then a thin tremor of a voice was heard from above. It was the captain; who, happening to ascend to the quarter-deck at the commencement of the scuffle, would gladly have returned to the cabin, but was prevented by the fear of ridicule. As the din increased, and it became evident that his officer was in serious trouble, he thought it would never do to stand leaning over the bulwarks, so he made his appearance on the forecastle, resolved, as his best policy, to treat the matter lightly.

"Why, why," he began, speaking pettishly, and very fast, "what's all this about?—Mr. Jermin, Mr. Jermin— carpenter, carpenter; what are you doing down there? Come on deck; come on deck."

Whereupon Doctor Long Ghost cries out in a squeak, "Ah! Miss Guy, is that you? Now, my dear, go right home, or you'll get hurt."

"Pooh, pooh! you, sir, whoever you are, I was not speaking to you; none of your nonsense. Mr. Jermin, I was talking to *you*; have the kindness to come on deck, sir; I want to see you."

"And how, in the devil's name, am I to get there?" cried the mate, furiously. "Jump down here, Captain Guy, and show yourself a man. Let me up, you Chips! unhand me, I say! Oh! I'll pay you for this, some day! Come on, Captain Guy!"

At this appeal, the poor man was seized with a perfect spasm of fidgets. "Pooh, pooh, carpenter; have done with

your nonsense! Let him up, sir; let him up! Do you hear?
Let Mr. Jermin come on deck! "

"Go along with you, Paper Jack," replied Beauty;
"this quarrel's between the mate and me; so go aft, where
you belong! "

As the captain once more dipped his head down the
scuttle to make answer, from an unseen hand, he received,
full in the face, the contents of a tin can of soaked biscuit
and tea-leaves. The doctor was not far off just then. Without waiting for any thing more, the discomfited gentleman,
with both hands to his streaming face, retreated to the
quarter-deck.

A few moments more, and Jermin, forced to a compro-
mise, followed after, in his torn frock and scarred face,
looking for all the world as if he had just disentangled himself from some intricate piece of machinery. For about
half an hour both remained in the cabin, where the mate's
rough tones were heard high above the low, smooth voice
of the captain.

Of all his conflicts with the men, this was the first in
which Jermin had been worsted; and he was proportionably enraged. Upon going below—as the steward afterward told us—he bluntly informed Guy that, for the
future, he might look out for his ship himself; for *his* part,
he was done with her, if that was the way he allowed his
officers to be treated. After many high words, the captain
finally assured him, that the first fitting opportunity the
carpenter should be cordially flogged; though, as matters
stood, the experiment would be a hazardous one. Upon
this Jermin reluctantly consented to drop the matter for
the present; and he soon drowned all thoughts of it in a
can of flip, which Guy had previously instructed the steward to prepare, as a sop to allay his wrath.

Nothing more ever came of this.

CHAPTER V.

LESS than forty-eight hours after leaving Nukuheva, the blue, looming island of St. Christina greeted us from afar. Drawing near the shore, the grim, black spars and waspish hull of a small man-of-war craft crept into view; the masts and yards lined distinctly against the sky. She was riding to her anchor in the bay, and proved to be a French corvette.

This pleased our captain exceedingly, and, coming on deck, he examined her from the mizzen rigging with his glass. His original intention was not to let go an anchor; but, counting upon the assistance of the corvette in case of any difficulty, he now changed his mind, and anchored alongside of her. As soon as a boat could be lowered, he then went off to pay his respects to the commander, and, moreover, as we supposed, to concert measures for the apprehension of the runaways.

Returning in the course of twenty minutes, he brought along with him two officers in undress and whiskers, and three or four drunken obstreperous old chiefs; one with his legs thrust into the armholes of a scarlet vest, another with a pair of spurs on his heels, and a third in a cocked hat and feather. In addition to these articles, they merely wore the ordinary costume of their race—a slip of native cloth about the loins. Indecorous as their behavior was, these worthies turned out to be a deputation from the reverend the clergy of the island; and the object of their visit was to put our ship under a rigorous "Taboo," to prevent the disorderly scenes and facilities for desertion which would ensue, were the natives—men and women —allowed to come off to us freely.

There was little ceremony about the matter. The priests went aside for a moment, laid their shaven old crowns together, and went over a little mummery. Whereupon, their leader tore a long strip from his girdle of white tappa, and handed it to one of the French officers, who, after explaining what was to be done, gave it to Jermin. The mate at once went out to the end of the flying jib boom, and fastened there the mystic symbol of the ban. This put to flight a party of girls who had been observed swimming toward us. Tossing their arms about, and splashing the water like porpoises, with loud cries of "taboo! taboo!" they turned about and made for the shore.

The night of our arrival, the mate and the Mowree were to stand "watch and watch," relieving each other every four hours; the crew, as is sometimes customary when lying at an anchor, being allowed to remain all night below. A distrust of the men, however, was, in the present instance, the principal reason for this proceeding. Indeed, it was all but certain, that some kind of attempt would be made at desertion; and, therefore, when Jermin's first watch came on at eight bells (midnight)—by which time all was quiet—he mounted to the deck with a flask of spirits in one hand, and the other in readiness to assail the first countenance that showed itself above the forecastle scuttle.

Thus prepared, he doubtless meant to stay awake; but for all that, he before long fell asleep; and slept with such hearty good-will too, that the men who left us that night might have been waked up by his snoring. Certain it was, the mate snored most strangely; and no wonder, with that crooked bugle of his. When he came to himself it was just dawn, but quite light enough to show two boats gone from the side. In an instant he knew what had happened.

Dragging the Mowree out of an old sail where he was napping, he ordered him to clear away another boat, and then darted into the cabin to tell the captain the news. Springing on deck again, he dove down into the forecastle for a couple of oarsmen, but hardly got there before there was a cry, and a loud splash heard over the side. It was the Mowree and the boat—into which he had just leaped to get ready for lowering—rolling over and over in the water.

The boat having at nightfall been hoisted up to its place over the starboard quarter, some one had so cut the tackles which held it there, that a moderate strain would at once part them. Bembo's weight had answered the purpose, showing that the deserters must have ascertained his specific gravity to a fibre of hemp. There was another boat remaining; but it was as well to examine it before attempting to lower. And it was well they did; for there was a hole in the bottom large enough to drop a barrel through: she had been scuttled most ruthlessly.

Jermin was frantic. Dashing his hat upon deck, he was about to plunge overboard and swim to the corvette for a cutter, when Captain Guy made his appearance and begged him to stay where he was. By this time the officer of the deck aboard the Frenchman had noticed our movements, and hailed to know what had happened. Guy informed him through his trumpet, and men to go in pursuit were instantly promised. There was a whistling of a boatswain's pipe, an order or two, and then a large cutter pulled out from the man-of-war's stern, and in half a dozen strokes was alongside. The mate leaped into her, and they pulled rapidly ashore.

Another cutter, carrying an armed crew, soon followed.

In an hour's time the first returned, towing the two whale boats, which had been found turned up like tortoises on the beach.

Noon came, and nothing more was heard from the deserters. Meanwhile Doctor Long Ghost and myself lounged about, cultivating an acquaintance, and gazing upon the shore scenery. The bay was as calm as death; the sun high and hot; and occasionally a still gliding canoe stole out from behind the headlands, and shot across the water.

And all the morning long our sick men limped about the deck, casting wistful glances inland, where the palm-trees waved and beckoned them into their reviving shades. Poor invalid rascals! How conducive to the restoration of their shattered health would have been those delicious groves! But hard-hearted Jermin assured them, with an oath, that foot of theirs should never touch the beach.

Toward sunset a crowd was seen coming down to the water. In advance of all were the fugitives—bareheaded

—their frocks and trowsers hanging in tatters, every face covered with blood and dust, and their arms pinioned behind them with green thongs. Following them up, was a shouting rabble of islanders, pricking them with the points of their long spears, the party from the corvette menacing them in flank with their naked cutlasses.

The bonus of a musket to the King of the Bay, and the promise of a tumbler full of powder for every man caught, had set the whole population on their track; and so successful was the hunt, that not only were that morning's deserters brought back, but five of those left behind on a former visit. The natives, however, were the mere hounds of the chase, raising the game in their coverts, but leaving the securing of it to the Frenchmen. Here, as elsewhere, the islanders have no idea of taking part in such a scuffle as ensues upon the capture of a party of desperate seamen.

The runaways were at once brought aboard, and, though they looked rather sulky, soon came round, and treated the whole affair as a frolicsome adventure.

CHAPTER VI.

WE TOUCH AT LA DOMINICA.

FEARFUL of spending another night in Hytyhoo, Captain Guy caused the ship to be got under way shortly after dark.

The next morning, when all supposed that we were fairly embarked for a long cruise, our course was suddenly altered for La Dominica, or Hivarhoo, an island just north of the one we had quitted. The object of this, as we learned, was to procure, if possible, several English sailors, who, according to the commander of the corvette, had recently gone ashore there from an American whaler and were desirous of shipping aboard of one of their own country vessels.

We made the land in the afternoon, coming abreast of a

shady glen opening from a deep bay, and winding by green defiles far out of sight. " Hands by the weather-main-brace! " roared the mate, jumping up on the bulwarks; and in a moment the prancing Julia, suddenly arrested in her course, bridled her head like a steed reined in, while the foam flaked under her bows.

This was the place where we expected to obtain the men; so a boat was at once got in readiness to go ashore. Now it was necessary to provide a picked crew—men the least likely to abscond. After considerable deliberation on the part of the captain and mate, four of the seamen were pitched upon as the most trustworthy; or rather they were selected from a choice assortment of suspicious characters as being of an inferior order of rascality.

Armed with cutlasses all round—the natives were said to be an ugly set—they were followed over the side by the invalid captain, who, on this occasion, it seems, was determined to signalize himself. Accordingly, in addition to his cutlass, he wore an old boarding belt, in which was thrust a brace of pistols. They at once shoved off.

My friend Long Ghost had, among other things which looked somewhat strange in a ship's forecastle, a capital spy-glass, and on the present occasion we had it in use.

When the boat neared the head of the inlet, though invisible to the naked eye, it was plainly revealed by the glass; looking no bigger than an egg-shell, and the men diminished to pigmies.

At last, borne on what seemed a long flake of foam the tiny craft shot up the beach amid a shower of sparkles. Not a soul was there. Leaving one of their number by the water, the rest of the pigmies stepped ashore, looking about them very circumspectly, pausing now and then hand to ear, and peering under a dense grove which swept down within a few paces of the sea. No one came, and to all appearances every thing was as still as the grave. Presently, he with the pistols, followed by the rest flourishing their bodkins, entered the wood and were soon lost to view. They did not stay long; probably anticipating some inhospitable ambush were they to stray any distance up the glen.

In a few moments they embarked again, and were soon riding pertly over the waves of the bay. All of a sudden the captain started to his feet—the boat spun round, and again made for the shore. Some twenty or thirty natives armed with spears which through the glass looked like reeds, had just come out of the grove, and were apparently shouting to the strangers not to be in such a hurry, but return and be sociable. But they were somewhat distrusted, for the boat paused about its length from the beach, when the captain standing up in its head delivered an address in pantomime, the object of which seemed to be, that the islanders should draw near. One of them stepped forward and made answer, seemingly again urging the strangers not to be diffident, but beach their boat. The captain declined, tossing his arms about in another pantomime. In the end he said something which made them shake their spears; whereupon he fired a pistol among them, which set the whole party running; while one poor little fellow, dropping his spear and clapping his hand behind him, limped away in a manner which almost made me itch to get a shot at his assailant.

Wanton acts of cruelty like this are not unusual on the part of sea captains landing at islands comparatively unknown. Even at the Pomotu group, but a day's sail from Tahiti, the islanders coming down to the shore have several times been fired at by trading schooners passing through their narrow channels; and this too as a mere amusement on the part of the ruffians.

Indeed, it is almost incredible, the light in which many sailors regard these naked heathens. They hardly consider them human. But it is a curious fact, that the more ignorant and degraded men are, the more contemptuously they look upon those whom they deem their inferiors.

All powers of persuasion being thus lost upon these foolish savages, and no hope left of holding further intercourse, the boat returned to the ship.

CHAPTER VII.

WHAT HAPPENED AT HANNAMANOO.

On the other side of the island was the large and populous bay of Hannamanoo, where the men sought might yet be found. But as the sun was setting by the time the boat came alongside, we got our off-shore tacks aboard and stood away for an offing. About daybreak we wore, and ran in, and by the time the sun was well up, entered the long, narrow channel dividing the islands of La Dominica and St. Christina.

On one hand was a range of steep green bluffs hundreds of feet high, the white huts of the natives here and there nestling like birdsnests in deep clefts gushing with verdure. Across the water, the land rolled away in bright hillsides, so warm and undulating, that they seemed almost to palpitate in the sun. On we swept, past bluff and grove, wooded glen and valley, and dark ravines lighted up far inland with wild falls of water. A fresh land-breeze filled our sails, the embayed waters were gentle as a lake, and every blue wave broke with a tinkle against our coppered prow.

On gaining the end of the channel we rounded a point, and came full upon the bay of Hannamanoo. This is the only harbor of any note about the island, though as far as a safe anchorage is concerned it hardly deserves the title.

Before we held any communication with the shore, an incident occurred which may convey some further idea of the character of our crew.

Having approached as near the land as we could prudently, our headway was stopped, and we awaited the arrival of a canoe which was coming out of the bay. All at once we got into a strong current, which swept us rapidly toward a rocky promontory forming one side of the harbor. The wind had died away; so two boats were at once lowered for the purpose of pulling the ship's head round. Before this could be done, the eddies were whirling upon all sides, and the rock so near, that it seemed as if one might leap upon it from the mast-head. Notwithstanding the speechless fright of the captain, and the hoarse shouts of the unappalled Jermin, the men handled the ropes as deliberately as possible, some of them chuckling at the prospect of going ashore, and others so eager for the vessel to strike, that they could hardly contain themselves. Unexpectedly a countercurrent befriended us, and assisted by the boats we were soon out of danger.

What a disappointment for our crew! All their little plans for swimming ashore from the wreck, and having a fine time of it for the rest of their days, thus cruelly nipt in the bud.

Soon after, the canoe came alongside. In it were eight or ten natives, comely, vivacious-looking youths, all gesture and exclamation; the red feathers in their headbands perpetually nodding. With them also came a stranger, a renegado from Christendom and humanity—a white man, in the South Sea girdle, and tattooed in the face. A broad blue band stretched across his face from ear to ear, and on his forehead was the taper figure of a blue shark, nothing but fins from head to tail.

Some of us gazed upon this man with a feeling akin to horror, no ways abated when informed that he had voluntarily submitted to this embellishment of his countenance. What an impress! Far worse than Cain's—*his* was perhaps a wrinkle, or a freckle, which some of our modern cosmetics might have effaced; but the blue shark was a mark indelible, which all the waters of Abana and Pharpar, rivers of Damascus, could never wash out. He was an Englishman, Lem Hardy he called himself, who had deserted from a trading brig touching at the island for wood and water some ten years previous. He had gone ashore as a sovereign power, armed with a musket and a bag of ammunition, and ready, if need were, to prosecute war on his own account. The country was divided by the hostile kings of several large valleys. With one of them, from whom he first received overtures, he formed an alliance, and became what he now was, the military leader of the tribe, and war-god of the entire island.

His campaigns beat Napoleon's. In one night-attack, his invincible musket, backed by the light infantry of spears and javelins, vanquished two clans, and the next morning brought all the others at the feet of his royal ally.

Nor was the rise of his domestic fortunes at all behind the Corsican's: three days after landing, the exquisitely tattooed hand of a princess was his; receiving along with the damsel as her portion, one thousand fathoms of fine tappa, fifty double-braided mats of split grass, four hundred hogs, ten houses in different parts of her native valley, and the sacred protection of an express edict of the Taboo, declaring his person inviolable forever.

Now, this man was settled for life, perfectly satisfied with his circumstances, and feeling no desire to return to his friends. " Friends," indeed, he had none. He told me his history. Thrown upon the world a foundling, his paternal origin was as much a mystery to him as the genealogy of Odin; and, scorned by every body, he fled the parish workhouse when a boy, and lanched upon the sea. He had followed it for several years, a dog before the mast, and now he had thrown it up forever.

And for the most part, it is just this sort of men—so many of whom are found among sailors—uncared for by a single soul, without ties, reckless, and impatient of the restraints of civilization, who are occasionally found quite at home upon the savage islands of the Pacific. And, glancing at their hard lot in their own country, what marvel at their choice?

According to the renegado, there was no other white man on the island; and as the captain could have no reason to suppose that Hardy intended to deceive us, he concluded that the Frenchmen were in some way or other mistaken in what they had told us. However, when our errand was made known to the rest of our visitors, one of them, a fine, stalwart fellow, his face all eyes and expression, volunteered for a cruise. All the wages he asked, was a red shirt, a pair of trowsers, and a hat, which were to be put on there and then; beside a plug of tobacco and a pipe. The bargain was struck directly; but Wymontoo afterward came

in with a codicil, to the effect that a friend of his, who had
come along with him, should be given ten whole sea-
biscuits, without crack or flaw, twenty perfectly new and
symmetrically straight nails, and one jackknife. This being
agreed to, the articles were at once handed over, the
native receiving them with great avidity, and in the absence of clothing, using his mouth as a pocket to put the
nails in. Two of them, however, were first made to take
the place of a pair of ear-ornaments, curiously fashioned
out of bits of whitened wood.

It now began breezing strongly from seaward, and no
time was to be lost in getting away from the land; so after
an affecting rubbing of noses between our new shipmate
and his countrymen, we sailed away with him.

To our surprise, the farewell shouts from the canoe, as
we dashed along under bellied royals, were heard unmoved
by our islander; but it was not long thus. That very
evening, when the dark blue of his native hills sunk in
the horizon, the poor savage leaned over the bulwarks,
dropped his head upon his chest, and gave way to irrepres-
sible emotions. The ship was plunging hard, and Wymontoo, sad to tell, in addition to his other pangs, was
terribly sea-sick.

CHAPTER VIII.

THE TATTOOERS OF LA DOMINICA.

For a while leaving Little Jule to sail away by herself, I
will here put down some curious information obtained
from Hardy.

The renegado had lived so long on the island, that its
customs were quite familiar; and I much lamented that,
from the shortness of our stay, he could not tell us more
than he did.

From the little intelligence gathered, however, I learned
to my surprise that, in some things, the people of Hivarhoo,

though of the same group of islands, differed considerably from my tropical friends in the valley of Typee.

As his tattooing attracted so much remark, Hardy had a good deal to say concerning the manner in which that art was practiced upon the island.

Throughout the entire cluster the tattooers of Hivarhoo enjoyed no small reputation. They had carried their art to the highest perfection, and the profession was esteemed most honorable. No wonder, then, that like genteel tailors, they rated their services very high; so much so, that none but those belonging to the higher classes could afford to employ them. So true was this, that the elegance of one's tattooing was in most cases a sure indication of birth and riches.

Professors in large practice lived in spacious houses, divided by screens of tappa into numerous little apartments, where subjects were waited upon in private. The arrangement chiefly grew out of a singular ordinance of the Taboo, which enjoined the strictest privacy upon all men, high and low, while under the hands of a tattooer. For the time, the slightest intercourse with others is prohibited, and the small portion of food allowed, is pushed under the curtain by an unseen hand. The restriction with regard to food, is intended to reduce the blood, so as to diminish the inflammation consequent upon puncturing the skin. As it is, this comes on very soon, and takes some time to heal; so that the period of seclusion generally embraces many days, sometimes several weeks.

All traces of soreness vanished, the subject goes abroad; but only again to return; for, on account of the pain, only a small surface can be operated upon at once; and as the whole body is to be more or less embellished by a process so slow, the studios alluded to are constantly filled. Indeed, with a vanity elsewhere unheard of, many spend no small portion of their days thus sitting to an artist.

To begin the work, the period of adolescence is esteemed the most suitable. After casting about for some eminent tattooer, the friends of the youth take him to his house, to have the outlines of the general plan laid out. It behooves the professor to have a nice eye, for a suit to be worn for life should be well cut.

Some tattooers, yearning after perfection, employ, at large wages, one or two men of the commonest order— vile fellows, utterly regardless of appearances, upon whom they first try their patterns and practice generally. Their backs remorselessly scrawled over, and no more canvas remaining, they are dismissed, and ever after go about, the scorn of their countrymen.

Hapless wights! thus martyred in the cause of the Fine Arts.

Beside the regular practitioners, there are a parcel of shabby, itinerant tattooers, who, by virtue of their calling, stroll unmolested from one hostile bay to another, doing their work dog-cheap for the multitude. They always repair to the various religious festivals, which gather great crowds. When these are concluded, and the places where they are held vacated even by the tattooers, scores of little tents of coarse tappa are left standing, each with a solitary inmate, who, forbidden to talk to his unseen neighbors, is obliged to stay there till completely healed. The itinerants are a reproach to their profession, mere cobblers, dealing in nothing but jagged lines and clumsy patches, and utterly incapable of soaring to those heights of fancy attained by the gentlemen of the faculty.

All professors of the arts love to fraternize; and so, in Hannamanoo, the tattooers came together in the chapters of their worshipful order. In this society, duly organized, and conferring degrees, Hardy, from his influence as a white, was a sort of honorary Grand Master. The blue shark, and a sort of Urim and Thummim engraven upon his chest, were the seal of his initiation. All over Hivarhoo are established these orders of tattooers. The way in which the renegado's came to be founded is this. A year or two after his landing there happened to be a season of scarcity, owing to the partial failure of the bread-fruit harvest for several consecutive seasons. This brought about such a falling off in the number of subjects for tattooing, that the profession became quite needy. The royal ally of Hardy, however, hit upon a benevolent expedient to provide for their wants, at the same time conferring a boon upon many of his subjects.

By sound of conch-shell it was proclaimed before the palace, on the beach, and at the head of the valley, that Noomai, King of Hannamanoo, and friend of Hardee-Hardee, the white, kept open heart and table for all tat-tooers whatsoever; but to entitle themselves to this hospi-tality, they were commanded to practice without fee upon the meanest native soliciting their services.

Numbers at once flocked to the royal abode, both artists and sitters. It was a famous time; and the buildings of the palace being " taboo " to all but the tattooers and chiefs, the sitters bivouacked on the common, and formed an extensive encampment.

The " Lora Tattoo," or the Time of Tattooing, will be long remembered. An enthusiastic sitter celebrated the event in verse. Several lines were repeated to us by Hardy, some of which, in a sort of colloquial chant he translated nearly thus:

> " Where is that sound?
> In Hannamanoo.
> And wherefore that sound?
> The sound of a hundred hammers,
> Tapping, tapping, tapping
>   The shark teeth.*
>
> " Where is that light?
> Round about the king's house.
> And the small laughter?
> The small, merry laughter it is
> Of the sons and daughters of the tattooed."

---

* The coloring matter is inserted by means of a shark's tooth attached to the end of a short stick, which is struck upon the other end with a small mallet of wood.

3

CHAPTER IX.

WE STEER TO THE WESTWARD—STATE OF AFFAIRS.

THE night we left Hannamanoo was bright and starry, and so warm, that when the watches were relieved, most of the men, instead of going below, flung themselves around the foremast.

Toward morning, finding the heat of the forecastle unpleasant, I ascended to the deck where every thing was noiseless. The Trades were blowing with a mild, steady strain upon the canvas, and the ship heading right out into the immense blank of the Western Pacific. The watch were asleep. With one foot resting on the rudder, even the man at the helm nodded, and the mate himself, with arms folded, was leaning against the capstan.

On such a night, and all alone, revery was inevitable. I leaned over the side, and could not help thinking of the strange objects we might be sailing over.

But my meditations were soon interrupted by a gray, spectral shadow cast over the heaving billows. It was the dawn, soon followed by the first rays of the morning. They flashed into view at one end of the arched night, like— to compare great things with small—the gleamings of Guy Fawkes's lantern in the vaults of the Parliament House. Before long, what seemed a live ember rested for a moment on the rim of the ocean, and at last the blood-red sun stood full and round in the level East, and the long sea-day began.

Breakfast over, the first thing attended to was the formal baptism of Wymontoo, who, after thinking over his affairs during the night, looked dismal enough.

There were various opinions as to a suitable appellation. Some maintained that we ought to call him "Sunday," that being the day we caught him; others, "Eighteen Forty-two," the then year of our Lord; while Doctor Long Ghost remarked, that he ought, by all means, to retain his original name, — Wymontoo-Hee, meaning (as he maintained), in the figurative language of the island, something analogous to one who had got himself into a scrape. The mate put an end to the discussion by sousing the poor fellow with a bucket of salt water, and bestowing upon him the nautical appellation of " Luff."

Though a certain mirthfulness succeeded his first pangs at leaving home, Wymontoo — we will call him thus — gradually relapsed into his former mood, and became very melancholy. Often I noticed him crouching apart in the forecastle, his strange eyes gleaming restlessly, and watching the slightest movement of the men. Many a time he must have been thinking of his bamboo hut, when they were talking of Sydney and its dance-houses.

We were now fairly at sea, though to what particular cruising-ground we were going, no one knew; and, to all appearances, few cared. The men, after a fashion of their own, began to settle down into the routine of sea-life, as if every thing was going on prosperously. Blown along over a smooth sea, there was nothing to do but steer the ship, and relieve the " lookouts " at the mast-heads. As for the sick, they had two or three more added to their number — the air of the island having disagreed with the constitutions of several of the runaways. To crown all, the captain again relapsed, and became quite ill.

The men fit for duty were divided into two small watches, headed respectively by the mate and the Mowree; the latter, by virtue of his being a harponeer, succeeding to the place of the second mate, who had absconded.

In this state of things whaling was out of the question; but in the face of every thing, Jermin maintained that the invalids would soon be well. However that might be, with the same pale blue sky overhead, we kept running steadily to the westward. Forever advancing, we seemed always in the same place, and every day was the former lived over again. We saw no ships, expected to see none. No sign of life was perceptible but the porpoises and other fish sporting under the bows like pups ashore. But, at intervals, the gray albatros, peculiar to these seas, came flapping his immense wings over us, and then skimmed away silently as if from a plague-ship. Or flights of the tropic bird, known among seamen as the " boatswain," wheeled round and round us, whistling shrilly as they flew.

The uncertainty hanging over our destination at this time, and the fact that we were abroad upon waters comparatively little traversed, lent an interest to this portion of the cruise which I shall never forget.

From obvious prudential considerations the Pacific has been principally sailed over in known tracts, and this is the reason why new islands are still occasionally discovered, by exploring ships and adventurous whalers, notwithstanding the great number of vessels of all kinds of late navigating this vast ocean. Indeed, considerable portions still remain wholly unexplored; and there is doubt as to the actual existence of certain shoals, and reefs, and small clusters of islands vaguely laid down in the charts. The mere circumstance, therefore, of a ship like ours penetrating into these regions, was sufficient to cause any reflecting mind to feel at least a little uneasy. For my own part, the many stories I had heard of ships striking at midnight upon unknown rocks, with all sail set, and a slumbering crew, often recurred to me, especially, as from the absence of discipline, and our being so short-handed, the watches at night were careless in the extreme.

But no thoughts like these were entertained by my reckless shipmates; and along we went, the sun every evening setting right ahead of our jib boom.

For what reason the mate was so reserved with regard to our precise destination was never made known. The stories he told us, I, for one, did not believe; deeming them all a mere device to lull the crew.

He said we were bound to a fine cruising ground, scarcely known to other whalemen, which he had himself discovered when commanding a small brig upon a former voyage. Here, the sea was alive with large whales, so tame, that all you had to do was to go up and kill them: they were too frightened to resist. A little to leeward of this was a small cluster of islands, where we were going to refit, abounding with delicious fruits, and peopled by a race

almost wholly unsophisticated by intercourse with strangers.

In order, perhaps, to guard against the possibility of
any one finding out the precise latitude and longitude of
the spot we were going to, Jermin never revealed to us the
ship's place at noon, though such is the custom aboard of
most vessels.

Meanwhile, he was very assiduous in his attention to
the invalids. Doctor Long Ghost having given up the keys
of the medicine-chest, they were handed over to him; and,
as physician, he discharged his duties to the satisfaction of
all. Pills and powders, in most cases, were thrown to the
fish, and in place thereof, the contents of a mysterious little
quarter cask were produced, diluted with water from the
" butt." His draughts were mixed on the capstan, in cocoa-
nut shells marked with the patients' names. Like shore
doctors, he did not eschew his own medicines, for his professional calls in the forecastle were sometimes made when he
was comfortably tipsy: nor did he omit keeping his invalids in good-humor, spinning his yarns to them, by the
hour, whenever he went to see them.

Owing to my lameness, from which I soon began to
recover, I did no active duty, except standing an occasional
" trick " at the helm. It was in the forecastle chiefly, that
I spent my time, in company with the Long Doctor, who
was at great pains to make himself agreeable. His books,
though sadly torn and battered, were an invaluable re-
source. I read them through again and again, including
a learned treatise on the yellow fever. In addition to these,
he had an old file of Sydney papers, and I soon became
intimately acquainted with the localities of all the adver-
tising tradesmen there. In particular, the rhetorical flourishes of Stubbs, the real-estate auctioneer, diverted me exceedingly, and I set him down as no other than a pupil
of Robins the Londoner.

Aside from the pleasure of his society, my intimacy
with Long Ghost was of great service to me in other
respects. His disgrace in the cabin only confirmed the
good-will of the democracy in the forecastle; and they not

only treated him in the most friendly manner, but looked up to him with the utmost deference, besides laughing heartily at all his jokes. As his chosen associate, this feeling for him extended to me, and gradually we came to be regarded in the light of distinguished guests. At meal-times we were always first served, and otherwise were treated with much respect.

Among other devices to kill time, during the frequent calms, Long Ghost hit upon the game of chess. With a jackknife, we carved the pieces quite tastefully out of bits of wood, and our board was the middle of a chest-lid, chalked into squares, which, in playing, we straddled at either end. Having no other suitable way of distinguishing the sets, I marked mine by tying round them little scarfs of black silk, torn from an old neck handkerchief. Putting them in mourning this way, the doctor said, was quite appropriate, seeing that they had reason to feel sad three games out of four. Of chess, the men never could make head nor tail; indeed, their wonder rose to such a pitch, that they at last regarded the mysterious movements of the game with something more than perplexity; and after puzzling over them through several long engagements, they came to the conclusion that we must be a couple of necromancers.

CHAPTER X.

A SEA-PARLOR DESCRIBED, WITH SOME OF ITS TENANTS.

I MAY as well give some idea of the place in which the doctor and I lived together so sociably.

Most persons know that a ship's forecastle embraces the forward part of the deck about the bowsprit: the same term, however, is generally bestowed upon the sailors' sleeping-quarters, which occupy a space immediately beneath, and are partitioned off by a bulkhead.

Planted right in the bows, or, as sailors say, in the very *eyes* of the ship, this delightful apartment is of a triangular shape, and is generally fitted with two tiers of rude bunks. Those of the Julia were in a most deplorable condition, mere wrecks, some having been torn down altogether to patch up others; and on one side there were but two standing. But with most of the men it made little difference whether they had a bunk or not, since, having no bedding, they had nothing to put in it but themselves.

Upon the boards of my own crib I spread all the old canvas and old clothes I could pick up. For a pillow, I wrapped an old jacket round a log. This helped a little the wear and tear of one's bones when the ship rolled.

Rude hammocks made out of old sails were in many cases used as substitutes for the demolished bunks; but the space they swung in was so confined, that they were far from being agreeable.

The general aspect of the forecastle was dungeon-like and dingy in the extreme. In the first place, it was not five feet from deck to deck, and even this space was encroached upon by two outlandish cross-timbers bracing the vessel, and by the sailors' chests, over which you must needs crawl in getting about. At meal-times, and especially when we indulged in after-dinner chat, we sat about the chests like a parcel of tailors.

In the middle of all, were two square, wooden columns, denominated in marine architecture " Bowsprit Bitts." They were about a foot apart, and between them, by a rusty chain, swung the forecastle lamp, burning day and night, and forever casting two long black shadows. Lower down, between the bitts, was a locker, or sailors' pantry, kept in abominable disorder, and sometimes requiring a vigorous cleaning and fumigation.

All over, the ship was in a most dilapidated condition; but in the forecastle it looked like the hollow of an old tree going to decay. In every direction the wood was damp and discolored, and here and there soft and porous. Moreover, it was hacked and hewed without mercy, the cook frequently helping himself to splinters for kindling-wood from the bitts and beams. Overhead, every carline was sooty, and here and there deep holes were burned in them, a freak of some drunken sailors on a voyage long previous.

From above, you entered by a plank, with two cleets, slanting down from the scuttle, which was a mere hole in the deck. There being no slide to draw over in case of emergency, the tarpaulin temporarily placed there, was little protection from the spray heaved over the bows; so that in any thing of a breeze the place was miserably wet. In a squall, the water fairly poured down in sheets like a cascade, swashing about, and afterward spirting up between the chests like the jets of a fountain.

Such were our accommodations aboard of the Julia; but bad as they were, we had not the undisputed possession of them. Myriads of cockroaches, and regiments of rats disputed the place with us. A greater calamity than this can scarcely befall a vessel in the South Seas.

So warm is the climate that it is almost impossible to get rid of them. You may seal up every hatchway, and fumigate the hull till the smoke forces itself out at the seams, and enough will survive to repeople the ship in an incredibly short period. In some vessels, the crews of which after a hard fight have given themselves up, as it were, for lost, the vermin seem to take actual possession, the sailors being mere tenants by sufferance. With Sperm Whale-men, hanging about the Line, as many of them do for a couple of years on a stretch, it is infinitely worse than with other vessels.

As for the Julia, these creatures never had such free and easy times as they did in her crazy old hull; every chink and cranny swarmed with them; they did not live among you, but you among them. So true was this, that the business of eating and drinking was better done in the dark than in the light of day.

Concerning the cockroaches, there was an extraordinary phenomenon, for which none of us could ever account.

Every night they had a jubilee. The first symptom was an unusual clustering and humming among the swarms lining the beams overhead, and the inside of the sleeping-

places. This was succeeded by a prodigious coming and
going on the part of those living out of sight. Presently
they all came forth; the larger sort racing over the chests
and planks; winged monsters darting to and fro in the air; and
the small fry buzzing in heaps almost in a state of fusion.

On the first alarm, all who were able darted on deck;
while some of the sick who were too feeble, lay perfectly
quiet—the distracted vermin running over them at
pleasure. The performance lasted some ten minutes, during which no hive ever hummed louder. Often it was
lamented by us that the time of the visitation could never
be predicted; it was liable to come upon us at any hour of
the night, and what a relief it was, when it happened to
fall in the early part of the evening.

Nor must I forget the rats: they did not forget me.
Tame as Trenck's mouse, they stood in their holes peering at you like old grandfathers in a doorway. Often they
darted in upon us at meal-times, and nibbled our food.
The first time they approached Wymontoo, he was actually
frightened; but becoming accustomed to it, he soon got
along with them much better then the rest. With curious
dexterity he seized the animals by their legs, and flung
them up the scuttle to find a watery grave.

But I have a story of my own to tell about these rats.
One day the cabin steward made me a present of some
molasses, which I was so choice of, that I kept it hid away
in a tin can in the farthest corner of my bunk. Faring as
we did, this molasses dropped upon a biscuit was a positive
luxury, which I shared with none but the doctor, and then
only in private. And sweet as the treacle was, how could
bread thus prepared and eaten in secret be otherwise than
pleasant.

One night our precious can ran low, and in canting it
over in the dark, something besides the molasses slipped
out. How long it had been there, kind Providence never revealed; nor were we over anxious to know; for we hushed
up the bare thought as quickly as possible. The creature
certainly died a luscious death, quite equal to Clarence's in
the butt of Malmsey.

CHAPTER XI.

GRAVE though he was at times, Doctor Long Ghost was a decided wag.

Every one knows what lovers of fun sailors are ashore —afloat, they are absolutely mad after it. So his pranks were duly appreciated.

The poor old black cook! Unlashing his hammock for the night, and finding a wet log fast asleep in it; and then waking in the morning with his woolly head tarred. Opening his coppers, and finding an old boot boiling away as saucy as could be, and sometimes cakes of pitch candying in his oven.

Baltimore's * tribulations were indeed sore; there was no peace for him day nor night. Poor fellow! he was altogether too good-natured. Say what they will about easy-tempered people, it is far better, on some accounts, to have the temper of a wolf. Who ever thought of taking liberties with gruff Black Dan!

The most curious of the doctor's jokes, was hoisting the men aloft by the foot or shoulder, when they fell asleep on deck during the night-watches.

Ascending from the forecastle on one occasion, he found every soul napping, and forthwith went about his capers. Fastening a rope's end to each sleeper, he rove the lines through a number of blocks, and conducted them all to the windlass; then, by heaving round cheerily, in spite of cries and struggles, he soon had them dangling aloft in all directions by arms and legs. Waked by the uproar, we rushed up from below, and found the poor fellows swinging in the moonlight from the tops and lower yard-arms, like a parcel of pirates gibbeted at sea by a cruiser.

---

* He was so called from the place of his birth, being a runaway Maryland slave.

Connected with this sort of diversion, was another prank of his. During the night some of those on deck would come below to light a pipe, or take a mouthful of beef and biscuit. Sometimes they fell asleep; and being missed directly that any thing was to be done, their shipmates often amused themselves by running them aloft with a pulley dropped down the scuttle from the fore-top.

One night, when all was perfectly still, I lay awake in the forecastle; the lamp was burning low and thick, and swinging from its blackened beam; and with the uniform motion of the ship, the men in the bunks rolled slowly from side to side; the hammocks swaying in unison.

Presently I heard a foot upon the ladder, and, looking up, saw a wide trowsers' leg. Immediately, Navy Bob, a stout, old Triton, stealthily descended, and at once went to groping in the locker after something to eat.

Supper ended, he proceeded to load his pipe. Now, for a good comfortable smoke at sea, there never was a better place than the Julia's forecastle at midnight. To enjoy the luxury, one wants to fall into a kind of dreamy revery, only known to the children of the weed. And the very atmosphere of the place, laden as it was with the snores of the sleepers, was inducive of this. No wonder, then, that after a while Bob's head sunk upon his breast; presently his hat fell off, the extinguished pipe dropped from his mouth, and the next moment he lay out on the chest as tranquil as an infant.

Suddenly an order was heard on deck, followed by the trampling of feet and the hauling of rigging. The yards were being braced, and soon after the sleeper was missed; for there was a whispered conference over the scuttle.

Directly a shadow glided across the forecastle and noiselessly approached the unsuspecting Bob. It was one of the watch with the end of a rope leading out of sight up the scuttle. Pausing an instant, the sailor pressed softly the chest of his victim, sounding his slumbers; and then hitching the cord to his ankle, returned to the deck.

Hardly was his back turned, when a long limb was thrust from a hammock opposite, and Doctor Long Ghost, leaping forth warily, whipped the rope from Bob's ankle, and fastened it like lightning to a great lumbering chest, the property of the man who had just disappeared.

Scarcely was the thing done, when lo! with a thundering bound, the clumsy box was torn from its fastenings, and banging from side to side, flew toward the scuttle. Here it jammed; and thinking that Bob, who was as strong as a windlass, was grappling a beam and trying to cut the line, the jokers on deck strained away furiously. On a sudden, the chest went aloft, and striking against the mast, flew open, raining down on the heads of the party a merciless shower of things too numerous to mention.

Of course the uproar roused all hands, and when we hurried on deck, there was the owner of the box, looking aghast at its scattered contents, and with one wandering hand taking the altitude of a bump on his head.

CHAPTER XII.

DEATH AND BURIAL OF TWO OF THE CREW.

THE mirthfulness, which, at times, reigned among us, was in strange and shocking contrast with the situation of some of the invalids. Thus, at least, did it seem to me, though not to others.

But an event occurred about this period, which, in removing by far the most pitiable cases of suffering, tended to make less grating to my feelings the subsequent conduct of the crew.

We had been at sea about twenty days, when two of the sick who had rapidly grown worse, died one night within an hour of each other.

One occupied a bunk right next to mine, and for several days had not risen from it. During this period he was often delirious, starting up and glaring around him, and sometimes wildly tossing his arms.

On the night of his decease, I retired shortly after the middle watch began, and waking from a vague dream of horrors, felt something clammy resting on me. It was the sick man's hand. Two or three times during the evening previous, he had thrust it into my bunk, and I had quietly removed it; but now I started and flung it from me. The arm fell stark and stiff, and I knew that he was dead.

Waking the men, the corpse was immediately rolled up in the strips of blanketing upon which it lay, and carried on deck. The mate was then called, and preparations made for an instantaneous burial. Laying the body out on the forehatch, it was stitched up in one of the hammocks, some " kentlege " being placed at the feet instead of shot. This done, it was borne to the gangway, and placed on a plank laid across the bulwarks. Two men supported the inside end. By way of solemnity, the ship's headway was then stopped by hauling aback the main-top-sail.

The mate, who was far from being sober, then staggered up, and holding on to a shroud, gave the word. As the plank tipped, the body slid off slowly, and fell with a splash into the sea. A bubble or two, and nothing more was seen.

" Brace forward! " The main-yard swung round to its place, and the ship glided on, while the corpse, perhaps, was still sinking.

We had tossed a shipmate to the sharks, but no one would have thought it, to have gone among the crew immediately after. The dead man had been a churlish, unsocial fellow, while alive, and no favorite; and now that he was no more, little thought was bestowed upon him. All that was said, was concerning the disposal of his chest, which, having been always kept locked, was supposed to contain money. Some one volunteered to break it open, and distribute its contents, clothing and all, before the captain should demand it.

While myself and others were endeavoring to dissuade them from this, all started at a cry from the forecastle. There could be no one there but two of the sick, unable to crawl on deck. We went below, and found one of them dying on a chest. He had fallen out of his hammock in a fit, and was insensible. The eyes were open and fixed, and his breath coming and going convulsively. The men shrunk from him; but the doctor, taking his hand, held it a few moments in his, and suddenly letting it fall, exclaimed, " He's gone! " The body was instantly borne up the ladder.

Another hammock was soon prepared, and the dead sailor stitched up as before. Some additional ceremony, however, was now insisted upon, and a Bible was called for. But none was to be had, not even a Prayer Book. When this was made known, Antone, a Portuguese, from the Cape-de-Verd Islands, stepped up, muttered something over the corpse of his countryman, and, with his finger, described upon the back of the hammock the figure of a large cross; whereupon it received the dead-lanch.

These two men both perished from the proverbial indiscretions of seamen, heightened by circumstances apparent; but had either of them been ashore under proper treatment, he would, in all human probability, have recovered.

Behold here the fate of a sailor! They give him the last toss, and no one asks whose child he was.

For the rest of that night there was no more sleep. Many stayed on deck until broad morning, relating to each other those marvelous tales of the sea which the occasion was calculated to call forth. Little as I believed in such things, I could not listen to some of these stories unaffected. Above all was I struck by one of the carpenter's.

On a voyage to India, they had a fever aboard, which carried off nearly half the crew in the space of a few days. After this the men never went aloft in the night-time, except in couples. When top-sails were to be reefed, phantoms were seen at the yard-arm ends; and in tacking ship, voices called aloud from the tops. The carpenter himself, going with another man to furl the main-top-gallant-sail in a squall, was nearly pushed from the rigging by an unseen hand; and his shipmate swore that a wet hammock was flirted in his face.

Stories like these were related as gospel truths, by those who declared themselves eye-witnesses.

It is a circumstance not generally known, perhaps, that, among ignorant seamen, Finlanders, or Finns, as they are more commonly called, are regarded with peculiar superstition. For some reason or other, which I never could get at, they are supposed to possess the gift of second sight, and the power to wreak supernatural vengeance upon those who offend them. On this account they have great influence among sailors, and two or three with whom I have sailed at different times, were persons well calculated to produce this sort of impression, at least upon minds disposed to believe in such things.

Now, we had one of these sea-prophets aboard; an old, yellow-haired fellow, who always wore a rude seal-skin cap of his own make, and carried his tobacco in a large pouch made of the same stuff. Van, as we called him, was a quiet, inoffensive man, to look at, and, among such a set, his occasional peculiarities had hitherto passed for nothing. At this time, however, he came out with a prediction, which was none the less remarkable from its absolute fulfillment, though not exactly in the spirit in which it was given out.

The night of the burial he laid his hand on the old horse-shoe nailed as a charm to the foremast, and solemnly told us that, in less than three weeks, not one quarter of our number would remain aboard the ship—by that time they would have left her forever.

Some laughed; Flash Jack called him an old fool; but among the men generally it produced a marked effect. For several days a degree of quiet reigned among us, and allusions of such a kind were made to recent events, as could be attributed to no other cause than the Finn's omen.

For my own part, what had lately come to pass was not without its influence. It forcibly brought to mind our really critical condition. Doctor Long Ghost, too, frequently revealed his apprehensions, and once assured me that he would give much to be safely landed upon any island around us.

Where we were, exactly, no one but the mate seemed to know, nor whither we were going. The captain—a mere cipher—was an invalid in his cabin; to say nothing more of so many of his men languishing in the forecastle.

Our keeping the sea under these circumstances, a matter strange enough at first, now seemed wholly unwarranted; and added to all, was the thought, that our fate was absolutely in the hand of the reckless Jermin. Were any thing to happen to him, we would be left without a navigator, for, according to Jermin himself, he had, from the commencement of the voyage, always kept the ship's reckoning, the captain's nautical knowledge being insufficient.

But considerations like these, strange as it may seem, seldom or never occurred to the crew. They were alive only to superstitious fears; and when, in apparent contradiction to the Finn's prophecy, the sick men rallied a little, they began to recover their former spirits, and the recollection of what had occurred insensibly faded from their minds. In a week's time, the unworthiness of Little Jule, as a sea vessel, always a subject of jest, now became more so than ever. In the forecastle, Flash Jack, with his knife, often dug into the dank, rotten planks ribbed between us and death, and flung away the splinters with some sea joke.

As to the remaining invalids, they were hardly ill enough to occasion any serious apprehension, at least for the present, in the breasts of such thoughtless beings as themselves. And even those who suffered the most, studiously refrained from any expression of pain.

The truth is, that among sailors as a class, sickness at sea is so heartily detested, and the sick so little cared for, that the greatest invalid generally strives to mask his sufferings. He has given no sympathy to others, and he expects none in return. Their conduct, in this respect, so opposed to their generous-hearted behavior ashore, painfully affects the landsman on his first intercourse with them as a sailor.

Sometimes, but seldom, our invalids inveighed against their being kept at sea, where they could be of no service, when they ought to be ashore and in the way of recov-

ery. But—" Oh! cheer up—cheer up, my hearties! "—
the mate would say. And after this fashion he put a stop
to their murmurings.

But there was one circumstance, to which heretofore I
have but barely alluded, that tended more than any thing
else to reconcile many to their situation. This was the receiving regularly, twice every day, a certain portion of
Pisco, which was served out at the capstan, by the steward,
in little tin measures called " tots."

The lively affection seamen have for strong drink is
well known; but in the South Seas, where it is so seldom
to be had, a thorough-bred sailor deems scarcely any price
too dear which will purchase his darling " tot." Nowadays,
American whalemen in the Pacific never think of carrying
spirits as a ration; and aboard of most of them, it is never
served out even in times of the greatest hardships. All
Sydney whalemen, however, still cling to the old custom,
and carry it as a part of the regular supplies for the voyage.

In port, the allowance of Pisco was suspended; with a
view, undoubtedly, of heightening the attractions of being
out of sight of land.

Now, owing to the absence of proper discipline, our
sick, in addition to what they took medicinally, often came
in for their respective " tots " convivially; and, added to
all this, the evening of the last day of the week was always
celebrated by what is styled on board of English vessels,
" The Saturday-night bottles." Two of these were sent
down into the forecastle, just after dark; one for the
starboard watch, and the other for the larboard.

By prescription, the oldest seaman in each claims the
treat as his, and, accordingly, pours out the good cheer
and passes it round like a lord doing the honors of his
table. But the Saturday-night bottles were not all. The
carpenter and cooper, in sea parlance, Chips and Bungs,
who were the " Cods," or leaders of the forecastle, in some
way or other, managed to obtain an extra supply, which
perpetually kept them in fine after-dinner spirits, and,
moreover, disposed them to look favorably upon a state
of affairs like the present.

But where were the sperm whales all this time? In good sooth, it made little matter where they were, since we were in no condition to capture them. About this time, indeed, the men came down from the mast-heads, where, until now, they had kept up the form of relieving each other every two hours. They swore they would go there no more. Upon this, the mate carelessly observed, that they would soon be where lookouts were entirely unnecessary, the whales he had in his eye (though Flash Jack said they were all in his) being so tame, that they made a practice of coming round ships, and scratching their backs against them.

Thus went the world of waters with us, some four weeks or more after leaving Hannamanoo.

CHAPTER XIII.

OUR DESTINATION CHANGED.

It was not long after the death of the two men, that Captain Guy was reported as fast declining, and in a day or two more, as dying. The doctor, who previously had refused to enter the cabin upon any consideration, now relented, and paid his old enemy a professional visit.

He prescribed a warm bath, which was thus prepared. The skylight being removed, a cask was lowered down into the cabin, and then filled with buckets of water from the ship's coppers. The cries of the patient, when dipped into this rude bath, were most painful to hear. They at last laid him on the transom, more dead than alive.

That evening, the mate was perfectly sober, and coming forward to the windlass, where we were lounging, summoned aft the doctor, myself, and two or three others of his favorites; when, in the presence of Bembo the Mowree, he spoke to us thus:

" I have something to say to ye, men. There's none but Bembo here as belongs aft, so I've picked ye out as the

best men for'ard to take counsel with, d'ye see, consarning
the ship. The captain's anchor is pretty nigh atrip; I
shouldn't wonder if he croaked afore morning. So what's
to be done? If we have to sew him up, some of those pirates there for'ard may take it into their heads to run off
with the ship, because there's no one at the tiller. Now,
I've detarmined what's best to be done; but I don't want
to do it unless I've good men to back me, and make
things all fair and square if ever we get home again."

We all asked what his plan was.

" I'll tell ye what it is, men. If the skipper dies, all agree
to obey my orders, and in less than three weeks I'll engage
to have five hundred barrels of sperm oil under hatches:
enough to give every mother's son of ye a handful of dollars when we get to Sydney. If ye don't agree to this, ye
won't have a farthing coming to ye." *

Doctor Long Ghost at once broke in. He said that such
a thing was not to be dreamt of; that if the captain died,
the mate was in duty bound to navigate the ship to the
nearest civilized port, and deliver her up into an English
consul's hands; when, in all probability, after a run ashore,
the crew would be sent home. Every thing forbade the
mate's plan. " Still," said he, assuming an air of indifference, " if the men say stick it out, stick it out say I; but
in that case, the sooner we get to those islands of yours the
better."

Something more he went on to say; and from the manner in which the rest regarded him, it was plain that our
fate was in his hands. It was finally resolved upon, that
if Captain Guy was no better in twenty-four hours, the
ship's head should be pointed for the island of Tahiti.

This announcement produced a strong sensation—the
sick rallied—and the rest speculated as to what was next
to befall us; while the doctor, without alluding to Guy,

---

* The men were shipped "by the lay;" in other words, they
received no wages; but, by the articles, were entitled to a certain
portion of the profits of the voyage.

congratulated me upon the prospect of soon beholding a place so famous as the island in question.

The night after the holding of the council, I happened to go on deck in the middle watch, and found the yards braced sharp up on the larboard tack, with the South East Trades strong on our bow. The captain was no better; and we were off for Tahiti.

CHAPTER XIV.

ROPE YARN.

WHILE gliding along on our way, I can not well omit some account of a poor devil we had among us, who went by the name of Rope Yarn, or Ropey.

He was a nondescript who had joined the ship as a landsman. Being so excessively timid and awkward, it was thought useless to try and make a sailor of him; so he was translated into the cabin as steward; the man previously filling that post, a good seaman, going among the crew and taking his place. But poor Ropey proved quite as clumsy among the crockery as in the rigging; and one day when the ship was pitching, having stumbled into the cabin with a wooden tureen of soup, he scalded the officers so that they didn't get over it in a week. Upon which, he was dismissed, and returned to the forecastle.

Now, nobody is so heartily despised as a pusillanimous, lazy, good-for-nothing land-lubber; a sailor has no bowels of compassion for him. Yet, useless as such a character may be in many respects, a ship's company is by no means disposed to let him reap any benefit from his deficiencies. Regarded in the light of a mechanical power, whenever there is any plain, hard work to be done, he is put to it like a lever; every one giving him a pry.

Then, again, he is set about all the vilest work. Is there a heavy job at tarring to be done, he is pitched neck and shoulders into a tar-barrel, and set to work at it. More-

over, he is made to fetch and carry like a dog. Like as
not, if the mate sends him after his quadrant, on the way
he is met by the captain, who orders him to pick some
oakum; and while he is hunting up a bit of rope, a sailor
comes along and wants to know what the deuse he's after,
and bids him be off to the forecastle.

"Obey the last order," is a precept inviolable at sea.
So the land-lubber, afraid to refuse to do any thing, rushes
about distracted, and does nothing: in the end receiving a
shower of kicks and cuffs from all quarters.

Added to his other hardships, he is seldom permitted to
open his mouth unless spoken to; and then, he might
better keep silent. Alas for him! if he should happen to
be any thing of a droll; for in an evil hour should he
perpetrate a joke, he would never know the last of it.

The witticisms of others, however, upon himself, must
be received in the greatest good-humor.

Woe be unto him, if at meal-times he so much as look
sideways at the beef-kid before the rest are helped.

Then he is obliged to plead guilty to every piece of
mischief which the real perpetrator refuses to acknowl-
edge; thus taking the place of that sneaking rascal, nobody,
ashore. In short, there is no end to his tribulations.

The land-lubber's spirits often sink, and the first result
of his being moody and miserable, is naturally enough an
utter neglect of his toilet.

The sailors perhaps ought to make allowances; but
heartless as they are, they do not. No sooner is his clean-
liness questioned, than they rise upon him like a mob of
the Middle Ages upon a Jew; drag him into the lee-scup-
pers, and strip him to the buff. In vain he bawls for mercy;
in vain calls upon the captain to save him.

Alas! I say again, for the land-lubber at sea. He is the
veriest wretch the watery world over. And such was Rope
Yarn; of all land-lubbers, the most lubberly and the most
miserable. A forlorn, stunted, hook-visaged mortal he was
too; one of those, whom you know at a glance to have
been tried hard and long in the furnace of affliction. His
face was an absolute puzzle; though sharp and sallow, it

had neither the wrinkles of age nor the smoothness of youth; so that for the soul of me, I could hardly tell whether he was twenty-five or fifty.

But to his history. In his better days, it seems he had been a journeyman baker in London, somewhere about Holborn; and on Sundays wore a blue coat and metal buttons, and spent his afternoons in a tavern, smoking his pipe and drinking his ale like a free and easy journeyman baker that he was. But this did not last long; for an intermeddling old fool was the ruin of him. He was told that London might do very well for elderly gentlemen and invalids; but for a lad of spirit, Australia was the Land of Promise. In a dark day Ropey wound up his affairs and embarked.

Arriving in Sydney with a small capital, and after a while waxing snug and comfortable by dint of hard kneading, he took unto himself a wife; and so far as *she* was concerned, might then have gone into the country and retired; for she effectually did his business. In short, the lady worked him woe in heart and pocket; and in the end, ran off with his till and his foreman. Ropey went to the sign of the Pipe and Tankard; got fuddled; and over his fifth pot meditated suicide—an intention carried out; for the next day he shipped as landsman aboard the Julia, South Seaman.

The ex-baker would have fared far better, had it not been for his heart. which was soft and underdone. A kind word made a fool of him; and hence most of the scrapes he got into. Two or three wags, aware of his infirmity, used to "draw him out" in conversation, whenever the most crabbed and choleric old seamen were present.

To give an instance. The watch below, just waked from their sleep, are all at breakfast; and Ropey, in one corner, is disconsolately partaking of its delicacies. Now, sailors newly waked are no cherubs; and therefore not a word is spoken, every body munching his biscuit, grim and unshaven. At this juncture an affable-looking scamp—Flash Jack—crosses the forecastle, tin can in hand, and seats himself beside the land-lubber.

"Hard fare this, Ropey," he begins; "hard enough, too, for them that's known better and lived in Lun'nun. I say now, Ropey, s'posing you were back to Holborn this morning, what would you have for breakfast, eh?"

"Have for breakfast!" cried Ropey, in a rapture. "Don't speak of it!"

"What ails that fellow?" here growled an old sea-bear, turning round savagely.

"Oh, nothing, nothing," said Jack; and then, leaning over to Rope Yarn, he bade him go on, but speak lower.

"Well, then," said he, in a smugged tone, his eyes lighting up like two lanterns, "well, then, I'd go to Mother Moll's that makes the great muffins: I'd go there, you know, and cock my foot on the 'ob, and call for a noggin o' somethink to begin with."

"And what then, Ropey?"

"Why then, Flashy," continued the poor victim, unconsciously warming with his theme; "why then, I'd draw my chair up and call for Betty, the gal wot tends to customers. Betty, my dear, says I, you looks charmin' this mornin'; give me a nice rasher of bacon and h'eggs Betty my love; and I wants a pint of h'ale, and three nice h'ot muffins and butter — and a slice of Cheshire; and Betty, I wants—"

"A shark-steak, and be hanged to you!" roared Black Dan, with an oath. Whereupon, dragged over the chests, the ill-starred fellow is pummeled on deck.

I always made a point of befriending poor Ropey when I could; and, for this reason, was a great favorite of his.

CHAPTER XV.

CHIPS AND BUNGS.

BOUND into port, Chips and Bungs increased their devotion to the bottle; and, to the unspeakable envy of the rest, these jolly companions—or "the Partners," as the men called them—rolled about deck, day after day, in the merriest mood imaginable.

But jolly as they were in the main, two more discreet tipplers it would be hard to find. No one ever saw them take any thing, except when the regular allowance was served out by the steward; and to make them quite sober and sensible, you had only to ask them how they contrived to keep otherwise. Sometime after, however, their secret leaked out.

The casks of Pisco were kept down the after-hatchway, which, for this reason, was secured with bar and padlock. The cooper, nevertheless, from time to time, effected a burglarious entry, by descending into the fore-hold; and then, at the risk of being jammed to death, crawling along over a thousand obstructions, to where the casks were stowed.

On the first expedition, the only one to be got at lay among others, upon its bilge, with the bung-hole well over. With a bit of iron hoop, suitably bent, and a good deal of prying and punching, the bung was forced in; and then the cooper's neck-handkerchief, attached to the end of the hoop, was drawn in and out—the absorbed liquor being deliberately squeezed into a small bucket.

Bungs was a man after a bar-keeper's own heart. Drinking steadily, until just manageably tipsy, he contrived to continue so; getting neither more nor less inebriated, but, to use his own phrase, remaining " just about right." When in this interesting state, he had a free lurch in his gait, a queer way of hitching up his waistbands, looked unnecessarily steady at you when speaking, and for the rest, was in very tolerable spirits. At these times, moreover, he was exceedingly patriotic; and in a most amusing way, frequently showed his patriotism whenever he happened to encounter Dunk, a good-natured, square-faced Dane, aboard.

It must be known here, by the bye, that the cooper had a true sailor admiration for Lord Nelson. But he entertained a very erroneous idea of the personal appearance of the hero. Not content with depriving him of an eye, and an arm, he stoutly maintained that he had also lost a leg in one of his battles. Under this impression, he sometimes hopped up to Dunk, with one leg curiously locked behind him into his right arm, at the same time closing an eye.

In this attitude he would call upon him to look up, and behold the man who gave his countrymen such a thrashing at Copenhagen. "Look you, Dunk," says he, staggering about, and winking hard with one eye, to keep the other shut, "Look you; one man—hang me, *half* a man—with one leg, one arm, one eye—hang me, with only a piece of a carcass, flogged your whole shabby nation. Do you deny it, you lubber?"

The Dane was a mule of a man, and understanding but little English, seldom made any thing of a reply; so the cooper generally dropped his leg, and marched off, with the air of a man who despised saying any thing further.

CHAPTER XVI.

WE ENCOUNTER A GALE.

THE mild blue weather we enjoyed after leaving the Marquesas, gradually changed as we ran farther south and approached Tahiti. In these generally tranquil seas, the wind sometimes blows with great violence; though, as every sailor knows, a spicy gale in the tropic latitudes of the Pacific, is far different from a tempest in the howling North Atlantic. We soon found ourselves battling with the waves, while the before mild Trades, like a woman roused, blew fiercely, but still warmly, in our face.

For all this, the mate carried sail without stint; and as for brave little Jule, she stood up to it well; and though once in a while floored in the trough of a sea, sprang to her keel again and showed play. Every old timber groaned —every spar buckled—every chafed cord strained; and yet, spite of all, she plunged on her way like a racer. Jermin, sea-jockey that he was, sometimes stood in the fore-chains, with the spray every now and then dashing

over him, and shouting out, " Well done, Jule—dive
into it, sweetheart. Hurrah! "

One afternoon there was a mighty queer noise aloft,
which set the men running in every direction. It was the
main-t'-gallant-mast. Crash! it broke off just above the cap,
and held there by the rigging, dashed with every roll,
from side to side, with all the hamper that belonged to
it. The yard hung by a hair, and at every pitch, thumped
against the cross-trees; while the sail streamed in ribbons,
and the loose ropes coiled, and thrashed the air, like
whip-lashes. " Stand from under! " and down came the
rattling blocks, like so many shot. The yard, with a snap
and a plunge, went hissing into the sea, disappeared, and
shot its full length out again. The crest of a great wave
then broke over it—the ship rushed by—and we saw
the stick no more.

While this lively breeze continued, Baltimore, our old
black cook, was in great tribulation.

Like most South Seamen, the Julia's " caboose," or
cook-house, was planted on the larboard side of the forecastle. Under such a press of canvas, and with the heavy
sea running, the barque, diving her bows under, now and
then shipped green glassy waves, which, breaking over the
head-rails, fairly deluged that part of the ship, and washed
clean aft. The caboose-house—thought to be firmly lashed
down to its place—served as a sort of breakwater to the
inundation.

About these times, Baltimore always wore what he called
his " gale-suit; " among other things, comprising a Sou'-
Wester and a huge pair of well anointed sea-boots, reaching
almost to his knees. Thus equipped for a ducking or a
drowning, as the case might be, our culinary high-priest
drew to the slides of his temple, and performed his sooty
rites in secret.

So afraid was the old man of being washed overboard,
that he actually fastened one end of a small line to his
waistbands, and coiling the rest about him, made use of
it as occasion required. When engaged outside, he unwound
the cord, and secured one end to a ring-bolt in the deck;

so that if a chance sea washed him off his feet, it could do nothing more.

One evening, just as he was getting supper, the Julia reared up on her stern, like a vicious colt, and when she settled again forward, fairly *dished* a tremendous sea. Nothing could withstand it. One side of the rotten head-bulwarks came in with a crash; it smote the caboose, tore it from its moorings, and after boxing it about, dashed it against the windlass, where it stranded. The water then poured along the deck like a flood, rolling over and over pots, pans, and kettles, and even old Baltimore himself, who went breaching along like a porpoise.

Striking the taffrail, the wave subsided, and washing from side to side, left the drowning cook high and dry on the after-hatch: his extinguished pipe still between his teeth, and almost bitten in two.

The few men on deck having sprung into the main-rigging, sailor-like, did nothing but roar at his calamity.

The same night, our flying-jib-boom snapped off like a pipestem, and our spanker-gaff came down by the run.

By the following morning, the wind in a great measure had gone down; the sea with it; and by noon we had repaired our damages as well as we could, and were sailing along as pleasantly as ever.

But there was no help for the demolished bulwarks; we had nothing to replace them; and so, whenever it breezed again, our dauntless craft went along with her splintered prow dripping, but kicking up her fleet heels just as high as before.

CHAPTER XVII.

THE CORAL ISLANDS.

How far we sailed to the westward after leaving the Marquesas, or what might have been our latitude and longitude at any particular time, or how many leagues we

voyaged on our passage to Tahiti, are matters, about which,
I am sorry to say, I can not with any accuracy enlighten
the reader. Jermin, as navigator, kept our reckoning; and,
as hinted before, kept it all to himself. At noon, he brought
out his quadrant, a rusty old thing, so odd-looking that
it might have belonged to an astrologer.

Sometimes, when rather flustered from his potations,
he went staggering about deck, instrument to eye, looking all over for the sun—a phenomenon which any sober
observer might have seen right overhead. How upon earth
he contrived, on some occasions, to settle his latitude, is
more than I can tell. The longitude, he must either have
obtained by the Rule of Three, or else by special revelation. Not that the chronometer in the cabin was seldom to
be relied on, or was any ways fidgety; quite the contrary;
it stood stock-still; and by that means, no doubt, the true
Greenwich time—at the period of its stopping, at least
—was preserved to a second.

The mate, however, in addition to his " Dead Reckoning," pretended to ascertain his meridian distance from
Bow Bells by an occasional lunar observation. This, I
believe, consists in obtaining with the proper instruments,
the angular distance between the moon and some one of
the stars. The operation generally requires two observers
to take sights, at one and the same time.

Now, though the mate *alone* might have been thought
well calculated for this, inasmuch as he generally saw
things double, the doctor was usually called upon to play
a sort of second quadrant to Jermin's first; and what with
the capers of both, they used to furnish a good deal of
diversion. The mate's tremulous attempts to level his
instrument at the star he was after, were comical enough.
For my own part, when he *did* catch sight of it, I hardly
knew how he managed to separate it from the astral host
revolving in his own brain.

However, by hook or by crook, he piloted us along; and
before many days, a fellow sent aloft to darn a rent in the

fore-top-sail, threw his hat into the air, and bawled out
" Land, ho! "

Land it was; but in what part of the South Seas, Jermin
alone knew, and some doubted whether even *he* did. But
no sooner was the announcement made, than he came
running on deck, spy-glass in hand, and clapping it to his
eye, turned round with the air of a man receiving indubi-
table assurance of something he was quite certain of before. The land was precisely that for which he had been
steering; and, with a wind, in less than twenty-four hours
we would sight Tahiti. What he said was verified.

The island turned out to be one of the Pomotu or Low
Group—sometimes called the Coral Islands—perhaps
the most remarkable and interesting in the Pacific. Lying
to the east of Tahiti, the nearest are within a day's sail of
that place.

They are very numerous; mostly small, low, and level;
sometimes wooded, but always covered with verdure. Many
are crescent-shaped; others resemble a horse-shoe in figure.
These last are nothing more than narrow circles of land,
surrounding a smooth lagoon, connected by a single opening with the sea. Some of the lagoons, said to have subter-
ranean outlets, have no visible ones; the inclosing island,
in such cases, being a complete zone of emerald. Other
lagoons still, are girdled by numbers of small, green islets,
very near to each other.

The origin of the entire group is generally ascribed to
the coral insect.

According to some naturalists, this wonderful little
creature, commencing its erections at the bottom of the
sea, after the lapse of centuries, carries them up to the
surface, where its labors cease. Here, the inequalities of
the coral collect all floating bodies; forming, after a time,
a soil, in which the seeds carried thither by birds, germi-
nate, and cover the whole with vegetation. Here and there,
all over this archipelago, numberless naked, detached coral
formations are seen, just emerging, as it were, from the
ocean. These would appear to be islands in the very pro-

cess of creation—at any rate, one involuntarily concludes so, on beholding them.*

As far as I know, there are but few bread-fruit trees in any part of the Pomotu group. In many places the cocoa-nut even does not grow; though, in others, it largely flourishes. Consequently, some of the islands are altogether uninhabited; others support but a single family; and in no place is the population very large. In some respects the natives resemble the Tahitians: their language, too, is very similar. The people of the southeasterly clusters—concerning whom, however, but little is known—have a bad name as cannibals; and for that reason their hospitality is seldom taxed by the mariner.

Within a few years past, missionaries from the Society group have settled among the leeward islands, where the natives have treated them kindly. Indeed, nominally, many of these people are now Christians; and, through the political influence of their instructors, no doubt, a short time since came under the allegiance of Pomaree, the Queen of Tahiti; with which island they always carried on considerable intercourse.

The Coral Islands are principally visited by the pearl-shell fishermen, who arrive in small schooners, carrying not more than five or six men.

For a long while the business was engrossed by Moerenhout, the French Consul at Tahiti, but a Dutchman by birth, who, in one year, is said to have sent to France fifty thousand dollars' worth of shells. The oysters are found in the lagoons, and about the reefs; and, for half-a-dozen nails a-day, or a compensation still less, the natives are hired to dive after them.

A great deal of cocoa-nut oil is also obtained in various

---

* The above is the popular idea on the subject. But of late, a theory directly the reverse has been started. Instead of regarding the phenomena last described as indicating any thing like an active, creative power now in operation, it is maintained, that, together with the entire group, they are merely the remains of a continent, long ago worn away, and broken up by the action of the sea.

places. Some of the uninhabited islands are covered with dense groves; and the ungathered nuts which have fallen year after year, lie upon the ground in incredible quantities. Two or three men, provided with the necessary apparatus for trying out the oil, will, in the course of a week or two, obtain enough to load one of the large sea-canoes.

Cocoa-nut oil is now manufactured in different parts of the South Seas, and forms no small part of the traffic carried on with trading vessels. A considerable quantity is annually exported from the Society Islands to Sydney. It is used in lamps and for machinery, being much cheaper than the sperm, and, for both purposes, better than the right-whale oil. They bottle it up in large bamboos, six or eight feet long; and these form part of the circulating medium of Tahiti.

To return to the ship. The wind dying away, evening came on before we drew near the island. But we had it in view during the whole afternoon.

It was small and round, presenting one enameled level, free from trees, and did not seem four feet above the water. Beyond it was another and larger island, about which a tropical sunset was throwing its glories; flushing all that part of the heavens, and making it flame like a vast dyed oriel illuminated.

The Trades scarce filled our swooning sails; the air was languid with the aroma of a thousand strange, flowering shrubs. Upon inhaling it, one of the sick, who had recently shown symptoms of scurvy, cried out in pain, and was carried below. This is no unusual effect in such instances.

On we glided, within less than a cable's length of the shore, which was margined with foam that sparkled all round. Within, nestled the still, blue lagoon. No living thing was seen, and, for aught we knew, we might have been the first mortals who had ever beheld the spot. The thought was quickening to the fancy; nor could I help dreaming of the endless grottoes and galleries, far below the reach of the mariner's lead.

And what strange shapes were lurking there! Think of those arch creatures, the mermaids, chasing each other in and out of the coral cells, and catching their long hair in the coral twigs!

CHAPTER XVIII.

TAHITI.

AT early dawn of the following morning we saw the Peaks of Tahiti. In clear weather they may be seen at the distance of ninety miles.

"Hivarhoo!" shouted Wymontoo, overjoyed, and running out upon the bowsprit when the land was first faintly descried in the distance. But when the clouds floated away, and showed the three peaks standing like obelisks against the sky; and the bold shore undulating along the horizon, the tears gushed from his eyes. Poor fellow! It was not Hivarhoo. Green Hivarhoo was many a long league off.

Tahiti is by far the most famous island in the South Seas; indeed, a variety of causes has made it almost classic. Its natural features alone distinguish it from the surrounding groups. Two round and lofty promontories, whose mountains rise nine thousand feet above the level of the ocean, are connected by a low, narrow isthmus; the whole being some one hundred miles in circuit. From the great central peaks of the larger peninsula—Orohena, Aorai, and Pirohitee—the land radiates on all sides to the sea in sloping green ridges. Between these are broad and shadowy valleys—in aspect, each a Tempe—watered with fine streams, and thickly wooded. Unlike many of the other islands, there extends nearly all round Tahiti, a belt of low, alluvial soil, teeming with the richest vegetation. Here, chiefly, the natives dwell.

Seen from the sea, the prospect is magnificent. It is one mass of shaded tints of green, from beach to mountain top; endlessly diversified with valleys, ridges, glens, and cascades. Over the ridges, here and there, the loftier peaks

fling their shadows, and far down the valleys. At the head
of these, the water-falls flash out into the sunlight as if
pouring through vertical bowers of verdure. Such en-
chantment, too, breathes over the whole, that it seems a
fairy world, all fresh and blooming from the hand of the
Creator.

Upon a near approach, the picture loses not its attractions. It is no exaggeration to say, that to a European
of any sensibility, who, for the first time, wanders back into
these valleys—away from the haunts of the natives—
the ineffable repose and beauty of the landscape is such,
that every object strikes him like something seen in a
dream; and for a time he almost refuses to believe that
scenes like these should have a commonplace existence.
No wonder that the French bestowed upon the island
the appellation of the New Cytherea. "Often," says
Bougainville, "I thought I was walking in the Garden of
Eden."

Nor, when first discovered, did the inhabitants of this
charming country at all diminish the wonder and admiration of the voyager. Their physical beauty and amiable
dispositions harmonized completely with the softness of
their clime. In truth, every thing about them was calculated to awaken the liveliest interest. Glance at their civil
and religious institutions. To their king, divine rights
were paid; while for poetry, their mythology rivaled that
of ancient Greece.

Of Tahiti, earlier and more full accounts were given,
than of any other island in Polynesia; and this is the reason
why it still retains so strong a hold on the sympathies of
all readers of South Sea voyages. The journals of its first
visitors, containing, as they did, such romantic descriptions
of a country and people before unheard of, produced a
marked sensation throughout Europe; and when the first
Tahitians were carried thither, Omai in London, and
Aotooroo in Paris, were caressed by nobles, scholars, and
ladies.

In addition to all this, several eventful occurrences,
more or less connected with Tahiti, have tended to increase

its celebrity. Over two centuries ago, Quiros, the Spaniard, is supposed to have touched at the island; and at intervals, Wallis, Byron, Cook, Bougainville, Vancouver, La Pérouse, and other illustrious navigators, refitted their vessels in its harbors. Here the famous Transit of Venus was observed, in 1769. Here the memorable mutiny of the Bounty afterward had its origin. It was to the pagans of Tahiti that the first regularly constituted Protestant missionaries were sent; and from their shores also, have sailed successive missions to the neighboring islands.

These, with other events, which might be mentioned, have united in keeping up the first interest which the place awakened; and the recent proceedings of the French have more than ever called forth the sympathies of the public.

CHAPTER XIX.

A SURPRISE.—MORE ABOUT BEMBO.

THE sight of the island was right welcome. Going into harbor, after a cruise is always joyous enough, and the sailor is apt to indulge in all sorts of pleasant anticipations. But to us, the occasion was heightened by many things peculiar to our situation.

Since steering for the land, our prospects had been much talked over. By many it was supposed, that should the captain leave the ship, the crew were no longer bound by her articles. This was the opinion of our forecastle Cokes; though, probably, it would not have been sanctioned by the Marine Courts of Law. At any rate, such was the state of both vessel and crew, that whatever might be the event, a long stay, and many holydays in Tahiti, were confidently predicted.

Every body was in high spirits. The sick, who had been improving day by day since the change in our destination, were on deck, and leaning over the bulwarks; some all animation, and others silently admiring an object unrivaled for its stately beauty—Tahiti from the sea.

The quarter-deck, however, furnished a marked contrast to what was going on at the other end of the ship. The Mowree was there, as usual, scowling by himself; and Jermin walked to and fro in deep thought, every now and then looking to windward, or darting into the cabin and quickly returning.

With all our light sails wooingly spread, we held on our way, until, with the doctor's glass, Papeetee, the village metropolis of Tahiti came into view. Several ships were descried lying in the harbor, and among them, one which loomed up black and large; her two rows of teeth proclaiming a frigate. This was the Reine Blanche, last from the Marquesas, and carrying at the fore, the flag of Rear Admiral Dupetit-Thouars. Hardly had we made her out, when the booming of her guns came over the water. She was firing a salute, which afterward turned out to be in honor of a treaty; or rather—as far as the natives were concerned—a forced cession of Tahiti to the French, that morning concluded.

The cannonading had hardly died away, when Jermin's voice was heard giving an order so unexpected that every one started. " Stand by to haul back the main-yard! "

" What's that mean? " shouted the men, " are we not going into port? "

" Tumble after here, and no words! " cried the mate; and in a moment the main-yard swung round, when, with her jib-boom pointing out to sea, the Julia lay as quiet as a duck. We all looked blank—what was to come next?

Presently the steward made his appearance, carrying a matress, which he spread out in the stern-sheets of the captain's boat; two or three chests, and other things belonging to his master, were similarly disposed of.

This was enough. A slight hint suffices for a sailor.

Still adhering to his resolution to keep the ship at sea in spite of every thing, the captain, doubtless, intended to set himself ashore, leaving the vessel under the mate, to resume her voyage at once; but after a certain period agreed upon, to touch at the island, and take him off. All this, of course, could easily be done, without approaching any nearer the land with the Julia than we now were. Invalid whaling captains often adopt a plan like this; but, in the present instance, it was wholly unwarranted; and, every thing considered, at war with the commonest principles of prudence and humanity. And, although, on Guy's part, this resolution showed more hardihood than he had ever been given credit for; it, at the same time, argued an unaccountable simplicity, in supposing that such a crew would, in any way, submit to the outrage.

It was soon made plain that we were right in our suspicions; and the men became furious. The cooper and carpenter volunteered to head a mutiny forthwith; and, while Jermin was below, four or five rushed aft to fasten down the cabin scuttle; others, throwing down the mainbraces, called out to the rest to lend a hand, and fill away for the land. All this was done in an instant; and things were looking critical, when Doctor Long Ghost and myself prevailed upon them to wait a while, and do nothing hastily; there was plenty of time, and the ship was completely in our power.

While the preparations were still going on in the cabin, we mustered the men together, and went into counsel upon the forecastle.

It was with much difficulty that we could bring these rash spirits to a calm consideration of the case. But the doctor's influence at last began to tell; and, with a few exceptions, they agreed to be guided by him; assured that, if they did so, the ship would eventually be brought to her anchors, without any one getting into trouble. Still they told us, up and down, that if peaceable means failed, they would seize Little Jule, and carry her into Papeetee, if they all swung for it; but, for the present, the captain should have his own way.

By this time every thing was ready; the boat was lowered and brought to the gangway; and the captain was helped on deck by the mate and steward. It was the first time we had seen him in more then two weeks, and he was greatly

altered. As if anxious to elude every eye, a broad-brimmed
Payta hat was pulled down over his brow; so that his face
was only visible when the brim flapped aside. By a sling,
rigged from the main-yard, the cook and Bembo now assisted in lowering him into the boat. As he went moaning
over the side, he must have heard the whispered maledictions of his crew.

While the steward was busy adjusting matters in the
boat, the mate, after a private interview with the Mowree,
turned round abruptly, and told us that he was going
ashore with the captain, to return as soon as possible. In
his absence, Bembo, as next in rank, would command;
there being nothing to do but keep the ship at a safe
distance from the land. He then sprang into the boat, and,
with only the cook and steward as oarsmen, steered for the
shore.

Guy's thus leaving the ship in the men's hands, contrary to the mate's advice, was another evidence of his
simplicity; for at this particular juncture, had neither the
doctor nor myself been aboard, there is no telling what
they might have done.

For the nonce, Bembo was captain; and, so far as mere
seamanship was concerned, he was as competent to command as any one. In truth, a better seaman never swore.
This accomplishment, by the by, together with a surprising familiarity with most nautical names and phrases, comprised about all the English he knew.

Being a harpooneer, and, as such, having access to the
cabin, this man, though not yet civilized, was, according
to sea usages, which know no exceptions, held superior to
the sailors; and therefore nothing was said against his
being left in charge of the ship; nor did it occasion any
surprise.

Some additional account must be given of Bembo. In
the first place, he was far from being liked. A dark, moody
savage, every body but the mate more or less distrusted
or feared him. Nor were these feelings unreciprocated.
Unless duty called, he seldom went among the crew. Hard

stories too were told about him; something, in particular, concerning an hereditary propensity to kill men and eat them. True, he came from a race of cannibals; but that was all that was known to a certainty.

Whatever unpleasant ideas were connected with the Mowree, his personal appearance no way lessened them. Unlike most of his countrymen, he was, if any thing, below the ordinary height; but then, he was all compact, and under his swart, tattooed skin, the muscles worked like steel rods. Hair, crisp, and coal-black, curled over shaggy brows, and ambushed small, intense eyes, always on the glare. In short, he was none of your effeminate barbarians.

Previous to this, he had been two or three voyages in Sydney whalemen; always, however, as in the present instance, shipping at the Bay of Islands, and receiving his discharge there on the homeward-bound passage. In this way, his countrymen frequently enter on board the colonial whaling vessels.

There was a man among us who had sailed with the Mowree on his first voyage, and he told me that he had not changed a particle since then.

Some queer things this fellow told me. The following is one of his stories. I give it for what it is worth; premising, however, that from what I know of Bembo, and the fool-hardy, dare-devil feats sometimes performed in the sperm-whale fishery, I believe in its substantial truth.

As may be believed, Bembo was a wild one after a fish; indeed, all New Zealanders engaged in this business are; it seems to harmonize sweetly with their blood-thirsty propensities. At sea, the best English they speak, is the South Seaman's slogan in lowering away, " A dead whale, or a stove boat! " Game to the marrow, these fellows are generally selected for harponeers; a post in which a nervous, timid man would be rather out of his element.

In darting, the harponeer, of course, stands erect in the head of the boat, one knee braced against a support. But Bembo disdained this; and was always pulled up to his fish, balancing himself right on the gunwale.

But to my story. One morning, at daybreak, they brought him up to a large, lone whale. He darted his harpoon, and missed; and the fish sounded. After a while, the monster rose again, about a mile off, and they made after him. But he was frightened, or "gallied," as they call it; and noon came, and the boat was still chasing him. In whaling, as long as the fish is in sight, and no matter what may have been previously undergone, there is no giving up, except when night comes; and nowadays, when whales are so hard to be got, frequently not even then. At last, Bembo's whale was alongside for the second time. He darted both harpoons; but, as sometimes happens to the best men, by some unaccountable chance, once more missed. Though it is well known that such failures *will* happen at times, they, nevertheless, occasion the bitterest disappointment to a boat's crew, generally expressed in curses both loud and deep. And no wonder. Let any man pull with might and main for hours and hours together, under a burning sun; and if it do not make him a little peevish, he is no sailor.

The taunts of the seamen may have maddened the Mowree; however it was, no sooner was he brought up again, than, harpoon in hand, he bounded upon the whale's back, and for one dizzy second was seen there. The next, all was foam and fury, and both were out of sight. The men sheered off, flinging overboard the line as fast as they could; while ahead, nothing was seen but a red whirlpool of blood and brine.

Presently, a dark object swam out; the line began to straighten; then smoked round the loggerhead, and, quick as thought, the boat sped like an arrow through the water. They were "fast," and the whale was running.

Where was the Mowree? His brown hand was on the boat's gunwale; and he was hauled aboard in the very midst of the mad bubbles that burst under the bows.

Such a man, or devil, if you will, was Bembo.

CHAPTER XX.

AFTER the captain left, the land-breeze died away; and, as is usual about these islands, toward noon it fell a dead calm. There was nothing to do but haul up the courses, run down the jib, and lay and roll upon the swells. The repose of the elements seemed to communicate itself to the men; and for a time, there was a lull.

Early in the afternoon, the mate, having left the captain at Papeetee, returned to the ship. According to the steward, they were to go ashore again right after dinner with the remainder of Guy's effects.

On gaining the deck, Jermin purposely avoided us, and went below without saying a word. Meanwhile, Long Ghost and I labored hard to diffuse the right spirit among the crew; impressing upon them that a little patience and management would, in the end, accomplish all that their violence could; and that, too, without making a serious matter of it.

For my own part, I felt that I was under a foreign flag; that an English consul was close at hand, and that sailors seldom obtain justice. It was best to be prudent. Still, so much did I sympathize with the men, so far, at least, as their real grievances were concerned; and so convinced was I of the cruelty and injustice of what Captain Guy seemed bent upon, that if need were, I stood ready to raise a hand.

In spite of all we could do, some of them again became most refractory, breathing nothing but downright mutiny. When we went below to dinner, these fellows stirred up such a prodigious tumult that the old hull fairly echoed. Many, and fierce too, were the speeches delivered, and uproarious the comments of the sailors. Among others, Long Jim, or —as the doctor afterward called him—Lacedæmonian Jim, rose in his place, and addressed the forecastle parliament in the following strain:

" Look ye, Britons! if, after what's happened, this here craft goes to sea with us, we are no men; and that's the way to say it. Speak the word, my livelies, and I'll pilot her in. I've been to Tahiti before, and I can do it." Whereupon, he sat down amid a universal pounding of chest-lids, and cymbaling of tin pans; the few invalids, who, as yet, had not been actively engaged with the rest, now taking part in the applause, creaking their bunk-boards and swinging their hammocks. Cries also were heard, of " Handspikes and a shindy! " " Out stunsails! " " Hurrah! "

Several now ran on deck, and, for the moment, I thought it was all over with us; but we finally succeeded in restoring some degree of quiet.

At last, by way of diverting their thoughts, I proposed that a " Round Robin " should be prepared and sent ashore to the consul, by Baltimore, the cook. The idea took mightily, and I was told to set about it at once. On turning to the doctor for the requisite materials, he told me he had none; there was not a fly-leaf, even, in any of his books. So, after great search, a damp, musty volume, entitled " A History of the most Atrocious and Bloody Piracies," was produced, and its two remaining blank leaves being torn out, were, by help of a little pitch, lengthened into one sheet. For ink, some of the soot over the lamp was then mixed with water, by a fellow of a literary turn; and an immense quill, plucked from a distended albatros' wing, which, nailed against the bowsprit bitts, had long formed an ornament of the forecastle, supplied a pen.

Making use of the stationery thus provided, I indited upon a chest-lid, a concise statement of our grievances; concluding with the earnest hope, that the consul would at once come off, and see how matters stood, for himself. Right beneath the note was described the circle about which the names were to be written; the great object of a Round Robin being to arrange the signatures in such a way, that, although they are all found in a ring, no man can be picked out as the leader of it.

Few among them had any regular names; many answering to some familiar title, expressive of a personal trait; or oftener still, to the name of the place from which they hailed; and in one or two cases were known by a handy syllable or two, significant of nothing in particular but the men who bore them. Some, to be sure, had, for the sake of formality, shipped under a feigned cognomen, or " Purser's name; " these, however, were almost forgotten by themselves; and so, to give the document an air of genuineness, it was decided that every man's name should be put down as it went among the crew. The annexed, therefore, as nearly as I can recall it, is something like a correct representation of the signatures. It is due the doctor, to say, that the circumscribed device was his.

Folded, and sealed with a drop of tar, the Round Robin was directed to " The English Consul, Tahiti;" and, handed to the cook, was by him delivered into that gentleman's hands as soon as the mate went ashore.

On the return of the boat, some time after dark, we learned a good deal from old Baltimore, who, having been allowed to run about as much as he pleased, had spent his time gossiping.

Owing to the proceedings of the French, every thing in Tahiti was in an uproar. Pritchard, the missionary consul, was absent in England; but his place was temporarily filled by one Wilson, an educated white man, born on the island, and the son of an old missionary of that name, still living.

With natives and foreigners alike, Wilson the younger was exceedingly unpopular, being held an unprincipled and dissipated man, a character verified by his subsequent conduct. Pritchard's selecting a man like this to attend to the duties of his office, had occasioned general dissatisfaction ashore.

Though never in Europe or America, the acting consul had been several voyages to Sydney in a schooner belonging to the mission; and therefore our surprise was lessened, when Baltimore told us, that he and Captain Guy were as sociable as could be—old acquaintances, in fact; and that the latter had taken up his quarters at Wilson's house. For us, this boded ill.

The mate was now assailed by a hundred questions as to what was going to be done with us. His only reply was, that in the morning the consul would pay us a visit, and settle every thing.

After holding our ground off the harbor during the night, in the morning a shore boat, manned by natives, was seen coming off. In it were Wilson and another white man, who proved to be a Doctor Johnson, an Englishman, and a resident physician of Papeetee.

Stopping our headway as they approached, Jermin advanced to the gangway to receive them. No sooner did the consul touch the deck, than he gave us a specimen of what he was.

"Mr. Jermin," he cried loftily, and not deigning to notice the respectful salutation• of the person addressed, "Mr. Jermin, tack ship, and stand off from the land."

Upon this, the men looked hard at him, anxious to see what sort of a looking "cove" he was. Upon inspection, he turned out to be an exceedingly minute "cove," with a viciously pugged nose, and a decidedly thin pair of legs. There was nothing else noticeable about him. Jermin, with ill assumed suavity, at once obeyed the order, and the ship's head soon pointed out to sea.

Now, contempt is as frequently produced at first sight as love; and thus was it with respect to Wilson. No one could look at him without conceiving a strong dislike, or a cordial desire to entertain such a feeling the first favorable opportunity. There was such an intolerable air of conceit about this man, that it was almost as much as one could do to refrain from running up and affronting him.

"So the *counselor* is come," exclaimed Navy Bob, who, like all the rest, invariably styled him thus, much to mine and the doctor's diversion. "Ay," said another, "and for no good, I'll be bound."

Such were some of the observations made, as Wilson and the mate went below conversing.

But no one exceeded the cooper in the violence with which he inveighed against the ship and every thing connected with her. Swearing like a trooper, he called the

main-mast to witness, that if he (Bungs) ever again went
out of sight of land in the Julia, he prayed Heaven that
a fate might be his—altogether too remarkable to be here
related.

Much had he to say also concerning the vileness of
what we had to eat—not fit for a dog; besides enlarging
upon the imprudence of intrusting the vessel longer to a
man of the mate's intemperate habits. With so many sick,
too, what could we expect to do in the fishery? It was no
use talking; come what come might, the ship must let go
her anchor.

Now, as Bungs, besides being an able seaman, a " Cod "
in the forecastle, and about the oldest man in it, was,
moreover, thus deeply imbued with feelings so warmly
responded to by the rest, he was all at once selected to
officiate as spokesman, so soon as the consul should see fit
to address us. The selection was made contrary to mine
and the doctor's advice; however, all assured us they
would keep quiet, and hear every thing Wilson had to say,
before doing any thing decisive.

We were not kept long in suspense; for very soon he
was seen standing in the cabin gangway, with the tarnished
tin case containing the ship's papers; and Jermin at once
sung out for the ship's company to muster on the quarter-
deck.

The Round-Robin.

CHAPTER XXI.

PROCEEDINGS OF THE CONSUL.

THE order was instantly obeyed, and the sailors ranged themselves, facing the consul.

They were a wild company; men of many climes—not at all precise in their toilet arrangements, but picturesque in their very tatters. My friend, the Long Doctor, was there too; and with a view, perhaps, of enlisting the sympathies of the consul for a gentleman in distress, had taken more than ordinary pains with his appearance. But among the sailors, he looked like a land-crane blown off to sea, and consorting with petrels.

The forlorn Rope Yarn, however, was by far the most remarkable figure. Land-lubber that he was, his outfit of sea-clothing had long since been confiscated; and he was now fain to go about in whatever he could pick up. His upper garment — an unsailor-like article of dress which he persisted in wearing, though torn from his back twenty times in the day—was an old " claw-hammer-jacket," or swallow-tail coat, formerly belonging to Captain Guy, and which had formed one of his perquisites when steward.

By the side of Wilson was the mate, bareheaded, his gray locks lying in rings upon his bronzed brow, and his keen eye scanning the crowd as if he knew their every thought. His frock hung loosely, exposing his round throat, mossy chest, and short and nervous arm embossed with pugilistic bruises, and quaint with many a device in India ink.

In the midst of a portentous silence, the consul unrolled his papers, evidently intending to produce an effect by the exceeding bigness of his looks.

" Mr. Jermin, call off their names; " and he handed him a list of the ship's company.

All answered but the deserters and the two mariners at the bottom of the sea.

It was now supposed that the Round Robin would be produced, and something said about it. But not so. Among the consul's papers, that unique document was thought to be perceived; but, if there, it was too much despised to be made a subject of comment. Some present, very justly regarding it as an uncommon literary production, had been anticipating all sorts of miracles therefrom; and were, therefore, much touched at this neglect.

" Well, men," began Wilson again after a short pause, " although you all look hearty enough, I'm told there are some sick among you. Now then, Mr. Jermin, call off the names on that sick-list of yours, and let them go over to the other side of the deck—I should like to see who they are."

" So, then," said he, after we had all passed over, " *you* are the sick fellows, are you? Very good: I shall have you seen to. You will go down into the cabin, one by one, to Doctor Johnson, who will report your respective cases to me. Such as he pronounces in a dying state I shall have sent ashore; the rest will be provided with every thing needful, and remain aboard."

At this announcement, we gazed strangely at each other, anxious to see who it was that looked like dying, and pretty nearly deciding to stay aboard and get well, rather than go ashore and be buried. There were some, nevertheless, who saw very plainly what Wilson was at, and they acted accordingly. For my own part, I resolved to assume as dying an expression as possible; hoping, that on the strength of it, I might be sent ashore, and so get rid of the ship without any further trouble.

With this intention, I determined to take no part in any thing that might happen, until my case was decided upon. As for the doctor, he had all along pretended to be more or less unwell; and by a significant look now given me, it was plain that he was becoming decidedly worse.

The invalids disposed of for the present, and one of them having gone below to be examined, the consul turned round to the rest, and addressed them as follows:

" Men, I'm going to ask you two or three questions—
let one of you answer yes or no, and the rest keep silent.
Now then: Have you any thing to say against your mate,
Mr. Jermin? " And he looked sharply among the sailors,
and, at last, right into the eye of the cooper, whom every
body was eying.

" Well, sir," faltered Bungs, " we can't say any thing
against Mr. Jermin's seamanship, but—"

" I want no *buts*," cried the consul, breaking in: " answer me *yes* or *no*—have you any thing to say against
Mr. Jermin? "

" I was going on to say, sir; Mr. Jermin's a very good
man; but then—" Here the mate looked marlingspikes at
Bungs; and Bungs, after stammering out something, looked
straight down to a seam in the deck, and stopped short.

A rather assuming fellow heretofore, the cooper had
sported many feathers in his cap; he was now showing the
white one.

" So much then for that part of the business," exclaimed
Wilson, smartly; " you have nothing to say against him,
I see."

Upon this, several seemed to be on the point of saying
a good deal; but disconcerted by the cooper's conduct,
checked themselves and the consul proceeded.

" Have you enough to eat, aboard? answer me, you man
who spoke before."

" Well, I don't know as to that," said the cooper, looking excessively uneasy, and trying to edge back, but pushed
forward again. " Some of that *salt horse* ain't as sweet as
it might be."

" That's not what I asked you," shouted the consul,
growing brave quite fast; " answer my questions as I put
them, or I'll find a way to make you."

This was going a little too far. The ferment, into which
the cooper's poltroonery had thrown the sailors, now
brooked no restraint; and one of them—a young American
who went by the name of Salem *—dashed out from

---

* So called from the place he hailed from; a well known seaport on the coast of Massachusetts.

among the rest, and fetching the cooper a blow, that sent him humming over toward the consul, flourished a naked sheath-knife in the air, and burst forth with " I'm the little fellow that can answer your questions; just put them to me once, counselor."

But the " counselor " had no more questions to ask just then; for at the alarming apparition of Salem's knife, and the extraordinary effect produced upon Bungs, he had popped his head down the companion-way, and was holding it there.

Upon the mate's assuring him, however, that it was all over, he looked up, quite flustered, if not frightened, but evidently determined to put as fierce a face on the matter as practicable. Speaking sharply, he warned all present to " look out; " and then repeated the question, whether there was enough to eat aboard. Every one now turned spokesman; and he was assailed by a perfect hurricane of yells, in which the oaths fell like hailstones.

" How's this! what d'ye mean? " he cried, upon the first lull; " who told you all to speak at once? Here, you man with the knife, you'll be putting some one's eyes out yet; d'ye hear, you sir? You seem to have a good deal to say, who are *you*, pray; where did *you* ship? "

" I'm nothing more nor a bloody *beech-comber*," * retorted Salem, stepping forward piratically and eying him; " and if you want to know, I shipped at the Islands about four months ago."

" Only four months ago? And here you have more to say than men who have been aboard the whole voyage; " and the consul made a dash at looking furious, but failed. " Let me hear no more from *you*, sir. Where's that respectable,

---

* This is a term much in vogue among sailors in the Pacific. It is applied to certain roving characters, who, without attaching themselves permanently to any vessel, ship now and then for a short cruise in a whaler; but upon the condition only of being honorably discharged the very next time the anchor takes hold of the bottom; no matter where. They are, mostly, a reckless, rollicking set, wedded to the Pacific, and never dreaming of ever doubling Cape Horn again on a homeward-bound passage. Hence, their reputation is a bad one.

gray-headed man, the cooper? *he's* the one to answer my questions."

"There's no 'spectable, gray-headed men aboard," returned Salem; "we're all a parcel of mutineers and pirates!"

All this time, the mate was holding his peace; and Wilson, now completely abashed, and at a loss what to do, took him by the arm, and walked across the deck. Returning to the cabin-scuttle, after a close conversation, he abruptly addressed the sailors, without taking any further notice of what had just happened.

"For reasons you all know, men, this ship has been placed in my hands. As Captain Guy will remain ashore for the present, your mate, Mr. Jermin, will command until his recovery. According to my judgment, there is no reason why the voyage should not be at once resumed; especially, as I shall see that you have two more harponeers, and enough good men to man three boats. As for the sick, neither you nor I have any thing to do with them; they will be attended to by Doctor Johnson; but I've explained that matter before. As soon as things can be arranged—in a day or two, at farthest—you will go to sea for a three months' cruise, touching here, at the end of it, for your captain. Let me hear a good report of you, now, when you come back. At present, you will continue lying off and on the harbor. I will send you fresh provisions as soon as I can get them. There: I've nothing more to say; go forward to your stations."

And, without another word, he wheeled round to descend into the cabin. But hardly had he concluded, before the incensed men were dancing about him on every side, and calling upon him to lend an ear. Each one for himself denied the legality of what he proposed to do; insisted upon the necessity for taking the ship in; and finally gave him to understand, roughly and roundly, that go to sea in her they would not.

In the midst of this mutinous uproar, the alarmed consul stood fast by the scuttle. His tactics had been decided upon beforehand; indeed, they must have been concerted ashore, between him and the captain; for all he said, as he now hurried below, was, "Go forward, men; I'm through with you: you should have mentioned these matters before: my arrangements are concluded: go forward, I say; I've nothing more to say to you." And, drawing over the slide of the scuttle, he disappeared.

Upon the very point of following him down, the attention of the exasperated seamen was called off to a party who had just then taken the recreant Bungs in hand. Amid a shower of kicks and cuffs, the traitor was borne along to the forecastle, where—I forbear to relate what followed.

CHAPTER XXII.

THE CONSUL'S DEPARTURE.

During the scenes just described, Doctor Johnson was engaged in examining the sick; of whom, as it turned out, all but two were to remain in the ship. He had evidently received his cue from Wilson.

One of the last called below into the cabin, just as the quarter-deck gathering dispersed, I came on deck quite incensed. My lameness, which, to tell the truth, was now much better, was put down as, in a great measure, affected; and my name was on the list of those who would be fit for any duty in a day or two. This was enough. As for Doctor Long Ghost, the shore physician, instead of extending to him any professional sympathy, had treated him very cavalierly. To a certain extent, therefore, we were now both bent on making common cause with the sailors.

I must explain myself here. All we wanted was to have the ship snugly anchored in Papeetee Bay; entertaining no doubt that, could this be done, it would in some way or other peaceably lead to our emancipation. Without a downright mutiny, there was but one way to accomplish this: to induce the men to refuse all further duty, unless it were to work the vessel in. The only difficulty lay in restraining them within proper bounds. Nor was it without certain misgivings, that I found myself so situated, that I must necessarily link myself, however guardedly, with such a desperate company; and in an enterprise too, of which it was hard to conjecture what might be the result. But any thing like neutrality was out of the question; and unconditional submission was equally so.

On going forward, we found them ten times more tumultuous than ever. After again restoring some degree of tranquillity, we once more urged our plan of quietly refusing duty, and awaiting the result. At first, few would hear of it; but in the end, a good number were convinced by our representations. Others held out. Nor were those who thought with us, in all things to be controlled.

Upon Wilson's coming on deck to enter his boat, he was beset on all sides; and, for a moment, I thought the ship would be seized before his very eyes.

" Nothing more to say to you, men; my arrangements are made. Go forward, where you belong. I'll take no insolence;" and, in a tremor, Wilson hurried over the side in the midst of a volley of execrations.

Shortly after his departure, the mate ordered the cook and steward into his boat; and saying that he was going to see how the captain did, left us, as before, under the charge of Bembo.

At this time we were lying becalmed, pretty close in with the land (having gone about again), our main-topsail flapping against the mast with every roll.

The departure of the consul and Jermin was followed by a scene absolutely indescribable. The sailors ran about deck like madmen; Bembo, all the while, leaning against the taffrail by himself, smoking his heathenish stone pipe, and never interfering.

The cooper, who that morning had got himself into a fluid of an exceedingly high temperature, now did his best to regain the favor of the crew. " Without distinction of party," he called upon all hands to step up, and partake of the contents of his bucket.

But it was quite plain that, before offering to intoxicate others, he had taken the wise precaution of getting well tipsy himself. He was now once more happy in the affection of his shipmates, who, one and all, pronounced him sound to the kelson.

The Pisco soon told; and, with great difficulty, we restrained a party in the very act of breaking into the after-hold in pursuit of more.

All manner of pranks were now played.

" Mast-head, there! what d'ye see? " bawled Beauty, hailing the main-truck through an enormous copper tunnel. " Stand by for stays," roared Flash Jack, hauling off with the cook's axe, at the fastenings of the main-stay. " Looky out for 'qualls! " shrieked the Portuguese, Antone, darting a handspike through the cabin sky-light. And " Heave round cheerly, men," sung out Navy Bob, dancing a hornpipe on the forecastle.

CHAPTER XXIII.

THE SECOND NIGHT OFF PAPEETEE.

Toward sunset, the mate came off, singing merrily, in the stern of his boat; and in attempting to climb up the side, succeeded in going plump into the water. He was rescued by the steward, and carried across the deck with many moving expressions of love for his bearer. Tumbled into the quarter-boat, he soon fell asleep, and waking about midnight, somewhat sobered, went forward among the men. Here, to prepare for what follows, we must leave him for a moment.

It was now plain enough, that Jermin was by no means unwilling to take the Julia to sea; indeed, there was nothing he so much desired; though what his reasons were, seeing our situation, we could only conjecture. Nevertheless, so it was; and having counted much upon his rough popularity with the men to reconcile them to a short cruise under him, he had consequently been disappointed in their behavior. Still, thinking that they would take a different view of the matter, when they came to know what fine times he had in store for them, he resolved upon trying a little persuasion.

So on going forward, he put his head down the fore-castle scuttle, and hailed us all quite cordially, inviting us down into the cabin; where, he said, he had something to make merry withal. Nothing loth, we went; and throwing ourselves along the transom, waited for the steward to serve us.

As the can circulated, Jermin, leaning on the table and occupying the captain's arm-chair secured to the deck, opened his mind as bluntly and freely as ever. He was by no means yet sober.

He told us we were acting very foolishly; that if we only stuck to the ship, he would lead us all a jovial life of it; enumerating the casks still remaining untapped in the Julia's wooden cellar. It was even hinted vaguely, that such a thing might happen as our not coming back for the captain; whom he spoke of but lightly; asserting, what he had often said before, that he was no sailor.

Moreover, and perhaps with special reference to Doctor Long Ghost and myself, he assured us generally, that if there were any among us studiously inclined, he would take great pleasure in teaching such the whole art and mystery of navigation, including the gratuitous use of his quadrant.

I should have mentioned, that previous to this, he had taken the doctor aside, and said something about reinstating him in the cabin with augmented dignity; beside throwing out a hint, that I myself, was in some way or other to be promoted. But it was all to no purpose; bent the men were upon going ashore, and there was no moving them.

At last he flew into a rage—much increased by the frequency of his potations—and with many imprecations, concluded by driving every body out of the cabin. We tumbled up the gangway in high good-humor.

Upon deck every thing looked so quiet, that some of the most pugnacious spirits actually lamented that there was so little prospect of an exhilarating disturbance before morning. It was not five minutes, however, ere these fellows were gratified.

Sydney Ben—said to be a runaway Ticket-of-Leave-Man,* and for reasons of his own, one of the few who still remained on duty—had, for the sake of the fun, gone down with the rest into the cabin; where Bembo, who meanwhile was left in charge of the deck, had frequently called out for him. At first, Ben pretended not to hear; but on being sung out for again and again, bluntly refused; at the same time, casting some illiberal reflections on the Mowree's maternal origin, which the latter had been long enough among sailors to understand as in the highest degree offensive. So just after the men came up from below, Bembo singled him out, and gave him such a cursing in his broken lingo, that it was enough to frighten one. The convict was the worse for liquor; indeed the Mowree had been tippling also, and before we knew it, a blow was struck by Ben, and the two men came together like magnets.

The Ticket-of-Leave-Man was a practiced bruiser; but the savage knew nothing of the art pugilistic: and so they were even. It was clear hugging and wrenching till both came to the deck. Here they rolled over and over in the middle of a ring which seemed to form of itself. At last the white man's head fell back, and his face grew purple. Bembo's teeth were at his throat. Rushing in all round, they hauled the savage off, but not until repeatedly struck on the head would he let go.

His rage was now absolutely demoniac; he lay glaring, and writhing on the deck, without attempting to rise. Cowed, as they supposed he was, from his attitude, the

---

* Some of the most " promising " convicts in New South Wales are hired out to the citizens as servants; thus being, in some degree, permitted to go at large, government, however, still claiming them as wards. They are provided with tickets, which they are obliged to show to any one who pleases to suspect their being abroad without warrant. Hence the above appellation. This was the doctor's explanation of the term.

men, rejoiced at seeing him thus humbled, left him; after rating him in sailor style, for a cannibal and a coward.

Ben was attended to, and led below.

Soon after this, the rest also, with but few exceptions, retired into the forecastle; and having been up nearly all the previous night, they quickly dropped about the chests and rolled into the hammocks. In an hour's time, not a sound could be heard in that part of the ship.

Before Bembo was dragged away, the mate had in vain endeavored to separate the combatants, repeatedly striking the Mowree; but the seamen interposing, at last kept him off.

And intoxicated as he was, when they dispersed, he knew enough to charge the steward—a steady seaman be it remembered—with the present safety of the ship; and then went below, where he fell directly into another drunken sleep.

Having remained upon deck with the doctor some time after the rest had gone below, I was just on the point of following him down, when I saw the Mowree rise, draw a bucket of water, and holding it high above his head, pour its contents right over him. This he repeated several times. There was nothing very peculiar in the act, but something else about him struck me. However, I thought no more of it, but descended the scuttle.

After a restless nap, I found the atmosphere of the forecastle so close, from nearly all the men being down at the same time, that I hunted up an old pea-jacket and went on deck; intending to sleep it out there till morning. Here I found the cook and steward, Wymontoo, Rope Yarn, and the Dane; who, being all quiet, manageable fellows, and holding aloof from the rest since the captain's departure, had been ordered by the mate not to go below until sunrise. They were lying under the lee of the bulwarks; two or three fast asleep, and the others smoking their pipes, and conversing.

To my surprise, Bembo was at the helm; but there being so few to stand there now, they told me, he had offered to take his turn with the rest, at the same time heading the watch; and to this, of course, they made no objection.

It was a fine, bright night; all moon and stars, and white crests of waves. The breeze was light, but freshening; and close hauled, poor little Jule, as if nothing had happened, was heading in for the land, which rose high and hazy in the distance.

After the day's uproar, the tranquillity of the scene was soothing, and I leaned over the side to enjoy it.

More than ever did I now lament my situation—but it was useless to repine, and I could not upbraid myself. So at last, becoming drowsy, I made a bed with my jacket under the windlass, and tried to forget myself.

How long I lay there, I can not tell; but as I rose, the first object that met my eye, was Bembo at the helm; his dark figure slowly rising and falling with the ship's motion against the spangled heavens behind. He seemed all impatience and expectation; standing at arm's length from the spokes, with one foot advanced, and his bare head thrust forward. Where I was, the watch were out of sight; and no one else was stirring; the deserted decks and broad white sails were gleaming in the moonlight.

Presently, a swelling, dashing sound came upon my ear, and I had a sort of vague consciousness that I had been hearing it before. The next instant I was broad awake and on my feet. Right ahead, and so near that my heart stood still, was a long line of breakers, heaving and frothing. It was the coral reef, girdling the island. Behind it, and almost casting their shadows upon the deck, were the sleeping mountains, about whose hazy peaks the gray dawn was just breaking. The breeze had freshened, and with a steady, gliding motion, we were running straight for the reef.

All was taken in at a glance; the fell purpose of Bembo was obvious, and with a frenzied shout to wake the watch, I rushed aft. They sprang to their feet bewildered; and after a short, but desperate scuffle, we tore him from the helm. In wrestling with him, the wheel—left for a moment unguarded—flew to leeward, thus, fortunately, bringing the

ship's head to the wind, and so retarding her progress.
Previous to this, she had been kept three or four points
free, so as to close with the breakers. Her headway now
shortened, I steadied the helm, keeping the sails just lifting, while we glided obliquely toward the land. To have
run off before the wind—an easy thing—would have been
almost instant destruction, owing to a curve of the reef in
that direction. At this time, the Dane and the steward
were still struggling with the furious Mowree, and the
others were running about irresolute and shouting.

But darting forward the instant I had the helm, the old
cook thundered on the forecastle with a handspike,
"Breakers! breakers close aboard!—'bout ship! 'bout ship!"

Up came the sailors, staring about them in stupid horror.

"Haul back the head-yards!" "Let go the lee fore-
brace!" "Ready about! about!" were now shouted on all
sides; while distracted by a thousand orders, they ran
hither and thither, fairly panic-stricken.

It seemed all over with us; and I was just upon the
point of throwing the ship full into the wind (a step,
which, saving us for the instant, would have sealed our
fate in the end), when a sharp cry shot by my ear like
the flight of an arrow.

It was Salem: "All ready for'ard; hard down!"

Round and round went the spokes—the Julia, with
her short keel, spinning to windward like a top. Soon,
the jib-sheets lashed the stays, and the men, more self-
possessed, flew to the braces.

"Main-sail haul!" was now heard, as the fresh breeze
streamed fore and aft the deck; and directly the after-
yards were whirled round.

In half-a-minute more, we were sailing away from the
land on the other tack, with every sail distended.

Turning on our heel within little more than a biscuit's
toss of the reef, no earthly power could have saved us, were
it not that, up to the very brink of the coral rampart,
there are no soundings.

CHAPTER XXIV.

OUTBREAK OF THE CREW.

THE purpose of Bembo had been made known to the men generally by the watch; and now that our salvation was certain, by an instinctive impulse they raised a cry, and rushed toward him.

Just before liberated by Dunk and the steward, he was standing doggedly by the mizen-mast; and, as the infuriated sailors came on, his bloodshot eye rolled, and his sheath-knife glittered over his head.

"Down with him!" "Strike him down!" "Hang him at the main-yard!" such were the shouts now raised. But he stood unmoved, and, for a single instant, they absolutely faltered.

"Cowards!" cried Salem, and he flung himself upon him. The steel descended like a ray of light; but did no harm; for the sailor's heart was beating against the Mowree's before he was aware.

They both fell to the deck, when the knife was instantly seized, and Bembo secured.

"For'ard! for'ard with him!" was again the cry; "give him a sea-toss!" "overboard with him!" and he was dragged along the deck, struggling and fighting with tooth and nail.

All this uproar immediately over the mate's head at last roused him from his drunken nap, and he came staggering on deck.

"What's this?" he shouted, running right in among them.

"It's the Mowree, zur; they are going to murder him, zur," here sobbed poor Rope Yarn, crawling close up to him.

"Avast! avast!" roared Jermin, making a spring toward Bembo, and dashing two or three of the sailors aside. At this moment the wretch was partly flung over the bulwarks, which shook with his frantic struggles. In vain the doctor and others tried to save him: the men listened to nothing.

"Murder and mutiny, by the salt sea!" shouted the mate; and dashing his arms right and left, he planted his iron hand upon the Mowree's shoulder.

"There are two of us now; and as you serve him, you serve me," he cried, turning fiercely round.

"Over with them together, then," exclaimed the carpenter, springing forward; but the rest fell back before the courageous front of Jermin, and, with the speed of thought, Bembo, unharmed, stood upon deck.

"Aft with ye!" cried his deliverer; and he pushed him right among the men, taking care to follow him up close. Giving the sailors no time to recover, he pushed the Mowree before him, till they came to the cabin scuttle, when he drew the slide over him, and stood still. Throughout, Bembo never spoke one word.

"Now for'ard where ye belong!" cried the mate, addressing the seamen, who by this time, rallying again, had no idea of losing their victim.

"The Mowree! the Mowree!" they shouted.

Here the doctor, in answer to the mate's repeated questions, stepped forward, and related what Bembo had been doing; a matter which the mate but dimly understood from the violent threatenings he had been hearing.

For a moment he seemed to waver; but at last, turning the key in the padlock of the slide, he breathed through his set teeth—"Ye can't have him; I'll hand him over to the consul; so for'ard with ye, I say: when there's any drowning to be done, I'll pass the word; so away with ye, ye blood-thirsty pirates!"

It was to no purpose that they begged or threatened: Jermin, although by no means sober, stood his ground manfully, and before long they dispersed, soon to forget every thing that had happened.

Though we had no opportunity to hear him confess it, Bembo's intention to destroy us was beyond all question. His only motive could have been, a desire to revenge the contumely heaped upon him the night previous, operating upon a heart irreclaimably savage, and at no time fraternally disposed toward the crew.

During the whole of this scene the doctor did his best to save him. But well knowing that all I could do, would have been equally useless, I maintained my place at the wheel. Indeed, no one but Jermin could have prevented this murder.

CHAPTER XXV.

JERMIN ENCOUNTERS AN OLD SHIPMATE.

During the morning of the day which dawned upon the events just recounted, we remained a little to leeward of the harbor, waiting the appearance of the consul, who had promised the mate to come off in a shore boat for the purpose of seeing him.

By this time the men had forced his secret from the cooper; and the consequence was, that they kept him continually coming and going from the after-hold. The mate must have known this; but he said nothing, notwithstanding all the dancing, and singing, and occasional fighting which announced the flow of the Pisco.

The peaceable influence which the doctor and myself had heretofore been exerting, was now very nearly at an end.

Confident, from the aspect of matters, that the ship, after all, would be obliged to go in; and learning, moreover, that the mate had said so, the sailors, for the present, seemed in no hurry about it; especially as the bucket of Bungs gave such generous cheer.

As for Bembo, we were told that, after putting him in double irons, the mate had locked him up in the captain's state-room, taking the additional precaution of keeping the cabin scuttle secured. From this time forward we never saw the Mowree again, a circumstance which will explain itself as the narrative proceeds.

Noon came, and no consul; and as the afternoon advanced without any word even from the shore, the mate was justly incensed; more especially, as he had taken great pains to keep perfectly sober against Wilson's arrival.

Two or three hours before sundown, a small schooner came out of the harbor, and headed over for the adjoining island of Imeeo, or Moreea, in plain sight, about fifteen miles distant. The wind failing, the current swept her down under our bows, where we had a fair glimpse of the natives on her decks.

There were a score of them, perhaps, lounging upon spread mats, and smoking their pipes. On floating so near, and hearing the maudlin cries of our crew, and beholding their antics, they must have taken us for a pirate; at any rate, they got out their sweeps, and pulled away as fast as they could; the sight of our two six-pounders, which, by way of a joke, were now run out of the side-ports, giving a fresh impetus to their efforts. But they had not gone far, when a white man, with a red sash about his waist, made his appearance on deck, the natives immediately desisting.

Hailing us loudly, he said he was coming aboard; and after some confusion on the schooner's decks, a small canoe was lanched overboard, and, in a minute or two, he was with us. He turned out to be an old shipmate of Jermin's, one Viner, long supposed dead, but now resident on the island.

The meeting of these men, under the circumstances, is one of a thousand occurrences appearing exaggerated in fiction; but, nevertheless, frequently realized in actual lives of adventure.

Some fifteen years previous, they had sailed together as officers of the bark Jane, of London, a South Seaman. Somewhere near the New Hebrides, they struck one night upon an unknown reef; and, in a few hours, the Jane went to pieces. The boats, however, were saved; some provisions also, a quadrant, and a few other articles. But several of the men were lost before they got clear of the wreck.

The three boats, commanded respectively by the captain, Jermin, and the third mate, then set sail for a small English settlement at the Bay of Islands in New Zealand. Of course they kept together as much as possible. After being at sea about a week, a Lascar in the captain's boat went crazy; and, it being dangerous to keep him, they tried to throw him overboard. In the confusion that ensued, the boat capsized from the sail's " jibing; " and a considerable sea running at the time, and the other boats being separated more than usual, only one man was picked up. The very next night it blew a heavy gale; and the remaining boats taking in all sail, made bundles of their oars, flung them overboard, and rode to them with plenty of line. When morning broke, Jermin and his men were alone upon the ocean; the third mate's boat, in all probability, having gone down.

After great hardships, the survivors caught sight of a brig, which took them on board, and eventually landed them in Sydney.

Ever since then our mate had sailed from that port, never once hearing of his lost shipmates, whom, by this time, of course, he had long given up. Judge, then, his feelings, when Viner, the lost third mate, the instant he touched the deck, rushed up and wrung him by the hand.

During the gale his line had parted; so that the boat, drifting fast to leeward, was out of sight by morning. Reduced, after this, to great extremities, the boat touched, for fruit, at an island of which they knew nothing. The natives, at first, received them kindly; but one of the men getting into a quarrel on account of a woman, and the rest taking his part, they were all massacred but Viner, who, at the time, was in an adjoining village. After staying on the island more than two years, he finally escaped in the boat of an American whaler, which landed him at Valparaiso. From this period he had continued to follow the seas, as a man before the mast, until, about eighteen months previous, when he went ashore at Tahiti, where he now owned the schooner we saw, in which he traded among the neighboring islands.

The breeze springing up again just after nightfall, Viner left us, promising his old shipmate to see him again, three days hence, in Papeetee harbor.

CHAPTER XXVI.

WE ENTER THE HARBOR.—JIM THE PILOT.

EXHAUSTED by the day's wassail, most of the men went below at an early hour, leaving the deck to the steward and two of the men remaining on duty; the mate, with Baltimore and the Dane, engaging to relieve them at midnight. At that hour, the ship—now standing off shore, under short sail—was to be tacked.

It was not long after midnight, when we were wakened in the forecastle by the lion roar of Jermin's voice, ordering a pull at the jib-halyards; and soon afterward, a handspike struck the scuttle, and all hands were called to take the ship into port.

This was wholly unexpected; but we learned directly, that the mate, no longer relying upon the consul, and renouncing all thought of inducing the men to change their minds, had suddenly made up his own. He was going to beat up to the entrance of the harbor, so as to show a signal for a pilot before sunrise.

Notwithstanding this, the sailors absolutely refused to assist in working the ship under any circumstances whatever: to all mine and the doctor's entreaties lending a deaf ear. Sink or strike, they swore they would have nothing more to do with her. This perverseness was to be attributed, in a great measure, to the effects of their late debauch.

With a strong breeze, all sail set, and the ship in the hands of four or five men, exhausted by two nights' watching, our situation was bad enough; especially as the mate seemed more reckless than ever, and we were now to tack ship several times close under the land.

Well knowing that if any thing untoward happened to the vessel before morning, it would be imputed to the conduct of the crew, and so lead to serious results, should they ever be brought to trial; I called together those on deck, to witness my declaration:—that now that the Julia was destined for the harbor (the only object for which *I*, at least, had been struggling), I was willing to do what I could, toward carrying her in safely. In this step I was followed by the doctor.

The hours passed anxiously until morning; when, being well to windward of the mouth of the harbor, we bore up for it, with the union-jack at the fore. No sign, however, of boat or pilot was seen; and after running close in several times, the ensign was set at the mizen-peak, union down in distress. But it was of no avail.

Attributing to Wilson this unaccountable remissness on the part of those ashore, Jermin, quite enraged, now determined to stand boldly in upon his own responsibility; trusting solely to what he remembered of the harbor on a visit there many years previous.

This resolution was characteristic. Even with a competent pilot, Papeetee Bay is considered a ticklish one to enter. Formed by a bold sweep of the shore, it is protected seaward by the coral reef, upon which the rollers break with great violence. After stretching across the bay, the barrier extends on toward Point Venus,* in the district of Matavai, eight or nine miles distant. Here there is an opening, by which ships enter, and glide down the smooth, deep canal, between the reef and the shore, to the harbor. But, by seamen generally, the leeward entrance is preferred, as the wind is extremely variable inside the reef. This latter entrance is a break in the barrier directly facing the bay and village of Papeetee. It is very narrow; and, from

---

* The most northerly point of the island; and so called from Cook's observatory being placed there during his first visit.

the baffling winds, currents, and sunken rocks, ships now and then grate their keels against the coral.

But the mate was not to be daunted; so, stationing what men he had at the braces, he sprang upon the bulwarks, and, bidding every body keep wide awake, ordered the helm up. In a few moments, we were running in. Being toward noon, the wind was fast leaving us, and, by the time the breakers were roaring on either hand, little more than steerage-way was left. But on we glided — smoothly and deftly; avoiding the green, darkling objects here and there strewn in our path: Jermin occasionally looking down in the water, and then about him, with the utmost calmness, and not a word spoken. Just fanned along thus, it was not many minutes ere we were past all danger, and floated into the placid basin within. This was the cleverest specimen of his seamanship that he ever gave us.

As we held on toward the frigate and shipping, a canoe, coming out from among them, approached. In it were a boy and an old man—both islanders; the former nearly naked, and the latter dressed in an old naval frock-coat. Both were paddling with might and main; the old man, once in a while, tearing his paddle out of the water; and, after rapping his companion over the head, both fell to with fresh vigor. As they came within hail, the old fellow, springing to his feet and flourishing his paddle, cut some of the queerest of capers; all the while jabbering something which at first we could not understand.

Presently we made out the following: —" Ah! you *pemi*, ah!—you come!—What for you come?—You be fine for come no pilot.—I say, you *hear?*—I say, you *ita maitai* (no good).—You *hear?*—You no pilot.—Yes, you d——me, you no pilot 't all; I d——you; you *hear?* "

This tirade, which showed plainly that, whatever the profane old rascal was at, he was in right good earnest, produced peals of laughter from the ship. Upon which, he seemed to get beside himself; and the boy, who, with suspended paddle, was staring about him, received a sound box over the head, which set him to work in a twinkling, and brought the canoe quite near. The orator now opening

afresh, it turned out that his vehement rhetoric was all
addressed to the mate, still standing conspicuously on the
bulwarks.

But Jermin was in no humor for nonsense; so, with a
sailor's blessing, he ordered him off. The old fellow then
flew into a regular frenzy, cursing and swearing worse than
any civilized being I ever heard.

"You *sabbee* * me?" he shouted. "You know me, ah?
Well: me *Jim,* me *pilot*—been pilot now long time."

"Ay," cried Jermin, quite surprised, as indeed we all
were, "you are the pilot, then, you old pagan. Why didn't
you come off before this?"

"Ah! me *sabbee,*—me know—you *piratee* (pirate)—see
you long time, but no me come—I *sabbee* you—you *ita
maitai nuee* (superlatively bad)."

"Paddle away with ye," roared Jermin, in a rage; "be
off! or I'll dart a harpoon at ye!"

But, instead of obeying the order, Jim, seizing his paddle,
darted the canoe right up to the gangway, and, in two
bounds, stood on deck. Pulling a greasy silk handkerchief
still lower over his brow, and improving the sit of his
frock-coat with a vigorous jerk, he then strode up to the
mate; and, in a more flowery style than ever, gave him to
understand that the redoubtable "Jim," himself, was before
him; that the ship was *his* until the anchor was down; and
he should like to hear what any one had to say to it.

As there now seemed little doubt that he was all he
claimed to be, the Julia was at last surrendered.

Our gentleman now proceeded to bring us to an anchor,
jumping up between the knight-heads, and bawling out
"Luff! luff! *keepy off! keepy off!*" and insisting upon each
time being respectfully responded to by the man at the
helm. At this time our steerage-way was almost gone; and
yet, in giving his orders, the passionate old man made as
much fuss as a white squall aboard the Flying Dutchman.

---

* A corruption of the French word *savoir,* much in use among
sailors of all nations, and hence made familiar to many of the
natives of Polynesia.

Jim turned out to be the regular pilot of the harbor; a post, be it known, of no small profit; and, in *his* eyes, at least, invested with immense importance.* Our unceremonious entrance, therefore, was regarded as highly insulting, and tending to depreciate both the dignity and lucrativeness of his office.

The old man is something of a wizard. Having an understanding with the elements, certain phenomena of theirs are exhibited for his particular benefit. Unusually clear weather, with a fine steady breeze, is a certain sign that a merchantman is at hand; whale-spouts seen from the harbor, are tokens of a whaling vessel's approach; and thunder and lightning, happening so seldom as they do, are proof positive that a man-of-war is drawing near.

In short, Jim, the pilot, is quite a character in his way; and no one visits Tahiti without hearing some curious story about him.

CHAPTER XXVII.

A GLANCE AT PAPEETEE.—
WE ARE SENT ABOARD THE FRIGATE.

THE village of Papeetee struck us all very pleasantly. Lying in a semicircle round the bay, the tasteful mansions of the chiefs and foreign residents impart an air of tropical elegance, heightened by the palm-trees waving here and there, and the deep-green groves of the Bread-Fruit in the background. The squalid huts of the common people are out of sight, and there is nothing to mar the prospect.

All round the water, extends a wide, smooth beach of

---

* For a few years past, more than one hundred and fifty sail have annually touched at Tahiti. They are principally whalemen, whose cruising-grounds lie in the vicinity. The harbor dues—going to the queen—are so high, that they have often been protested against. Jim, I believe, gets five silvers dollars for every ship brought in.

mixed pebbles and fragments of coral. This forms the thoroughfare of the village; the handsomest houses all facing it—the fluctuations of the tides * being so inconsiderable, that they cause no inconvenience.

The Pritchard residence—a fine large building—occupies a site on one side of the bay: a green lawn slopes off to the sea; and in front waves the English flag. Across the water, the tricolor also, and the stars and stripes, distinguish the residences of the other consuls.

What greatly added to the picturesqueness of the bay at this time, was the condemned hull of a large ship, which at the farther end of the harbor lay bilged upon the beach, its stern settled low in the water, and the other end high and dry. From where we lay, the trees behind seemed to lock their leafy boughs over its bowsprit; which, from its position, looked nearly upright.

She was an American whaler, a very old craft. Having sprung a leak at sea, she had made all sail for the island, to heave down for repairs. Found utterly unseaworthy, however, her oil was taken out and sent home in another vessel; the hull was then stripped and sold for a trifle.

Before leaving Tahiti, I had the curiosity to go over this poor old ship, thus stranded on a strange shore. What were my emotions, when I saw upon her stern the name of a small town on the river Hudson! She was from the noble stream on whose banks I was born; in whose waters I had a hundred times bathed. In an instant, palm-trees and elms—canoes and skiffs—church spires and bamboos— all mingled in one vision of the present and the past.

But we must not leave Little Jule.

At last the wishes of many were gratified; and like an aeronaut's grapnel, her rusty little anchor was caught in the coral groves at the bottom of Papeetee Bay. This must

---

* The Newtonian theory concerning the tides does not hold good at Tahiti; where, throughout the year, the waters uniformly commence ebbing at noon and midnight, and flow about sunset and daybreak. Hence the term Tooerar-Po is used alike to express high-water and midnight.

have been more than forty days after leaving the Marquesas.

The sails were yet unfurled, when a boat came alongside with our esteemed friend Wilson, the consul.

"How's this, how's this, Mr. Jermin?" he began, looking very savage as he touched the deck. "What brings you in without orders?"

"You did not come off to us, as you promised, sir; and there was no hanging on longer with nobody to work the ship," was the blunt reply.

"So the infernal scoundrels held out—did they? Very good, I'll make them *sweat* for it," and he eyed the scowling men with unwonted intrepidity. The truth was, he felt safer *now*, than when outside the reef.

"Muster the mutineers on the quarter-deck," he continued. "Drive them aft, sir, sick and well: I have a word to say to them."

"Now, men," said he, "you think it's all well with you, I suppose. You wished the ship in, and here she is. Captain Guy's ashore, and you think you must go too: but we'll see about that—I'll miserably disappoint you." (These last were his very words.) "Mr. Jermin, call off the names of those who did not refuse duty, and let them go over to the starboard side."

This done, a list was made out of the "mutineers," as he was pleased to call the rest. Among these, the doctor and myself were included; though the former stepped forward, and boldly pleaded the office held by him when the vessel left Sydney. The mate also—who had always been friendly—stated the service rendered by myself two nights previous, as well as my conduct when he announced his intention to enter the harbor. For myself, I stoutly maintained, that according to the tenor of the agreement made with Captain Guy, my time aboard the ship had expired—the cruise being virtually at an end, however it had been brought about—and I claimed my discharge.

But Wilson would hear nothing. Marking something in my manner, nevertheless, he asked my name and country; and then observed with a sneer, "Ah, you are the lad, I see, that wrote the Round Robin; I'll take good care of *you*, my fine fellow—step back, sir."

As for poor Long Ghost, he denounced him as a " Sydney Flash-Gorger; " though what under heaven he meant by that euphonious title, is more than I can tell. Upon this, the doctor gave him such a piece of his mind, that the consul furiously commanded him to hold his peace, or he would instantly have him seized into the rigging, and flogged. There was no help for either of us—we were judged by the company we kept.

All were now sent forward; not a word being said as to what he intended doing with us.

After a talk with the mate, the consul withdrew, going aboard the French frigate, which lay within a cable's length. We now suspected his object; and since matters had come to this pass, were rejoiced at it. In a day or two the Frenchman was to sail for Valparaiso, the usual place of rendezvous for the English squadron in the Pacific; and doubtless, Wilson meant to put us on board, and send us thither to be delivered up. Should our conjecture prove correct, all we had to expect, according to our most experienced shipmates, was the fag end of a cruise in one of her majesty's ships, and a discharge before long at Portsmouth.

We now proceeded to put on all the clothes we could—frock over frock, and trowsers over trowsers—so as to be in readiness for removal at a moment's warning. Armed ships allow nothing superfluous to litter up the deck; and therefore, should we go aboard the frigate, our chests and their contents would have to be left behind.

In an hour's time, the first-cutter of the Reine Blanche came alongside, manned by eighteen or twenty sailors, armed with cutlasses and boarding-pistols—the officers, of course, wearing their side-arms, and the consul in an official cocked hat, borrowed for the occasion. The boat was painted a "pirate black," its crew were a dark, grim-looking set, and the officers uncommonly fierce-looking little Frenchmen. On the whole they were calculated to intimidate — the consul's object, doubtless, in bringing them.

Summoned aft again, every one's name was called separately; and being solemnly reminded that it was his last chance to escape punishment, was asked if he still refused duty. The response was instantaneous: "Ay, sir, I do." In some cases followed up by divers explanatory observations, cut short by Wilson's ordering the delinquent into the cutter. As a general thing, the order was promptly obeyed —some taking a sequence of hops, skips, and jumps, by way of showing, not only their unimpaired activity of body, but their alacrity in complying with all reasonable requests.

Having avowed their resolution not to pull another rope of the Julia's—even if at once restored to perfect health —all the invalids, with the exception of the two to be set ashore, accompanied us into the cutter. They were in high spirits; so much so, that something was insinuated about their not having been quite as ill as pretended.

The cooper's name was the last called; we did not hear what he answered, but he stayed behind. Nothing was done about the Mowree.

Shoving clear from the ship, three loud cheers were raised; Flash Jack and others receiving a sharp reprimand for it from the consul.

"Good-by, Little Jule," cried Navy Bob, as we swept under the bows. "Don't fall overboard, Ropey," said another to the poor land-lubber, who, with Wymontoo, the Dane, and others left behind, was looking over at us from the forecastle.

"Give her three more!" cried Salem, springing to his feet and whirling his hat round. "You sacre dam raskeel," shouted the lieutenant of the party, bringing the flat of his sabre across his shoulders, "you now keepy steel."

The doctor and myself, more discreet, sat quietly in the bow of the cutter; and for my own part, though I did not repent what I had done, my reflections were far from being enviable.

CHAPTER XXVIII.

RECEPTION FROM THE FRENCHMAN.

In a few moments, we were paraded in the frigate's gangway; the first lieutenant—an elderly, yellow-faced officer, in an ill-cut coat and tarnished gold lace—coming up, and frowning upon us.

This gentleman's head was a mere bald spot; his legs, sticks; in short, his whole physical vigor seemed exhausted in the production of one enormous moustache. Old Gamboge, as he was forthwith christened, now received a paper from the consul; and, opening it, proceeded to compare the goods delivered with the invoice.

After being thoroughly counted, a meek little midshipman was called, and we were soon after given in custody to half-a-dozen sailor-soldiers—fellows with tarpaulins and muskets. Preceded by a pompous functionary (whom we took for one of the ship's corporals, from his ratan and the gold lace on his sleeve), we were now escorted down the ladders to the berth-deck.

Here we were politely handcuffed, all round; the man with the bamboo evincing the utmost solicitude in giving us a good fit from a large basket of the articles of assorted sizes.

Taken by surprise at such an uncivil reception, a few of the party demurred; but all coyness was, at last, overcome; and finally our feet were inserted into heavy anklets of iron, running along a great bar bolted down to the deck. After this, we considered ourselves permanently established in our new quarters.

" The deuse take their old iron! " exclaimed the doctor; " if I'd known this, I'd stayed behind.".

" Ha, ha! " cried Flash Jack, " you're in for it, Doctor Long Ghost."

" My hands and feet are, any way," was the reply.

They placed a sentry over us; a great lubber of a fellow, who marched up and down with a dilapidated old cutlass of most extraordinary dimensions. From its length we had some idea that it was expressly intended to keep a crowd in order—reaching over the head of half-a-dozen, say, so as to get a cut at somebody behind.

"Mercy!" ejaculated the doctor with a shudder, "what a sensation it must be to be killed by such a tool."

We fasted till night, when one of the boys came along with a couple of "kids" containing a thin, saffron-colored fluid, with oily particles floating on top. The young wag told us this was soup: it turned out to be nothing more than oleaginous warm water. Such as it was, nevertheless, we were fain to make a meal of it, our sentry being attentive enough to undo our bracelets. The "kids" passed from mouth to mouth, and were soon emptied.

The next morning, when the sentry's back was turned, some one, whom we took for an English sailor, tossed over a few oranges, the rinds of which we afterward used for cups.

On the second day nothing happened worthy of record. On the third, we were amused by the following scene.

A man, whom we supposed a boatswain's mate, from the silver whistle hanging from his neck, came below, driving before him a couple of blubbering boys, and followed by a whole troop of youngsters in tears. The pair, it seemed, were sent down to be punished by command of an officer; the rest had accompanied them out of sympathy.

The boatswain's mate went to work without delay, seizing the poor little culprits by their loose frocks, and using a ratan without mercy. The other boys wept, clasped their hands, and fell on their knees; but in vain; the boatswain's mate only hit out at them; once in a while making them yell ten times louder than ever.

In the midst of the tumult, down comes a midshipman, who, with a great air, orders the man on deck, and running in among the boys, sets them to scampering in all directions.

The whole of this proceeding was regarded with infinite scorn by Navy Bob, who, years before, had been captain of the foretop on board a line-of-battle ship. In his estimation, it was a lubberly piece of business throughout: they did things differently in the English navy.

CHAPTER XXIX.

THE REINE BLANCHE.

I CAN not forbear a brief reflection upon the scene ending the last chapter.

The ratanning of the young culprits, although significant of the imperfect discipline of a French man-of-war, may also be considered as in some measure characteristic of the nation.

In an American or English ship, a boy, when flogged, is either lashed to the breech of a gun, or brought right up to the gratings, the same way the men are. But as a general rule, he is never punished beyond his strength. You seldom or never draw a cry from the young rogue. He bites his tongue, and stands up to it like a hero. If practicable (which is not always the case), he makes a point of smiling under the operation. And so far from his companions taking any compassion on him, they always make merry over his misfortunes. Should he turn baby and cry, they are pretty sure to give him afterward a sly pounding in some dark corner.

This tough training produces its legitimate results.* The boy becomes, in time, a thorough-bred tar, equally ready to strip and take a dozen on board his own ship, or, cutlass in hand, dash pell-mell on board the enemy's. Whereas the young Frenchman, as all the world knows,

---

* I do not wish to be understood as applauding the flogging system practiced in men-of-war. As long, however, as navies are needed, there is no substitute for it. War being the greatest of evils, all its accessories necessarily partake of the same character; and this is about all that can be said in defense of flogging.

makes but an indifferent seaman; and though, for the most part, he fights well enough, some how or other he seldom fights well enough to beat.

How few sea-battles have the French ever won! But more: how few ships have they ever carried *by the board* —that true criterion of naval courage! But not a word against French bravery—there is plenty of it; but not of the right sort. A Yankee's, or an Englishman's is the downright Waterloo " game." The French fight better on land; and not being essentially a maritime people, they ought to stay there. The best of shipwrights, they are no sailors.

And this carries me back to the Reine Blanche, as noble a specimen of what wood and iron can make, as ever floated.

She was a new ship: the present her maiden cruise. The greatest pains having been taken in her construction, she was accounted the " crack " craft in the French navy. She is one of the heavy sixty-gun frigates now in vogue all over the world, and which we Yankees were the first to introduce. In action, these are the most murderous vessels ever lanched.

The model of the Reine Blanche has all that warlike comeliness only to be seen in a fine fighting-ship. Still, there is a good deal of French flummery about her—brass-plates and other gewgaws, stuck on all over, like baubles on a handsome woman.

Among other things, she carries a stern gallery resting on the uplifted hands of two Caryatides, larger than life. You step out upon this from the commodore's cabin. To behold the rich hangings, and mirrors, and mahogany within, one is almost prepared to see a bevy of ladies trip forth on the balcony for an airing.

But come to tread the gun-deck, and all thoughts like these are put to flight. Such batteries of thunderbolt hurlers! with a sixty-eight-pounder or two thrown in as make-weights. On the spar-deck, also, are carronades of enormous caliber.

Recently built, this vessel, of course, had the benefit of the latest improvements. I was quite amazed to see on what high principles of art, some exceedingly simple things were done. But your Gaul is scientific about every thing; what other people accomplish by a few hard knocks, he delights in achieving by a complex arrangement of the pulley, lever, and screw.

What demi-semi-quavers in a French air! In exchanging naval courtesies, I have known a French band play " Yankee Doodle " with such a string of variations that no one but a " pretty 'cute " Yankee could tell what they were at.

In the French navy they have no marines; their men, taking turns at carrying the musket, are sailors one moment, and soldiers the next; a fellow running aloft in his line-frock to-day, to-morrow stands sentry at the admiral's cabin-door. This is fatal to any thing like proper sailor pride. To make a man a seaman, he should be put to no other duty. Indeed, a thorough tar is unfit for any thing else; and what is more, this fact is the best evidence of his being a true sailor.

On board the Reine Blanche, they did not have enough to eat; and what they *did* have, was not of the right sort. Instead of letting the sailors file their teeth against the rim of a hard sea-biscuit, they baked their bread daily in pitiful little rolls. Then they had no " grog; " as a substitute, they drugged the poor fellows with a thin, sour wine—the juice of a few grapes, perhaps, to a pint of the juice of water-facets. Moreover, the sailors asked for meat, and they gave them soup; a rascally substitute, as they well knew.

Ever since leaving home, they had been on " short allowance." At the present time, those belonging to the boats —and thus getting an occasional opportunity to run ashore —frequently sold their rations of bread to some less fortunate shipmate for sixfold its real value.

Another thing tending to promote dissatisfaction among the crew was, their having such a devil of a fellow for a captain. He was one of those horrid naval bores—a great disciplinarian. In port, he kept them constantly exercising yards and sails, and manœuvering with the boats;

and at sea, they were forever at quarters; running in and out the enormous guns, as if their arms were made for nothing else. Then there was the admiral aboard, also; and, no doubt, *he* too had a paternal eye over them.

In the ordinary routine of duty, we could not but be struck with the listless, slovenly behavior of these men; there was nothing of the national vivacity in their movements; nothing of the quick precision perceptible on the deck of a thoroughly disciplined armed vessel.

All this, however, when we came to know the reason, was no matter of surprise; three fourths of them were pressed men. Some old merchant sailors had been seized the very day they landed from distant voyages; while the landsmen, of whom there were many, had been driven down from the country in herds, and so sent to sea.

At the time, I was quite amazed to hear of press-gangs in a day of comparative peace; but the anomaly is accounted for by the fact, that, of late, the French have been building up a great military marine, to take the place of that which Nelson gave to the waves of the sea at Trafalgar. But it is to be hoped, that they are not building their ships for the people across the channel to take. In case of a war, what a fluttering of French ensigns there would be!

Though I say the French are no sailors, I am far from seeking to underrate them as a people. They are an ingenious and right gallant nation. And, as an American, I take pride in asserting it.

CHAPTER XXX.

THEY TAKE US ASHORE. —— WHAT HAPPENED THERE.

FIVE days and nights, if I remember right, we were aboard the frigate. On the afternoon of the fifth, we were told that the next morning she sailed for Valparaiso.

Rejoiced at this, we prayed for a speedy passage. But, as it turned out, the consul had no idea of letting us off so easily. To our no small surprise, an officer came along toward night, and ordered us out of irons. Being then mustered in the gangway, we were escorted into a cutter alongside, and pulled ashore.

Accosted by Wilson as we struck the beach, he delivered us up to a numerous guard of natives, who at once conducted us to a house near by. Here we were made to sit down under a shade without; and the consul and two elderly European residents passed by us, and entered.

After some delay, during which we were much diverted by the hilarious good-nature of our guard—one of our number was called out for, followed by an order for him to enter the house alone.

On returning a moment after, he told us we had little to encounter. It had simply been asked, whether he still continued of the same mind; on replying yes, something was put down upon a piece of paper, and he was waved outside. All being summoned in rotation, my own turn came at last.

Within, Wilson and his two friends were seated magisterially at a table—an inkstand, a pen, and a sheet of paper, lending quite a business-like air to the apartment. These three gentlemen, being arrayed in coats and pantaloons, looked respectable, at least in a country where complete suits of garments are so seldom met with. One present essayed a solemn aspect; but having a short neck and a full face, only made out to look stupid.

It was this individual who condescended to take a paternal interest in myself. After declaring my resolution with respect to the ship unalterable, I was proceeding to withdraw, in compliance with a sign from the consul, when the stranger turned round to him, saying, " Wait a minute, if you please, Mr. Wilson; let me talk to that youth. Come here, my young friend: I'm extremely sorry to see you associated with these bad men; do you know what it will end in? "

"Oh, that's the lad that wrote the Round Robin," interposed the consul. "He and that rascally doctor are at the bottom of the whole affair—go outside, sir."

I retired as from the presence of royalty; backing out with many bows.

The evident prejudice of Wilson against both the doctor and myself, was by no means inexplicable. A man of any education before the mast is always looked upon with dislike by his captain; and, never mind how peaceable he may be, should any disturbance arise, from his intellectual superiority, he is deemed to exert an underhand influence against the officers.

Little as I had seen of Captain Guy, the few glances cast upon me after being on board a week or so, were sufficient to reveal his enmity—a feeling quickened by my undisguised companionship with Long Ghost, whom he both feared and cordially hated. Guy's relations with the consul, readily explains the latter's hostility.

The examination over, Wilson and his friends advanced to the doorway; when the former, assuming a severe expression, pronounced our perverseness, infatuation in the extreme. Nor was there any hope left: our last chance for pardon was gone. Even were we to become contrite, and crave permission to return to duty, it would not now be permitted.

"Oh! get along with your gammon, *counselor*," exclaimed Black Dan, absolutely indignant that his understanding should be thus insulted.

Quite enraged, Wilson bade him hold his peace; and then, summoning a fat old native to his side, addressed him in Tahitian, giving directions for leading us away to a place of safe keeping.

Hereupon, being marshaled in order, with the old man at our head, we were put in motion, with loud shouts, along a fine pathway, running far on, through wide groves of the cocoa-nut and bread-fruit.

The rest of our escort trotted on beside us in high good-humor; jabbering broken English, and in a hundred ways giving us to understand that Wilson was no favorite of theirs, and that we were prime, good fellows for holding out as we did. They seemed to know our whole history.

The scenery around was delightful. The tropical day was fast drawing to a close; and from where we were, the sun looked like a vast red fire burning in the woodlands—its rays falling aslant through the endless ranks of trees, and every leaf fringed with flame. Escaped from the confined decks of the frigate, the air breathed spices to us; streams were heard flowing; green boughs were rocking; and far inland, all sunset flushed, rose the still, steep peaks of the island.

As we proceeded, I was more and more struck by the picturesqueness of the wide, shaded road. In several places, durable bridges of wood were thrown over large water-courses; others were spanned by a single arch of stone. In any part of the road, three horsemen might have ridden abreast.

This beautiful avenue—by far the best thing which civilization has done for the island—is called by foreigners " the Broom Road," though for what reason I do not know. Originally planned for the convenience of the missionaries journeying from one station to another, it almost completely encompasses the larger peninsula; skirting for a distance of at least sixty miles along the low, fertile lands bordering the sea. But on the side next Taiarboo, or the lesser peninsula, it sweeps through a narrow, secluded valley, and thus crosses the island in that direction.

The uninhabited interior, being almost impenetrable from the densely wooded glens, frightful precipices, and sharp mountain ridges absolutely inaccessible, is but little known, even to the natives themselves; and so, instead of striking directly across from one village to another, they follow the Broom Road round and round.*

---

* Concerning the singular ignorance of the natives respecting their own country, it may be here observed, that a considerable inland lake—Whaiherea by name—is known to exist, although their accounts of it strangely vary. Some told me it had no bottom, no outlet, and no inlet; others, that it fed all the streams on the island. A sailor of my acquaintance said, that he once visited this

It is by no means, however, altogether traveled on foot; horses being now quite plentiful. They were introduced from Chili; and possessing all the gayety, fleetness, and docility of the Spanish breed, are admirably adapted to the tastes of the higher classes, who as equestrians have become very expert. The missionaries and chiefs never think of journeying except in the saddle; and at all hours of the day, you see the latter galloping along at full speed. Like the Sandwich Islanders, they ride like Pawnee-Loups.

For miles and miles I have traveled the Broom Road, and never wearied of the continual change of scenery. But wherever it leads you—whether through level woods, across grassy glens, or over hills waving with palms—the bright blue sea on one side, and the green mountain pinnacles on the other, are always in sight.

CHAPTER XXXI.

THE CALABOOZA BERETANEE.

About a mile from the village we came to a halt.

It was a beautiful spot. A mountain stream here flowed at the foot of a verdant slope; on one hand, it murmured along until the waters, spreading themselves upon a beach of small, sparkling shells, trickled into the sea; on the other, was a long defile, where the eye pursued a gleaming, sinuous thread, lost in shade and verdure.

The ground next the road was walled in by a low, rude parapet of stones; and, upon the summit of the slope beyond, was a large, native house, the thatch dazzling white, and, in shape, an oval.

----

marvelous lake, as one of an exploring party from an English sloop-of-war. It was found to be a great curiosity: very small, deep, and green; a choice well of water bottled up among the mountains, and abounding with delicious fish.

" Calabooza! Calabooza Beretanee! " (the English Jail),
cried our conductor, pointing to the building.

For a few months past, having been used by the consul as
a house of confinement for his refractory sailors, it was thus
styled to distinguish it from similar places in and about
Papeetee.

Though extremely romantic in appearance, on a near
approach it proved but ill adapted to domestic comfort. In
short, it was a mere shell, recently built, and still un-
finished. It was open all round, and tufts of grass were
growing here and there under the very roof. The only
piece of furniture was the " stocks," a clumsy machine for
keeping people in one place, which, I believe, is pretty
much out of date in most countries. It is still in use,
however, among the Spaniards in South America; from
whom, it seems, the Tahitians have borrowed the contrivance, as well as the name by which all places of confinement are known among them.

The stocks were nothing more than two stout timbers,
about twenty feet in length, and precisely alike. One was
placed edgeways on the ground, and the other resting on
top, left, at regular intervals along the seam, several round
holes, the object of which was evident at a glance.

By this time, our guide had informed us, that he went
by the name of " *Capin Bob* " (Captain Bob); and a hearty
old Bob he proved. It was just the name for him. From the
first, so pleased were we with the old man, that we cheerfully acquiesced in his authority.

Entering the building, he set us about fetching heaps
of dry leaves to spread behind the stocks for a couch. A
trunk of a small cocoa-nut tree was then placed for a
bolster—rather a hard one, but the natives are used to it.
For a pillow, they use a little billet of wood, scooped out,
and standing on four short legs—a sort of head-stool.

These arrangements completed, Captain Bob proceeded
to " hannapar," or secure us, for the night. The upper
timber of the machine being lifted at one end, and our
ankles placed in the semicircular spaces of the lower one,
the other beam was then dropped; both being finally se-

cured together by an old iron hoop at either extremity. This initiation was performed to the boisterous mirth of the natives, and diverted ourselves not a little.

Captain Bob now bustled about, like an old woman seeing the children to bed. A basket of baked " taro," or Indian turnip, was brought in, and we were given a piece all round. Then a great counterpane, of coarse, brown " tappa," was stretched over the whole party; and, after sundry injunctions to " moee-moee," and be " maitai "— in other words, to go to sleep, and be good boys—we were left to ourselves, fairly put to bed and tucked in.

Much talk was now had concerning our prospects in life; but the doctor and I, who lay side by side, thinking the occasion better adapted to meditation, kept pretty silent; and, before long, the rest ceased conversing, and, wearied with loss of rest on board the frigate, were soon sound asleep.

After sliding from one revery into another, I started, and gave the doctor a pinch. He was dreaming, however; and, resolved to follow his example, I troubled him no more.

How the rest managed, I know not; but, for my own part, I found it very hard to get asleep. The consciousness of having one's foot *pinned*; and the impossibility of getting it anywhere else than just where it was, was most distressing.

But this was not all: there was no way of lying but straight on your back; unless, to be sure, one's limb went round and round in the ankle, like a swivel. Upon getting into a sort of doze, it was no wonder this uneasy posture gave me the nightmare. Under the delusion that I was about some gymnastics or other, I gave my unfortunate member such a twitch, that I started up with the idea that some one was dragging the stocks away.

Captain Bob and his friends lived in a little hamlet hard by; and when morning showed in the East, the old gentleman came forth from that direction likewise, emerging from a grove, and saluting us loudly as he approached.

Finding every body awake, he set us at liberty; and, leading us down to the stream, ordered every man to strip and bathe.

" All han's, my boy, hanna-hanna, wash! " he cried. Bob was a linguist, and had been to sea in his day, as he many a time afterward told us.

At this moment, we were all alone with him; and it would have been the easiest thing in the world to have given him the slip; but he seemed to have no idea of such a thing; treating us so frankly and cordially, indeed, that even had we thought of running, we would have been ashamed of attempting it. He very well knew, nevertheless (as we ourselves were not slow in finding out), that, for various reasons, any attempt of the kind, without some previously arranged plan for leaving the island, would be certain to fail.

As Bob was a rare one every way, I must give some account of him. There was a good deal of "personal appearance " about him; in short, he was a corpulent giant, over six feet in height, and literally as big round as a hogshead. The enormous bulk of some of the Tahitians has been frequently spoken of by voyagers.

Beside being the English consul's jailer, as it were, he carried on a little Tahitian farming; that is to say, he owned several groves of the bread-fruit and palm, and never hindered their growing. Close by was a " taro " patch of his, which he occasionally visited.

Bob seldom disposed of the produce of his lands; it was all needed for domestic consumption. Indeed, for gormandizing, I would have matched him against any three common-council-men at a civic feast.

A friend of Bob's told me, that, owing to his voraciousness, his visits to other parts of the island were much dreaded; for, according to Tahitian customs, hospitality without charge is enjoined upon every one; and though it is reciprocal in most cases, in Bob's it was almost out of the question. The damage done to a native larder in one of his morning calls, was more than could be made good by his entertainer's spending the holydays with him.

The old man, as I have hinted, had, once upon a time, been a cruise or two in a whaling-vessel; and, therefore, he prided himself upon his English. Having acquired what he knew of it in the forecastle, he talked little else than sailor phrases, which sounded whimsically enough.

I asked him one day how old he was. " Olee? " he exclaimed, looking very profound in consequence of thoroughly understanding so subtile a question—" Oh! very olee—'tousand 'ear—more—big man when Capin Tootee (Captain Cook) heavey in sight." (In sea parlance, came into view.)

This was a thing impossible; but adapting my discourse to the man, I rejoined—" Ah! you see Capin Tootee— well, how you like him? "

" Oh! he maitai: (good) friend of me, and know my wife."

On my assuring him strongly, that he could not have been born at the time, he explained himself by saying, that he was speaking of his father, all the while. This, indeed, might very well have been.

It is a curious fact, that all these people, young and old, will tell you that they have enjoyed the honor of a personal acquaintance with the great navigator; and if you listen to them, they will go on and tell anecdotes without end. This springs from nothing but their great desire to please; well knowing that a more agreeable topic for a white man could not be selected. As for the anachronism of the thing, they seem to have no idea of it: days and years are all the same to them.

After our sunrise bath, Bob once more placed us in the stocks, almost moved to tears at subjecting us to so great a hardship; but he could not treat us otherwise, he said, on pain of the consul's displeasure. How long we were to be confined, he did not know; nor what was to be done with us in the end.

As noon advanced, and no signs of a meal were visible, some one inquired whether we were to be boarded, as well as lodged, at the Hotel de Calabooza?

"Vast heavey" (avast heaving, or wait a bit)—said Bob—"kow-kow" (food) "come ship by by."

And, sure enough, along comes Rope Yarn with a wooden bucket of the Julia's villainous biscuit. With a grin, he said it was a present from Wilson; it was all we were to get that day. A great cry was now raised; and well was it for the land-lubber, that he had a pair of legs, and the men could not use theirs. One and all, we resolved not to touch the bread, come what come might; and so we told the natives.

Being extravagantly fond of ship-biscuit—the harder the better—they were quite overjoyed; and offered to give us every day, a small quantity of baked bread-fruit and Indian turnip in exchange for the bread. This we agreed to; and every morning afterward, when the bucket came, its contents were at once handed over to Bob and his friends, who never ceased munching until nightfall.

Our exceedingly frugal meal of bread-fruit over, Captain Bob waddled up to us with a couple of long poles hooked at one end, and several large baskets of woven cocoa-nut branches.

Not far off was an extensive grove of orange-trees in full bearing; and myself and another were selected to go with him, and gather a supply for the party. When we went in among the trees, the sumptuousness of the orchard was unlike any thing I had ever seen; while the fragrance shaken from the gently waving boughs, regaled our senses most delightfully.

In many places the trees formed a dense shade, spreading overhead a dark, rustling vault, groined with boughs, and studded here and there with the ripened spheres, like gilded balls. In several places, the overladen branches were borne to the earth, hiding the trunk in a tent of foliage. Once fairly in the grove, we could see nothing else; it was oranges all round.

To preserve the fruit from bruising, Bob, hooking the twigs with his pole, let them fall into his basket. But this would not do for us. Seizing hold of a bough, we brought such a shower to the ground, that our old friend was fain to run from under. Heedless of remonstrance, we then reclined in the shade, and feasted to our heart's content. Heaping up the baskets afterward, we returned to our comrades, by whom our arrival was hailed with loud plaudits; and in a marvelously short time, nothing was left of the oranges we brought, but the rinds.

While inmates of the Calabooza, we had as much of the fruit as we wanted; and to this cause, and others that might be mentioned, may be ascribed the speedy restoration of our sick to comparative health.

The orange of Tahiti is delicious—small and sweet, with a thin, dry rind. Though now abounding, it was unknown before Cook's time, to whom the natives are indebted for so great a blessing. He likewise introduced several other kinds of fruit; among these were the fig, pineapple, and lemon, now seldom met with. The lime still grows, and some of the poorer natives express the juice to sell to the shipping. It is highly valued as an anti-scorbutic. Nor was the variety of foreign fruits and vegetables which were introduced, the only benefit conferred by the first visitors to the Society group. Cattle and sheep were left at various places. More of them anon.

Thus, after all that of late years has been done for these islanders, Cook and Vancouver may, in one sense at least, be considered their greatest benefactors.

CHAPTER XXXII.

PROCEEDINGS OF THE FRENCH AT TAHITI.

As I happened to arrive at the island at a very interesting period in its political affairs, it may be well to give some little account here of the proceedings of the French, by way of episode to the narrative. My information was obtained at the time from the general reports then rife among the natives, as well as from what I learned upon a subsequent visit, and reliable accounts which I have seen since reaching home.

It seems, that for some time back the French had been making repeated ineffectual attempts to plant a Roman Catholic mission here. But, invariably treated with contumely, they sometimes met with open violence; and, in every case, those directly concerned in the enterprise were ultimately forced to depart. In one instance, two priests, Laval and Caret, after enduring a series of persecutions, were set upon by the natives, maltreated, and finally carried aboard a small trading schooner, which eventually put them ashore at Wallis' island—a savage place—some two thousand miles to the westward.

Now, that the resident English missionaries authorized the banishment of these priests, is a fact undenied by themselves. I was also repeatedly informed, that by their inflammatory harangues they instigated the riots which preceded the sailing of the schooner. At all events, it is certain that their unbounded influence with the natives would easily have enabled them to prevent every thing that took place on this occasion, had they felt so inclined.

Melancholy as such an example of intolerance on the part of Protestant missionaries must appear, it is not the only one, and by no means the most flagrant, which might be presented. But I forbear to mention any others; since they have been more than hinted at by recent voyagers, and their repetition here would perhaps be attended with no good effect. Besides, the conduct of the Sandwich Island missionaries in particular, has latterly much amended in this respect.

The treatment of the two priests formed the principal ground (and the only justifiable one) upon which Dupetit-Thouars demanded satisfaction; and which subsequently led to his seizure of the island. In addition to other things, he also charged, that the flag of Moerenhout, the consul, had been repeatedly insulted, and the property of a certain French resident violently appropriated by the government. In the latter instance, the natives were perfectly in the right. At that time, the law against the traffic in ardent spirits (every now and then suspended and revived) happened to be in force; and finding a large quantity on the premises of Victor, a low, knavish adventurer from Marseilles, the Tahitians pronounced it forfeit.

For these, and similar alledged outrages, a large pecuniary restitution was demanded ($10,000), which there being no exchequer to supply, the island was forthwith seized, under cover of a mock treaty, dictated to the chiefs on the gun-deck of Dupetit-Thouars' frigate. But, notwithstanding this formality, there now seems little doubt that the downfall of the Pomarees was decided upon at the Tuilleries.

After establishing the Protectorate, so called, the rear-admiral sailed; leaving M. Bruat governor, assisted by Reine and Carpègne, civilians, named members of the Council of Government, and Moerenhout, the consul, now made Commissioner Royal. No soldiers, however, were landed, until several months afterward. As men, Reine and Carpègne were not disliked by the natives; but Bruat and Moerenhout they bitterly detested. In several interviews with the poor queen, the unfeeling governor sought to terrify her into compliance with his demands; clapping his hand upon his sword, shaking his fist in her face, and swearing violently. "Oh, king of a great nation," said Pomaree, in her letter to Louis Philippe, "fetch away this man; I and my people can not endure his evil doings. He is a shameless man."

Although the excitement among the natives did not wholly subside upon the rear-admiral's departure, no overt act of violence immediately followed. The queen had fled to Imeeo; and the dissensions among the chiefs, together with the ill advised conduct of the missionaries, prevented a union upon some common plan of resistance. But the great body of the people, as well as their queen, confidently relied upon the speedy interposition of England—a nation bound to them by many ties, and which, more than once, had solemnly guarantied their independence.

As for the missionaries, they openly defied the French governor, childishly predicting fleets and armies from

Britain. But what is the welfare of a spot like Tahiti, to the mighty interests of France and England! There was a remonstrance on one side, and a reply on the other; and there the matter rested. For once in their brawling lives, St. George and St. Denis were hand and glove; and they were not going to cross sabres about Tahiti.

During my stay upon the island, so far as I could see, there was little to denote that any change had taken place in the government. Such laws as they had were administered the same as ever; the missionaries went about unmolested, and comparative tranquillity everywhere prevailed. Nevertheless, I sometimes heard the natives inveighing against the French (no favorites, by the by, throughout Polynesia), and bitterly regretting that the queen had not, at the outset, made a stand.

In the house of the chief Adeea, frequent discussions took place, concerning the ability of the island to cope with the French: the number of fighting men and muskets among the natives were talked of, as well as the propriety of fortifying several heights overlooking Papeetee. Imputing these symptoms to the mere resentment of a recent outrage, and not to any determined spirit of resistance, I little anticipated the gallant, though useless warfare, so soon to follow my departure.

At a period subsequent to my first visit, the island, which before was divided into nineteen districts, with a native chief over each, in capacity of governor and judge, was, by Bruat, divided into four. Over these he set as many recreant chiefs, Kitoti, Tati, Utamai, and Paraita; to whom he paid $1000 each, to secure their assistance in carrying out his evil designs.

The first blood shed, in any regular conflict, was at Mahanar, upon the peninsula of Taraiboo. The fight originated in the seizure of a number of women from the shore, by men belonging to one of the French vessels of war. In this affair, the islanders fought desperately, killing about fifty of the enemy and losing ninety of their own number. The French sailors and marines, who, at the time, were reported to be infuriated with liquor, gave no quarter;

and the survivors only saved themselves by fleeing to the mountains. Subsequently, the battles of Hararparpi and Fararar were fought, in which the invaders met with indifferent success.

Shortly after the engagement at Hararparpi, three Frenchmen were waylaid in a pass of the valleys, and murdered by the incensed natives. One was Lefèvre, a notorious scoundrel, and a spy, whom Bruat had sent to conduct a certain Major Fergus (said to be a Pole), to the hiding-place of four chiefs, whom the governor wished to seize and execute. This circumstance violently inflamed the hostility of both parties.

About this time, Kitoti, a depraved chief, and the pliant tool of Bruat, was induced by him to give a great feast in the Vale of Paree, to which all his countrymen were invited. The governor's object was to gain over all he could to his interests; he supplied an abundance of wine and brandy, and a scene of bestial intoxication was the natural consequence. Before it came to this, however, several speeches were made by the islanders. One of these, delivered by an aged warrior, who had formerly been at the head of the celebrated Aeorai Society, was characteristic. " This is a very good feast," said the reeling old man, " and the wine also is very good; but you evil-minded Wee-Wees (French), and you false-hearted men of Tahiti, are all very bad."

By the latest accounts, most of the islanders still refuse to submit to the French; and what turn events may hereafter take, it is hard to predict. At any rate, these disorders must accelerate the final extinction of their race.

Along with the few officers left by Dupetit-Thouars, were several French priests, for whose unobstructed exertions in the dissemination of their faith, the strongest guaranties were provided by an article of the treaty. But no one was bound to offer them facilities; much less a luncheon, the first day they went ashore. True, they had plenty of gold; but to the natives it was anathema—taboo —and, for several hours and some odd minutes, they would not touch it. Emissaries of the Pope and the devil, as the strangers were considered—the smell of sulphur hardly yet shaken out of their canonicals—what islander would venture to jeopardize his soul, and call down a blight on his bread-fruit, by holding any intercourse with them! That morning the priests actually picknicked in a grove of cocoa-nut trees; but, before night, Christian hospitality—in exchange for a commercial equivalent of hard dollars—was given them in an adjoining house.

Wanting in civility, as the conduct of the English missionaries may be thought, in withholding a decent reception to these persons, the latter were certainly to blame in needlessly placing themselves in so unpleasant a predicament. Under far better auspices, they might have settled upon some one of the thousand unconverted isles of the Pacific, rather than have forced themselves thus, upon a people already professedly Christians.

CHAPTER XXXIII.

WE RECEIVE CALLS AT THE HOTEL DE CALABOOZA.

OUR place of confinement being open all round, and so near the Broom Road, of course we were in plain sight of every body passing; and, therefore, we had no lack of visitors among such an idle, inquisitive set, as the Tahitians. For a few days, they were coming and going continually; while thus ignobly fast by the foot, we were fain to give passive audience.

During this period, we were the lions of the neighborhood; and, no doubt, strangers from the distant villages were taken to see the " Karhowrees " (white men), in the same way that countrymen, in a city, are gallanted to the Zoological Gardens.

All this gave us a fine opportunity of making observations. I was painfully struck by the considerable number of sickly or deformed persons; undoubtedly made so by a virulent complaint, which, under native treatment, almost invariably affects, in the end, the muscles and bones of the body. In particular, there is a distortion of the back, most unsightly to behold, originating in a horrible form of the malady.

Although this, and other bodily afflictions, were un-known before the discovery of the islands by the whites, there are several cases found of the Fa-Fa, or Elephan-tiasis—a native disease, which seems to have prevailed among them from the earliest antiquity. Affecting the legs and feet alone, it swells them, in some instances, to the girth of a man's body, covering the skin with scales. It might be supposed, that one, thus afflicted, would be incapable of walking; but, to all appearance, they seem to be nearly as active as any body; apparently, suffering no pain, and bearing the calamity with a degree of cheerfulness truly marvelous.

The Fa-Fa is very gradual in its approaches, and years elapse before the limb is fully swollen. Its origin is as-cribed by the natives to various causes; but the general im-pression seems to be, that it arises, in most cases, from the eating of unripe bread-fruit and Indian turnip. So far as I could find out, it is not hereditary. In no stage do they attempt a cure; the complaint being held incurable.

Speaking of the Fa-Fa, reminds me of a poor fellow, a sailor, whom I afterward saw at Roorootoo, a lone island, some two days' sail from Tahiti.

The island is very small, and its inhabitants nearly extinct. We sent a boat off to see whether any yams were to be had, as formerly, the yams of Roorootoo were as famous among the islands round about, as Sicily oranges in the Mediterranean. Going ashore, to my surprise, I was accosted, near a little shanty of a church, by a white man, who limped forth from a wretched hut. His hair and beard were unshorn, his face deadly pale and haggard, and one limb swelled with the Fa-Fa to an incredible bigness. This was the first instance of a foreigner suffering from it, that I had ever seen, or heard of; and the spectacle shocked me accordingly.

He had been there for years. From the first symptoms, he could not believe his complaint to be what it really was, and trusted it would soon disappear. But when it became plain, that his only chance for recovery was a speedy change of climate, no ship would receive him as a sailor: to think of being taken as a passenger, was idle. This speaks little for the humanity of sea captains; but the truth is, that those in the Pacific have little enough of the virtue; and, nowadays, when so many charitable appeals are made to them, they have become callous.

I pitied the poor fellow from the bottom of my heart; but nothing could I do, as our captain was inexorable. " Why," said he, " here we are—started on a six months' cruise—I can't put back; and he is better off on the island than at sea. So on Roorootoo he must die." And probably he did.

I afterward heard of this melancholy object, from two seamen. His attempts to leave were still unavailing, and his hard fate was fast closing in.

Notwithstanding the physical degeneracy of the Tahitians as a people, among the chiefs, individuals of personable figures are still frequently met with; and, occasionally, majestic-looking men, and diminutive women as lovely as the nymphs who, nearly a century ago, swam round the ships of Wallis. In these instances, Tahitian beauty is quite as seducing as it proved to the crew of the Bounty; the young girls being just such creatures as a poet would picture in the tropics—soft, plump, and dreamy-eyed.

The natural complexion of both sexes is quite light; but the males appear much darker, from their exposure to the sun. A dark complexion, however, in a man, is highly esteemed, as indicating strength of both body and soul. Hence there is a saying, of great antiquity among them,

> " If dark the cheek of the mother,
> The son will sound the war-conch;
> If strong her frame, he will give laws."

With this idea of manliness, no wonder the Tahitians regard all pale and tepid-looking Europeans, as weak and feminine; whereas, a sailor, with a cheek like the breast of a roast turkey, is held a lad of brawn: to use their own phrase, a " taata tona," or man of bones.

Speaking of bones, recalls an ugly custom of theirs, now obsolete—that of making fish-hooks and gimblets out of those of their enemies. This beats the Scandinavians turning people's skulls into cups and saucers.

But to return to the Calabooza Beretanee. Immense was the interest we excited among the throngs that called there; they would stand talking about us by the hour, growing most unnecessarily excited too, and dancing up and down with all the vivacity of their race. They invariably sided with us; flying out against the consul, and denouncing him as " Ita maitai nuee," or very bad exceedingly. They must have borne him some grudge or other.

Nor were the women, sweet souls, at all backward in visiting. Indeed, they manifested even more interest than the men; gazing at us with eyes full of a thousand meanings, and conversing with marvelous rapidity. But, alas! inquisitive though they were, and, doubtless, taking some passing compassion on us, there was little real feeling in them after all, and still less sentimental sympathy. Many of them laughed outright at us, noting only what was ridiculous in our plight.

I think it was the second day of our confinement, that a wild, beautiful girl burst into the Calabooza, and, throwing herself into an arch attitude, stood afar off, and gazed at us. She was a heartless one:—tickled to death with Black Dan's nursing his chafed ankle, and indulging in certain moral reflections on the consul and Captain Guy. After laughing her fill at him, she condescended to notice the rest; glancing from one to another, in the most methodical and provoking manner imaginable. Whenever any thing struck her comically, you saw it like a flash— her finger leveled instantaneously, and, flinging herself back, she gave loose to strange, hollow little notes of laughter, that sounded like the bass of a music-box, playing a lively air with the lid down.

Now, I knew not, that there was any thing in my own appearance calculated to disarm ridicule; and, indeed, to have looked at all heroic, under the circumstances, would have been rather difficult. Still, I could not but feel exceedingly annoyed at the prospect of being screamed at in turn, by this mischievous young witch, even though she were but an islander. And, to tell a secret, her beauty had something to do with this sort of feeling; and, pinioned as I was, to a log, and clad most unbecomingly, I began to grow sentimental.

Ere her glance fell upon me, I had, unconsciously, thrown myself into the most graceful attitude I could assume, leaned my head upon my hand, and summoned up as abstracted an expression as possible. Though my face was averted, I soon felt it flush, and knew that the glance was on me: deeper and deeper grew the flush, and not a sound of laughter.

Delicious thought! she was moved at the sight of me. I could stand it no longer, but started up. Lo! there she was; her great hazel eyes rounding and rounding in her head, like two stars, her whole frame in a merry quiver, and an expression about the mouth that was sudden and violent death to any thing like sentiment.

The next moment she spun round, and, bursting from peal to peal of laughter, went racing out of the Calabooza; and, in mercy to me, never returned.

CHAPTER XXXIV.

LIFE AT THE CALABOOZA.

A few days passed; and, at last, our docility was rewarded by some indulgence on the part of Captain Bob.

He allowed the entire party to be at large during the day; only enjoining upon us always to keep within hail. This, to be sure, was in positive disobedience to Wilson's orders; and so, care had to be taken that he should not

9

hear of it. There was little fear of the natives telling him; but strangers traveling the Broom Road might. By way of precaution, boys were stationed as scouts along the road. At sight of a white man, they sounded the alarm; when we all made for our respective holes (the stocks being purposely left open): the beam then descended, and we were prisoners. As soon as the traveler was out of sight, of course, we were liberated.

Notwithstanding the regular supply of food which we obtained from Captain Bob and his friends, it was so small, that we often felt most intolerably hungry. We could not blame them for not bringing us more, for we soon became aware that they had to pinch themselves, in order to give us what they did; beside, they received nothing for their kindness but the daily bucket of bread.

Among a people, like the Tahitians, what we call " hard times," can only be experienced in a scarcity of edibles; yet, so destitute are many of the common people, that this most distressing consequence of civilization may be said, with them, to be ever present. To be sure, the natives about the Calabooza, had abundance of limes and oranges; but what were *these* good for, except to impart a still keener edge to appetites which there was so little else to gratify? During the height of the bread-fruit season, they fare better; but, at other times, the demands of the shipping exhaust the uncultivated resources of the island; and the lands being mostly owned by the chiefs, the inferior orders have to suffer for their cupidity. Deprived of their nets, many of them would starve.

As Captain Bob insensibly remitted his watchfulness, and we began to stroll farther and farther from the Calabooza, we managed, by a systematic foraging upon the country round about, to make up for some of our deficiencies. And fortunate it was, that the houses of the wealthier natives were just as open to us as those of the most destitute; we were treated as kindly in one as the other.

Once in a while, we came in at the death of a chief's pig; the noise of whose slaughtering was generally to be heard at a great distance. An occasion like this gathers the neighbors together, and they have a bit of a feast, where a stranger is always welcome. A good loud squeal, therefore, was music in our ears. It showed something going on in that direction.

Breaking in upon the party tumultuously, as we did, we always created a sensation. Sometimes, we found the animal still alive and struggling; in which case, it was generally dropped at our approach. To provide for these emergencies, Flash Jack generally repaired to the scene of operations with a sheath knife between his teeth, and a club in his hand. Others were exceedingly officious in singeing off the bristles, and disemboweling. Doctor Long Ghost and myself, however, never meddled with these preliminaries, but came to the feast itself, with unimpaired energies.

Like all lank men, my long friend had an appetite of his own. Others occasionally went about seeking what they might devour, but *he* was always on the alert.

He had an ingenious way of obviating an inconvenience which we all experienced at times. The islanders seldom use salt with their food; so he begged Rope Yarn to bring him some from the ship; also a little pepper, if he could; which, accordingly, was done. This he placed in a small leather wallet—a " monkey bag " (so called by sailors)— usually worn as a purse about the neck.

" In my poor opinion," said Long Ghost, as he tucked the wallet out of sight, " it behooves a stranger, in Tahiti, to have his knife in readiness, and his caster slung."

CHAPTER XXXV.

VISIT FROM AN OLD ACQUAINTANCE.

WE had not been many days ashore, when Doctor Johnson was espied coming along the Broom Road.

We had heard that he meditated a visit, and suspected what he was after. Being upon the consul's hands, all our expenses were of course payable by him in his official capacity; and, therefore, as a friend of Wilson, and sure of good pay, the shore doctor had some idea of allowing us to run up a bill with him. True, it was rather awkward to ask us to take medicines, which, on board the ship, he told us were not needed. However, he resolved to put a bold face on the matter, and give us a call.

His approach was announced by one of the scouts, upon which some one suggested that we should let him enter, and then put him in the stocks. But Long Ghost proposed better sport. What it was, we shall presently see.

Very bland and amiable, Doctor Johnson advanced, and, resting his cane on the stocks, glanced to right and left, as we lay before him. " Well, my lads "—he began—"how do you find yourselves to-day? "

Looking very demure, the men made some rejoinder; and he went on.

" Those poor fellows I saw the other day—the sick, I mean—how are they? " and he scrutinized the company. At last, he singled out one who was assuming a most un-earthly appearance, and remarked, that he looked as if he were extremely ill. " Yes," said the sailor dolefully, " I'm afeard, doctor, I'll soon be losing the number of my mess! " (a sea phrase, for departing this life) and he closed his eyes, and moaned.

" *What* does he say? " said Johnson, turning round eagerly.

" Why," exclaimed Flash Jack, who volunteered as interpreter, " he means he's going to *croak* " (die).

" *Croak*! and what does that mean, applied to a patient? "

" Oh! I understand," said he, when the word was ex-plained; and he stepped over the stocks, and felt of the man's pulse.

" What's his name? " he asked, turning this time to old Navy Bob.

" We calls him Jingling Joe," replied that worthy.

" Well then, men, you must take good care of poor Joseph; and I will send him a powder, which must be taken

according to the directions. Some of you know how to read,
I presume? "

" That ere young cove does," replied Bob, pointing
toward the place where I lay, as if he were directing attention to a sail at sea.

After examining the rest—some of whom were really
invalids, but convalescent, and others only pretending to
be laboring under divers maladies, Johnson turned round,
and addressed the party.

" Men," said he, " if any more of you are ailing, speak
up, and let me know. By order of the consul, I'm to call
every day; so if any of you are at all sick, it's my duty to
prescribe for you. This sudden change from ship fare to
shore living, plays the deuse with you sailors, so be cautious
about eating fruit. Good-day! I'll send you the medicines
the first thing in the morning."

Now, I am inclined to suspect that with all his want of
understanding, Johnson must have had some idea that we
were quizzing him. Still, that was nothing, so long as it
answered his purpose; and therefore, if he *did* see through
us, he never showed it.

Sure enough, at the time appointed, along came a native
lad with a small basket of cocoa-nut stalks, filled with
powders, pillboxes, and vials, each with names and directions written in a large, round hand. The sailors, one
and all, made a snatch at the collection, under the strange
impression that some of the vials were seasoned with
spirits. But, asserting his privilege as physician, to the first
reading of the labels, Doctor Long Ghost was at last permitted to take possession of the basket.

The first thing lighted upon, was a large vial, labeled
—" For William—rub well in."

This vial certainly had a spirituous smell; and upon
handling it to the patient, he made a summary internal
application of its contents. The doctor looked aghast.

There was now a mighty commotion. Powders and pills
were voted mere drugs in the market, and the holders of
vials were pronounced lucky dogs. Johnson must have
known enough of sailors to make some of his medicines

palatable—this, at least, Long Ghost suspected. Certain it was, every one took to the vials; if at all spicy, directions were unheeded, their contents all going one road.

The largest one of all, quite a bottle indeed, and having a sort of burnt brandy odor, was labeled—"For Daniel, drink freely, and until relieved." This, Black Dan proceeded to do; and would have made an end of it at once, had not the bottle, after a hard struggle, been snatched from his hands, and passed round, like a jovial decanter. The old tar had complained of the effects of an immoderate eating of fruit.

Upon calling the following morning, our physician found his precious row of patients reclining behind the stocks, and doing "as well as could be expected."

But the pills and powders were found to have been perfectly inactive: probably because none had been taken. To make them efficacious, it was suggested that, for the future, a bottle of Pisco should be sent along with them. According to Flash Jack's notions, unmitigated medical compounds were but dry stuff at the best, and needed something good to wash them down.

Thus far, our own M. D., Doctor Long Ghost, after starting the frolic, had taken no further part in it; but on the physician's third visit, he took him to one side, and had a private confabulation. What it was, exactly, we could not tell; but from certain illustrative signs and gestures, I fancied that he was describing the symptoms of some mysterious disorganization of the vitals, which must have come on within the hour. Assisted by his familiarity with medical terms, he seemed to produce a marked impression. At last, Johnson went his way, promising aloud that he would send Long Ghost what he desired.

When the medicine boy came along the following morning, the doctor was the first to accost him, walking off with a small purple vial. This time, there was little else in the basket but a case bottle of the burnt brandy cordial, which, after much debate, was finally disposed of by some one pouring the contents, little by little, into the half of a cocoa-nut shell, and so giving all who desired, a glass. No further medicinal cheer remaining, the men dispersed.

An hour or two passed, when Flash Jack directed attention to my long friend, who, since the medicine boy left, had not been noticed till now. With eyes closed, he was lying behind the stocks, and Jack was lifting his arm and letting it fall as if life were extinct. On running up with the rest, I at once connected the phenomenon with the mysterious vial. Searching his pocket, I found it, and holding it up, it proved to be laudanum. Flash Jack, snatching it from my hand in a rapture, quickly informed all present, what it was; and with much glee, proposed a nap for the company. Some of them not comprehending him exactly, the apparently defunct Long Ghost—who lay so still that I a little suspected the genuineness of his sleep—was rolled about as an illustration of the virtues of the vial's contents. The idea tickled every body mightily; and throwing themselves down, the magic draught was passed from hand to hand. Thinking that, as a matter of course, they must at once become insensible, each man, upon taking his sip, fell back and closed his eyes.

There was little fear of the result, since the narcotic was equally distributed. But, curious to see how it would operate, I raised myself gently after a while, and looked around. It was about noon, and perfectly still; and as we all daily took the siesta, I was not much surprised to find every one quiet. Still, in one or two instances, I thought I detected a little peeping.

Presently, I heard a footstep, and saw Doctor Johnson approaching.

And perplexed enough did he look at the sight of his prostrate file of patients, plunged apparently, in such unaccountable slumbers.

"Daniel," he cried, at last, punching in the side with his cane, the individual thus designated—"Daniel, my good fellow, get up! do you hear?"

But Black Dan was immovable; and he poked the next sleeper.

"Joseph, Joseph! come, wake up! it's me, Doctor Johnson."

But Jingling Joe, with mouth open, and eyes shut, was not to be started.

"Bless my soul!" he exclaimed, with uplifted hands and cane, "what's got into 'em? I say, *men*"—he shouted, running up and down—"come to life, men! what under the sun's the matter with you?" and he struck the stocks, and bawled with increased vigor.

At last he paused, folded his hands over the head of his cane, and steadfastly gazed upon us. The notes of the nasal orchestra were rising and falling upon his ear, and a new idea suggested itself.

"Yes, yes; the rascals must have been getting boozy. Well, it's none of my business—I'll be off;" and off he went.

No sooner was he out of sight, than nearly all started to their feet, and a hearty laugh ensued.

Like myself, most of them had been watching the event from under a sly eyelid. By this time, too, Doctor Long Ghost was as wide awake as any body. What were his reasons for taking laudanum,—if, indeed, he took any whatever, —is best known to himself; and, as it is neither mine nor the reader's business, we will say no more about it.

CHAPTER XXXVI.

WE ARE CARRIED BEFORE THE CONSUL AND CAPTAIN.

WE had been inmates of the Calabooza Beretanee about two weeks, when, one morning, Captain Bob, coming from the bath, in a state of utter nudity, brought into the building an armful of old tappa, and began to dress to go out.

The operation was quite simple. The tappa—of the coarsest kind—was in one long, heavy piece; and, fastening one end to a column of Habiscus wood, supporting the Calabooza, he went off a few paces, and putting the other about his waist, wound himself right up to the post. This unique costume, in rotundity something like a farthingale, added immensely to his large bulk; so much so, that he fairly waddled in his gait. But he was only adhering to the fashion of his fathers; for, in the olden time, the " Kihee," or big girdle, was quite the mode for both sexes. Bob, despising recent innovations, still clung to it. He was a gentleman of the old school—one of the last of the Kihees.

He now told us, that he had orders to take us before the consul. Nothing loth, we formed in procession; and, with the old man at our head, sighing and laboring like an engine, and flanked by a guard of some twenty natives, we started for the village.

Arrived at the consular office, we found Wilson there, and four or five Europeans, seated in a row facing us; probably with the view of presenting as judicial an appearance as possible.

On one side was a couch, where Captain Guy reclined. He looked convalescent; and, as we found out, intended soon to go aboard his ship. He said nothing, but left every thing to the consul.

The latter now rose, and, drawing forth a paper from a large roll, tied with red tape, commenced reading aloud.

It purported to be, " The affidavit of John Jermin, first officer of the British Colonial Barque Julia; Guy, Master;" and proved to be a long statement of matters, from the time of leaving Sydney, down to our arrival in the harbor. Though artfully drawn up, so as to bear hard against every one of us, it was pretty correct in the details; excepting, that it was wholly silent as to the manifold derelictions of the mate himself—a fact which imparted unusual significance to the concluding sentence, " And furthermore, this deponent sayeth not."

No comments were made, although we all looked round for the mate, to see whether it was possible that he could have authorized this use of his name. But he was not present.

The next document produced, was the deposition of the captain himself. As on all other occasions, however, he had very little to say for himself, and it was soon set aside.

The third affidavit, was that of the seamen remaining aboard the vessel, including the traitor Bungs, who, it seemed, had turned ship's evidence. It was an atrocious piece of exaggeration, from beginning to end; and those who signed it could not have known what they were about. Certainly Wymontoo did not, though his mark was there. In vain the consul commanded silence during the reading of this paper; comments were shouted out upon every paragraph.

The affidavits read, Wilson, who, all the while, looked as stiff as a poker, solemnly drew forth the ship's articles from their tin case. This document was a discolored, musty, bilious-looking affair, and hard to read. When finished, the consul held it up; and, pointing to the marks of the ship's company, at the bottom, asked us, one by one, whether we acknowledged the same for our own.

" What's the use of asking that? " said Black Dan; " Captain Guy there, knows as well as we they are."

" Silence, sir! " said Wilson, who, intending to produce a suitable impression by this ridiculous parade, was not a little mortified by the old sailor's bluntness.

A pause of a few moments now ensued; during which the bench of judges communed with Captain Guy, in a low tone, and the sailors canvassed the motives of the consul in having the affidavits taken.

The general idea seemed to be, that it was done with a view of " bouncing," or frightening us into submission. Such proved to be the case; for Wilson, rising to his feet again, addressed us as follows: —

" You see, men, that every preparation has been made to send you to Sydney for trial. The Rosa (a small Australian schooner, lying in the harbor) will sail for that place in the course of ten days, at farthest. The Julia sails on a cruise this day week. Do you still refuse duty? "

We did.

Hereupon the consul and captain exchanged glances; and the latter looked bitterly disappointed.

Presently I noticed Guy's eye upon me; and, for the first time, he spoke, and told me to come near. I stepped forward.

" Was it not you that was taken off the island? "

" It was."

" It is *you* then who owe your life to my humanity. Yet this is the gratitude of a sailor, Mr. Wilson! "

" Not so, sir." And I at once gave him to understand, that I was perfectly acquainted with his motives in sending a boat into the bay; his crew was reduced, and he merely wished to procure the sailor whom he expected to find there. The *ship* was the means of my deliverance, and no thanks to the benevolence of its captain.

Doctor Long Ghost also, had a word to say. In two masterly sentences he summed up Captain Guy's character, to the complete satisfaction of every seaman present.

Matters were now growing serious; especially as the sailors became riotous, and talked about taking the consul and the captain back to the Calabooza with them.

The other judges fidgeted, and loudly commanded silence. It was at length restored; when Wilson, for the last time addressing us, said something more about the Rosa and Sydney, and concluded by reminding us, that a week would elapse ere the Julia sailed.

Leaving these hints to operate for themselves, he dismissed the party, ordering Captain Bob and his friends to escort us back whence we came.

CHAPTER XXXVII.

THE FRENCH PRIESTS PAY THEIR RESPECTS.

A DAY or two after the events just related, we were lounging in the Calabooza Beretanee, when we were honored by a visit from three of the French priests; and as about the only notice ever taken of us by the English missionaries, was their leaving their cards for us in the shape of a package of tracts, we could not help thinking, that the Frenchmen, in making a personal call, were at least much better bred.

By this time they had settled themselves down quite near our habitation. A pleasant little stroll down the Broom Road, and a rustic cross peeped through the trees; and soon you came to as charming a place as one would wish to see: a soft knoll, planted with old bread-fruit trees; in front, a savannah, sloping to a grove of palms, and, between these, glimpses of blue, sunny waves.

On the summit of the knoll, was a rude chapel, of bamboos; quite small, and surmounted by the cross. Between the canes, at nightfall, the natives stole peeps at a small portable altar; a crucifix to correspond, and gilded candlesticks and censers. Their curiosity carried them no further; nothing could induce them to worship there. Such queer ideas as they entertained, of the hated strangers! Masses and chants were nothing more than evil spells. As for the priests themselves, they were no better than diabolical sorcerers; like those who, in old times, terrified their fathers.

Close by the chapel, was a range of native houses; rented from a chief, and handsomely furnished. Here lived the priests; and, very comfortably, too. They looked sanctimonious enough abroad; but that went for nothing: since, at home, in their retreat, they were a club of Friar Tucks; holding priestly wassail over many a good cup of red brandy, and rising late in the morning.

Pity it was, they couldn't marry—pity for the ladies of the island, I mean, and the cause of morality; for what business had the ecclesiastical old bachelors, with such a set of trim little native handmaidens? These damsels were their first converts; and devoted ones they were.

The priests, as I said before, were accounted necromancers: the appearance of two of our three visitors might have justified the conceit.

They were little, dried-up Frenchmen, in long, straight gowns of black cloth, and unsightly three-cornered hats—

so preposterously big, that, in putting them on, the reverend fathers seemed extinguishing themselves.

Their companion was dressed differently. He wore a sort of yellow, flannel morning-gown, and a broad-brimmed Manilla hat. Large and portly, he was also hale and fifty; with a complexion like an autumnal leaf—handsome blue eyes—fine teeth, and a racy Milesian brogue. In short, he was an Irishman; Father Murphy, by name; and, as such, pretty well known, and very thoroughly disliked, throughout all the Protestant missionary settlements in Polynesia. In early youth, he had been sent to a religious seminary in France; and, taking orders there, had, but once or twice afterward, revisited his native land.

Father Murphy marched up to us briskly; and the first words he uttered were, to ask whether there were any of his countrymen among us. There were two of them; one, a lad of sixteen—a bright, curly-headed rascal—and, being a young Irishman, of course, his name was Pat. The other, was an ugly, and rather melancholy-looking scamp; one M'Gee, whose prospects in life had been blasted by a premature transportation to Sydney. This was the report, at least, though it might have been scandal.

In most of my shipmates, were some redeeming qualities; but about M'Gee, there was nothing of the kind; and forced to consort with him, I could not help regretting, a thousand times, that the gallows had been so tardy. As if impelled, against her will, to send him into the world, Nature had done all she could to insure his being taken for what he was. About the eyes, there was no mistaking him; with a villainous cast in one, they seemed suspicious of each other.

Glancing away from him at once, the bluff priest rested his gaze on the good-humored face of Pat, who, with a pleasant roguishness, was " twigging " the enormous hats (or " Hytee Belteezers," as land beavers are called by sailors), from under which, like a couple of snails, peeped the two little Frenchmen.

Pat and the priest were both from the same town in Meath; and, when this was found out, there was no end to the questions of the latter. To him, Pat seemed a letter from home, and said a hundred times as much.

After a long talk between these two, and a little broken English from the Frenchmen, our visitors took leave; but Father Murphy had hardly gone a dozen rods, when back he came, inquiring whether we were in want of any thing.

"Yes," cried one, "something to eat." Upon this, he promised to send us some fresh wheat bread, of his own baking; a great luxury in Tahiti.

We all felicitated Pat upon picking up such a friend, and told him his fortune was made.

The next morning, a French servant of the priest's made his appearance, with a small bundle of clothing for our young Hibernian; and the promised bread for the party. Pat, being out at the knees and elbows, and, like the rest of us, not full inside, the present was acceptable all round.

In the afternoon, Father Murphy himself came along; and, in addition to his previous gifts, gave Pat a good deal of advice: said he was sorry to see him in limbo, and that he would have a talk with the consul about having him set free.

We saw nothing more of him for two or three days; at the end of which time he paid us another call, telling Pat, that Wilson was inexorable, having refused to set him at liberty, unless to go aboard the ship. This, the priest now besought him to do forthwith; and so escape the punishment which, it seems, Wilson had been hinting at to his intercessor. Pat, however, was stanch against entreaties; and, with all the ardor of a sophomorean sailor, protested his intention to hold out to the last. With none of the meekness of a good little boy about him, the blunt youngster stormed away at such a rate, that it was hard to pacify him; and the priest said no more.

How it came to pass—whether from Murphy's speaking to the consul, or otherwise, we could not tell—but the next day, Pat was sent for by Wilson, and being escorted to the village by our good old keeper, three days elapsed before he returned.

Bent upon reclaiming him, they had taken him on board the ship; feasted him in the cabin; and, finding that of no avail, down they thrust him into the hold, in double irons, and on bread and water. All would not do; and so he was sent back to the Calabooza. Boy that he was, they must have counted upon his being more susceptible to discipline than the rest.

The interest felt in Pat's welfare, by his benevolent countryman, was very serviceable to the rest of us; especially as we all turned Catholics, and went to mass every morning, much to Captain Bob's consternation. Upon finding it out, he threatened to keep us in the stocks, if we did not desist. He went no farther than this, though; and so, every few days, we strolled down to the priest's residence, and had a mouthful to eat, and something generous to drink. In particular, Dr. Long Ghost and myself became huge favorites with Pat's friend; and many a time he regaled us from a quaint-looking traveling-case for spirits, stowed away in one corner of his dwelling. It held four square flasks, which, somehow or other, always contained just enough to need emptying. In truth, the fine old Irishman was a rosy fellow in canonicals. His countenance and his soul were always in a glow. It may be ungenerous to reveal his failings, but he often talked thick, and sometimes was perceptibly eccentric in his gait.

I never drink French brandy, but I pledge Father Murphy. His health again! And many jolly proselytes may he make in Polynesia!

CHAPTER XXXVIII.

LITTLE JULE SAILS WITHOUT US.

To make good the hint thrown out by the consul upon the conclusion of the Farce of the Affidavits, we were again brought before him within the time specified.

It was the same thing over again: he got nothing out of us, and we were remanded; our resolute behavior annoying him prodigiously.

What we observed, led us to form the idea, that on first learning the state of affairs on board the Julia, Wilson must have addressed his invalid friend, the captain, something in the following style:

"Guy, my poor fellow, don't worry yourself now about those rascally sailors of yours. I'll dress them out for you— just leave it all to me, and set your mind at rest."

But handcuffs and stocks, big looks, threats, dark hints, and depositions, had all gone for naught.

Conscious that, as matters now stood, nothing serious could grow out of what had happened; and never dreaming that our being sent home for trial, had ever been really thought of, we thoroughly understood Wilson, and laughed at him accordingly.

Since leaving the Julia, we had caught no glimpse of the mate; but we often heard of him.

It seemed that he remained on board, keeping house in the cabin for himself and Viner; who, going to see him according to promise, was induced to remain a guest. These two cronies now had fine times; tapping the captain's quarter-casks, playing cards on the transom, and giving balls of an evening to the ladies ashore. In short, they cut up so many queer capers, that the missionaries complained of them to the consul; and Jermin received a sharp reprimand.

This so affected him, that he drank still more freely than before; and one afternoon, when mellow as a grape, he took umbrage at a canoe full of natives, who, on being hailed from the deck to come aboard and show their papers, got frightened, and paddled for the shore. Lowering a boat instantly, he equipped Wymontoo and the Dane with a cutlass apiece, and seizing another himself, off they started in pursuit, the ship's ensign flying in the boat's stern. The alarmed islanders, beaching their canoe, with loud cries fled through the village, the mate after them, slashing his naked weapon to right and left. A crowd soon collected; and the " Karhowree toonee," or crazy stranger, was quickly taken before Wilson.

Now, it so chanced, that in a native house hard by, the consul and Captain Guy were having a quiet game at cribbage by themselves, a decanter on the table standing sentry. The obstreperous Jermin was brought in; and finding the two thus pleasantly occupied, it had a soothing effect upon him; and he insisted upon taking a hand at the cards, and a drink of the brandy. As the consul was nearly as tipsy as himself, and the captain dared not object for fear of giving offense, at it they went,—all three of them — and made a night of it; the mate's delinquencies being summarily passed over, and his captors sent away.

An incident worth relating grew out of this freak.

There wandered about Papeetee, at this time, a shriveled little fright of an Englishwoman, known among sailors as " Old Mother Tot." From New Zealand to the Sandwich Islands, she had been all over the South Seas; keeping a rude hut of entertainment for mariners, and supplying them with rum and dice. Upon the missionary islands, of course, such conduct was severely punishable; and at various places, Mother Tot's establishment had been shut up, and its proprietor made to quit in the first vessel that could be hired to land her elsewhere. But, with a perseverance invincible, wherever she went, she always started afresh; and so became notorious everywhere.

By some wicked spell of hers, a patient, one-eyed little cobbler followed her about, mending shoes for white men, doing the old woman's cooking, and bearing all her abuse without grumbling. Strange to relate, a battered Bible was seldom out of his sight; and whenever he had leisure, and his mistress' back was turned, he was forever poring over it. This pious propensity used to enrage the old crone past belief; and oftentimes she boxed his ears with the book, and tried to burn it. Mother Tot and her man Josy were, indeed, a curious pair.

But to my story.

A week or so after our arrival in the harbor, the old lady had once again been hunted down, and forced for the time to abandon her nefarious calling. This was brought about chiefly by Wilson, who, for some reason unknown, had contracted the most violent hatred for her; which, on her part, was more than reciprocated.

10

Well: passing, in the evening, where the consul and his party were making merry, she peeped through the bamboos of the house; and straightway resolved to gratify her spite.

The night was very dark; and providing herself with a huge ship's lantern, which usually swung in her hut, she waited till they came forth. This happened about midnight; Wilson making his appearance, supported by two natives, holding him up by the arms. These three went first; and just as they got under a deep shade, a bright light was thrust within an inch of Wilson's nose. The old hag was kneeling before him, holding the lantern with uplifted hands.

" Ha, ha! my fine *counselor*," she shrieked; " ye persecute a lone old body like me for selling rum—do ye? And here ye are, carried home drunk—Hoot! ye villain, I scorn ye! " And she spat upon him.

Terrified at the apparition, the poor natives—arrant believers in ghosts—dropped the trembling consul, and fled in all directions. After giving full vent to her rage, Mother Tot hobbled away, and left the three revelers to stagger home the best way they could.

The day following our last interview with Wilson, we learned that Captain Guy had gone on board his vessel, for the purpose of shipping a new crew. There was a round bounty offered; and a heavy bag of Spanish dollars, with the Julia's articles ready for signing, were laid on the capstan-head.

Now, there was no lack of idle sailors ashore, mostly " Beachcombers," who had formed themselves into an organized gang, headed by one Mack, a Scotchman, whom they styled the Commodore. By the laws of the fraternity, no member was allowed to ship on board a vessel, unless granted permission by the rest. In this way the gang controlled the port, all discharged seamen being forced to join them.

To Mack and his men our story was well known; indeed, they had several times called to see us; and of course, as sailors and congenial spirits, they were hard against Captain Guy.

Deeming the matter important, they came in a body to the Calabooza, and wished to know, whether, all things considered, we thought it best for any of them to join the Julia.

Anxious to pack the ship off as soon as possible, we answered, by all means. Some went so far as to laud the Julia to the skies, as the best and fastest of ships. Jermin too, as a good fellow, and a sailor every inch, came in for *his* share of praise; and as for the captain—quiet man, he would never trouble any one. In short, every inducement we could think of was presented; and Flash Jack ended by assuring the beachcombers solemnly, that now we were all well and hearty, nothing but a regard to principle, prevented us from returning on board ourselves.

The result was, that a new crew was finally obtained, together with a steady New Englander for second mate, and three good whalemen for harponeers. In part, what was wanting for the ship's larder was also supplied; and as far as could be done in a place like Tahiti, the damages the vessel had sustained were repaired. As for the Mowree, the authorities refusing to let him be put ashore, he was carried to sea in irons, down in the hold. What eventually became of him, we never heard.

Ropey, poor, poor Ropey, who a few days previous had fallen sick, was left ashore at the sailor hospital at Townor, a small place upon the beach between Papeetee and Mata-vai. Here, some time after, he breathed his last. No one knew his complaint: he must have died of hard times. Several of us saw him interred in the sand, and I planted a rude post to mark his resting-place.

The cooper, and the rest who had remained aboard from the first, of course, composed part of the Julia's new crew.

To account for the conduct, all along, of the consul and captain, in trying so hard to alter our purpose with respect to the ship, the following statement is all that is requisite. Beside an advance of from fifteen to twenty-five dollars demanded by every sailor shipping at Tahiti, an additional sum for each man so shipped, has to be paid into the hands of the government, as a charge of the port. Beside this, the men—with here and there an exception—will only ship for one cruise, thus becoming entitled to a discharge before the vessel reaches home; which, in time, creates the necessity of obtaining other men, at a similar cost. Now, the Julia's exchequer was at low-water mark, or rather, it was quite empty; and to meet these expenses, a good part of what little oil there was aboard, had to be sold for a song to a merchant of Papeetee.

It was Sunday in Tahiti, and a glorious morning, when Captain Bob, waddling into the Calabooza, startled us by announcing "Ah—my boy—shippy you, harree—maky sail!" In other words, the Julia was off.

The beach was quite near, and in this quarter altogether uninhabited; so down we ran, and, at a cable's length, saw little Jule gliding past—top-gallant-sails hoisting, and a boy aloft with one leg thrown over the yard, loosing the fore-royal. The decks were all life and commotion; the sailors on the forecastle singing "Ho, cheerly men!" as they catted the anchor; and the gallant Jermin, bareheaded as his wont, standing up on the bowsprit, and issuing his orders. By the man at the helm, stood Captain Guy, very quiet and gentlemanly, and smoking a cigar. Soon the ship drew near the reef, and altering her course, glided out through the break, and went on her way.

Thus disappeared little Jule, about three weeks after entering the harbor; and nothing more have I ever heard of her.

CHAPTER XXXIX.

JERMIN SERVES US A GOOD TURN.—FRIENDSHIPS IN POLYNESIA.

THE ship out of the way, we were quite anxious to know what was going to be done with us. On this head, Captain Bob could tell us nothing; no further at least, than that he still considered himself responsible for our safe-

keeping. However, he never put us to bed any more; and
we had every thing our own way.

The day after the Julia left, the old man came up to us
in great tribulation, saying that the bucket of bread was
no longer forthcoming, and that Wilson had refused to send
any thing in its place. One and all, we took this for a
hint to disperse quietly, and go about our business. Nevertheless, we were not to be shaken off so easily; and taking a
malicious pleasure in annoying our old enemy, we resolved,
for the present, to stay where we were. For the part he had
been acting, we learned that the consul was the laughing-
stock of all the foreigners ashore, who frequently twitted
him upon his hopeful protegées of the Calabooza Beretanee.

As we were wholly without resources, so long as we
remained on the island no better place than Captain Bob's
could be selected for an abiding-place. Beside, we heartily
loved the old gentleman, and could not think of leaving
him; so, telling him to give no thought as to wherewithal
we should be clothed and fed, we resolved, by extending
and systematizing our foraging operations, to provide for
ourselves.

We were greatly assisted by a parting legacy of Jermin's.
To him we were indebted for having all our chests sent
ashore, and every thing left therein. They were placed in the
custody of a petty chief living near by, who was instructed
by the consul not to allow them to be taken away; but we
might call and make our toilets whenever we pleased.

We went to see Mahinee, the old chief; Captain Bob
going along, and stoutly insisting upon having the chattels
delivered up. At last this was done; and in solemn procession the chests were borne by the natives to the Calabooza. Here, we disposed them about quite tastefully; and
made such a figure, that in the eyes of old Bob and his
friends, the Calabooza Beretanee was by far the most
sumptuously furnished saloon in Tahiti.

Indeed, so long as it remained thus furnished, the native
courts of the district were held there; the judge, Mahinee,
and his associates, sitting upon one of the chests, and the
culprits and spectators thrown at full length upon the

ground, both inside of the building, and under the shade of the trees without; while, leaning over the stocks as from a gallery, the worshipful crew of the Julia looked on, and canvassed the proceedings.

I should have mentioned before, that previous to the vessel's departure, the men had bartered away all the clothing they could possibly spare; but now, it was resolved to be more provident.

The contents of the chests were of the most miscellaneous description:—sewing utensils, marling-spikes, strips of calico, bits of rope, jackknives; nearly every thing, in short, that a seaman could think of. But of wearing apparel, there was little but old frocks, remnants of jackets, and legs of trowsers, with now and then the foot of a stocking. These, however, were far from being valueless; for, among the poorer Tahitians, every thing European is highly esteemed. They come from "Beretanee, Fenooa Pararee" (Britain, Land of Wonders), and that is enough.

The chests themselves were deemed exceedingly precious, especially those with unfractured locks, which would absolutely click, and enable the owner to walk off with the key. Scars, however, and bruises, were considered great blemishes. One old fellow, smitten with the doctor's large mahogany chest (a well filled one, by the by), and finding infinite satisfaction in merely sitting thereon, was detected in the act of applying a healing ointment to a shocking scratch which impaired the beauty of the lid.

There is no telling the love of a Tahitian for a sailor's trunk. So ornamental is it held as an article of furniture in his hut, that the women are incessantly tormenting their husbands to bestir themselves, and make them a present of one. When obtained, no pier-table just placed in a drawing-room, is regarded with half the delight. For these reasons, then, our coming into possession of our estate at this time, was an important event.

The islanders are much like the rest of the world; and the news of our good fortune brought us troops of "tayos" or friends, eager to form an alliance after the national custom, and do our slightest bidding.

The really curious way in which all the Polynesians are in the habit of making bosom friends at the shortest possible notice, is deserving of remark. Although, among a people like the Tahitians, vitiated as they are by sophisticating influences, this custom has in most cases degenerated into a mere mercenary relation, it nevertheless had its origin in a fine, and in some instances, heroic sentiment, formerly entertained by their fathers.

In the annals of the island are examples of extravagant friendships, unsurpassed by the story of Damon and Pythias: in truth, much more wonderful; for, notwithstanding the devotion—even of life in some cases—to which they led, they were frequently entertained at first sight for some stranger from another island.

Filled with love and admiration for the first whites who came among them, the Polynesians could not testify the warmth of their emotions more strongly, than by instantaneously making their abrupt proffer of friendship. Hence, in old voyages we read of chiefs coming off from the shore in their canoes, and going through with strange antics, expressive of this desire. In the same way, their inferiors accosted the seamen; and thus the practice has continued in some islands down to the present day.

There is a small place, not many days' sail from Tahiti, and seldom visited by shipping, where the vessel touched to which I then happened to belong.

Of course, among the simple-hearted natives, we had a friend all round. Mine was Poky, a handsome youth, who never could do enough for me. Every morning at sunrise, his canoe came alongside loaded with fruits of all kinds; upon being emptied, it was secured by a line to the bowsprit, under which it lay all day long, ready at any time to carry its owner ashore on an errand.

Seeing him so indefatigable, I told Poky one day, that I was a virtuoso in shells and curiosities of all kinds. That was enough; away he paddled for the head of the bay, and I never saw him again for twenty-four hours. The next morning, his canoe came gliding slowly along the shore, with the full-leaved bough of a tree for a sail. For the purpose of keeping the things dry, he had also built a sort of platform just behind the prow, railed in with green wicker-work; and here was a heap of yellow bananas and cowree shells; young cocoa-nuts and antlers of red coral; two or three pieces of carved wood; a little pocket-idol, black as jet, and rolls of printed tappa.

We were given a holyday; and upon going ashore, Poky, of course, was my companion and guide. For this, no mortal could be better qualified; his native country was not large, and he knew every inch of it. Gallanting me about, every one was stopped and ceremoniously introduced to Poky's " tayo karhowree nuee " or his particular white friend.

He showed me all the lions; but more than all, he took me to see a charming lioness—a young damsel—the daughter of a chief—the reputation of whose charms had spread to the neighboring islands, and even brought suitors therefrom. Among these was Tooboi, the heir of Tamatoy, King of Raiatair, one of the Society Isles. The girl was certainly fair to look upon. Many heavens were in her sunny eyes; and the outline of that arm of hers, peeping forth from a capricious tappa robe, was the very curve of beauty.

Though there was no end to Poky's attentions, not a syllable did he ever breathe of reward; but sometimes he looked very knowing. At last the day came for sailing, and with it, also, his canoe, loaded down to the gunwale with a sea stock of fruits. Giving him all I could spare from my chest, I went on deck to take my place at the windlass; for the anchor was weighing. Poky followed, and heaved with me at the same handspike.

The anchor was soon up; and away we went out of the bay with more than twenty shallops towing astern. At last they left us; but long as I could see him at all, there was Poky, standing alone and motionless in the bow of his canoe.

END OF PART I.

PART II.

CHAPTER XL.

WE TAKE UNTO OURSELVES FRIENDS.

THE arrival of the chests made my friend, the doctor, by far the wealthiest man of the party. So much the better for me, seeing that I had little or nothing myself; though from our intimacy, the natives courted my favor almost as much as his.

Among others, Kooloo was a candidate for my friendship; and being a comely youth, quite a buck in his way, I accepted his overtures. By this, I escaped the importunities of the rest; for be it known, that, though little inclined to jealousy in love matters, the Tahitian will hear of no rivals in his friendship.

Kooloo, running over his qualifications as a friend, first of all informed me, that he was a " Mickonaree," thus declaring his communion with the church.

The way this " tayo " of mine expressed his regard, was by assuring me over and over again, that the love he bore me was " nuee, nuee, nuee," or infinitesimally extensive. All over these seas, the word " nuee " is significant of quantity. Its repetition is like placing ciphers at the right hand of a numeral; the more places you carry it out to, the greater the sum. Judge, then, of Kooloo's esteem. Nor is the allusion to the ciphers at all inappropriate, seeing that, in themselves, Kooloo's professions turned out to be worthless. He was, alas! as sounding brass and a tinkling cymbal; one of those who make no music unless the clapper be silver.

In the course of a few days, the sailors, like the doctor and myself, were cajoled out of every thing, and our "tayos," all round, began to cool off quite sensibly. So remiss did they become in their attentions, that we could no longer rely upon their bringing us the daily supply of food, which all of them had faithfully promised.

As for Kooloo, after sponging me well, he one morning played the part of a retrograde lover; informing me, that his affections had undergone a change; he had fallen in love at first sight with a smart sailor, who had just stepped ashore quite flush from a lucky whaling-cruise.

It was a touching interview, and with it, our connection dissolved. But the sadness which ensued would soon have been dissipated, had not my sensibilities been wounded by his indelicately sporting some of my gifts very soon after this transfer of his affections. Hardly a day passed, that I did not meet him on the Broom Road, airing himself in a Regatta shirt, which I had given him in happier hours.

He went by with such an easy saunter too, looking me pleasantly in the eye, and merely exchanging the cold salute of the road:—"Yar onor, boyoee," a mere side-walk how d'ye do. After several experiences like this, I began to entertain a sort of respect for Kooloo, as quite a man of the world. In good sooth, he turned out to be one; in one week's time giving me the cut direct, and lounging by without even nodding. He must have taken me for part of the landscape.

Before the chests were quite empty, we had a grand washing in the stream of our best raiment, for the purpose of looking tidy, and visiting the European chapel in the village. Every Sunday morning it is open for divine service, some member of the mission officiating. This was the first time we ever entered Papeetee unattended by an escort.

In the chapel there were about forty people present, including the officers of several ships in harbor. It was an energetic discourse, and the pulpit cushion was well pounded. Occupying a high seat in the synagogue, and stiff as a flag-staff, was our beloved guardian, Wilson. I shall never forget his look of wonder when his interesting wards filed in at the doorway, and took up a seat directly facing him.

Service over, we waited outside in hopes of seeing more of him; but sorely annoyed at the sight of us, he reconnoitered from the window, and never came forth until we had started for home.

CHAPTER XLI.

WE LEVY CONTRIBUTIONS ON THE SHIPPING.

SCARCELY a week went by after the Julia's sailing, when, with the proverbial restlessness of sailors, some of the men began to grow weary of the Calabooza Beretanee, and resolved to go boldly among the vessels in the bay, and offer to ship.

The thing was tried; but though strongly recommended by the commodore of the beachcombers, in the end they were invariably told by the captains to whom they applied, that they bore an equivocal character ashore, and would not answer. So often were they repulsed, that we pretty nearly gave up all thoughts of leaving the island in this way; and growing domestic again, settled down quietly at Captain Bob's.

It was about this time, that the whaling-ships, which have their regular seasons for cruising, began to arrive at Papeetee; and of course their crews frequently visited us. This is customary all over the Pacific. No sailor steps ashore, but he straightway goes to the " Calabooza," where he is almost sure to find some poor fellow or other in confinement for desertion, or alledged mutiny, or something of that sort. Sympathy is proffered, and if need be, tobacco. The latter, however, is most in request; as a solace to the captive, it is invaluable.

Having fairly carried the day against both consul and captain, we were objects of even more than ordinary interest to these philanthropists; and they always cordially applauded our conduct. Besides, they invariably brought along something in the way of refreshments; occasionally smuggling in a little Pisco. Upon one occasion, when there was quite a number present, a calabash was passed round, and a pecuniary collection taken up for our benefit.

One day a new comer proposed, that two or three of us should pay him a sly, nocturnal visit aboard his ship; engaging to send us away well freighted with provisions. This was not a bad idea; nor were we at all backward in acting upon it. Night after night every vessel in the harbor was visited in rotation, the foragers borrowing Captain Bob's canoe for the purpose. As we all took turns at this—two by two—in due course it came to Long Ghost and myself, for the sailors invariably linked us together. In such an enterprise, I somewhat distrusted the doctor, for he was no sailor, and very tall; and a canoe is the most ticklish of navigable things. However, it could not be helped; and so we went.

But a word about the canoes, before we go any further. Among the Society Islands, the art of building them, like all native accomplishments, has greatly deteriorated; and they are now the most inelegant, as well as the most insecure of any in the South Seas. In Cook's time, according to his account, there was at Tahiti a royal fleet of seventeen hundred and twenty large war-canoes, handsomely carved, and otherwise adorned. At present, those used are quite small; nothing more than logs hollowed out, sharpened at one end, and then lanched into the water.

To obviate a certain rolling propensity, the Tahitians, like all Polynesians, attach to them what sailors call an "outrigger." It consists of a pole floating alongside, parallel to the canoe, and connected with it by a couple of cross sticks, a yard or more in length. Thus equipped, the canoe can not be overturned, unless you overcome the buoyancy of the pole, or lift it entirely out of the water.

Now, Captain Bob's "gig" was exceedingly small; so small, and of such a grotesque shape, that the sailors christened it the Pill Box; and by this appellation it always went. In fact, it was a sort of "sulky," meant for a solitary paddler, but on an emergency, capable of floating two or three. The outrigger was a mere switch, alternately rising in air, and then depressed in the water.

Assuming the command of the expedition, upon the strength of my being a sailor, I packed the Long Doctor with a paddle in the bow, and then shoving off, leaped into the stern; thus leaving him to do all the work, and reserving to myself the dignified sinecure of steering. All would have gone well, were it not that my paddler made such clumsy work, that the water spattered, and showered down upon us without ceasing. Continuing to ply his tool, however, quite energetically, I thought he would improve after a while, and so let him alone. But by and by, getting wet through with this little storm we were raising, and seeing no signs of its clearing off, I conjured him, in mercy's name, to stop short, and let me wring myself out. Upon this, he suddenly turned round, when the canoe gave a roll, the outrigger flew overhead, and the next moment came rap on the doctor's skull, and we were both in the water.

Fortunately, we were just over a ledge of coral, not half-a-fathom under the surface. Depressing one end of the filled canoe, and letting go of it quickly, it bounced up, and discharged great part of its contents; so that we easily baled out the remainder, and again embarked. This time, my comrade coiled himself away in a very small space; and enjoining upon him not to draw a single unnecessary breath, I proceeded to urge the canoe along by myself. I was astonished at his docility, never speaking a word, and stirring neither hand nor foot; but the secret was, he was unable to swim, and in case we met with a second mishap, there were no more ledges beneath to stand upon. " Drowning's but a shabby way of going out of the world," he exclaimed, upon my rallying him; " and I'm not going to be guilty of it."

At last, the ship was at hand, and we approached with much caution, wishing to avoid being hailed by any one from the quarter-deck. Dropping silently under her bows, we heard a low whistle—the signal agreed upon—and presently a goodly sized bag was lowered over to us.

We cut the line, and then paddled away as fast as we could, and made the best of our way home. Here, we found the rest waiting impatiently.

The bag turned out to be well filled with sweet potatoes boiled, cubes of salt beef and pork, and a famous sailors' pudding, what they call " duff," made of flour and water, and of about the consistence of an underdone brick. With these delicacies, and keen appetites, we went out into the moonlight, and had a nocturnal picknick.

CHAPTER XLII.

MOTOO-OTOO.—A TAHITIAN CASUIST.

THE Pill-Box was sometimes employed for other purposes than that described in the last chapter. We sometimes went a-pleasuring in it.

Right in the middle of Papeetee harbor is a bright, green island, one circular grove of waving palms, and scarcely a hundred yards across. It is of coral formation; and all round, for many rods out, the bay is so shallow, that you might wade anywhere. Down in these waters, as transparent as air, you see coral plants of every hue and shape imaginable:—antlers, tufts of azure, waving reeds like stalks of grain, and pale green buds and mosses. In some places, you look through prickly branches down to a snow-white floor of sand, sprouting with flinty bulbs; and crawling among these are strange shapes:—some bristling with spikes, others clad in shining coats-of-mail, and here and there, round forms all spangled with eyes.

The island is called Motoo-Otoo; and around Motoo-Otoo have I often paddled of a white moonlight night, pausing now and then to admire the marine gardens beneath.

The place is the private property of the queen, who has a residence there—a melancholy-looking range of bamboo houses—neglected and falling to decay among the trees.

Commanding the harbor as it does, her majesty has done all she could to make a fortress of the island. The margin has been raised and leveled, and built up with a low parapet of hewn blocks of coral. Behind the parapet, are ranged at wide intervals, a number of rusty old cannon, of all fashions and calibres. They are mounted upon lame, decrepit-looking carriages, ready to sink under the useless burden of bearing them up. Indeed, two or three have given up the ghost altogether, and the pieces they sustained lie half-buried among their bleaching bones. Several of the cannon are spiked; probably with a view of making them more formidable; as they certainly must be to any one undertaking to fire them off.

Presented to Pomaree at various times by captains of British armed ships, these poor old " dogs of war," thus toothless and turned out to die, formerly bayed in full pack, as the battle hounds of Old England.

There was something about Motoo-Otoo that struck my fancy; and I registered a vow to plant my foot upon its soil, notwithstanding an old bareheaded sentry menaced me in the moonlight with an unsightly musket. As my canoe drew scarcely three inches of water, I could paddle close up to the parapet without grounding; but every time I came near, the old man ran toward me, pushing his piece forward, but never clapping it to his shoulder. Thinking he only meant to frighten me, I at last dashed the canoe right up to the wall, purposing a leap. It was the rashest act of my life; for never did cocoa-nut come nearer getting demolished, than mine did then. With the stock of his gun, the old warder fetched a tremendous blow, which I managed to dodge; and then falling back, succeeded in paddling out of harm's reach.

He must have been dumb; for never a word did he utter; but grinning from ear to ear, and with his white cotton robe streaming in the moonlight, he looked more like the spook of the island than any thing mortal.

I tried to effect my object by attacking him in the rear—
but he was all front; running about the place as I paddled,
and presenting his confounded musket wherever I went.
At last I was obliged to retreat; and to this day my vow
remains unfulfilled.

It was a few days after my repulse from before the walls
of Motoo Otoo, that I heard a curious case of casuistry
argued between one of the most clever and intelligent
natives I ever saw in Tahiti, a man by the name of Arheetoo,
and our learned Theban of a doctor.

It was this:—whether it was right and lawful for any
one, being a native, to keep the European Sabbath, in
preference to the day set apart as such by the missionaries,
and so considered by the islanders in general.

It must be known, that the missionaries of the good
ship Duff, who more than half-a-century ago established
the Tahitian reckoning, came hither by the way of the
Cape of Good Hope; and by thus sailing to the eastward,
lost one precious day of their lives all round, getting about
that much in advance of Greenwich time. For this reason,
vessels coming round Cape Horn—as they most all do
nowadays—find it Sunday in Tahiti, when, according to
their own view of the matter, it ought to be Saturday.
But as it won't do to alter the log, the sailors keep their
Sabbath, and the islanders theirs.

This confusion perplexes the poor natives mightily; and
it is to no purpose that you endeavor to explain so incomprehensible a phenomenon. I once saw a worthy old
missionary essay to shed some light on the subject; and
though I understood but few of the words employed, I
could easily get at the meaning of his illustrations. They
were something like the following:

"Here," says he, "you see this circle" (describing a
large one on the ground with a stick): "very good; now
you see this spot here" (marking a point in the perimeter):
"well; this is Beretanee (England), and I'm going to sail
round to Tahiti. Here I go, then; (following the circle
round), and there goes the sun (snatching up another stick,

and commissioning a bandy-legged native to travel round
with it in a contrary direction). Now then, we are both
off, and both going away from each other; and here you
see I have arrived at Tahiti (making a sudden stop); and
look now, where Bandy Legs is! "

But the crowd strenuously maintained, that Bandy Legs
ought to be somewhere above them in the atmosphere; for
it was a traditionary fact, that the people from the Duff
came ashore when the sun was high overhead. And here
the old gentleman, being a very good sort of man, doubtless,
but no astronomer, was obliged to give up.

Arheetoo, the casuist alluded to, though a member of
the church, and extremely conscientious about what
Sabbath he kept, was more liberal in other matters. Learning that I was something of a " mickonaree " (in this
sense, a man able to read, and cunning in the use of the
pen), he desired the slight favor of my forging for him a
set of papers; for which, he said, he would be much obliged,
and give me a good dinner of roast pig and Indian turnip
in the bargain.

Now, Arheetoo was one of those who board the shipping
for their washing; and the competition being very great
(the proudest chiefs not disdaining to solicit custom in
person, though the work is done by their dependents),
he had decided upon a course suggested by a knowing
sailor, a friend of his. He wished to have manufactured a
set of certificates, purporting to come from certain man-
of-war and merchant captains, known to have visited the
island; recommending him as one of the best getters up
of fine linen in all Polynesia.

At this time, Arheetoo had known me but two hours;
and, as he made the proposition very coolly, I thought it
rather presumptuous, and told him so. But as it was quite
impossible to convey a hint, that there was a slight impropriety in the thing, I did not resent the insult, but simply
declined.

11

CHAPTER XLIII.

ONE IS JUDGED BY THE COMPANY HE KEEPS.

ALTHOUGH, from its novelty, life at Captain Bob's was pleasant enough, for the time; there were some few annoyances connected with it, any thing but agreeable to a " soul of sensibility."

Prejudiced against us by the malevolent representations of the consul and others, many worthy foreigners ashore regarded us as a set of lawless vagabonds; though, truth to speak, better behaved sailors never stepped on the island, nor any who gave less trouble to the natives. But, for all this, whenever we met a respectably dressed European, ten to one he shunned us, by going over to the other side of the road. This was very unpleasant, at least to myself; though, certes, it did not prey upon the minds of the others.

To give an instance.

Of a fine evening in Tahiti—but they are all fine evenings there—you may see a bevy of silk bonnets and parasols passing along the Broom Road: perhaps a band of pale, little white urchins—sickly exotics—and, oftener still, sedate, elderly gentlemen, with canes; at whose appearance the natives, here and there, slink into their huts. These are the missionaries, their wives, and children, taking a family airing. Sometimes, by the by, they take horse, and ride down to Point Venus and back; a distance of several miles. At this place is settled the only survivor of the first missionaries that landed—an old, white-headed, saint-like man, by the name of Wilson, the father of our friend, the consul.

The little parties on foot were frequently encountered; and, recalling, as they did, so many pleasant recollections of home and the ladies, I really longed for a dress coat and beaver, that I might step up and pay my respects. But, situated as I was, this was out of the question. On one occasion, however, I received a kind, inquisitive glance, from a matron in gingham. Sweet lady! I have not forgotten her: her gown was a plaid.

But a glance, like hers, was not always bestowed.

One evening, passing the verandah of a missionary's dwelling, the dame, his wife, and a pretty, blond young girl, with ringlets, were sitting there, enjoying the seabreeze, then coming in, all cool and refreshing, from the spray of the reef. As I approached, the old lady peered hard at me; and her very cap seemed to convey a prim rebuke. The blue, English eyes, by her side, were also bent on me. But, oh Heavens! what a glance to receive, from such a beautiful creature! As for the mob cap, not a fig did I care for it; but, to be taken for any thing but a cavalier, by the ringleted one, was absolutely unendurable.

I resolved on a courteous salute, to show my goodbreeding if nothing more. But, happening to wear a sort of turban—hereafter to be particularly alluded to—there was no taking it off and putting it on again, with any thing like dignity. At any rate, then, here goes a bow. But, another difficulty presented itself: my loose frock was so voluminous, that I doubted whether any spinal curviture would be perceptible.

" Good-evening, ladies," exclaimed I, at last, advancing winningly; " a delightful air from the sea, ladies."

Hysterics and hartshorn! who would have thought it? The young lady screamed, and the old one came near fainting. As for myself, I retreated, in double quick time; and scarcely drew breath, until safely housed in the Calabooza.

CHAPTER XLIV.

CATHEDRAL OF PAPOAR.—THE CHURCH OF THE COCOA-NUTS.

On Sundays I always attended the principal native church on the outskirts of the village of Papeetee, and not far from the Calabooza Beretanee. It was esteemed the best specimen of architecture in Tahiti.

Of late, they have built their places of worship with more reference to durability than formerly. At one time, there were no less than thirty-six on the island—mere barns, tied together with thongs, which went to destruction in a very few years.

One, built many years ago in this style, was a most remarkable structure. It was erected by Pomaree II., who, on this occasion, showed all the zeal of a royal proselyte. The building was over seven hundred feet in length, and of a proportionate width; the vast ridge-pole was at intervals supported by a row of thirty-six cylindrical trunks of the bread-fruit tree; and, all round, the wall-plates rested on shafts of the palm. The roof—steeply inclining to within a man's height of the ground — was thatched with leaves, and the sides of the edifice were open. Thus spacious was the Royal Mission Chapel of Papoar.

At its dedication, three distinct sermons were, from different pulpits, preached to an immense concourse gathered from all parts of the island.

As the chapel was built by the king's command, nearly as great a multitude was employed in its construction, as swarmed over the scaffolding of the great temple of the Jews. Much less time, however, was expended. In less than three weeks from planting the first post, the last tier of palmetto-leaves drooped from the eaves, and the work was done.

Apportioned to the several chiefs and their dependents, the labor, though immense, was greatly facilitated by every one's bringing his post, or his rafter, or his pole strung with thatching, ready for instant use. The materials thus prepared being afterward secured together by thongs, there was literally " neither hammer, nor axe, nor any tool of iron heard in the house while it was building. "

But the most singular circumstance connected with this South Sea cathedral, remains to be related. As well for the beauty, as the advantages of such a site, the islanders love to dwell near the mountain streams; and so, a considerable brook, after descending from the hills and watering the

valley, was bridged over in three places, and swept clean
through the chapel.

Flowing waters! what an accompaniment to the songs
of the sanctuary; mingling with them, the praises and
thanksgivings of the green solitudes inland.

But the chapel of the Polynesian Solomon has long
since been deserted. Its thousand rafters of habiscus have
decayed, and fallen to the ground; and now, the stream
murmurs over them in its bed.

The present metropolitan church of Tahiti is very unlike the one just described. It is of moderate dimensions,
boarded over, and painted white. It is furnished also with
blinds, but no sashes; indeed, were it not for the rustic
thatch, it would remind one of a plain chapel at home.

The wood-work was all done by foreign carpenters, of
whom there are always several about Papeetee.

Within, its aspect is unique, and can not fail to interest
a stranger. The rafters overhead are bound round with
fine matting of variegated dyes; and all along the ridge-
pole, these trappings hang pendent, in alternate bunches
of tassels and deep fringes of stained grass. The floor is
composed of rude planks. Regular aisles run between
ranges of native settees, bottomed with crossed braids of
the cocoa-nut fibre, and furnished with backs.

But the pulpit, made of a dark, lustrous wood, and
standing at one end, is by far the most striking object. It is
preposterously lofty; indeed, a capital bird's-eye view of
the congregation ought to be had from its summit.

Nor does the church lack a gallery, which runs round
on three sides, and is supported by columns of the cocoa-
nut tree.

Its facings are here and there daubed over with a tawdry
blue; and in other places (without the slightest regard to
uniformity), patches of the same color may be seen. In their
ardor to decorate the sanctuary, the converts must have
borrowed each a brush full of paint, and zealously daubed
away at the first surface that offered.

As hinted, the general impression is extremely curious.
Little light being admitted, and every thing being of a

dark color, there is an indefinable Indian aspect of duski-
ness, throughout. A strange, woody smell, also—more or
less pervading every considerable edifice in Polynesia—is
at once perceptible. It suggests the idea of worm-eaten
idols packed away in some old lumber-room at hand.

For the most part, the congregation attending this
church is composed of the better and wealthier orders—
the chiefs and their retainers; in short, the rank and fashion
of the island. This class is infinitely superior in personal
beauty and general healthfulness to the " marenhoar," or
common people; the latter having been more exposed to
the worst and most debasing evils of foreign intercourse.
On Sundays, the former are invariably arrayed in their
finery; and thus appear to the best advantage. Nor are they
driven to the chapel, as some of their inferiors are to other
places of worship; on the contrary, capable of maintaining
a handsome exterior, and possessing greater intelligence,
they go voluntarily.

In respect of the woodland colonnade supporting its
galleries, I called this chapel the Church of the Cocoa-
nuts.

It was the first place for Christian worship in Polynesia
that I had seen; and the impression upon entering during
service was all the stronger. Majestic-looking chiefs, whose
fathers had hurled the battle-club, and old men who had
seen sacrifices smoking upon the altars of Oro, were there.
And hark! hanging from the bough of a bread-fruit tree
without, a bell is being struck with a bar of iron by a native
lad. In the same spot, the blast of the war-conch had often
resounded. But to the proceedings within.

The place is well filled. Everywhere meets the eye the
gay calico draperies worn on great occasions by the higher
classes, and forming a strange contrast of patterns and
colors. In some instances, these are so fashioned as to resemble as much as possible, European garments. This is
in excessively bad taste. Coats and pantaloons, too, are here
and there seen; but they look awkwardly enough, and take
away from the general effect.

But it is the array of countenances that most strikes you. Each is suffused with the peculiar animation of the Polynesians, when thus collected in large numbers. Every robe is rustling, every limb in motion, and an incessant buzzing going on throughout the assembly. The tumult is so great, that the voice of the placid old missionary, who now rises, is almost inaudible. Some degree of silence is at length obtained through the exertions of half-a-dozen strapping fellows, in white shirts and no pantaloons. Running in among the settees, they are at great pains to inculcate the impropriety of making a noise, by creating a most unnecessary racket themselves. This part of the service was quite comical.

There is a most interesting Sabbath School connected with the church; and the scholars, a vivacious, mischievous set, were in one part of the gallery. I was amused by a party in a corner. The teacher sat at one end of the bench, with a meek little fellow by his side. When the others were disorderly, this young martyr received a rap; intended, probably, as a sample of what the rest might expect, if they didn't amend.

Standing in the body of the church, and leaning against a pillar, was an old man, in appearance very different from others of his countrymen. He wore nothing but a coarse, scant mantle, of faded tappa; and from his staring, bewildered manner, I set him down as an aged bumpkin from the interior, unaccustomed to the strange sights and sounds of the metropolis. This old worthy was sharply reprimanded for standing up, and thus intercepting the view of those behind; but not comprehending exactly what was said to him, one of the white liveried gentry made no ceremony of grasping him by the shoulders, and fairly crushing him down into a seat.

During all this, the old missionary in the pulpit—as well as his associates beneath, never ventured to interfere—leaving every thing to native management. With South Sea islanders, assembled in any numbers, there is no other way of getting along.

CHAPTER XLV.

A MISSIONARY'S SERMON; WITH SOME REFLECTIONS.

SOME degree of order at length restored, the service was continued, by singing. The choir was composed of twelve or fifteen ladies of the mission, occupying a long bench to the left of the pulpit. Almost the entire congregation joined in.

The first air fairly startled me; it was the brave tune of Old Hundred, adapted to a Tahitian psalm. After the graceless scenes I had recently passed through, this circumstance, with all its accessories, moved me forcibly.

Many voices around were of great sweetness and compass. The singers, also, seemed to enjoy themselves mightly; some of them pausing, now and then, and looking round, as if to realize the scene more fully. In truth, they sang right joyously, despite the solemnity of the tune.

The Tahitians have much natural talent for singing; and, on all occasions, are exceedingly fond of it. I have often heard a stave or two of psalmody, hummed over by rakish young fellows, like a snatch from an opera.

With respect to singing, as in most other matters, the Tahitians widely differ from the people of the Sandwich Islands; where the parochial flocks may be said rather to *bleat* than *sing*.

The psalm concluded, a prayer followed. Very considerately, the good old missionary made it short; for the congregation became fidgety and inattentive as soon as it commenced.

A chapter of the Tahitian Bible was now read; a text selected; and the sermon began. It was listened to with more attention than I had anticipated.

Having been informed, from various sources, that the discourses of the missionaries, being calculated to engage the attention of their simple auditors, were, naturally enough, of a rather amusing description to strangers; in short, that they had much to say about steamboats, lord mayor's coaches, and the way fires are put out in London,

I had taken care to provide myself with a good interpreter, in the person of an intelligent Hawaiian sailor, whose acquaintance I had made.

"Now, Jack," said I, before entering, "hear every word, and tell me what you can, as the missionary goes on."

Jack's was not, perhaps, a critical version of the discourse; and, at the time, I took no notes of what he said. Nevertheless, I will here venture to give what I remember of it; and, as far as possible, in Jack's phraseology, so as to lose nothing by a double translation.

"Good friends, I glad to see you; and I very well like to have some talk with you to-day. Good friends, very bad times in Tahiti; it make me weep. Pomaree is gone—the island no more yours, but the Wee-Wee's (French). Wicked priests here, too; and wicked idols in woman's clothes, and brass chains.*

"Good friends, no you speak, or look at them—but I know you won't—they belong to a set of robbers—the wicked Wee-Wees. Soon these bad men be made to go very quick. Beretanee ships of thunder come, and away they go. But no more 'bout this now. I speak more by by.

"Good friends, many whale-ships here now; and many bad men come in 'em. No good sailors living—that you know very well. They come here, 'cause so bad they no keep 'em home.

"My good little girls, no run after sailors—no go where they go; they harm you. Where they come from, no good people talk to 'em—just like dogs. Here, they talk to Pomaree, and drink *arva* with great Poofai.*

"Good friends, this very small island, but very wicked, and very poor; these two go together. Why Beretanee so great? Because that island good island, and send *mikonaree*†

* Meaning the showy image of the Virgin in the little Catholic chapel.

* The word "arva," as here employed, means brandy. Poofai was one of the highest chiefs on the island, and a jolly companion.

† This word, evidently a corruption of "missionary," is used under various significations by the natives. Sometimes, it is applied to a communicant of the Church. But, above, it has its original meaning.

to poor *kannaka*.‡ In Beretanee, every man rich: plenty things to buy; and plenty things to sell. Houses bigger than Pomaree's, and more grand. Every body, too, ride about in coaches, bigger than hers;§ and wear fine tappa every day. (Several luxurious appliances of civilization were here enumerated, and described.)

" Good friends, little to eat left at my house. Schooner from Sydney no bring bag of flour; and kannaka no bring pig and fruit enough. Mickonaree do great deal for kannaka; kannaka do little for mickonaree. So, good friends, weave plenty of cocoa-nut baskets, fill 'em, and bring 'em to-morrow."

Such was the substance of great part of this discourse; and, whatever may be thought of it, it was specially adapted to the minds of the islanders; who are susceptible to no impressions, except from things palpable, or novel and striking. To them, a dry sermon would be dry indeed.

The Tahitians can hardly ever be said to reflect: they are all impulse; and so, instead of expounding dogmas, the missionaries give them the large type, pleasing cuts, and short, and easy lessons of the primer. Hence, any thing like a permanent religious impression, is seldom or never produced.

In fact, there is, perhaps, no race upon earth, less disposed, by nature, to the monitions of Christianity, than the people of the South Sea. And this assertion is made, with full knowledge of what is called the " Great Revival at the Sandwich Islands," about the year 1836; when several thousands were, in the course of a few weeks, admitted into the bosom of the Church. But this result was brought about by no sober moral convictions; as an almost instantaneous relapse into every kind of licentiousness, soon afterward testified. It was the legitimate effect of a morbid feeling, engendered by the sense of severe physical wants, preying

---

‡ A word generally used by foreigners to designate the natives of Polynesia.

§ Pomaree, some time previous, had received a present of a chariot from Queen Victoria. It was afterward sent to Oahu (Sandwich Islands), and there sold to pay her debts.

upon minds excessively prone to superstition; and, by fanatical preaching, inflamed into the belief, that the gods of the missionaries were taking vengeance upon the wickedness of the land.*

It is a noteworthy fact, that those very traits in the Tahitians, which induced the London Missionary Society to regard them as the most promising subjects for conversion; and which led, moreover, to the selection of their island as the very first field for missionary labor, eventually proved the most serious obstruction. An air of softness in their manners, great apparent ingenuousness and docility, at first misled; but these were the mere accompaniments of an indolence, bodily and mental; a constitutional voluptuousness; and an aversion to the least restraint; which, however fitted for the luxurious state of nature, in the tropics, are the greatest possible hinderances to the strict moralities of Christianity.

Added to all this, is a quality inherent in Polynesians; and more akin to hypocrisy than any thing else. It leads them to assume the most passionate interest, in matters for which they really feel little or none whatever; but in which, those whose power they dread, or whose favor they court, they believe to be at all affected. Thus, in their heathen state, the Sandwich Islanders actually knocked out their teeth, tore their hair, and mangled their bodies with shells, to testify their inconsolable grief at the demise of a high chief, or member of the royal family. And yet, Vancouver relates, that, on such an occasion, upon which he happened to be present, those apparently the most abandoned to their feelings, immediately assumed the utmost light-heartedness, on receiving the present of a penny whistle, or a Dutch looking-glass. Similar instances, also, have come under my own observation.

The following is an illustration of the trait alluded to, as occasionally manifested among the converted Polynesians.

At one of the Society Islands—Raiatair, I believe—the natives, for special reasons, desired to commend themselves

---

* At this period, many of the population were upon the verge of starvation.

particularly to the favor of the missionaries. Accordingly, during divine service, many of them behaved in a manner, otherwise unaccountable, and precisely similar to their behavior as heathens. They pretended to be wrought up to madness by the preaching which they heard. They rolled their eyes; foamed at the mouth; fell down in fits; and so, were carried home. Yet, strange to relate, all this was deemed the evidence of the power of the Most High; and, as such, was heralded abroad.

But, to return to the Church of the Cocoa-nuts. The blessing pronounced, the congregation disperse; enlivening the Broom Road with their waving mantles. On either hand, they disappear down the shaded pathways, which lead off from the main route, conducting to hamlets in the groves, or to the little marine villas upon the beach. There is considerable hilarity; and you would suppose them just from an old-fashioned "hevar," or jolly heathen dance. Those who carry Bibles, swing them carelessly from their arms, by cords of sinnate.

The Sabbath is no ordinary day with the Tahitians. So far as doing any work is concerned, it is scrupulously observed. The canoes are hauled up on the beach; the nets are spread to dry. Passing by the hen-coop huts, on the roadside, you find their occupants idle, as usual; but less disposed to gossip. After service, repose broods over the whole island; the valleys reaching inland look stiller than ever.

In short, it is Sunday—their "Taboo Day;" the very word, formerly expressing the sacredness of their pagan observances, now proclaiming the sanctity of the Christian Sabbath.

CHAPTER XLVI.

SOMETHING ABOUT THE KANNAKIPPERS.

A WORTHY young man, formerly a friend of mine (I speak of Kooloo with all possible courtesy, since after our intimacy there would be an impropriety in doing otherwise)—this worthy youth, having some genteel notions of retirement, dwelt in a " maroo boro," or bread-fruit shade, a pretty nook in a wood, midway between the Calabooza Beretanee and the Church of Cocoa-nuts. Hence, at the latter place, he was one of the most regular worshipers.

Kooloo was a blade. Standing up in the congregation in all the bravery of a striped calico shirt, with the skirts rakishly adjusted over a pair of white sailor trowsers, and hair well anointed with cocoa-nut oil, he ogled the ladies with an air of supreme satisfaction. Nor were his glances unreturned.

But such looks as the Tahitian belles cast at each other: frequently turning up their noses at the advent of a new cotton mantle recently imported in the chest of some amorous sailor. Upon one occasion, I observed a group of young girls, in tunics of coarse, soiled sheeting, disdainfully pointing at a damsel in a flaming red one. " Oee tootai owree! " said they with ineffable scorn, " itai maitai! " (you are a good-for-nothing huzzy, no better than you should be).

Now, Kooloo communed with the church; so did all these censorious young ladies. Yet after eating bread-fruit at the Eucharist, I knew several of them, the same night, to be guilty of some sad derelictions.

Puzzled by these things, I resolved to find out, if possible, what ideas, if any, they entertained of religion; but as one's spiritual concerns are rather delicate for a stranger to meddle with, I went to work as adroitly as I could.

Farnow, an old native who had recently retired from active pursuits, having thrown up the business of being a sort of running footman to the queen, had settled down in a snug little retreat, not fifty rods from Captain Bob's. His selecting our vicinity for his residence, may have been with some view to the advantages it afforded for introducing his three daughters into polite circles. At any rate, not averse to receiving the attentions of so devoted a gallant as the doctor, the sisters (communicants, be it remembered) kindly extended to him, free permission to visit them sociably, whenever he pleased.

We dropped in one evening, and found the ladies at home. My long friend engaged his favorites, the two younger girls, at the game of " Now," or hunting a stone under three piles of tappa. For myself, I lounged on a mat with Ideea the eldest, dallying with her grass fan, and improving my knowledge of Tahitian.

The occasion was well adapted to my purpose, and I began.

" Ah, Ideea, mickonaree oee? " the same as drawling out—" By the by, Miss Ideea, do you belong to the church? "

" Yes, me mickonaree," was the reply.

But the assertion was at once qualified by certain reservations; so curious, that I can not forbear their relation.

" Mickonaree *ena* " (church member *here*), exclaimed she, laying her hand upon her mouth, and a strong emphasis on the adverb. In the same way, and with similar exclamations, she touched her eyes and hands. This done, her whole air changed in an instant; and she gave me to understand, by unmistakable gestures, that in certain other respects she was not exactly a " mickonaree." In short, Ideea was

> " A sad good Christian at the heart—
> A very heathen in the carnal part." *

The explanation terminated in a burst of laughter, in which all three sisters joined; and for fear of looking silly, the doctor and myself. As soon as good-breeding would permit, we took leave.

The hypocrisy in matters of religion, so apparent in all Polynesian converts, is most injudiciously nourished in Tahiti, by a zealous, and in many cases, a coercive superintendence over their spiritual well-being. But it is only manifested with respect to the common people, their superiors being exempted.

On Sunday mornings, when the prospect is rather small for a full house in the minor churches, a parcel of fellows

---

* Pope. (Epistle to a lady.)

are actually sent out with ratans into the highways and byways as whippers-in of the congregation. This is a sober fact.†

These worthies constitute a religious police; and you always know them by the great white diapers they wear. On week days, they are quite as busy as on Sundays; to the great terror of the inhabitants, going all over the island, and spying out the wickedness thereof.

Moreover, they are the collectors of fines—levied generally in grass mats—for obstinate non-attendance upon divine worship, and other offenses amenable to the ecclesiastical judicature of the missionaries.

Old Bob called these fellows " kannakippers," a corruption, I fancy, of our word constable.

He bore them a bitter grudge; and one day, drawing near home, and learning that two of them were just then making a domiciliary visit at his house, he ran behind a bush; and as they came forth, two green bread-fruit from a hand unseen, took them each between the shoulders. The sailors in the Calabooza were witnesses to this, as well as several natives; who, when the intruders were out of sight, applauded Captain Bob's spirit in no measured terms; the ladies present vehemently joining in. Indeed, the kannakippers have no greater enemies than the latter. And no wonder: the impertinent varlets, popping into their houses at all hours, are forever prying into their peccadilloes.

Kooloo, who at times was patriotic and pensive, and mourned the evils under which his country was groaning, frequently inveighed against the statute, which thus authorized an utter stranger to interfere with domestic arrangements. He himself—quite a ladies' man—had often been annoyed thereby. He considered the kannakippers a bore.

Besides their confounded inquisitiveness, they add insult to injury, by making a point of dining out every day at

† With abhorrence and disgust the custom is alluded to by a late benevolent visitor at the island. See page 763 of the " Memoirs of the Life and Gospel Labors of the late Daniel Wheeler." A work hereafter to be more particularly alluded to.

some hut within the limits of their jurisdiction. As for the gentleman of the house, his meek endurance of these things is amazing. But " good easy man," there is nothing for him but to be as hospitable as possible.

These gentry are indefatigable. At the dead of night prowling round the houses, and in the daytime hunting amorous couples in the groves. Yet in one instance, the chase completely baffled them.

It was thus.

Several weeks previous to our arrival at the island, some one's husband and another person's wife, having taken a mutual fancy for each other, went out for a walk. The alarm was raised, and with hue and cry they were pursued; but nothing was seen of them again until the lapse of some ninety days; when we were called out from the Calabooza to behold a great mob inclosing the lovers, and escorting them for trial to the village.

Their appearance was most singular. The girdle excepted, they were quite naked; their hair was long, burned yellow at the ends, and entangled with burs; and their bodies scratched and scarred in all directions. It seems, that acting upon the " love in a cottage " principle, they had gone right into the interior; and throwing up a hut in an uninhabited valley, had lived there, until in an unlucky stroll, they were observed and captured.

They were subsequently condemned to make one hundred fathoms of Broom Road—a six months' work, if not more.

Often, when seated in a house, conversing quietly with its inmates, I have known them betray the greatest confusion at the sudden announcement of a kannakipper's being in sight. To be reported by one of these officials as a " Tootai Owree " (in general, signifying a bad person or disbeliever in Christianity), is as much dreaded as the forefinger of Titus Oates was, leveled at an alledged papist.

But the islanders take a sly revenge upon them. Upon entering a dwelling, the kannakippers oftentimes volunteer a pharisaical prayer-meeting: hence, they go in secret by the name of " Boora-Artuas," literally, " Pray-to-Gods."

CHAPTER XLVII.

EXCEPT where the employment of making "tappa" is inflicted as a punishment, the echoes of the cloth-mallet have long since died away in the listless valleys of Tahiti. Formerly, the girls spent their mornings like ladies at their tambour frames; *now*, they are lounged away in almost utter indolence. True, most of them make their own garments; but this comprises but a stitch or two; the ladies of the mission, by the by, being entitled to the credit of teaching them to sew.

The "kihee whihenee," or petticoat, is a mere breadth of white cotton, or calico; loosely enveloping the person, from the waist to the feet. Fastened simply, by a single tuck, or by twisting the upper corners together, this garment frequently becomes disordered; thus affording an opportunity of being coquettishly adjusted. Over the "kihee," they wear a sort of gown, open in front, very loose, and as negligent as you please. The ladies here, never dress for dinner.

But what shall be said of those horrid hats! Fancy a bunch of straw, plaited into the shape of a coal-scuttle, and stuck, bolt upright, on the crown; with a yard or two of red ribbon, flying about like kite-strings. Milliners of Paris, what would ye say to them! Though made by the natives, they are said to have been first contrived and recommended by the missionaries' wives; a report, which, I really trust, is nothing but scandal.

Curious to relate, these things for the head, are esteemed exceedingly becoming. The braiding of the straw is one of the few employments of the higher classes; all of which, but minister to the silliest vanity. The young girls, however, wholly eschew the hats; leaving those dowdy old souls, their mothers, to make frights of themselves.

As for the men, those who aspire to European garments, seem to have no perception of the relation subsisting between the various parts of a gentleman's costume. To the wearer of a coat, for instance, pantaloons are by no means indispensable; and, a bell-crowned hat and a girdle, are full dress. The young sailor, for whom Kooloo deserted me, presented him with a shaggy old pea-jacket; and, with this buttoned up to his chin, under a tropical sun, he promenaded the Broom Road, quite elated. Doctor Long Ghost, who saw him thus, ran away with the idea, that he was under medical treatment at the time—in the act of taking, what the quacks call, a "sweat."

A bachelor friend of Captain Bob rejoiced in the possession of a full European suit; in which he often stormed the ladies' hearts. Having a military leaning, he ornamented the coat with a great scarlet patch on the breast; and mounted it also, here and there, with several regimental buttons, slyly cut from the uniform of a parcel of drunken marines, sent ashore on a holyday from a man-of-war. But, in spite of the ornaments, the dress was not exactly the thing. From the tightness of the cloth across the shoulders, his elbows projected from his sides, like an ungainly rider's; and his ponderous legs were jammed so hard into his slim, nether garments, that the threads of every seam showed; and, at every step, you looked for a catastrophe.

In general, there seems to be no settled style of dressing among the males: they wear any thing they can get; in some cases, awkwardly modifying the fashions of their fathers, so as to accord with their own altered views of what is becoming.

But ridiculous as many of them now appear, in foreign habiliments, the Tahitians presented a far different appearance in the original national costume; which was graceful in the extreme, modest to all but the prudish, and peculiarly adapted to the climate. But the short kilts of dyed tappa, the tasseled maroes, and other articles formerly worn, are, at the present day, prohibited by law, as indecorous. For what reason necklaces and garlands of flowers, among the women, are also forbidden, I never could learn; but, it is said, that they were associated, in some way, with a forgotten heathen observance.

Many pleasant, and, seemingly, innocent sports and pastimes, are likewise interdicted. In old times, there were several athletic games practiced; such as wrestling, foot-racing, throwing the javelin, and archery. In all these they greatly excelled; and, for some, splendid festivals were instituted. Among their everyday amusements, were dancing, tossing the football, kite-flying, flute-playing, and singing traditional ballads; *now*, all punishable offenses; though most of them have been so long in disuse that they are nearly forgotten.

In the same way, the " Opio," or festive harvest-home of the bread-fruit, has been suppressed; though, as described to me, by Captain Bob, it seemed wholly free from any immoral tendency. Against tattooing, of any kind, there is a severe law.

That this abolition of their national amusements and customs, was not willingly acquiesced in, is shown in the frequent violation of many of the statutes inhibiting them; and, especially, in the frequency with which their " hevars," or dances, are practiced in secret.

Doubtless, in thus denationalizing the Tahitians, as it were, the missionaries were prompted by a sincere desire for good; but the effect has been lamentable. Supplied with no amusements, in place of those forbidden, the Tahitians, who require more recreation than other people, have sunk into a listlessness, or indulge in sensualites, a hundred times more pernicious, than all the games ever celebrated in the Temple of Tanee.

CHAPTER XLVIII.

TAHITI AS IT IS.

As in the last few chapters, several matters connected with the general condition of the natives have been incidentally touched upon, it may be well not to leave so important a subject in a state calculated to convey erroneous impressions. Let us bestow upon it, therefore, something more than a mere cursory glance.

But in the first place, let it be distinctly understood, that in all I have to say upon this subject, both here and elsewhere, I mean no harm to the missionaries nor their cause; I merely desire to set forth things as they actually exist.

Of the results which have flowed from the intercourse of foreigners with the Polynesians, including the attempts to civilize and christianize them by the missionaries, Tahiti, on many accounts, is obviously the fairest practical example. Indeed, it may now be asserted, that the experiment of christianizing the Tahitians, and improving their social condition by the introduction of foreign customs, has been fully tried. The present generation have grown up under the auspices of their religious instructors. And although it may be urged, that the labors of the latter have at times been more or less obstructed by unprincipled foreigners, still, this in no wise renders Tahiti any the less a fair illustration; for, with obstacles like these, the missionaries in Polynesia must always, and everywhere struggle.

Nearly sixty years have elapsed since the Tahitian mission was started; and during this period, it has received the unceasing prayers and contributions of its friends abroad. Nor has any enterprise of the kind called forth more devotion on the part of those directly employed in it.

It matters not, that the earlier laborers in the work, although strictly conscientious, were, as a class, ignorant, and, in many cases, deplorably bigoted: such traits have, in some degree, characterized the pioneers of all faiths. And although in zeal and disinterestedness, the missionaries now on the island are, perhaps, inferior to their predecessors, they have, nevertheless, in their own way at least, labored hard to make a Christian people of their charge.

Let us now glance at the most obvious changes wrought in their condition.

The entire system of idolatry has been done away; together with several barbarous practices engrafted thereon.

But this result is not so much to be ascribed to the missionaries, as to the civilizing effects of a long and constant intercourse with whites of all nations; to whom, for many years, Tahiti has been one of the principal places of resort in the South Seas. At the Sandwich Islands, the potent institution of the Taboo, together with the entire paganism of the land, was utterly abolished by a voluntary act of the natives, some time previous to the arrival of the first missionaries among them.

The next most striking change in the Tahitians is this. From the permanent residence among them of influential and respectable foreigners, as well as from the frequent visits of ships-of-war, recognizing the nationality of the island, its inhabitants are no longer deemed fit subjects for the atrocities practiced upon mere savages; and hence, secure from retaliation, vessels of all kinds now enter their harbors with perfect safety.

But let us consider what results are directly ascribable to the missionaries alone.

In all cases, they have striven hard to mitigate the evils resulting from the commerce with the whites in general. Such attempts, however, have been rather injudicious, and often ineffectual: in truth, a barrier almost insurmountable is presented in the dispositions of the people themselves. Still, in this respect, the morality of the islanders is, upon the whole, improved by the presence of the missionaries.

But the greatest achievement of the latter, and one which in itself is most hopeful and gratifying is, that they have translated the entire Bible into the language of the island; and I have myself known several who were able to read it with facility. They have also established churches, and schools for both children and adults; the latter, I regret to say, are now much neglected; which must be ascribed, in a great measure, to the disorders growing out of the proceedings of the French.

It were unnecessary here, to enter diffusely into matters connected with the internal government of the Tahitian churches and schools. Nor, upon this head, is my information copious enough to warrant me in presenting details. But we do not need them. We are merely considering general *results*, as made apparent in the moral and religious condition of the island at large.

Upon a subject like this, however, it would be altogether too assuming for a single individual to decide; and so, in place of my own random observations, which may be found elsewhere, I will here present those of several known authors, made under various circumstances, at different periods, and down to a comparative late date. A few very brief extracts will enable the reader to mark for himself what progressive improvement, if any, has taken place.

Nor must it be overlooked, that of these authorities, the two first in order are largely quoted by the Right Reverend M. Russell, in a work composed for the express purpose of imparting information on the subject of Christian missions in Polynesia. And he frankly acknowledges, moreover, that they are such as " can not fail to have great weight with the public." *

After alluding to the manifold evils entailed upon the natives by foreigners, and their singularly inert condition; and after somewhat too severely denouncing the undeniable errors of the mission, Kotzebue, the Russian navigator, says, "A religion like this, which forbids every innocent pleasure, and cramps or annihilates every mental power, is a libel on the divine founder of Christianity. It is true, that the religion of the missionaries has, with a great deal of evil, effected some good. It has restrained the vices of theft and incontinence; but it has given birth to ignorance, hypocrisy, and a hatred of all other modes of faith, which was once foreign to the open and benevolent character of the Tahitian."†

Captain Beechey says, that while at Tahiti, he saw scenes " which must have convinced the greatest skeptic of the thor-

---

* Polynesia: or an Historical Account of the Principal Islands of the South Sea: By the Right Rev. M. Russell, LL.D. (Harpers' Family Library Edition), p. 96.

† A New Voyage round the World in the years 1823-24-25-26: By Otto Von Kotzebue, Post Captain in the Russian Imperial Service (London, 1830; 2 vols. 8vo.), vol. i., p. 168.

oughly immoral condition of the people, and which would force him to conclude, as Turnbull ‡ did, many years previous, that their intercourse with the Europeans had tended to debase, rather than exalt their condition."§

About the year 1834, Daniel Wheeler, an honest-hearted Quaker, prompted by motives of the purest philanthropy, visited, in a vessel of his own, most of the missionary settlements in the South Seas. He remained some time at Tahiti; receiving the hospitalities of the missionaries there, and, from time to time, exhorting the natives.

After bewailing their social condition, he frankly says of their religious state, " Certainly, appearances are unpromising; and however unwilling to adopt such a conclusion, there is reason to apprehend, that Christian principle is a great rarity." *

Such, then, is the testimony of good and unbiased men, who have been upon the spot; but, how comes it to differ so widely from impressions of others at home? Simply thus: instead of estimating the result of missionary labors by the number of heathens who have actually been made to understand and practice (in some measure, at least) the precepts of Christianity, this result has been unwarrantably inferred from the number of those, who, without any understanding of these things, have in any way been induced to abandon idolatry and conform to certain outward observances.

By authority of some kind or other, exerted upon the natives through their chiefs, and prompted by the hope of some worldly benefit to the latter, and not by appeals to the reason, have conversions in Polynesia been in most cases brought about.

---

‡ The author of a Voyage round the World, in the years 1800-1804 (3 vols. 8vo., London, 1805).

§ Narrative of a Voyage to the Pacific and Bherring's Straits, under the command of Captain F. W. Beechey, R.N. (London, 1831), vol. i., p. 287.

* Memoirs of the Life and Gospel Labors of the late Daniel Wheeler, a minister of the Society of Friends (London, 1842, 8vo.), p. 757.

Even in one or two instances—so often held up as wonderful examples of divine power—where the natives have impulsively burned their idols, and rushed to the waters of baptism, the very suddenness of the change has but indicated its unsoundness. Williams, the martyr of Erromanga, relates an instance where the inhabitants of an island professing Christianity, voluntarily assembled, and solemnly revived all their heathen customs.

All the world over, facts are more eloquent than words; and the following will show in what estimation the missionaries themselves hold the present state of Christianity and morals among the converted Polynesians.

On the island of Imeeo (attached to the Tahitian mission), is a seminary under the charge of the Rev. Mr. Simpson and wife, for the education of the children of the missionaries, exclusively. Sent home—in many cases, at a very early age—to finish their education, the pupils here are taught nothing but the rudiments of knowledge; nothing more than may be learned in the native schools. Notwithstanding this, the two races are kept as far as possible from associating; the avowed reason being, to preserve the young whites from moral contamination. The better to insure this end, every effort is made to prevent them from acquiring the native language.

They went even further at the Sandwich Islands; where, a few years ago, a play-ground for the children of the missionaries was inclosed with a fence many feet high, the more effectually to exclude the wicked little Hawaiians.

And yet, strange as it may seem, the depravity among the Polynesians, which renders precautions like these necessary, was in a measure unknown before their intercourse with the whites. The excellent Captain Wilson, who took the first missionaries out to Tahiti, affirms, that the people of that island had, in many things, "more refined ideas of decency than ourselves." * Vancouver, also, has some

---

* A Missionary Voyage to the South Pacific Ocean, Appendix, pp. 336, 342.

noteworthy ideas on this subject, respecting the Sandwich Islanders.†

That the immorality alluded to is continually increasing, is plainly shown in the numerous, severe, and perpetually violated laws against licentiousness of all kinds, in both groups of islands.

It is hardly to be expected, that the missionaries would send home accounts of this state of things. Hence, Captain Beechey, in alluding to the "Polynesian Researches" of Ellis, says, that the author has impressed his readers with a a far more elevated idea of the moral condition of the Tahitians, and the degree of civilization to which they have attained, than they deserve; or, at least, than the facts which came under his observation, authorized. He then goes on to say, that in his intercourse with the islanders, "they had no fear of him, and consequently acted from the impulse of their natural feelings; so that he was the better enabled to obtain a correct knowledge of their real disposition and habits." *

From my own familiar intercourse with the natives, this last reflection still more forcibly applies to myself.

CHAPTER XLIX.

SAME SUBJECT CONTINUED.

WE have glanced at their moral and religious condition; let us see how it is with them socially, and in other respects.

It has been said, that the only way to civilize a people, is to form in them habits of industry. Judged by this principle, the Tahitians are less civilized now than formerly. True, their constitutional indolence is excessive; but surely, if the spirit of Christianity is among them, so unchristian

---

† See Vancouver's Voyages, 4to. edition, vol. i., p. 172.
* Beechey's Narrative, p. 269.

a vice ought to be, at least, partially remedied. But the reverse is the fact. Instead of acquiring new occupations, old ones have been discontinued.

As previously remarked, the manufacture of tappa is nearly obsolete in many parts of the island. So, too, with that of the native tools and domestic utensils; very few of which are now fabricated, since the superiority of European wares has been made so evident.

This, however, would be all very well, were the natives to apply themselves to such occupations as would enable them to supply the few articles they need. But they are far from doing so; and the majority being unable to obtain European substitutes, for many things before made by themselves, the inevitable consequence is seen in the present wretched and destitute mode of life among the common people. To me, so recently from a primitive valley of the Marquesas, the aspect of most of the dwellings of the poorer Tahitians, and their general habits, seemed any thing but tidy; nor could I avoid a comparison, immeasurably to the disadvantage of these partially civilized islanders.

In Tahiti, the people have nothing to do; and idleness, everywhere, is the parent of vice. " There is scarcely any thing," says the good old Quaker Wheeler, "so striking, or pitiable, as their aimless, nerveless mode of spending life."

Attempts have repeatedly been made, to rouse them from their sluggishness; but in vain. Several years ago, the cultivation of cotton was introduced; and, with their usual love of novelty, they went to work with great alacrity; but the interest excited quickly subsided, and now, not a pound of the article is raised.

About the same time, machinery for weaving was sent out from London; and a factory was started at Afrehitoo, in Imeeo. The whiz of the wheels and spindles brought in volunteers from all quarters, who deemed it a privilege to be admitted to work: yet, in six months, not a boy could be hired; and the machinery was knocked down, and packed off to Sydney.

It was the same way with the cultivation of the sugar-cane, a plant indigenous to the island; peculiarly fitted to the soil and climate, and of so excellent a quality, that Bligh took slips of it to the West Indies. All the plantations went on famously, for a while; the natives swarming in the fields, like ants, and making a prodigious stir. What few plantations now remain, are owned and worked by whites; who would rather pay a drunken sailor eighteen or twenty Spanish dollars a month, than hire a sober native for his " fish and taro."

It is well worthy remark here, that every evidence of civilization among the South Sea Islands, directly pertains to foreigners; though the fact of such evidence existing at all, is usually urged as a proof of the elevated condition of the natives. Thus, at Honolulu, the capital of the Sandwich Islands, there are fine dwelling-houses, several hotels, and barber-shops, ay, even billiard-rooms; but all these are owned and used, be it observed, by whites. There are tailors and blacksmiths, and carpenters also; but not one of them is a native.

The fact is, that the mechanical and agricultural employments of civilized life, require a kind of exertion altogether too steady and sustained, to agree with an indolent people like the Polynesians. Calculated for a state of nature, in a climate providentially adapted to it, they are unfit for any other. Nay, as a race, they can not otherwise long exist.

The following statement speaks for itself.

About the year 1777, Captain Cook estimated the population of Tahiti at about two hundred thousand.* By a regular census, taken some four or five years ago, it was found to be only nine thousand.† This amazing decrease, not only shows the malignancy of the evils necessary to

---

* " I was convinced," he adds, " that from the vast swarms that everywhere appeared, this estimate was not at all too great."

† For an allusion to this census, see one of the chapters on Tahiti, in the volumes of the U. S. Exploring Expedition. And, for the almost incredible depopulation of the Sandwich Islands, in recent years, see the same work. The progressive decrease, in certain districts, for a considerable period, is there marked.

Ruschenberger, an intelligent surgeon in the United States Navy, takes the following instance from the records kept on the islands. The district of Rohalo, in Hawaii, at one time numbered 8679 souls: four produce it; but, from the fact, the inference unavoidably follows, that all the wars, child murders, and other depopulating causes, alledged to have existed in former times, were nothing in comparison to them.

These evils, of course, are solely of foreign origin. To say nothing of the effects of drunkenness, the occasional inroads of the small-pox, and other things, which might be mentioned, it is sufficient to allude to a virulent disease, which now taints the blood of at least two thirds of the common people of the island; and, in some form or other, is transmitted from father to son.

Their first horror and consternation at the earlier ravages of this scourge, were pitiable in the extreme. The very name bestowed upon it, is a combination of all that is horrid and unmentionable to a civilized being.

Distracted with their sufferings, they brought forth their sick before the missionaries, when they were preaching, and cried out, " Lies, lies! you tell us of salvation; and, behold, we are dying. We want no other salvation, than to live in this world. Where are there any saved through your speech? Pomaree is dead; and we are all dying with your cursed diseases. When will you give over? "

At present, the virulence of the disorder, in individual cases, has somewhat abated; but the poison is only the more widely diffused.

" How dreadful and appalling," breaks forth old Wheeler, " the consideration, that the intercourse of distant nations should have entailed upon these poor, untutored islanders, a curse unprecedented, and unheard of, in the annals of history."

In view of these things, who can remain blind to the fact, that, so far as mere temporal felicity is concerned, the Tahitians are far worse off now, than formerly; and although their circumstances, upon the whole, are bettered

---

years after, the population was 6175: decrease, in that time, 2504. No extraordinary cause is assigned for this depopulation. Vide A Voyage round the World, in the years 1835-36-37. By W. S. Ruschenberger, M.D. (Philadelphia, 1838, 8vo.) The chapter on the Sandwich Islands.

by the presence of the missionaries, the benefits conferred by the latter become utterly insignificant, when confronted with the vast preponderance of evil brought about by other means.

Their prospects are hopeless. Nor can the most devoted efforts, now exempt them from furnishing a marked illustration of a principle, which history has always exemplified. Years ago brought to a stand, where all that is corrupt in barbarism and civilization unite, to the exclusion of the virtues of either state; like other uncivilized beings, brought into contact with Europeans, they must here remain stationary until utterly extinct.

The islanders themselves, are mournfully watching their doom. Several years since, Pomaree II. said to Tyerman and Bennet, the deputies of the London Missionary Society, "You have come to see me at a very bad time. Your ancestors came in the time of men, when Tahiti was inhabited: you are come to behold just the remnant of my people."

Of like import, was the prediction of Teearmoar, the high-priest of Paree; who lived over a hundred years ago. I have frequently heard it chanted, in a low, sad tone, by aged Tahitians: —

> "A harree ta fow,
> A toro ta farraro,
> A now ta tararta."

> The palm-tree shall grow,
> The coral shall spread,
> But man shall cease.

CHAPTER L.

SOMETHING HAPPENS TO LONG GHOST.

WE will now return to the narrative.

The day before the Julia sailed, Dr. Johnson paid his last call. He was not quite so bland as usual. All he wanted was the men's names to a paper, certifying to their having received from him sundry medicaments, therein mentioned. This voucher, endorsed by Captain Guy, secured his pay. But he would not have obtained for it the sailors' signs manual, had either the doctor or myself been present at the time.

Now, my long friend wasted no love upon Johnson; but for reasons of his own, hated him heartily: all the same thing in one sense; for either passion argues an object deserving thereof. And so, to be hated cordially, is only a left-handed compliment; which shows how foolish it is to be bitter against any one.

For my own part, I merely felt a cool, purely incidental, and passive contempt for Johnson, as a selfish, mercenary apothecary; and hence, I often remonstrated with Long Ghost, when he flew out against him, and heaped upon him all manner of scurrilous epithets. In his professional brother's presence, however, he never acted thus; maintaining an amiable exterior, to help along the jokes which were played.

I am now going to tell another story, in which my long friend figures with the physician: I do not wish to bring one or the other of them too often upon the stage; but as the thing actually happened, I must relate it.

A few days after Johnson *presented his bill*, as above mentioned, the doctor expressed to me his regret, that although he (Johnson) had apparently been played off for our entertainment, yet, nevertheless, he had made money out of the transaction. And I wonder, added the doctor, if that now, he can not expect to receive any further pay, he could be induced to call again.

By a curious coincidence, not five minutes after making this observation, Doctor Long Ghost himself fell down in an unaccountable fit; and without asking any body's leave, Captain Bob, who was by, at once dispatched a boy, hot foot, for Johnson.

Meanwhile, we carried him into the Calabooza; and the natives, who assembled in numbers, suggested various modes of treatment. One rather energetic practitioner was for holding the patient by the shoulders, while somebody tugged

at his feet. This resuscitatory operation was called the
"Potata;" but thinking our long comrade sufficiently
lengthy without additional stretching, we declined *potataing*
him.

Presently the physician was spied coming along the
Broom Road at a great rate, and so absorbed in the business
of locomotion, that he heeded not the imprudence of being
in a hurry in a tropical climate. He was in a profuse perspiration; which must have been owing to the warmth of
his feelings, notwithstanding we had supposed him a man
of no heart. But his benevolent haste upon this occasion
was subsequently accounted for: it merely arose from professional curiosity, to behold a case most unusual in his
Polynesian practice. Now, under certain circumstances,
sailors, generally so frolicsome, are exceedingly particular
in having every thing conducted with the strictest propriety.
Accordingly, they deputed me, as his intimate friend, to
sit at Long Ghost's head, so as to be ready to officiate as
"spokesman;" and answer all questions propounded; the
rest to keep silent.

"What's the matter?" exclaimed Johnson, out of breath,
and bursting into the Calabooza: "how did it happen?—
speak quick!" and he looked at Long Ghost.

I told him how the fit came on.

"Singular"—he observed—"very: good enough pulse;"
and he let go of it, and placed his hand upon the heart.

"But what's all that frothing at the mouth?" he continued; "and bless me! look at the abdomen!"

The region thus denominated, exhibited the most
unaccountable symptoms. A low, rumbling sound was
heard; and a sort of undulation was discernible beneath the
thin cotton frock.

"Colic, sir?" suggested a by-stander.

"Colic be hanged!" shouted the physician; "who ever
heard of any body in a trance of the colic?"

During this, the patient lay upon his back, stark and
straight, giving no signs of life except those above mentioned.

"I'll bleed him!" cried Johnson at last—"run for a
calabash, one of you!"

" Life ho! " here sung out Navy Bob, as if he had just spied a sail.

" What under the sun's the matter with him! " cried the physician, starting at the appearance of the mouth, which had jerked to one side, and there remained fixed.

" Pr'aps it's St. Witus's hornpipe," suggested Bob.

" Hold the calabash! "—and the lancet was out in a moment.

But before the deed could be done, the face became natural;—a sigh was heaved;—the eyelids quivered, opened, closed; and Long Ghost, twitching all over, rolled on his side, and breathed audibly. By degrees, he became sufficiently recovered to speak.

After trying to get something coherent out of him, Johnson withdrew; evidently disappointed in the scientific interest of the case. Soon after his departure, the doctor sat up; and upon being asked what upon earth ailed him, shook his head mysteriously. He then deplored the hardship of being an invalid in such a place, where there was not the slightest provision for his comfort. This awakened the compassion of our good old keeper, who offered to send him to a place where he would be better cared for. Long Ghost acquiesced; and being at once mounted upon the shoulders of four of Captain Bob's men, was marched off in state, like the Grand Lama of Thibet.

Now, I do not pretend to account for his remarkable swoon; but his reason for suffering himself to be thus removed from the Calabooza, was strongly suspected to be nothing more than a desire to insure more regularity in his dinner-hour; hoping that the benevolent native to whom he was going, would set a good table.

The next morning, we were all envying his fortune; when of a sudden, he bolted in upon us, looking decidedly out of humor.

" Hang it! " he cried, " I'm worse off than ever; let me have some breakfast! " We lowered our slender bag of ship-stores from a rafter, and handed him a biscuit. While this was being munched, he went on and told us his story.

"After leaving here, they trotted me back into a valley, and left me in a hut, where an old woman lived by herself. This must be the nurse, thought I; and so I asked her to kill a pig, and bake it; for I felt my appetite returning. '*Ita! ita!—oee mattee—mattee nuee*'—(no, no; you too sick.) 'The devil *mattee* ye,' said I — 'give me something to eat!' But nothing could be had. Night coming on, I had to stay. Creeping into a corner, I tried to sleep; but it was to no purpose;—the old crone must have had the quinsy, or something else; and she kept up such a wheezing and choking, that at last I sprang up, and groped after her; but she hobbled away like a goblin; and that was the last of her. As soon as the sun rose, I made the best of my way back; and here I am."

He never left us more, nor ever had a second fit.

CHAPTER LI.

WILSON GIVES US THE CUT.—DEPARTURE FOR IMEEO.

ABOUT three weeks after the Julia's sailing, our condition began to be a little precarious. We were without any regular supply of food; the arrival of ships was growing less frequent; and, what was worse yet, all the natives but good old Captain Bob, began to tire of us. Nor was this to be wondered at; we were obliged to live upon their benevolence, when they had little enough for themselves. Beside, we were sometimes driven to acts of marauding: such as kidnapping pigs, and cooking them in the groves; at which their proprietors were by no means pleased.

In this state of affairs, we determined to march off to the consul in a body; and, as he had brought us to these straits, demand an adequate maintenance.

On the point of starting, Captain Bob's men raised the most outrageous cries, and tried to prevent us. Though

13

hitherto we had strolled about wherever we pleased, this grand conjunction of our whole force upon one particular expedition, seemed to alarm them. But we assured them, that we were not going to assault the village; and so, after a good deal of gibberish, they permitted us to leave.

We went straight to the Pritchard residence, where the consul dwelt. This house—to which I have before referred —is quite commodious. It has a wide verandah, glazed windows, and other appurtenances of a civilized mansion. Upon the lawn in front are palm-trees standing erect here and there, like sentinels. The Consular Office, a small building by itself, is inclosed by the same picket which fences in the lawn.

We found the office closed; but, in the verandah of the dwelling-house, was a lady performing a tonsorial operation on the head of a prim-looking, elderly European, in a low, white cravat;—the most domestic little scene I had witnessed since leaving home. Bent upon an interview with Wilson, the sailors now deputed the doctor to step forward as a polite inquirer after his health.

The pair stared very hard as he advanced; but no ways disconcerted, he saluted them gravely, and inquired for the consul.

Upon being informed that he had gone down to the beach, we proceeded in that direction; and soon met a native, who told us, that apprised of our vicinity, Wilson was keeping out of the way. We resolved to meet him; and passing through the village, he suddenly came walking toward us; having apparently made up his mind that any attempt to elude us would be useless.

" What do you want of me, you rascals? " he cried—a greeting which provoked a retort in no measured terms. At this juncture, the natives began to crowd round, and several foreigners strolled along. Caught in the very act of speaking to such disreputable acquaintances, Wilson now fidgeted, and moved rapidly toward his office; the men following. Turning upon them incensed, he bade them be off—he would have nothing more to say to us; and then, hurriedly addressing Captain Bob in Tahitian, he hastened on, and never stopped till the postern of Pritchard's wicket was closed behind him.

Our good old keeper was now highly excited, bustling about in his huge petticoats, and conjuring us to return to the Calabooza. After a little debate, we acquiesced.

This interview was decisive. Sensible that none of the charges brought against us would stand, yet unwilling formally to withdraw them, the consul now wished to get rid of us altogether; but without being suspected of encouraging our escape. Thus only could we account for his conduct.

Some of the party, however, with a devotion to principle truly heroic, swore they would never leave him, happen what might. For my own part, I began to long for a change; and as there seemed to be no getting away in a ship, I resolved to hit upon some other expedient. But first, I cast about for a comrade; and of course the long doctor was chosen. We at once laid our heads together; and for the present, resolved to disclose nothing to the rest.

A few days previous, I had fallen in with a couple of Yankee lads, twins, who, originally deserting their ship at Fanning's Island (an uninhabited spot, but exceedingly prolific in fruit of all kinds), had, after a long residence there, roved about among the Society group. They were last from Imeeo—the island immediately adjoining—where they had been in the employ of two foreigners, who had recently started a plantation there. These persons, they said, had charged them to send over from Papeetee, if they could, two white men for field-laborers.

Now, all but the prospect of digging and delving, suited us exactly; but the opportunity for leaving the island was not to be slighted; and so we held ourselves in readiness to return with the planters; who, in a day or two, were expected to visit Papeetee in their boat.

At the interview which ensued, we were introduced to them as Peter and Paul; and they agreed to give Peter and Paul fifteen silver dollars a month, promising something more, should we remain with them permanently. What they wanted, was men who would stay. To elude the natives

—many of whom not exactly understanding our relations with the consul, might arrest us, were they to see us departing—the coming midnight was appointed for that purpose.

When the hour drew nigh, we disclosed our intention to the rest. Some upbraided us for deserting them; others applauded, and said, that on the first opportunity they would follow our example. At last, we bade them farewell. And there would now be a serene sadness in thinking over the scene—since we never saw them again—had not all been dashed by M'Gee's picking the doctor's pocket of a jackknife, in the very act of embracing him.

We stole down to the beach, where, under the shadow of a grove, the boat was waiting. After some delay, we shipped the oars, and pulling outside of the reef, set the sail; and with a fair wind, glided away for Imeeo.

It was a pleasant trip. The moon was up—the air, warm —the waves, musical—and all above was the tropical night, one purple vault hung round with soft, trembling stars.

The channel is some five leagues wide. On one hand, you have the three great peaks of Tahiti lording it over ranges of mountains and valleys; and on the other, the equally romantic elevations of Imeeo, high above which a lone peak, called by our companions, "the Marling-spike," shot up its verdant spire.

The planters were quite sociable. They had been seafaring men, and this, of course, was a bond between us. To strengthen it, a flask of wine was produced, one of several which had been procured in person from the French admiral's steward; for whom the planters, when on a former visit to Papeetee, had done a good turn, by introducing the amorous Frenchman to the ladies ashore. Besides this, they had a calabash filled with wild boar's meat, baked yams, bread-fruit, and Tombez potatoes. Pipes and tobacco also were produced; and while regaling ourselves, plenty of stories were told about the neighboring islands.

At last we heard the roar of the Imeeo reef; and gliding through a break, floated over the expanse within, which was smooth as a young girl's brow, and beached the boat.

CHAPTER LII.

THE VALLEY OF MARTAIR.

WE went up through groves to an open space, where we heard voices, and a light was seen glimmering from out a bamboo dwelling. It was the planters' retreat; and in their absence, several girls were keeping house, assisted by an old native, who, wrapped up in tappa, lay in the corner, smoking.

A hasty meal was prepared, and after it we essayed a nap; but, alas! a plague, little anticipated, prevented. Unknown in Tahiti, the musquitoes here fairly eddied round us. But more of them anon.

We were up betimes, and strolled out to view the country. We were in the valley of Martair; shut in, on both sides, by lofty hills. Here and there, were steep cliffs, gay with flowering shrubs, or hung with pendulous vines, swinging blossoms in the air. Of considerable width at the sea, the vale contracts as it runs inland; terminating, at the distance of several miles, in a range of the most grotesque elevations, which seem embattled with turrets and towers, grown over with verdure, and waving with trees. The valley itself, is a wilderness of woodland; with links of streams flashing through, and narrow pathways, fairly tunneled through masses of foliage.

All alone, in this wild place, was the abode of the planters; the only one back from the beach—their sole neighbors, the few fishermen and their families, dwelling in a small grove of cocoa-nut trees, whose roots were washed by the sea.

The cleared tract which they occupied, comprised some thirty acres, level as a prairie, part of which was under cultivation; the whole being fenced in, by a stout palisade of trunks and boughs of trees, staked firmly in the ground. This was necessary, as a defense against the wild cattle and hogs over-running the island.

Thus far, Tombez potatoes * were the principal crop raised; a ready sale for them being obtained among the shipping touching at Papeetee. There was a small patch of the *taro*, or Indian turnip, also; another of yams; and, in one corner, a thrifty growth of the sugar-cane, just ripening.

On the side of the inclosure, next the sea, was the house; newly built of bamboos, in the native style. The furniture consisted of a couple of sea-chests, an old box, a few cooking utensils, and agricultural tools; together with three fowling-pieces, hanging from a rafter; and two enormous hammocks swinging in opposite corners, and composed of dried bullocks' hides, stretched out with poles.

The whole plantation was shut in by a dense forest; and, close by the house, a dwarfed " Aoa," or species of banian-tree, had purposely been left twisting over the palisade, in the most grotesque manner, and thus made a pleasant shade. The branches of this curious tree afforded low perches, upon which the natives frequently squatted, after the fashion of their race, and smoked and gossiped by the hour.

We had a good breakfast of fish—speared by the natives, before sunrise, on the reef—pudding of Indian turnip, fried bananas, and roasted bread-fruit.

During the repast, our new friends were quite sociable and communicative. It seems that, like nearly all uneducated foreigners, residing in Polynesia, they had, some time previous, deserted from a ship; and, having heard a good deal about the money to be made by raising supplies for whaling-vessels, they determined upon embarking in the business. Strolling about, with this intention, they, at last, came to Martair; and, thinking the soil would suit, set themselves to work. They began, by finding out the owner of the particular spot coveted, and then making a " tayo " of him.

---

* Perhaps the finest sweet potato in the world. It derives its name from a district of Peru, near Cape Blanco, very favorable to its growth; where, also, it is extensively cultivated: the root is very large; sometimes as big as a good-sized melon.

He turned out to be Tonoi, the chief of the fishermen; who, one day, when exhilarated with brandy, tore his meager tappa from his loins, and gave me to know, that he was allied by blood with Pomaree herself; and that his mother came from the illustrious race of pontiffs, who, in old times, swayed their bamboo crosier over all the pagans of Imeeo. A regal, and right reverend lineage! But, at the time I speak of, the dusky noble was in decayed circumstances, and therefore, by no means unwilling to alienate a few useless acres. As an equivalent, he received from the strangers two or three rheumatic old muskets, several red woolen shirts, and a promise to be provided for in his old age: he was always to find a home with the planters.

Desirous of living on the cozy footing of a father-in-law, he frankly offered his two daughters for wives; but as such, they were politely declined; the adventurers, though not averse to courting, being unwilling to entangle themselves in a matrimonial alliance, however splendid in point of family.

Tonoi's men, the fishermen of the grove, were a sad set. Secluded, in a great measure, from the ministrations of the missionaries, they gave themselves up to all manner of lazy wickedness. Strolling among the trees of a morning, you came upon them napping on the shady side of a canoe hauled up among the bushes; lying under a tree smoking; or, more frequently still, gambling with pebbles; though, a little tobacco excepted, what they gambled for at their outlandish games, it would be hard to tell. Other idle diversions they had also, in which they seemed to take great delight. As for fishing, it employed but a small part of their time. Upon the whole, they were a merry, indigent, godless race.

Tonoi, the old sinner, leaning against the fallen trunk of a cocoa-nut tree, invariably squandered his mornings at pebbles; a gray-headed rook of a native regularly plucking him of every other stick of tobacco obtained from his friends, the planters. Toward afternoon, he strolled back to their abode; where he tarried till the next morning, smoking and snoozing, and, at times, prating about the hapless fortunes of the House of Tonoi. But like any other easy-going old dotard, he seemed for the most part perfectly content with cheerful board and lodging.

On the whole, the valley of Martair was the quietest place imaginable. Could the musquitoes be induced to emigrate, one might spend the month of August there quite pleasantly. But this was not the case with the luckless Long Ghost and myself; as will presently be seen.

CHAPTER LIII.

FARMING IN POLYNESIA.

THE planters were both whole-souled fellows; but in other respects, as unlike as possible.

One was a tall, robust Yankee, born in the backwoods of Maine, sallow, and with a long face;—the other was a short little Cockney, who had first clapped his eyes on the Monument.

The voice of Zeke, the Yankee, had a twang like a cracked viol; and Shorty (as his comrade called him), clipped the aspirate from every word beginning with one. The latter, though not the tallest man in the world, was a good-looking young fellow, of twenty-five. His cheeks were dyed with the fine Saxon red, burned deeper from his roving life; his blue eye opened well, and a profusion of fair hair curled over a well shaped head.

But Zeke was no beauty. A strong, ugly man, he was well adapted for manual labor; and that was all. His eyes were made to see with, and not for ogling. Compared with the Cockney, he was grave, and rather taciturn; but there was a deal of good old humor bottled up in him, after all. For the rest, he was frank, good-hearted, shrewd, and resolute; and like Shorty, quite illiterate.

Though a curious conjunction, the pair got along together famously. But, as no two men were ever united in any enterprise, without one getting the upper hand of the other; so, in most matters, Zeke had his own way. Shorty, too, had imbibed from him a spirit of invincible industry; and Heaven only knows what ideas of making a fortune on their plantation.

We were much concerned at this; for the prospect of their setting us in their own persons an example of downright hard labor, was any thing but agreeable. But it was now too late to repent what we had done.

The first day—thank fortune—we did nothing. Having treated us as guests thus far, they no doubt thought it would be wanting in delicacy, to set us to work before the compliments of the occasion were well over. The next morning, however, they both looked business-like, and we were put to.

" Wall, b'ys " (boys), said Zeke, knocking the ashes out of his pipe, after breakfast—" we must get at it. Shorty, give Peter there (the doctor), the big hoe, and Paul the other, and let's be off." Going to a corner, Shorty brought forth three of the implements; and distributing them impartially, trudged on after his partner, who took the lead with something in the shape of an axe.

For a moment left alone in the house, we looked at each other, quaking. We were each equipped with a great, clumsy piece of a tree, armed at one end with a heavy, flat mass of iron.

The cutlery part—especially adapted to a primitive soil—was an importation from Sydney; the handles must have been of domestic manufacture. " Hoes "—so called —we had heard of, and seen; but they were harmless, in comparison with the tools in our hands.

" What's to be done with them? " inquired I of Peter.

" Lift them up and down," he replied; " or put them in motion, some way or other. Paul, we are in a scrape— but hark! they are calling; " and shouldering the hoes, off we marched.

Our destination was the farther side of the plantation, where the ground, cleared in part, had not yet been broken up; but they were now setting about it. Upon halting, I

asked why a plough was not used: some of the young wild
steers might be caught, and trained for draught.

Zeke replied, that, for such a purpose, no cattle, to his
knowledge, had ever been used in any part of Polynesia.
As for the soil of Martair, so obstructed was it with roots,
crossing and recrossing each other at all points, that no
kind of a plough could be used to advantage. The heavy
Sydney hoes were the only thing for such land.

Our work was now before us; but, previous to commencing operations, I endeavored to engage the Yankee in a
little further friendly chat, concerning the nature of virgin
soils in general, and that of the valley of Martair in particular. So masterly a stratagem made Long Ghost brighten
up; and he stood by ready to join in. But what our friend
had to say about agriculture, all referred to the particular
part of his plantation upon which we stood; and having
communicated enough on this head, to enable us to set to
work to the best advantage, he fell to, himself; and Shorty,
who had been looking on, followed suit.

The surface, here and there, presented closely ampu-
tated branches of what had once been a dense thicket. They
seemed purposely left projecting, as if to furnish a handle,
whereby to drag out the roots beneath. After loosening the
hard soil, by dint of much thumping and pounding, the
Yankee jerked one of the roots, this way and that, twisting
it round and round, and then tugging at it horizontally.

" Come! lend us a hand! " he cried, at last; and, running
up, we all four strained away in concert. The tough obsta-
cle convulsed the surface with throes and spasms; but stuck
fast, notwithstanding.

" Dumn it! " cried Zeke, " we'll have to get a rope; run
to the house, Shorty, and fetch one."

The end of this being attached, we took plenty of room,
and strained away once more.

" Give us a song, Shorty," said the doctor; who was
rather sociable, on a short acquaintance. Where the work
to be accomplished is any way difficult, this mode of
enlivening toil is quite efficacious among sailors. So, willing

to make every thing as cheerful as possible, Shorty struck up, " Were you ever in Dumbarton? " a marvelously inspiring, but somewhat indecorous windlass chorus.

At last, the Yankee cast a damper on his enthusiasm, by exclaiming, in a pet, " Oh! dumn your singing! keep quiet, and pull away! " This we now did, in the most uninteresting silence; until, with a jerk, that made every elbow hum, the root dragged out; and, most inelegantly, we all landed upon the ground. The doctor, quite exhausted, stayed there; and, deluded into believing, that, after so doughty a performance, we would be allowed a cessation of toil, took off his hat, and fanned himself.

" Rayther a hard customer, that, Peter," observed the Yankee, going up to him: " but it's no use for any on 'em to hang back; for, I'm dumned if they haint got to come out, whether or no. Hurrah! let's get at it agin! "

" Mercy! " ejaculated the doctor, rising slowly, and turning round. " He'll be the death of us! "

Falling to with our hoes again, we worked singly, or together, as occasion required, until " Nooning Time " came.

The period, so called by the planters, embraced about three hours in the middle of the day; during which it was so excessively hot, in this still, brooding valley, shut out from the Trades, and only open toward the leeward side of the island, that labor in the sun was out of the question. To use a hyperbolical phrase of Shorty's, " It was 'ot enough to melt the nose h'off a brass monkey."

Returning to the house, Shorty, assisted by old Tonoi, cooked the dinner; and, after we had all partaken thereof, both the Cockney and Zeke threw themselves into one of the hammocks, inviting us to occupy the other. Thinking it no bad idea, we did so; and, after skirmishing with the musquitoes, managed to fall into a doze. As for the planters, more accustomed to " Nooning," they, at once, presented a nuptial back to each other; and were soon snoring away at a great rate. Tonoi snoozed on a mat, in one corner.

At last, we were roused by Zeke's crying out, " Up! b'ys; up! rise, and shine; time to get at it agin! "

Looking at the doctor, I perceived, very plainly, that he had decided upon something.

In a languid voice, he told Zeke, that he was not very well: indeed, that he had not been himself for some time past; though a little rest, no doubt, would recruit him. The Yankee, thinking, from this, that our valuable services might be lost to him altogether, were he too hard upon us at the outset, at once begged us both to consult our own feelings, and not exert ourselves for the present, unless we felt like it. Then—without recognizing the fact, that my comrade claimed to be actually unwell—he simply suggested, that, since he was so *tired*, he had better, perhaps, swing in his hammock for the rest of the day. If agreeable, however, I myself, might accompany him upon a little bullock hunting excursion, in the neighboring hills. In this proposition, I gladly acquiesced; though Peter, who was a great sportsman, put on a long face. The muskets and ammunition were forthwith got down from overhead; and, every thing being then ready, Zeke cried out, " Tonoi! come; aramai! (get up) we want you for pilot. Shorty, my lad, look arter things, you know; and, if you likes, why, there's them roots in the field yonder."

Having thus arranged his domestic affairs to please himself, though little to Shorty's satisfaction, I thought; he slung his powder-horn over his shoulder, and we started. Tonoi was, at once, sent on in advance; and, leaving the plantation, he struck into a path, which led toward the mountains.

After hurrying through the thickets for some time, we came out into the sunlight, in an open glade, just under the shadow of the hills. Here, Zeke pointed aloft, to a beetling crag, far distant; where a bullock, with horns thrown back, stood like a statue.

CHAPTER LIV.

SOME ACCOUNT OF THE WILD CATTLE IN POLYNESIA.

BEFORE we proceed further, a word or two concerning these wild cattle, and the way they came on the island.

Some fifty years ago, Vancouver left several bullocks, sheep, and goats, at various places in the Society group. He instructed the natives to look after the animals carefully; and by no means to slaughter any, until a considerable stock had accumulated.

The sheep must have died off; for I never saw a solitary fleece in any part of Polynesia. The pair left, were an ill assorted couple, perhaps; separated in disgust, and died without issue.

As for the goats, occasionally you come across a black, misanthropic ram, nibbling the scant herbage of some height inaccessible to man, in preference to the sweet grasses of the valley below. The goats are not very numerous.

The bullocks, coming of a prolific ancestry, are a hearty set, racing over the island of Imeeo in considerable numbers; though in Tahiti, but few of them are seen. At the former place, the original pair must have scampered off to the interior, since it is now so thickly populated by their wild progeny. The herds are the private property of Queen Pomaree; from whom the planters had obtained permission to shoot for their own use, as many as they pleased.

The natives stand in great awe of these cattle; and for this reason, are excessively timid in crossing the island, preferring rather to sail round to an opposite village in their canoes.

Tonoi abounded in bullock stories; most of which, by the by, had a spice of the marvelous. The following is one of these.

Once upon a time, he was going over the hills with a brother—now no more—when a great bull came bellowing out of a wood, and both took to their heels. The old chief sprang into a tree; his companion, flying in an

opposite direction, was pursued, and in the very act of
reaching up to a bough, trampled under foot. The unhappy
man was then gored—tossed in the air—and finally run
away with on the bull's horns. More dead than alive,
Tonoi waited till all was over, and then made the best
of his way home. The neighbors, armed with two or three
muskets, at once started to recover, if possible, his unfortunate brother's remains. At nightfall, they returned without
discovering any trace of him; but the next morning, Tonoi
himself caught a glimpse of a bullock, marching across the
mountain's brow, with a long dark object borne aloft on his
horns.

Having referred to Vancouver's attempts to colonize the
islands with useful quadrupeds, we may as well say something concerning his success upon Hawaii, one of the largest
islands in the whole Polynesian Archipelago; and which
gives the native name to the well known cluster named by
Cook in honor of Lord Sandwich.

Hawaii is some one hundred leagues in circuit, and
covers an area of over four thousand square miles. Until
within a few years past, its interior was almost unknown,
even to the inhabitants themselves, who, for ages, had been
prevented from wandering thither, by certain strange superstitions. Pelee, the terrific goddess of the volcanoes Mount
Roa and Mount Kea,* was supposed to guard all the passes
to the extensive valleys lying round their base. There are
legends of her having chased with streams of fire several
impious adventurers. Near Hilo, a jet-black cliff is shown,
with the vitreous torrent apparently pouring over into the
sea: just as it cooled after one of these supernatural
eruptions.

To these inland valleys, and the adjoining hillsides,

---

* Perhaps the most remarkable volcanoes in the world. For
very interesting accounts of three adventurous expeditions to their
summits (seventeen thousand feet above the level of the sea), see
Lord Byron's Voyage of H. B. M. Ship Blonde; Ellis's Journal of a
Visit to the Sandwich Islands; and Wilkes' Narrative of the U. S.
Exploring Expedition.

which are clothed in the most luxuriant vegetation, Vancouver's bullocks soon wandered; and unmolested for a long period, multiplied in vast herds.

Some twelve or fifteen years ago, the natives, losing sight of their superstitions, and learning the value of the hides in commerce, began hunting the creatures that wore them; but being very fearful and awkward in a business so novel, their success was small; and it was not until the arrival of a party of Spanish hunters, men regularly trained to their calling upon the plains of California, that the work of slaughter was fairly begun.

The Spaniards were showy fellows, tricked out in gay blankets, leggins worked with porcupine quills, and jingling spurs. Mounted upon trained Indian mares, these heroes pursued their prey up to the very base of the burning mountains; making the profoundest solitudes ring with their shouts, and flinging the lasso under the very nose of the vixen goddess Pelee. Hilo, a village upon the coast, was their place of resort; and thither flocked roving whites from all the islands of the group. As pupils of the dashing Spaniards, many of these dissipated fellows, quaffing too freely of the stirrup-cup, and riding headlong after the herds, when they reeled in the saddle, were unhorsed and killed.

This was about the year 1835, when the present king, Tammahamaha III. was a lad. With royal impudence, laying claim to the sole property of the cattle, he was delighted with the idea of receiving one of every two silver dollars paid down for their hides; so, with no thought for the future, the work of extermination went madly on. In three years' time, eighteen thousand bullocks were slain, almost entirely upon the single island of Hawaii.

The herds being thus nearly destroyed, the sagacious young prince imposed a rigorous "taboo" upon the few surviving cattle, which was to remain in force for ten years. During this period—not yet expired—all hunting is forbidden, unless directly authorized by the king.

The massacre of the cattle extended to the hapless goats. In one year, three thousand of their skins were sold to the merchants of Honolulu, fetching a *quartilia*, or a shilling sterling apiece.

After this digression, it is time to run on after Tonoi and the Yankee.

CHAPTER LV.

A HUNTING RAMBLE WITH ZEKE.

AT the foot of the mountain, a steep path went up among rocks and clefts, mantled with verdure. Here and there were green gulfs, down which it made one giddy to peep. At last we gained an overhanging, wooded shelf of land which crowned the heights; and along this, the path, well shaded, ran like a gallery.

In every direction, the scenery was enchanting. There was a low, rustling breeze; and below, in the vale, the leaves were quivering; the sea lay, blue and serene, in the distance; and inland the surface swelled up, ridge after ridge, and peak upon peak, all bathed in the Indian haze of the Tropics, and dreamy to look upon. Still valleys, leagues away, reposed in the deep shadows of the mountains; and here and there, water-falls lifted up their voices in the solitude. High above all, and central, the " Marling-spike " lifted its finger. Upon the hillsides, small groups of bullocks were seen; some quietly browsing; others slowly winding into the valleys.

We went on, directing our course for a slope of the hills, a mile or two further, where the nearest bullocks were seen.

We were cautious in keeping to windward of them; their sense of smell and hearing being, like those of all wild creatures, exceedingly acute.

As there was no knowing that we might not surprise some other kind of game in the coverts through which we were passing, we crept along warily.

The wild hogs of the island are uncommonly fierce; and as they often attack the natives, I could not help following Tonoi's example of once in a while peeping in under the foliage. Frequent retrospective glances also, served to assure me that our retreat was not cut off.

As we rounded a clump of bushes, a noise behind them, like the crackling of dry branches, broke the stillness. In an instant, Tonoi's hand was on a bough, ready for a spring, and Zeke's finger touched the trigger of his piece. Again the stillness was broken; and thinking it high time to get ready, I brought my musket to my shoulder.

" Look sharp! " cried the Yankee; and dropping on one knee, he brushed the twigs aside. Presently, off went his piece; and with a wild snort, a black, bristling boar—his cherry red lip curled up by two glittering tusks—dashed, unharmed, across the path, and crashed through the opposite thicket. I saluted him with a charge as he disappeared; but not the slightest notice was taken of the civility.

By this time, Tonoi, the illustrious descendant of the Bishops of Imeeo, was twenty feet from the ground. " Aramai! come down, you old fool! " cried the Yankee; " the pesky critter's on t'other side of the island afore this.

" I rayther guess," he continued, as we began reloading, " that we've spoiled sport by firing at that ere 'tarnal hog. Them bullocks' heard the racket, and is flinging their tails about now on the keen jump. Quick, Paul, and let's climb that rock yonder, and see if so be there's any in sight."

But none were to be seen, except at such a distance that they looked like ants.

As evening was now at hand, my companion proposed our returning home forthwith; and then, after a sound night's rest, starting in the morning upon a good day's hunt with the whole force of the plantation.

Following another path, in descending into the valley, we passed through some nobly wooded land on the face of the mountain.

One variety of tree particularly attracted my attention. The dark mossy stem, over seventy feet high, was perfectly branchless for many feet above the ground, when it shot out in broad boughs laden with lustrous leaves of the deepest green. And all round the lower part of the trunk, thin, slab-like buttresses of bark, perfectly smooth, and radiating from a common center, projected along the ground for at least two yards. From below, these natural props tapered upward until gradually blended with the trunk itself. There were signs of the wild cattle having sheltered themselves behind them. Zeke called this the canoe-tree; as in old times it supplied the navies of the Kings of Tahiti. For canoe-building, the wood is still used. Being extremely dense, and impervious to worms, it is very durable.

Emerging from the forest, when half-way down the hillside, we came upon an open space, covered with ferns and grass, over which a few lonely trees were casting long shadows in the setting sun. Here, a piece of ground some hundred feet square, covered with weeds and brambles, and sounding hollow to the tread, was inclosed by a ruinous wall of stones. Tonoi said it was an almost forgotten burial-place, of great antiquity, where no one had been interred since the islanders had been Christians. Sealed up in dry, deep vaults, many a dead heathen was lying here.

Curious to prove the old man's statement, I was anxious to get a peep at the catacombs; but hermetically overgrown with vegetation, as they were, no aperture was visible.

Before gaining the level of the valley, we passed by the site of a village, near a water-course, long since deserted. There was nothing but stone walls, and rude dismantled foundations of houses, constructed of the same material. Large trees and brush-wood were growing rankly among them.

I asked Tonoi how long it was since any one had lived here. " Me, *tammaree* (boy)—plenty *kannaker* (men) Martair," he replied. " Now, only poor *pehe kannaka* (fishermen) left—me born here."

Going down the valley, vegetation of every kind presented a different aspect from that of the high land.

Chief among the trees of the plain on this island, is the " *Ati*," large and lofty, with a massive trunk, and broad, laurel-shaped leaves. The wood is splendid. In

Tahiti, I was shown a narrow, polished plank, fit to make a cabinet for a king. Taken from the heart of the tree, it was of a deep, rich scarlet, traced with yellow veins, and in some places clouded with hazel.

In the same grove with the regal "*Ati*," you may see the beautiful flowering "*Hotoo;*" its pyramid of shining leaves diversified with numberless small, white blossoms.

Planted with trees as the valley is, almost throughout its entire length, I was astonished to observe so very few which were useful to the natives: not one in a hundred was a cocoa-nut or bread-fruit tree.

But here Tonoi again enlightened me. In the sanguinary religious hostilities which ensued upon the conversion to Christianity of the first Pomaree, a war party from Tahiti destroyed (by "girdling" the bark) entire groves of these invaluable trees. For some time afterward, they stood stark and leafless in the sun; sad monuments of the fate which befell the inhabitants of the valley.

CHAPTER LVI.

MUSQUITOES.

THE night following the hunting trip, Long Ghost and myself, after a valiant defense, had to fly the house on account of the musquitoes.

And here I can not avoid relating a story, rife among the natives, concerning the manner in which these insects were introduced upon the island.

Some years previous, a whaling captain, touching at an adjoining bay, got into difficulty with its inhabitants, and at last carried his complaint before one of the native tribunals; but receiving no satisfaction, and deeming himself aggrieved, he resolved upon taking signal revenge. One night, he towed a rotten old water-cask ashore, and left it in a neglected *Taro* patch, where the ground was warm and moist. Hence the musquitoes.

I tried my best to learn the name of this man: and hereby do what I can to hand it down to posterity. It was Coleman —Nathan Coleman. The ship belonged to Nantucket.

When tormented by the musquitoes, I found much relief in coupling the word " Coleman " with another of one syllable, and pronouncing them together energetically.

The doctor suggested a walk to the beach, where there was a long, low shed tumbling to pieces, but open lengthwise to a current of air which he thought might keep off the musquitoes. So thither we went.

The ruin partially sheltered a relic of times gone by, which, a few days after, we examined with much curiosity. It was an old war-canoe, crumbling to dust. Being supported by the same rude blocks upon which, apparently, it had years before been hollowed out, in all probability it had never been afloat.

Outside, it seemed originally stained of a green color, which, here and there, was now changed into a dingy purple. The prow terminated in a high, blunt beak; both sides were covered with carving; and upon the stern was something which Long Ghost maintained to be the arms of the royal House of Pomaree. The device had an heraldic look, certainly—being two sharks with the talons of hawks clawing a knot left projecting from the wood.

The canoe was at least forty feet long, about two wide, and four deep. The upper part—consisting of narrow planks laced together with cords of sinnate—had in many places fallen off, and lay decaying upon the ground. Still, there were ample accommodations left for sleeping; and in we sprang—the doctor into the bow, and I, into the stern. I soon fell asleep; but waking suddenly, cramped in every joint from my constrained posture, I thought, for an instant, that I must have been prematurely screwed down in my coffin.

Presenting my compliments to Long Ghost, I asked how it fared with *him*.

" Bad enough," he replied, as he tossed about in the outlandish rubbish lying in the bottom of our couch. " Pah! how these old mats smell! "

As he continued talking in this exciting strain for some time, I at last made no reply, having resumed certain mathematical reveries to induce repose. But finding the multiplication-table of no avail, I summoned up a grayish image of chaos in a sort of sliding fluidity, and was just falling into a nap on the strength of it, when I heard a solitary and distinct buzz. The hour of my calamity was at hand. One blended hum, the creature darted into the canoe like a small sword-fish; and I out of it.

Upon getting into the open air, to my surprise, there was Long Ghost, fanning himself wildly with an old paddle. He had just made a noiseless escape from a swarm, which had attacked his own end of the canoe.

It was now proposed to try the water; so a small fishing canoe, hauled up near by, was quickly lanched; and paddling a good distance off, we dropped overboard the native contrivance for an anchor—a heavy stone, attached to a cable of braided bark. At this part of the island, the encircling reef was close to the shore, leaving the water within smooth, and extremely shallow.

It was a blessed thought! We knew nothing till sunrise, when the motion of our aquatic cot awakened us. I looked up, and beheld Zeke wading toward the shore, and towing us after him by the bark cable. Pointing to the reef, he told us we had had a narrow escape.

It was true enough; the water-sprites had rolled our stone out of its noose, and we had floated away.

CHAPTER LVII.

THE SECOND HUNT IN THE MOUNTAINS.

FAIR dawned, over the hills of Martair, the jocund morning of our hunt.

Every thing had been prepared for it overnight; and, when we arrived at the house, a good breakfast was spread by Shorty: and old Tonoi was bustling about like an innkeeper. Several of his men, also, were in attendance, to accompany us with calabashes of food; and, in case we met with any success, to officiate as bearers of burdens, on our return.

Apprised, the evening previous, of the meditated sport, the doctor had announced his willingness to take part therein.

Now, subsequent events made us regard this expedition as a shrewd device of the Yankee's. Once get us off on a pleasure trip, and with what face could we afterward refuse to work? Beside, he enjoyed all the credit of giving us a holyday. Nor did he omit assuring us, that, work or play, our wages were all the while running on.

A dilapidated old musket of Tonoi's, was borrowed for the doctor. It was exceedingly short and heavy, with a clumsy lock, which required a strong finger to pull the trigger. On trying the piece, by firing at a mark, Long Ghost was satisfied that it could not fail of doing execution: the charge went one way, and he the other.

Upon this, he endeavored to negotiate an exchange of muskets with Shorty; but the Cockney was proof against his blandishments; at last he intrusted his weapon to one of the natives to carry for him.

Marshaling our forces, we started for the head of the valley; near which, a path ascended to a range of high land, said to be a favorite resort of the cattle.

Shortly after gaining the heights, a small herd, some way off, was perceived entering a wood. We hurried on; and, dividing our party, went in after them, at four different points; each white man followed by several natives.

I soon found myself in a dense covert; and, after looking round, was just emerging into a clear space, when I heard a report, and a bullet knocked the bark from a tree near by. The same instant, there was a trampling and crashing; and five bullocks, nearly abreast, broke into view across the opening, and plunged right toward the spot where myself and three of the islanders were standing.

They were small, black, vicious-looking creatures; with short, sharp horns, red nostrils, and eyes like coals of fire. On they came—their dark woolly heads hanging down.

By this time, my island backers were roosting among the trees. Glancing round, for an instant, to discover a retreat in case of emergency, I raised my piece, when a voice cried out, from the wood, " Right between the 'orns, Paul! right between the 'orns! " Down went my barrel, in range with a small white tuft on the forehead of the headmost one; and, letting him have it, I darted to one side. As I turned again, the five bullocks shot by like a blast, making the air eddy in their wake.

The Yankee now burst into view, and saluted them in flank. Whereupon, the fierce little bull with the tufted forehead, flirted his long tail over his buttocks; kicked out, with his hind feet, and shot forward a full length. It was nothing but a graze; and, in an instant, they were out of sight, the thicket into which they broke rocking overhead, and marking their progress.

The action over, the heavy artillery came up, in the person of the Long Doctor, with his blunderbuss.

" Where are they? " he cried, out of breath.

" A mile or two h'off, by this time," replied the Cockney. " Lord, Paul! you ought to've sent an 'ail stone into that little black 'un."

While excusing my want of skill, as well as I could, Zeke, rushing forward, suddenly exclaimed, " Creation! what are you 'bout there, Peter? "

Peter, incensed at our ill luck, and ignorantly imputing it to the cowardice of our native auxiliaries, was bringing his piece to bear upon his trembling squire—the musket carrier—now descending a tree.

Pulling trigger, the bullet went high over his head; and, hopping to the ground, bellowing like a calf, the fellow ran away as fast as his heels could carry him. The rest followed us, after this, with fear and trembling.

After forming our line of march anew, we went on for several hours, without catching a glimpse of the game; the reports of the muskets having been heard at a great distance. At last, we mounted a craggy height, to obtain a wide view of the country. From this place, we beheld three cattle, quietly browsing in a green opening of a wood below; the trees shutting them in all round.

A general reëxamination of the muskets now took place, followed by a hasty lunch from the calabashes: we then started. As we descended the mountain-side, the cattle were in plain sight, until we entered the forest, when we lost sight of them for a moment; but only to see them again, as we crept close up to the spot where they grazed.

They were a bull, a cow, and a calf. The cow was lying down in the shade, by the edge of the wood; the calf, sprawling out before her in the grass, licking her lips; while old Taurus himself stood close by, casting a paternal glance at this domestic little scene, and conjugally elevating his nose in the air.

"Now then," said Zeke, in a whisper, "let's take the poor creeturs, while they are huddled together. Crawl along, b'ys; crawl along. Fire together, mind; and not 'till I say the word."

We crept up to the very edge of the open ground, and knelt behind a clump of bushes; resting our leveled barrels among the branches. The slight rustling was heard. Taurus turned round, dropped his head to the ground, and sent forth a low, sullen bellow; then snuffed the air. The cow rose on her fore knees, pitched forward alarmedly, and stood upon her legs; while the calf, with ears pricked, got right underneath her. All three were now grouped, and, in an instant would be off.

"I take the bull," cried our leader; "fire!"

The calf fell like a clod; its dam uttered a cry, and thrust her head into the thicket; but she turned, and came moaning up to the lifeless calf, going round and round it, snuffing fiercely with her bleeding nostrils. A crashing in the wood, and a loud roar, announced the flying bull.

Soon, another shot was fired, and the cow fell. Leaving some of the natives to look after the dead cattle, the rest of us hurried on after the bull; his dreadful bellowings guiding us to the spot where he lay. Wounded in the shoulder, in his fright and agony he had bounded into the wood; but when we came up to him, he had sunk to the earth in a green hollow, thrusting his black muzzle into a pool of his own blood, and tossing it over his hide in clots.

The Yankee brought his piece to a rest; and, the next instant, the wild brute sprang into the air, and with his fore legs crouching under him, fell dead.

Our island friends were now in high spirits; all courage and alacrity. Old Tonoi thought nothing of taking poor Taurus himself by the horns, and peering into his glazed eyes.

Our ship knives were at once in request; and, skinning the cattle, we hung them high up by cords of bark from the boughs of a tree. Withdrawing into a covert, we there waited for the wild hogs; which, according to Zeke, would soon make their appearance, lured by the smell of blood. Presently, we heard them coming, in two or three different directions; and, in a moment, they were tearing the offal to pieces.

As only one shot at these creatures could be relied on, we intended firing simultaneously; but, somehow or other, the doctor's piece went off by itself, and one of the hogs dropped. The others then breaking into the thicket, the rest of us sprang after them; resolved to have another shot at all hazards.

The Cockney darted among some bushes; and, a few moments after, we heard the report of his musket, followed by a quick cry. On running up, we saw our comrade doing battle with a young devil of a boar, as black as night, whose snout had been partly torn away. Firing when the game was in full career, and coming directly toward him, Shorty had been assailed by the enraged brute; it was now crunching the breech of the musket, with which he had tried to club it; Shorty holding fast to the barrel, and fingering his waist for a knife. Being in advance of the others, I clapped my gun to the boar's head, and so put an end to the contest.

Evening now coming on, we set to work loading our carriers. The cattle were so small, that a stout native could walk off with an entire quarter; brushing through thickets, and descending rocks without an apparent effort: though, to tell the truth, no white man present could have done the thing with any ease. As for the wild hogs, none of the islanders could be induced to carry Shorty's; some invincible superstition being connected with its black color. We were, therefore, obliged to leave it. The other, a spotted one, being slung by green thongs to a pole, was marched off with by two young natives.

With our bearers of burdens ahead, we then commenced our return down the valley. Half-way home, darkness overtook us in the woods; and torches became necessary. We stopped, and made them of dry palm branches; and then, sending two lads on in advance, for the purpose of gathering fuel to feed the flambeaux, we continued our journey.

It was a wild sight. The torches, waved aloft, flashed through the forest; and, where the ground admitted, the islanders went along on a brisk trot, notwithstanding they bent forward under their loads. Their naked backs were stained with blood; and occasionally, running by each other, they raised wild cries, which startled the hillsides.

CHAPTER LVIII.

THE HUNTING-FEAST; AND A VISIT TO AFREHITOO.

Two bullocks and a boar! No bad trophies of our day's sport. So by torchlight we marched into the plantation, the wild hog rocking from its pole, and the doctor singing an old hunting-song—Tally-ho! the chorus of which swelled high above the yells of the natives.

We resolved to make a night of it. Kindling a great fire just outside the dwelling, and hanging one of the heifer's quarters from a limb of the banian-tree, every one was at liberty to cut and broil for himself. Baskets of roasted

bread-fruit, and plenty of taro pudding; bunches of bananas, and young cocoa-nuts, had also been provided by
the natives against our return.

The fire burned bravely, keeping off the musquitoes,
and making every man's face glow like a beaker of Port.
The meat had the true wild-game flavor, not at all impaired by our famous appetites, and a couple of flasks of
white brandy, which Zeke, producing from his secret store,
circulated freely.

There was no end to my long comrade's spirits. After
telling his stories, and singing his songs, he sprang to his
feet, clasped a young damsel of the grove round the waist,
and waltzed over the grass with her. But there's no telling
all the pranks he played that night. The natives, who delight in a wag, emphatically pronounced him " maitai."

It was long after midnight ere we broke up; but when
the rest had retired, Zeke, with the true thrift of a Yankee,
salted down what was left of the meat.

The next day was Sunday; and at my request, Shorty
accompanied me to Afrehitoo—a neighboring bay, and
the seat of a mission, almost directly opposite Papeetee. In
Afrehitoo is a large church and school-house, both quite
dilapidated; and planted amid shrubbery on a fine knoll,
stands a very tasteful cottage, commanding a view across
the channel. In passing, I caught sight of a graceful calico
skirt disappearing from the piazza through a doorway. The
place was the residence of the missionary.

A trim little sail-boat was dancing out at her moorings,
a few yards from the beach.

Straggling over the low lands in the vicinity were several
native huts—untidy enough—but much better every way,
than most of those in Tahiti.

We attended service at the church, where we found but
a small congregation; and after what I had seen in Papeetee,
nothing very interesting took place. But the audience had
a curious, fidgety look, which I knew not how to account for,
until we ascertained that a sermon with the eighth commandment for a text was being preached.

It seemed that there lived an Englishman in the district, who, like our friends, the planters, was cultivating Tombez potatoes for the Papeetee market.

In spite of all his precautions, the natives were in the habit of making nocturnal forays into his inclosure, and carrying off the potatoes. One night he fired a fowling-piece, charged with pepper and salt, at several shadows which he discovered stealing across his premises. They fled. But it was like seasoning any thing else: the knaves stole again with a greater relish than ever; and the very next night, he caught a party in the act of roasting a basket full of potatoes under his own cooking-shed. At last, he stated his grievances to the missionary; who, for the benefit of his congregation, preached the sermon we heard.

Now, there were no thieves in Martair; but then, the people of the valley were bribed to be honest. It was a regular business transaction between them and the planters. In consideration of so many potatoes " to them in hand, duly paid," they were to abstain from all depredations upon the plantation. Another security against roguery, was the permanent residence upon the premises, of their chief, Tonoi.

On our return to Martair, in the afternoon, we found the doctor and Zeke making themselves comfortable. The latter was reclining on the ground, pipe in mouth, watching the doctor, who, sitting like a Turk, before a large iron kettle, was slicing potatoes and Indian turnip, and now and then shattering splinters from a bone; all of which, by turns, were thrown into the pot. He was making what he called " Bullock broth."

In gastronomic affairs, my friend was something of an artist; and by way of improving his knowledge, did nothing the rest of the day but practice in what might be called Experimental Cookery: broiling and grilling, and deviling slices of meat, and subjecting them to all sorts of igneous operations. It was the first fresh beef that either of us had tasted in more than a year.

" Oh, ye'll pick up arter a while, Peter," observed Zeke toward night, as Long Ghost was turning a great rib over the coals—" what d'ye think, Paul? "

"He'll get along, I dare say," replied I; "he only wants to get those cheeks of his tanned." To tell the truth, I was not a little pleased to see the doctor's reputation as an invalid fading away so fast; especially, as on the strength of his being one, he had promised to have such easy times of it, and very likely too, at my expense.

CHAPTER LIX.

THE MURPHIES.

DOZING in our canoe the next morning about daybreak, we were wakened by Zeke's hailing us loudly from the beach.

Upon paddling up, he told us that a canoe had arrived overnight, from Papeetee, with an order from a ship lying there, for a supply of his potatoes; and as they must be on board the vessel by noon, he wanted us to assist in bringing them down to his sail-boat.

My long comrade was one of those, who, from always thrusting forth the wrong foot foremost when they rise, or committing some other indiscretion of the limbs, are more or less crabbed or sullen before breakfast. It was in vain, therefore, that the Yankee deplored the urgency of the case, which obliged him to call us up thus early:—the doctor only looked the more glum, and said nothing in reply.

At last, by way of getting up a little enthusiasm for the occasion, the Yankee exclaimed quite spiritedly, "What d'ye say, then, b'ys, shall we git at it?"

"Yes, in the devil's name!" replied the doctor, like a snapping turtle; and we moved on to the house. Notwithstanding his ungracious answer, he probably thought that after the gastronomic performance of the day previous, it would hardly do to hang back. At the house, we found Shorty ready with the hoes; and we at once repaired to the farther side of the inclosure, where the potatoes had yet to be taken out of the ground.

The rich, tawny soil seemed specially adapted to the crop; the great yellow murphies rolling out of the hills like eggs from a nest.

My comrade really surprised me by the zeal with which he applied himself to his hoe. For my own part, exhilarated by the cool breath of the morning, I worked away like a good fellow. As for Zeke and the Cockney, they seemed mightily pleased at this evidence of our willingness to exert ourselves.

It was not long ere all the potatoes were turned out; and then came the worst of it: they were to be lugged down to the beach, a distance of at least a quarter of a mile. And there being no such thing as a barrow, or cart, on the island, there was nothing for it but spinal-marrows and broad shoulders. Well knowing that this part of the business would be any thing but agreeable, Zeke did his best to put as encouraging a face upon it as possible; and giving us no time to indulge in desponding thoughts, gleefully directed our attention to a pile of rude baskets—made of stout stalks—which had been provided for the occasion. So, without more ado, we helped ourselves from the heap; and soon we were all four staggering along under our loads.

The first trip down, we arrived at the beach together: Zeke's enthusiastic cries proving irresistible. A trip or two more, however, and my shoulders began to grate in their sockets; while the doctor's tall figure acquired an obvious stoop. Presently, we both threw down our baskets, protesting we could stand it no longer. But our employers, bent, as it were, upon getting the work out of us by a silent appeal to our moral sense, toiled away without pretending to notice us. It was as much as to say, " There, men, we've been boarding and lodging ye for the last three days; and yesterday ye did nothing earthly but eat; so stand by now, and look at us working, if ye dare." Thus driven to it, then, we resumed our employment. Yet, in spite of all we could do, we lagged behind Zeke and Shorty, who, breathing hard, and perspiring at every pore, toiled away without pause or cessation. I almost wickedly wished, that they would load themselves down with one potato too many.

Gasping as I was with my own hamper, I could not, for the life of me, help laughing at Long Ghost. There he went:—his long neck thrust forward, his arms twisted behind him to form a shelf for his basket to rest on; and his stilts of legs every once in a while giving way under him, as if his knee-joints slipped either way.

"There! I carry no more!" he exclaimed all at once, flinging his potatoes into the boat, where the Yankee was just then stowing them away.

"Oh, then," said Zeke, quite briskly, "I guess you and Paul had better try the 'barrel-machine'—come along, I'll fix ye out in no time;" and, so saying, he waded ashore, and hurried back to the house, bidding us follow.

Wondering what upon earth the "barrel-machine" could be, and rather suspicious of it, we limped after. On arriving at the house, we found him getting ready a sort of sedan-chair. It was nothing more than an old barrel, suspended by a rope from the middle of a stout oar. Quite an ingenious contrivance of the Yankee's; and his proposed arrangement with regard to mine and the doctor's shoulders, was equally so.

"There now!" said he, when every thing was ready, "there's no back-breaking about this; you can stand right up under it, you see: jist try it once;" and he politely rested the blade of the oar on my comrade's right shoulder, and the other end on mine, leaving the barrel between us.

"Jist the thing!" he added, standing off admiringly, while we remained in this interesting attitude.

There was no help for us; with broken hearts and backs we trudged back to the field; the doctor all the while saying masses.

Upon starting with the loaded barrel, for a few paces we got along pretty well, and were constrained to think the idea not a bad one. But we did not long think so. In less than five minutes we came to a dead halt, the springing and buckling of the clumsy oar being almost unendurable.

"Let's shift ends," cried the doctor, who did not quite relish the blade of the stick, which was cutting into the blade of his shoulder.

At last, by stages short and frequent, we managed to shamble down to the beach, where we again dumped our cargo, in something of a pet.

"Why not make the natives help?" asked Long Ghost, rubbing his shoulder.

"Natives be dumned!" said the Yankee, "twenty on 'em ain't worth one white man. They never was meant to work any, them chaps; and they knows it, too, for dumned little work any on 'em ever does."

But notwithstanding this abuse, Zeke was at last obliged to press a few of the bipeds into service. "Aramai!" (come here) he shouted to several, who, reclining on a bank, had hitherto been critical observers of our proceedings; and, among other things, had been particularly amused by the performance with the sedan-chair.

After making these fellows load their baskets together, the Yankee filled his own, and then drove them before him, down to the beach. Probably he had seen the herds of panniered mules, driven in this way by mounted Indians, along the great road from Callao to Lima.

The boat at last loaded, the Yankee, taking with him a couple of natives, at once hoisted sail, and stood across the channel for Papeetee.

The next morning at breakfast, old Tonoi ran in, and told us that the voyagers were returning. We hurried down to the beach, and saw the boat gliding toward us, with a dozing islander at the helm, and Zeke standing up in the bows, jingling a small bag of silver, the proceeds of his cargo.

CHAPTER LX.

WHAT THEY THOUGHT OF US IN MARTAIR.

SEVERAL quiet days now passed away, during which, we just worked sufficiently to sharpen our appetites; the planters leniently exempting us from any severe toil.

Their desire to retain us became more and more evident; which was not to be wondered at; for, beside esteeming us from the beginning a couple of civil, good-natured fellows, who would soon become quite at home with them, they were not slow in perceiving, that we were far different from the common run of rovers; and that our society was both entertaining and instructive to a couple of solitary, illiterate men, like themselves.

In a literary point of view, indeed, they soon regarded us with emotions of envy and wonder; and the doctor was considered nothing short of a prodigy. The Cockney found out, that he (the doctor) could read a book upside down, without even so much as spelling the big words beforehand; and the Yankee, in the twinkling of an eye, received from him the sum total of several arithmetical items, stated aloud, with the view of testing the extent of his mathematical lore.

Then, frequently, in discoursing upon men and things, my long comrade employed such imposing phrases, that, upon one occasion, they actually remained uncovered while he talked.

In short, their favorable opinion of Long Ghost in particular, rose higher and higher every day; and they began to indulge in all manner of dreams concerning the advantages to be derived from employing so learned a laborer. Among other projects revealed, was that of building a small craft of some forty tons, for the purpose of trading among the neighboring islands. With a native crew, we would then take turns cruising over the tranquil Pacific; touching here and there, as caprice suggested, and collecting romantic articles of commerce;—beach-de-mer, the pearl-oyster, arrow-root, ambergris, sandal-wood, cocoa-nut oil, and edible birdsnests.

This South Sea yachting was delightful to think of; and straightway, the doctor announced his willingness to navigate the future schooner clear of all shoals and reefs whatsoever. His impudence was audacious. He enlarged upon the science of navigation; treated us to a dissertation on Mercator's Sailing and the Azimuth compass; and went into an inexplicable explanation of, the Lord only knows what plan of his, for infallibly settling the longitude.

Whenever my comrade thus gave the reins to his fine fancy, it was a treat to listen, and therefore I never interfered; but, with the planters, sat in mute admiration before him. This apparent self-abasement on my part, must have been considered as truly indicative of our respective merits; for, to my no small concern, I quickly perceived, that in the estimate formed of us, Long Ghost began to be rated far above myself. For aught I knew, indeed, he might have privately thrown out a hint concerning the difference in our respective stations aboard the Julia; or else, the planters must have considered him some illustrious individual, for certain inscrutable reasons, going incog. With this idea of him, his undisguised disinclination for work became venial; and, entertaining such views of extending their business, they counted more upon his ultimate value to them as a man of science, than as a mere ditcher.

Nor did the humorous doctor forbear to foster an opinion every way so advantageous to himself; at times, for the sake of the joke, assuming airs of superiority over myself, which, though laughable enough, were sometimes annoying.

To tell the plain truth, things at last came to such a pass, that I told him, up and down, that I had no notion to put up with his pretensions; if he were going to play the gentleman, I was going to follow suit; and then, there would quickly be an explosion.

At this he laughed heartily; and after some mirthful chat, we resolved upon leaving the valley, as soon as we could do so with a proper regard to politeness.

At supper, therefore, the same evening, the doctor hinted at our intention.

Though much surprised, and vexed, Zeke moved not a muscle. " Peter," said he at last—very gravely—and after mature deliberation, " would you like to do the *cooking?* It's easy work; and you needn't do any thing else. Paul's heartier; he can work in the field when it suits him; and before long, we'll have ye at something more agreeable:—won't we, Shorty?"

Shorty assented.

Doubtless, the proposed arrangement was a snug one; especially the sinecure for the doctor; but I by no means relished the functions allotted to myself—they were too indefinite. Nothing final, however, was agreed upon;—our intention to leave was revealed, and that was enough for the present. But, as we said nothing further about going, the Yankee must have concluded, that we might yet be induced to remain. He redoubled his endeavors to make us contented.

It was during this state of affairs, that one morning, before breakfast, we were set to weeding in a potato-patch; and the planters being engaged at the house, we were left to ourselves.

Now, though the pulling of weeds was considered by our employers an easy occupation (for which reason, they had assigned it to us), and although as a garden recreation, it may be pleasant enough, for those who like it—still, long persisted in, the business becomes excessively irksome.

Nevertheless, we toiled away for some time, until the doctor, who from his height, was obliged to stoop at a very acute angle, suddenly sprang upright; and, with one hand propping his spinal column, exclaimed, "Oh, that one's joints were but provided with holes to drop a little oil through!"

Vain as the aspiration was, for his proposed improvement upon our species, I cordially responded thereto; for every vertebra in my spine was articulating its sympathy.

Presently, the sun rose over the mountains, inducing that deadly morning languor, so fatal to early exertion in a warm climate. We could stand it no longer; but, shouldering our hoes, moved on to the house, resolved to impose no more upon the good-nature of the planters, by continuing one moment longer in an occupation so extremely uncongenial.

We freely told them so. Zeke was exceedingly hurt, and said every thing he could think of to alter our determination; but, finding all unavailing, he very hospitably urged us not to be in any hurry about leaving; for we might stay with him as guests until we had time to decide upon our future movements.

We thanked him sincerely; but replied, that the following morning, we must turn our backs upon the hills of Martair.

CHAPTER LXI.

PREPARING FOR THE JOURNEY.

DURING the remainder of the day we loitered about, talking over our plans.

The doctor was all eagerness to visit Tamai, a solitary inland village, standing upon the banks of a considerable lake of the same name, and embosomed among groves. From Afrehitoo you went to this place by a lonely pathway, leading through the wildest scenery in the world. Much, too, we had heard concerning the lake itself, which abounded in such delicious fish, that, in former times, angling parties occasionally came over to it, from Papeetee.

Upon its banks, moreover, grew the finest fruit of the islands, and in their greatest perfection. The "Ve," or Brazilian plum, here attained the size of an orange; and the gorgeous "Arheea," or red apple of Tahiti, blushed with deeper dyes than in any of the seaward valleys.

Beside all this, in Tamai dwelt the most beautiful and unsophisticated women in the entire Society group. In short, the village was so remote from the coast, and had been so much less affected by recent changes than other places that, in most things, Tahitian life was here seen, as formerly existing in the days of young Otoo, the boy-king, in Cook's time.

After obtaining from the planters all the information which was needed, we decided upon penetrating to the village; and after a temporary sojourn there, to strike the beach again, and journey round to Taloo, a harbor on the opposite side of the island.

We at once put ourselves in traveling trim. Just previous to leaving Tahiti, having found my wardrobe reduced to two suits (frock and trowsers, both much the worse for wear), I had quilted them together for mutual preservation (after a fashion peculiar to sailors); engrafting a red frock upon a blue one, and producing thereby a choice variety in the way of clothing. This was the extent of my wardrobe. Nor was the doctor by any means better off. His improvidence had at last driven him to don the nautical garb; but by this time, his frock—a light cotton one—had almost given out, and he had nothing to replace it. Shorty very generously offered him one which was a little less ragged; but the alms was proudly refused; Long Ghost preferring to assume the ancient costume of Tahiti—the " *Roora.*"

This garment, once worn as a festival dress, is now seldom met with; but Captain Bob had often shown us one which he kept as an heirloom. It was a cloak, or mantle of yellow tappa, precisely similar to the "*poncho*," worn by the South-American Spaniards. The head being slipped through a slit in the middle, the robe hangs about the person in ample drapery. Tonoi obtained sufficient coarse brown tappa to make a short mantle of this description; and in five minutes the doctor was equipped. Zeke, eying his *toga* critically, reminded its proprietor, that there were many streams to ford, and precipices to scale, between Martair and Tamai; and if he traveled in petticoats, he had better hold them up.

Besides other deficiencies, we were utterly shoeless. In the free and easy Pacific, sailors seldom wear shoes; mine had been tossed overboard the day we met the Trades; and except in one or two tramps ashore, I had never worn any since. In Martair, they would have been desirable; but none were to be had. For the expedition we meditated, however, they were indispensable. Zeke, being the owner of a pair of huge, dilapidated boots, hanging from a rafter like saddle-bags, the doctor succeeded in exchanging for them a case-knife, the last valuable article in his possession.

For myself, I made sandals from a bullock's hide, such as are worn by the Indians in California. They are made in a minute; the sole, rudely fashioned to the foot, being confined across the instep by three straps of leather.

Our headgear deserves a passing word. My comrade's was a brave old Panama hat, made of grass, almost as fine as threads of silk; and so elastic, that upon rolling it up, it sprang into perfect shape again. Set off by the jaunty slouch of this Spanish sombrero, Doctor Long Ghost, in this and his Roora, looked like a mendicant grandee.

Nor was my own appearance in an Eastern turban less distinguished. The way I came to wear it was this. My hat having been knocked overboard, a few days before reaching Papeetee, I was obliged to mount an abominable wad of parti-colored worsted—what sailors call a Scotch cap. Every one knows the elasticity of knit wool; and this Caledonian head-dress crowned my temples so effectually, that the confined atmosphere engendered was prejudicial to my curls. In vain I tried to ventilate the cap: every gash made, seemed to heal whole in no time. Then such a continual chafing as it kept up in a hot sun.

Seeing my dislike to the thing, Kooloo, my worthy friend, prevailed upon me to bestow it upon him. I did so; hinting that a good boiling might restore the original brilliancy of the colors.

It was then that I mounted the turban. Taking a new Regatta frock of the doctor's, which was of a gay calico, and winding it round my head in folds, I allowed the sleeves to droop behind—thus forming a good defense against the sun, though in a shower it was best off. The pendent sleeves adding much to the effect, the doctor always called me the Bashaw with Two Tails.

Thus arrayed, we were ready for Tamai; in whose green saloons, we counted upon creating no small sensation.

CHAPTER LXII.

TAMAI.

Long before sunrise, the next morning, my sandals were laced on, and the doctor had vaulted into Zeke's boots.

Expecting to see us again before we went to Taloo, the planters wished us a pleasant journey; and, on parting, very generously presented us with a pound or two of what sailors call "plug" tobacco; telling us to cut it up into small change; the Virginian weed being the principal circulating medium on the island.

Tamai, we were told, was not more than three or four leagues distant; so making allowances for a wild road, a few hours to rest at noon, and our determination to take the journey leisurely, we counted upon reaching the shores of the lake some time in the flush of the evening.

For several hours we went on slowly through wood and ravine, and over hill and precipice, seeing nothing but occasional herds of wild cattle, and often resting; until we found ourselves, about noon, in the very heart of the island.

It was a green, cool hollow among the mountains, into which we at last descended with a bound. The place was gushing with a hundred springs, and shaded over with great solemn trees, on whose mossy boles the moisture stood in beads. Strange to say, no traces of the bullocks ever having been here were revealed. Nor was there a sound to be heard, nor a bird to be seen, nor any breath of wind stirring the leaves. The utter solitude and silence were oppressive; and after peering about under the shades, and seeing nothing but ranks of dark, motionless trunks, we hurried across the hollow, and ascended a steep mountain opposite.

Midway up, we rested where the earth had gathered about the roots of three palms, and thus formed a pleasant lounge, from which we looked down upon the hollow, now one dark-green tuft of woodland at our feet. Here we brought forth a small calabash of "*poee*," a parting present from Tonoi. After eating heartily, we obtained fire by two sticks, and throwing ourselves back, puffed forth our fatigue in wreaths of smoke. At last we fell asleep; nor did we waken till the sun had sunk so low, that its rays darted in upon us under the foliage.

Starting up, we then continued our journey; and as we gained the mountain top—there, to our surprise, lay the lake and village of Tamai. We had thought it a good league off. Where we stood, the yellow sunset was still lingering; but over the valley below, long shadows were stealing—the rippling green lake reflecting the houses and trees, just as they stood along its banks. Several small canoes, moored here and there to posts in the water, were dancing upon the waves; and one solitary fisherman was paddling over to a grassy point. In front of the houses, groups of natives were seen; some thrown at full length upon the ground, and others indolently leaning against the bamboos.

With whoop and halloo, we ran down the hills, the villagers soon hurrying forth to see who were coming. As we drew near, they gathered round, all curiosity to know what brought the " karhowries " into their quiet country. The doctor contriving to make them understand the purely social object of our visit, they gave us a true Tahitian welcome; pointing into their dwellings, and saying they were ours as long as we chose to remain.

We were struck by the appearance of these people, both men and women; so much more healthful than the inhabitants of the bays. As for the young girls, they were more retiring and modest, more tidy in their dress, and far fresher and more beautiful than the damsels of the coast. A thousand pities, thought I, that they should bury their charms in this nook of a valley.

That night we abode in the house of Rartoo, a hospitable old chief. It was right on the shore of the lake; and at supper, we looked out through a rustling screen of foliage upon the surface of the starlit water.

The next day we rambled about, and found a happy little community, comparatively free from many deplorable evils to which the rest of their countrymen are subject. Their time, too, was more occupied. To my surprise, the manufacture of tappa was going on in several buildings. European calicoes were seldom seen, and not many articles of foreign origin of any description.

The people of Tamai were nominally Christians; but being so remote from ecclesiastical jurisdiction, their religion sat lightly upon them. We had been told, even, that many heathenish games and dances still secretly lingered in their valley.

Now the prospect of seeing an old-fashioned " hevar," or Tahitian reel, was one of the inducements which brought us here; and so, finding Rartoo rather liberal in his religious ideas, we disclosed our desire. At first, he demurred; and shrugging his shoulders like a Frenchman, declared it could not be brought about—was a dangerous matter to attempt, and might bring all concerned into trouble. But we overcame all this, convinced him that the thing could be done, and a " hevar," a genuine pagan fandango, was arranged for that very night.

CHAPTER LXIII.

A DANCE IN THE VALLEY.

THERE were some ill-natured people—tell-tales—it seemed, in Tamai; and hence there was a deal of mystery about getting up the dance.

An hour or two before midnight, Rartoo entered the house, and, throwing robes of tappa over us, bade us follow at a distance behind him; and, until out of the village, hood our faces. Keenly alive to the adventure, we obeyed. At last, after taking a wide circuit, we came out upon the farthest shore of the lake. It was a wide, dewy space; lighted up by a full moon, and carpeted with a minute species of fern, growing closely together. It swept right down to the water, showing the village opposite, glistening among the groves.

Near the trees, on one side of the clear space, was a ruinous pile of stones, many rods in extent; upon which had formerly stood a temple of Oro. At present, there was nothing but a rude hut, planted on the lowermost terrace. It seemed to have been used as a " *tappa herree*; " or house for making the native cloth.

Here, we saw lights gleaming from between the bamboos, and casting long, rod-like shadows upon the ground without. Voices also were heard. We went up, and had a peep at the dancers; who were getting ready for the ballet. They were some twenty in number; waited upon by hideous old crones, who might have been duennas. Long Ghost proposed to send the latter packing; but Rartoo said it would never do, and so they were permitted to remain.

We tried to effect an entrance at the door, which was fastened; but, after a noisy discussion with one of the old witches within, our guide became fidgety, and, at last, told us to desist, or we would spoil all. He then led us off to a distance, to await the performance; as the girls, he said, did not wish to be recognized. He, furthermore, made us promise to remain where we were, until all was over, and the dancers had retired.

We waited impatiently; and, at last, they came forth. They were arrayed in short tunics of white tappa; with garlands of flowers on their heads. Following them, were the duennas, who remained clustering about the house, while the girls advanced a few paces; and, in an instant, two of them, taller than their companions, were standing, side by side, in the middle of a ring, formed by the clasped hands of the rest. This movement was made in perfect silence.

Presently, the two girls join hands overhead; and, crying out, " Ahloo! ahloo! " wave them to and fro. Upon which, the ring begins to circle slowly; the dancers moving sideways, with their arms a little drooping. Soon they quicken their pace; and, at last, fly round and round: bosoms heaving, hair streaming, flowers dropping, and every sparkling eye circling in what seemed a line of light.

Meanwhile, the pair within are passing and repassing each other incessantly. Inclining sideways, so that their long hair falls far over, they glide this way and that; one foot continually in the air, and their fingers thrown forth, and twirling in the moonbeams.

"Ahloo! ahloo!" again cry the dance queens; and, coming together in the middle of the ring, they once more lift up the arch, and stand motionless.

"Ahloo! ahloo!" Every link of the circle is broken; and the girls, deeply breathing, stand perfectly still. They pant hard and fast, a moment or two; and then, just as the deep flush is dying away from their faces, slowly recede, all round; thus enlarging the ring.

Again the two leaders wave their hands, when the rest pause; and now, far apart, stand in the still moonlight, like a circle of fairies. Presently, raising a strange chant, they softly sway themselves, gradually quickening the movement, until, at length, for a few passionate moments, with throbbing bosoms and glowing cheeks, they abandon themselves to all the spirit of the dance, apparently lost to every thing around. But soon subsiding again into the same languid measure, as before, they become motionless; and then, reeling forward on all sides, their eyes swimming in their heads, join in one wild chorus, and sink into each other's arms.

Such is the Lory-Lory, I think they call it; the dance of the backsliding girls of Tamai.

While it was going on, we had as much as we could do, to keep the doctor from rushing forward and seizing a partner.

They would give us no more "hevars" that night; and Rartoo fairly dragged us away to a canoe, hauled up on the lake shore; when we reluctantly embarked, and, paddling over to the village, arrived there in time for a good nap before sunrise.

The next day, the doctor went about, trying to hunt up the overnight dancers. He thought to detect them by their late rising; but never was man more mistaken; for, on first sallying out, the whole village was asleep, waking up in concert about an hour after. But, in the course of the day, he came across several, whom he at once charged with taking part in the " hevar." There were some prim-looking fellows standing by (visiting elders from Afrehitoo, perhaps), and the girls looked embarrassed; but parried the charge most skillfully.

Though soft as doves, in general, the ladies of Tamai are, nevertheless, flavored with a slight tincture of what we queerly enough call the " *devil*;" and they showed it on the present occasion. For when the doctor pressed one rather hard, she all at once turned round upon him, and, giving him a box on the ear, told him to "hanree perrar! " (be off with himself.)

CHAPTER LXIV.

MYSTERIOUS.

THERE was a little old man, of a most hideous aspect, living in Tamai, who, in a coarse mantle of tappa, went about the village, dancing, and singing, and making faces. He followed us about, wherever we went; and, when unobserved by others, plucked at our garments, making frightful signs for us to go along with him somewhere, and see something.

It was in vain, that we tried to get rid of him. Kicks and cuffs, even, were at last resorted to; but, though he howled like one possessed, he would not go away, but still haunted us. At last, we conjured the natives to rid us of him; but they only laughed; so, we were forced to endure the dispensation as well as we could.

On the fourth night of our visit, returning home late from paying a few calls through the village, we turned a dark corner of trees, and came full upon our goblin friend;

as usual, chattering, and motioning with his hands. The doctor, venting a curse, hurried forward; but, from some impulse or other, I stood my ground, resolved to find out what this unaccountable object wanted of us. Seeing me pause, he crept close up to me, peered into my face, and then retreated, beckoning me to follow; which I did.

In a few moments the village was behind us; and with my guide in advance, I found myself in the shadow of the heights overlooking the farther side of the valley. Here, my guide paused, until I came up with him; when, side by side, and without speaking, we ascended the hill.

Presently, we came to a wretched hut, barely distinguishable in the shade cast by the neighboring trees. Pushing aside a rude, sliding door, held together with thongs, the goblin signed me to enter. Within, it looked dark as pitch; so, I gave him to understand that he must strike a light, and go in before me. Without replying, he disappeared in the darkness; and, after groping about, I heard two sticks rubbing together, and directly saw a spark. A native taper was then lighted, and I stooped, and entered.

It was a mere kennel. Foul old mats, and broken cocoanut shells, and calabashes were strown about the floor of earth; and overhead, I caught glimpses of the stars through chinks in the roof. Here and there, the thatch had fallen through, and hung down in wisps.

I now told him to set about what he was going to do, or produce whatever he had to show without delay. Looking round fearfully, as if dreading a surprise, he commenced turning over and over the rubbish in one corner. At last, he clutched a calabash, stained black, and with the neck broken off; on one side of it was a large hole. Something seemed to be stuffed away in the vessel; and after a deal of poking at the aperture, a musty old pair of sailor trowsers was drawn forth; and, holding them up eagerly, he inquired, how many pieces of tobacco I would give for them.

Without replying, I hurried away; the old man chasing me, and shouting as I ran, until I gained the village. Here, I dodged him, and made my way home, resolved never to disclose so inglorious an adventure.

To no purpose, the next morning, my comrade besought me to enlighten him: I preserved a mysterious silence.

The occurrence served me a good turn, however, so long as we abode in Tamai; for the old clothesman never afterward troubled me; but forever haunted the doctor, who, in vain, supplicated Heaven to be delivered from him.

CHAPTER LXV.

THE HEGIRA, OR FLIGHT.

" I SAY, doctor," cried I, a few days after my adventure with the goblin, as, in the absence of our host, we were one morning lounging upon the matting in his dwelling, smoking our reed pipes, " Tamai's a thriving place; why not settle down? "

" Faith! " said he, " not a bad idea, Paul. But do you fancy they'll let us stay, though?"

" Why, certainly: they would be overjoyed to have a couple of karhowrees for townsmen."

" Gad! you're right, my pleasant fellow. Ha! ha! I'll put up a banana-leaf as physician from London—deliver lectures on Polynesian antiquities—teach English in five lessons, of one hour each—establish power-looms for the manufacture of tappa—lay out a public park in the middle of the village, and found a festival in honor of Captain Cook! "

" But, surely, not without stopping to take breath," observed I.

The doctor's projects, to be sure, were of a rather visionary cast; but we seriously thought, nevertheless, of prolonging our stay in the valley for an indefinite period; and, with this understanding, we were turning over various plans for spending our time pleasantly, when several women came running into the house, and hurriedly besought us to *heree! heree!* (make our escape), crying out something about the *mickonarees.*

Thinking that we were about to be taken up under the act for the suppression of vagrancy, we flew out of the house, sprang into a canoe before the door, and paddled with might and main over to the opposite side of the lake.

Approaching Rartoo's dwelling, was a great crowd, among which we perceived several natives, who, from their partly European dress, we were certain did not reside in Tamai.

Plunging into the groves, we thanked our stars that we had thus narrowly escaped being apprehended as runaway seamen, and marched off to the beach. This, at least, was what we thought we had escaped.

Having fled the village, we could not think of prowling about its vicinity, and then returning; in doing so, we might be risking our liberty again. We therefore determined upon journeying back to Martair; and setting our faces thitherward, we reached the planters' house about night-fall. They gave us a cordial reception, and a hearty supper; and we sat up talking until a late hour.

We now prepared to go round to Taloo, a place from which we were not far off when at Tamai; but wishing to see as much of the island as we could, we preferred returning to Martair, and then going round by way of the beach.

Taloo, the only frequented harbor of Imeeo, lies on the western side of the island, almost directly over against Martair. Upon one shore of the bay stands the village of Partoowye, a missionary station. In its vicinity is an extensive sugar plantation—the best in the South Seas, perhaps—worked by a person from Sydney.

The patrimonial property of the husband of Pomaree, and every way a delightful retreat, Partoowye was one of the occasional residences of the court. But at the time I write of, it was permanently fixed there, the queen having fled thither from Tahiti.

Partoowye, they told us, was, by no means, the place Papeetee was. Ships seldom touched, and very few foreigners were living ashore. A solitary whaler, however, was reported to be lying in the harbor, wooding and watering, and said to be in want of men.

All things considered, I could not help looking upon Taloo as offering "a splendid opening " for us adventurers. To say nothing of the facilities presented for going to sea in the whaler, or hiring ourselves out as day laborers in the sugar plantation, there were hopes to be entertained of being promoted to some office of high trust and emolument, about the person of her majesty, the queen.

Nor was this expectation altogether Quixotic. In the train of many Polynesian princes, roving whites are frequently found: gentlemen pensioners of state, basking in the tropical sunshine of the court, and leading the pleasantest lives in the world. Upon islands little visited by foreigners, the first seaman that settles down, is generally domesticated in the family of the head chief or king; where he frequently discharges the functions of various offices, elsewhere filled by as many different individuals. As historiographer, for instance, he gives the natives some account of distant countries; as commissioner of the arts and sciences, he instructs them in the use of the jackknife, and the best way of shaping bits of iron hoop into spearheads; and as interpreter to his majesty, he facilitates intercourse with strangers; besides instructing the people generally in the uses of the most common English phrases, civil and profane; but oftener the latter.

These men generally marry well; often—like Hardy of Hannamanoo—into the blood royal.

Sometimes they officiate as personal attendant, or First Lord in Waiting, to the king. At Amboi, one of the Tonga Islands, a vagabond Welshman bends his knee as cupbearer to his cannibal majesty. He mixes his morning cup of " arva," and, with profound genuflections, presents it in a cocoa-nut bowl, richly carved. Upon another island of the same group, where it is customary to bestow no small pains in dressing the hair—frizzing it out by a curious process, into an enormous Pope's-head—an old man-of-war's-man fills the post of barber to the king. And as his majesty is not very neat, his mop is exceedingly populous; so that, when Jack is not engaged in dressing the head intrusted to his charge, he busies himself in gently titillating it—a sort of skewer being actually worn about in the patient's hair for that special purpose.

Even upon the Sandwich Islands, a low rabble of foreigners is kept about the person of Tammahammaha, for the purpose of ministering to his ease or enjoyment.

Billy Loon, a jolly little negro, tricked out in a soiled blue jacket, studded all over with rusty bell-buttons, and garnished with shabby gold lace, is the royal drummer and pounder of the tambourine. Joe, a wooden-legged Portu-guese, who lost his leg by a whale, is violinist; and Mordecai, as he is called, a villainous-looking scamp, going about with his cups and balls in a side pocket, diverts the court with his jugglery. These idle rascals receive no fixed salary, being altogether dependent upon the casual bounty of their master. Now and then they run up a score at the Dance Houses in Honolulu, where the illustrious Tamma-hammaha III. afterward calls and settles the bill.

A few years since, an auctioneer to his majesty, came near being added to the retinue of state. It seems that he was the first man who had practiced his vocation on the Sand-wich Islands; and delighted with the sport of bidding upon his wares, the king was one of his best customers. At last he besought the man to leave all and follow him, and he should be handsomely provided for at court. But the auctioneer refused; and so the ivory hammer lost the chance of being borne before him on a velvet cushion, when the next king went to be crowned.

But it was not as strolling players, nor as footmen out of employ, that the doctor and myself looked forward to our approaching introduction to the court of the Queen of Tahiti. On the contrary, as before hinted we expected to swell the appropriations of bread-fruit and cocoa-nuts on the Civil List, by filling some honorable office in her gift.

We were told, that to resist the usurpation of the French, the queen was rallying about her person all the foreigners she could. Her partiality for the English and Americans was well known; and this was an additional ground for

16

our anticipating a favorable reception. Zeke had informed us, moreover, that by the queen's counselors at Partoowye, a war of aggression against the invaders at Papeetee had been seriously thought of. Should this prove true, a surgeon's commission for the doctor, and a lieutenancy for myself, were certainly counted upon in our sanguine expectations.

Such, then, were our views, and such our hopes in projecting a trip to Taloo. But in our most lofty aspirations, we by no means lost sight of any minor matters which might help us to promotion. The doctor had informed me, that he excelled in playing the fiddle. I now suggested, that as soon as we arrived at Partoowye, we should endeavor to borrow a violin for him; or if this could not be done, that he should manufacture some kind of a substitute, and thus equipped, apply for an audience of the queen. Her well known passion for music would at once secure his admittance; and so, under the most favorable auspices, bring about our introduction to her notice.

"And who knows," said my waggish comrade, throwing his head back, and performing an imaginary air by briskly drawing one arm across the other, "who knows, that I may not fiddle myself into her majesty's good graces, so as to become a sort of Rizzio to the Tahitian princess."

CHAPTER LXVI.

HOW WE WERE TO GET TO TALOO.

THE inglorious circumstances of our somewhat premature departure from Tamai, filled the sagacious doctor, and myself, with sundry misgivings for the future.

Under Zeke's protection, we were secure from all impertinent interference in our concerns, on the part of the natives. But as friendless wanderers over the island, we ran the risk of being apprehended as runaways, and as such, sent back to Tahiti. The truth is, that the rewards constantly offered for the apprehension of deserters from ships, induce some of the natives to eye all strangers suspiciously.

A passport was therefore desirable; but such a thing had never been heard of in Imeeo. At last, Long Ghost suggested, that as the Yankee was well known, and much respected all over the island, we should endeavor to obtain from him some sort of paper, not only certifying to our having been in his employ, but also to our not being highwaymen, kidnappers, nor yet runaway seamen. Even written in English, a paper like this would answer every purpose; for the unlettered natives, standing in great awe of the document, would not dare to molest us until acquainted with its purport. Then, if it came to the worst, we might repair to the nearest missionary, and have the passport explained.

Upon informing Zeke of these matters, he seemed highly flattered with the opinion we entertained of his reputation abroad; and he agreed to oblige us. The doctor at once offered to furnish him with a draught of the paper; but he refused, saying he would write it himself. With a rooster's quill, therefore, a bit of soiled paper, and a stout heart, he set to work. Evidently, he was not accustomed to composition; for his literary throes were so violent, that the doctor suggested that some sort of a Cæsarian operation might be necessary.

The precious paper was at last finished; and a great curiosity it was. We were much diverted with his reasons for not dating it.

"In this here dumned climmate," he observed, "a feller can't keep the run of the months, no how; cause there's no seasons; no summer and winter, to go by. One's etarnally thinkin' it's always July, it's so pesky hot."

A passport provided, we cast about for some means of getting to Taloo.

The island of Imeeo is very nearly surrounded by a regular breakwater of coral, extending within a mile or less of the shore. The smooth canal within, furnishes the best means of communication with the different settlements; all of which, with the exception of Tamai, are right upon the water. And so indolent are the Imeeose, that they think nothing of going twenty or thirty miles round the island in a canoe, in order to reach a place not a quarter of that distance by land. But as hinted before, the fear of the bullocks has something to do with this.

The idea of journeying in a canoe struck our fancy quite pleasantly; and we at once set about chartering one, if possible. But none could we obtain. For not only did we have nothing to pay for hiring one, but we could not expect to have it loaned; inasmuch as the good-natured owner would, in all probability, have to walk along the beach as we paddled, in order to bring back his property when we had no further use for it.

At last, it was decided to commence our journey on foot; trusting that we would soon fall in with a canoe going our way, in which we might take passage.

The planters said we would find no beaten path: —all we had to do was to follow the beach; and however inviting it might look inland, on no account must we stray from it. In short, the longest way round was the nearest way to Taloo. At intervals, there were little hamlets along the shore, besides lonely fishermen's huts here and there, where we could get plenty to eat without pay; so there was no necessity to lay in any store.

Intending to be off before sunrise the next morning, so as to have the benefit of the coolest part of the day, we bade our kind hosts farewell, overnight; and then, repairing to the beach, we lanched our floating pallet, and slept away merrily till dawn.

CHAPTER LXVII.

THE JOURNEY ROUND THE BEACH.

It was on the fourth day of the first month of the Hegira, or Flight from Tamai (we now reckoned our time thus), that, rising bright and early, we were up and away out of the valley of Martair, before the fishermen even were stirring.

It was the earliest dawn. The morning only showed itself along the lower edge of a bank of purple clouds, pierced by the misty peaks of Tahiti. The tropical day seemed too languid to rise. Sometimes, starting fitfully, it decked the clouds with faint edgings of pink and gray, which, fading away, left all dim again. Anon, it threw out thin, pale rays, growing lighter and lighter, until at last, the golden morning sprang out of the East with a bound— darting its bright beams hither and thither, higher and higher, and sending them, broadcast, over the face of the heavens.

All balmy from the groves of Tahiti, came an indolent air, cooled by its transit over the waters; and grateful under foot, was the damp and slightly yielding beach, from which the waves seemed just retired.

The doctor was in famous spirits; removing his Roora, he went splashing into the sea; and, after swimming a few yards, waded ashore, hopping, skipping, and jumping along the beach; but very careful to cut all his capers in the direction of our journey.

Say what they will of the glowing independence one feels in the saddle, give me the first morning flush of your cheery pedestrian!

Thus exhilarated, we went on, as light-hearted and care-free, as we could wish.

And here, I can not refrain from lauding the very superior inducements which most intertropical countries afford, not only to mere rovers like ourselves, but to penniless people, generally. In these genial regions, one's wants are naturally diminished; and those which remain are easily gratified: fuel, house-shelter, and, if you please, clothing, may be entirely dispensed with.

How different, our hard northern latitudes! Alas! the lot of a "poor devil," twenty degrees north of the tropic of Cancer, is indeed pitiable.

At last, the beach contracted to hardly a yard's width, and the dense thicket almost dipped into the sea. In place of the smooth sand, too, we had sharp fragments of broken coral, which made traveling exceedingly unpleasant. " Lord! my foot! " roared the doctor, fetching it up for inspection, with a galvanic fling of the limb. A sharp splinter had thrust itself into the flesh, through a hole in his boot. My sandals were worse yet; their soles taking a sort of fossil impression of every thing trod upon.

Turning round a bold sweep of the beach, we came upon a piece of fine, open ground, with a fisherman's dwelling in the distance, crowning a knoll which rolled off into the water.

The hut proved to be a low, rude erection, very recently thrown up; for the bamboos were still green as grass, and the thatching, fresh and fragrant as meadow hay. It was open upon three sides; so that, upon drawing near, the domestic arrangements within were in plain sight. No one was stirring; and nothing was to be seen but a clumsy old chest of native workmanship, a few calabashes, and bundles of tappa hanging against a post; and a heap of something, we knew not what, in a dark corner. Upon close inspection, the doctor discovered it to be a loving old couple, locked in each other's arms, and rolled together in a tappa mantle.

" Halloa! Darby! " he cried, shaking the one with a beard. But Darby heeded him not; though Joan, a wrinkled old body, started up in affright, and yelled aloud. Neither of us attempting to gag her, she presently became quiet; and after staring hard, and asking some unintelligible questions, she proceeded to rouse her still slumbering mate.

What ailed him, we could not tell; but there was no waking him. Equally in vain were all his dear spouse's cuffs, pinches, and other endearments; he lay like a log, face up, and snoring away like a cavalry trumpeter.

" Here, my good woman," said Long Ghost, " just let *me* try;" and, taking the patient right by his nose, he so lifted him bodily, into a sitting position, and held him there until his eyes opened. When this event came to pass, Darby looked round like one stupefied; and then, springing to his feet, backed away into a corner, from which place, we became the objects of his earnest and respectful attention.

" Permit me, my dear Darby, to introduce to you my esteemed friend and comrade, Paul," said the doctor, gallanting me up with all the grimace and flourish imaginable. Upon this, Darby began to recover his faculties, and surprised us not a little, by talking a few words of English. So far as could be understood, they were expressive of his having been aware, that there were two " karhowrees " in the neighborhood; that he was glad to see us, and would have something for us to eat in no time.

How he came by his English, was explained to us before we left. Some time previous, he had been a denizen of Papeetee, where the native language is broidered over with the most classic sailor phrases. He seemed to be quite proud of his residence there; and alluded to it, in the same significant way, in which a provincial informs you, that in his time he has resided in the capital. The old fellow was disposed to be garrulous; but being sharp-set, we told him to get breakfast; after which we would hear his anecdotes. While employed among the calabashes, the strange, antiquated fondness between these old semi-savages was really amusing. I made no doubt, that they were saying to each other, " yes, my love "—" no, my life," just in the same way that some young couples do, at home.

They gave us a hearty meal; and while we were discussing its merits, they assured us, over and over again, that they expected nothing in return for their attentions; more: we were at liberty to stay as long as we pleased; and as long as we *did* stay, their house and every thing they had, was no longer theirs, but ours; still more: they themselves were our slaves—the old lady, to a degree that was altogether superfluous. This, now, is Tahitian hospitality! Self-immolation upon one's own hearthstone for the benefit of the guest.

The Polynesians carry their hospitality to an amazing extent. Let a native of Waiurar, the westernmost part of Tahiti, make his appearance as a traveler at Partoowye, the most easternly village of Imeeo; though a perfect stranger, the inhabitants on all sides accost him at their doorways, inviting him to enter, and make himself at home. But the traveler passes on, examining every house attentively; until at last, he pauses before one which suits him, and then exclaiming, "ah, ena maitai" (this one will do, I think), he steps in, and makes himself perfectly at ease; flinging himself upon the mats, and very probably calling for a nice young cocoa-nut, and a piece of toasted bread-fruit, sliced thin, and done brown.

Curious to relate, however, should a stranger carrying it thus bravely, be afterward discovered to be without a house of his own, why, he may thenceforth go a-begging for his lodgings. The "karhowrees," or white men, are exceptions to this rule. Thus is it precisely as in civilized countries; where those who have houses and lands, are incessantly bored to death with invitations to come and live in other people's houses; while many a poor gentleman who inks the seams of his coat, and to whom the like invitation would be really acceptable, may go and sue for it. But to the credit of the ancient Tahitians, it should here be observed, that this blemish upon their hospitality is only of recent origin, and was wholly unknown in old times. So told me, Captain Bob.

In Polynesia, it is esteemed " a great hit," if a man succeed in marrying into a family, to which the best part of the community is related (Heaven knows it is otherwise with us). The reason is, that when he goes a-traveling, the greater number of houses are the more completely at his service.

Receiving a paternal benediction from old Darby and Joan, we continued our journey; resolved to stop at the very next place of attraction which offered.

Nor did we long stroll for it. A fine walk along a beach of shells, and we came to a spot, where, with trees here and there, the land was all meadow, sloping away to the water, which stirred a sedgy growth of reeds bordering its margin. Close by, was a little cove, walled in with coral, where a fleet of canoes was dancing up and down. A few paces distant, on a natural terrace overlooking the sea, were several native dwellings, newly thatched, and peeping into view out of the foliage, like summer-houses.

As we drew near, forth came a burst of voices; and presently, three gay girls, overflowing with life, health, and youth; and full of spirits and mischief. One was arrayed in a flaunting robe of calico; and her long black hair was braided behind in two immense tresses, joined together at the ends, and wreathed with the green tendrils of a vine. From her self-possessed and forward air, I fancied she might be some young lady from Papeetee, on a visit to her country relations. Her companions wore mere slips of cotton cloth; their hair was disheveled; and though very pretty, they betrayed the reserve and embarassment, characteristic of the provinces.

The little gipsy first mentioned, ran up to me with great cordiality; and giving the Tahitian salutation, opened upon me such a fire of questions, that there was no understanding, much less answering them. But our hearty welcome to Loohooloo, as she called the hamlet, was made plain enough. Meanwhile, Doctor Long Ghost gallantly presented an arm to each of the other young ladies; which, at first, they knew not what to make of; but at last, taking it for some kind of joke, accepted the civility.

The names of these three damsels were at once made known by themselves; and being so exceedingly romantic, I can not forbear particularizing them. Upon my comrade's arms, then, were hanging Night and Morning, in the persons of Farnowar, or the Day-Born, and Farnoopoo, or the Night-Born. She with the tresses, was very appropriately styled Marhar-Rarrar, the Wakeful, or Bright-Eyed.

By this time, the houses were emptied of the rest of their inmates—a few old men and women, and several strapping young fellows rubbing their eyes and yawning. All crowded round, putting questions as to whence we came. Upon being informed of our acquaintance with Zeke, they were delighted; and one of them recognized the boots worn by the doctor. " Keekee (Zeke) maitai," they cried, " nuee nuee hanna hanna portarto "—(makes plenty of potatoes).

There was now a little friendly altercation, as to who should have the honor of entertaining the strangers. At last, a tall old gentleman, by name Marharvai, with a bald head and white beard, took us each by the hand, and led us into his dwelling. Once inside, Marharvai, pointing about with his staff, was so obsequious in assuring us that his house was ours, that Long Ghost suggested, he might as well hand over the deed.

It was drawing near noon; so after a light lunch of roasted bread-fruit, a few whiffs of a pipe, and some lively chatting, our host admonished the company to lie down, and take the everlasting siesta. We complied; and had a social nap all round.

CHAPTER LXVIII.

A DINNER-PARTY IN IMEEO.

It was just in the middle of the merry, mellow after-noon, that they ushered us to dinner, underneath a green shelter of palm boughs; open all round, and so low at the eaves, that we stooped to enter.

Within, the ground was strewn over with aromatic ferns —called " nahee "—freshly gathered; which, stirred under foot, diffused the sweetest odor. On one side was a row of yellow mats, inwrought with fibres of bark, stained a bright red. Here, seated after the fashion of the Turk, we looked out, over a verdant bank, upon the mild, blue, endless Pacific. So far round had we skirted the island, that the view of Tahiti was now intercepted.

Upon the ferns before us, were laid several layers of broad, thick " pooroo " leaves; lapping over, one upon the other. And upon these were placed, side by side, newly plucked banana leaves, at least two yards in length, and very wide; the stalks were withdrawn, so as to make them lie flat. This green cloth was set out and garnished, in the manner following: —

First, a number of " pooroo " leaves, by way of plates, were ranged along on one side; and by each was a rustic nut-bowl, half-filled with sea-water, and a Tahitian roll, or small bread-fruit, roasted brown. An immense flat cala-bash, placed in the centre, was heaped up with numberless small packages of moist, steaming leaves: in each was a small fish, baked in the earth, and done to a turn. This pyramid of a dish, was flanked on either side by an orna-mental calabash. One was brimming with the golden-hued " poee," or pudding, made from the red plantain of the mountains: the other was stacked up with cakes of the Indian turnip, previously macerated in a mortar, kneaded with the milk of the cocoa-nut, and then baked. In the spaces between the three dishes, were piled young cocoa-nuts, stripped of their husks. Their eyes had been opened and enlarged; so that each was a ready-charged goblet.

There was a sort of side-cloth in one corner, upon which, in bright, buff jackets, lay the fattest of bananas; " avees," red-ripe; guavas, with the shadows of their crimson pulp flushing through a transparent skin, and almost coming and going there like blushes; oranges, tinged, here and there, berry-brown; and great, jolly melons, which rolled about in very portliness. Such a heap! All ruddy, ripe, and round —bursting with the good cheer of the tropical soil, from which they sprang!

" A land of orchards! " cried the doctor, in a rapture; and he snatched a morsel from a sort of fruit of which gentlemen of the sanguine temperament are remarkably fond; namely, the ripe cherry lips of Miss Day-Born, who stood looking on.

Marharvai allotted seats to his guests; and the meal began. Thinking that his hospitality needed some acknow-ledgment, I rose, and pledged him in the vegetable wine of the cocoa-nut; merely repeating the ordinary salutation, " Yar onor boyoee." Sensible that some compliment, after the fashion of white men, was paid him, with a smile, and a courteous flourish of the hand, he bade me be seated. No people, however refined, are more easy and graceful in their manners than the Imeeose.

The doctor, sitting next our host, now came under his special protection. Laying before his guest one of the packages of fish, Marharvai opened it; and commended its contents to his particular regards. But my comrade was one of those, who, on convivial occasions, can always take care of themselves. He ate an indefinite number of " Pehee Lee Lees " (small fish), his own and next neighbor's breadfruit; and helped himself, to right and left, with all the ease of an accomplished diner-out.

" Paul," said he, at last, " you don't seem to be getting along; why don't you try the pepper sauce? " and, by way of example, he steeped a morsel of food into his nutful of sea-water. On following suit, I found it quite piquant, though rather bitter; but, on the whole, a capital substitute for salt. The Imeeose invariably use sea-water in this way, deeming it quite a treat; and considering that their country is surrounded by an ocean of catsup, the luxury can not be deemed an expensive one.

The fish were delicious; the manner of cooking them in the ground, preserving all the juices, and rendering them exceedingly sweet and tender. The plantain pudding was almost cloying; the cakes of Indian turnip, quite palatable; and the roasted bread-fruit, crisp as toast.

During the meal, a native lad walked round and round the party; carrying a long staff of bamboo. This he occasionally tapped upon the cloth, before each guest; when a white clotted substance dropped forth, with a savor not unlike that of a curd. This proved to be " Lownee," an excellent relish, prepared from the grated meat of ripe cocoa-nuts, moistened with cocoa-nut milk and salt water, and kept perfectly tight, until a little past the saccharine stage of fermentation.

Throughout the repast there was much lively chatting among the islanders, in which their conversational powers quite exceeded ours. The young ladies, too, showed themselves very expert in the use of their tongues, and contributed much to the gayety which prevailed.

Nor did these lively nymphs suffer the meal to languish; for upon the doctor's throwing himself back, with an air of much satisfaction, they sprang to their feet, and pelted him with oranges and guavas. This, at last, put an end to the entertainment.

By a hundred whimsical oddities, my long friend became a great favorite with these people; and they bestowed upon him a long, comical title, expressive of his lank figure and Roora combined. The latter, by the by, never failed to excite the remark of every body we encountered.

The giving of nicknames is quite a passion with the people of Tahiti and Imeeo. No one, with any peculiarity, whether of person or temper, is exempt; not even strangers.

A pompous captain of a man-of-war, visiting Tahiti for the second time, discovered that, among the natives, he went by the dignified title of " Atee Poee "—literally, Poee Head, or Pudding Head. Nor is the highest rank among themselves any protection. The first husband of the present queen was commonly known in the court circles, as " Pot Belly." He carried the greater part of his person before him, to be sure, and so did the gentlemanly George IV.— but what a title for a king consort!

Even " Pomaree " itself, the royal patronymic, was. originally, a mere nickname; and literally signifies, one talking through his nose. The first monarch of that name, being on a war party, and sleeping overnight among the mountains, awoke one morning with a cold in his head; and some wag of a courtier, had no more manners than to vulgarize him thus.

How different from the volatile Polynesian in this, as in all other respects, is our grave and decorous North American Indian. While the former bestows a name, in accordance with some humorous or ignoble trait, the latter seizes upon what is deemed the most exalted or warlike: and hence, among the red tribes, we have the truly patrician appellations of " White Eagles," " Young Oaks," " Fiery Eyes," and " Bended Bows."

CHAPTER LXIX.

THE COCOA-PALM.

WHILE the doctor and the natives were taking a digestive nap after dinner, I strolled forth to have a peep at the country, which could produce so generous a meal.

To my surprise, a fine strip of land in the vicinity of the hamlet, and protected seaward by a grove of cocoa-nut and bread-fruit trees, was under high cultivation. Sweet potatoes, Indian turnips, and yams were growing; also melons, a few pine-apples, and other fruits. Still more pleasing was the sight, of young bread-fruit and cocoa-nut trees set out with great care, as if, for once, the improvident Polynesian had thought of his posterity. But this was the only instance of native thrift which ever came under my observation. For, in all my rambles over Tahiti and Imeeo, nothing so much struck me as the comparative scarcity of these trees in many places where they ought to abound. Entire valleys, like Martair, of inexhaustible fertility, are abandoned to all the rankness of untamed vegetation. Alluvial flats bordering the sea, and watered by streams from the mountains, are overgrown with a wild, scrub guava-bush, introduced by foreigners, and which spreads with such fatal rapidity, that the natives, standing still while it grows, anticipate its covering the entire island. Even tracts of clear land, which, with so little pains, might be made to wave with orchards, lie wholly neglected.

When I considered their unequaled soil and climate, thus unaccountably slighted, I often turned in amazement upon the natives about Papeetee; some of whom all but starve in their gardens run to waste. Upon other islands which I have visited, of similar fertility, and wholly unreclaimed from their first discovered condition, no spectacle of this sort was presented.

The high estimation in which many of their fruit-trees are held by the Tahitians and Imeeose—their beauty in the landscape—their manifold uses, and the facility with which they are propagated, are considerations which render the remissness alluded to still more unaccountable. The cocoa-palm is as an example; a tree by far the most important production of Nature in the Tropics. To the Polynesian, it is emphatically the Tree of Life; transcending even the bread-fruit in the multifarious uses to which it is applied.

Its very aspect is imposing. Asserting its supremacy by an erect and lofty bearing, it may be said to compare with other trees, as man with inferior creatures.

The blessings it confers are incalculable. Year after year, the islander reposes beneath its shade, both eating and drinking of its fruit; he thatches his hut with its boughs, and weaves them into baskets to carry his food; he cools himself with a fan platted from the young leaflets, and shields his head from the sun by a bonnet of the leaves; sometimes he clothes himself with the cloth-like substance which wraps round the base of the stalks, whose elastic rods, strung with filberts, are used as a taper; the larger nuts, thinned and polished, furnish him with a beautiful goblet: the smaller ones, with bowls for his pipes; the dry husks kindle his fires; their fibres are twisted into fishing-lines and cords for his canoes; he heals his wounds with a balsam compounded from the juice of the nut; and with the oil extracted from its meat, embalms the bodies of the dead.

The noble trunk itself is far from being valueless. Sawn into posts, it upholds the islander's dwelling; converted into charcoal, it cooks his food; and supported on blocks of stone, rails in his lands. He impels his canoe through the water with a paddle of the wood, and goes to battle with clubs and spears of the same hard material.

In pagan Tahiti a cocoa-nut branch was the symbol of regal authority. Laid upon the sacrifice in the temple, it made the offering sacred; and with it, the priests chastised and put to flight the evil spirits which assailed them. The supreme majesty of Oro, the great god of their mythology, was declared in the cocoa-nut log from which his image was rudely carved. Upon one of the Tonga Islands, there stands a living tree, revered itself as a deity. Even upon the

Sandwich Islands, the cocoa-palm retains all its ancient reputation; the people there having thought of adopting it as the national emblem.

The cocoa-nut is planted as follows: Selecting a suitable place, you drop into the ground a fully ripe nut, and leave it. In a few days, a thin, lance-like shoot forces itself through a minute hole in the shell, pierces the husk, and soon unfolds three pale-green leaves in the air; while originating, in the same soft white sponge which now completely fills the nut, a pair of fibrous roots, pushing away the stoppers which close two holes in an opposite direction, penetrate the shell, and strike vertically into the ground. A day or two more, and the shell and husk, which, in the last and germinating stage of the nut, are so hard that a knife will scarcely make any impression, spontaneously burst by some force within; and, henceforth, the hardy young plant thrives apace; and needing no culture, pruning, or attention of any sort, rapidly advances to maturity. In four or five years it bears; in twice as many more, it begins to lift its head among the groves, where, waxing strong, it flourishes for near a century.

Thus, as some voyager has said, the man who but drops one of these nuts into the ground, may be said to confer a greater, and more certain benefit upon himself and posterity, than many a life's toil in less genial climes.

The fruitfulness of the tree is remarkable. As long as it lives, it bears; and without intermission. Two hundred nuts, besides innumerable white blossoms of others, may be seen upon it at one time; and though a whole year is required to bring any one of them to the germinating point, no two, perhaps, are at one time in precisely the same stage of growth.

The tree delights in a maritime situation. In its greatest perfection, it is perhaps found right on the sea-shore, where its roots are actually washed. But such instances are only met with upon islands where the swell of the sea is prevented from breaking on the beach by an encircling reef. No saline flavor is perceptible in the nut produced in such a place. Although it bears in any soil, whether upland or bottom, it does not flourish vigorously inland; and I have frequently observed, that when met with far up the valleys, its tall stem inclines seaward, as if pining after a more genial region.

It is a curious fact, that if you deprive the cocoa-nut tree of the verdant tuft at its head, it dies at once; and if allowed to stand thus, the trunk, which, when alive, is encased in so hard a bark, as to be almost impervious to a bullet, molders away, and, in an incredibly short period, becomes dust. This is, perhaps, partly owing to the peculiar constitution of the trunk, a mere cylinder of minute hollow reeds, closely packed, and very hard; but when exposed at top, peculiarly fitted to convey moisture and decay through the entire stem.

The finest orchard of cocoa-palms I know, and the only plantation of them I ever saw at the islands, is one that stands right upon the southern shore of Papeetee Bay. They were set out by the first Pomaree, almost half-a-century ago; and the soil being especially adapted to their growth, the noble trees now form a magnificent grove, nearly a mile in extent. No other plant, scarcely a bush, is to be seen within its precincts. The Broom Road passes through its entire length.

At noonday, this grove is one of the most beautiful, serene, witching places that ever was seen. High overhead, are ranges of green rustling arches; through which the sun's rays come down to you in sparkles. You seem to be wandering through illimitable halls of pillars; everywhere you catch glimpses of stately aisles, intersecting each other at all points. A strange silence, too, reigns far and near; the air, flushed with the mellow stillness of a sunset.

But after the long morning calms, the sea-breeze comes in; and creeping over the tops of these thousand trees, they nod their plumes. Soon the breeze freshens; and you hear the branches brushing against each other; and the flexible trunks begin to sway. Toward evening, the whole grove is rocking to and fro; and the traveler on the Broom Road is startled by the frequent falling of the nuts, snapped from their brittle stems. They come flying through the air, ring-

17

ing like jugglers' balls; and often bound along the ground for many rods.

CHAPTER LXX.

LIFE AT LOOHOOLOO.

FINDING the society at Loohooloo very pleasant, the young ladies, in particular, being extremely sociable; and, moreover, in love with the famous good cheer of old Marharvai, we acquiesced in an invitation of his, to tarry a few days longer. We might then, he said, join a small canoe party, which was going to a place a league or two distant. So averse to all exertion are these people, that they really thought the prospect of thus getting rid of a few miles' walking, would prevail with us, even if there were no other inducement.

The people of the hamlet, as we soon discovered, formed a snug little community of cousins; of which our host seemed the head. Marharvai, in truth, was a petty chief, who owned the neighboring lands. And as the wealthy, in most cases, rejoice in a numerous kindred, the family footing upon which every body visited him, was, perhaps, ascribable to the fact, of his being the lord of the manor. Like Captain Bob, he was, in some things, a gentleman of the old school—a stickler for the customs of a past and pagan age.

Nowhere else, except in Tamai, did we find the manners of the natives less vitiated by recent changes. The old-fashioned Tahitian dinner they gave us on the day of our arrival, was a fair sample of their general mode of living.

Our time passed delightfully. The doctor went his way, and I mine. With a pleasant companion, he was forever strolling inland, ostensibly to collect botanical specimens; while I, for the most part, kept near the sea; sometimes taking the girls an aquatic excursion in a canoe.

Often we went fishing; not dozing over stupid hooks and lines, but leaping right into the water, and chasing our prey over the coral rocks, spear in hand.

Spearing fish is glorious sport. The Imeeose, all round the island, catch them in no other way. The smooth shallows between the reef and the shore, and, at low water, the reef itself, being admirably adapted to this mode of capturing them. At almost any time of the day—save ever the sacred hour of noon—you may see the fish-hunters pursuing their sport; with loud halloos, brandishing their spears, and splashing through the water in all directions. Sometimes a solitary native is seen, far out upon a lonely shallow, wading slowly along, with eye intent and poised spear.

But the best sport of all, is going out upon the great reef itself, by torch-light. The natives follow this recreation with as much spirit as a gentleman of England does the chase; and take full as much delight in it.

The torch is nothing more than a bunch of dry reeds, bound firmly together: the spear, a long, light pole, with an iron head, on one side barbed.

I shall never forget the night, that old Marharvai and the rest of us, paddling off to the reef, leaped at midnight upon the coral ledges with waving torches and spears. We were more than a mile from the land; the sullen ocean, thundering upon the outside of the rocks, dashed the spray in our faces, almost extinguishing the flambeaux; and, far as the eye could reach, the darkness of sky and water was streaked with a long, misty line of foam, marking the course of the coral barrier. The wild fishermen, flourishing their weapons, and yelling like so many demons to scare their prey, sprang from ledge to ledge, and sometimes darted their spears in the very midst of the breakers.

But fish-spearing was not the only sport we had at Loohooloo. Right on the beach was a mighty old cocoa-nut tree, the roots of which had been underwashed by the waves, so that the trunk inclined far over its base. From the tuft of the tree, a stout cord of bark depended, the end of which swept the water several yards from the shore.

This was a Tahitian swing. A native lad seizes hold of the cord, and, after swinging to and fro quite leisurely, all at once sends himself fifty or sixty feet from the water, rushing through the air like a rocket. I doubt whether any of our rope-dancers would attempt the feat. For my own part, I had neither head nor heart for it; so, after sending a lad aloft with an additional cord, by way of security, I constructed a large basket of green boughs, in which I and some particular friends of mine, used to swing over sea and land by the hour.

CHAPTER LXXI.

WE START FOR TALOO.

BRIGHT was the morning, and brighter still the smiles of the young ladies who accompanied us, when we sprang into a sort of family canoe—wide and roomy—and bade adieu to the hospitable Marharvai and his tenantry. As we paddled away, they stood upon the beach, waving their hands, and crying out, " aroha! aroha! " (farewell! farewell!) as long as we were within hearing.

Very sad at parting with them, we endeavored, nevertheless, to console ourselves in the society of our fellow-passengers. Among these were two old ladies; but as they said nothing to us, we will say nothing about them; nor any thing about the old men who managed the canoe. But of the three mischievous, dark-eyed young witches, who lounged in the stern of that comfortable old island gondola, I have a great deal to say.

In the first place, one of them was Marhar-Rarrar, the Bright-Eyed; and, in the second place, neither she nor the romps, her companions, ever dreamed of taking the voyage, until the doctor and myself announced our intention; their going along was nothing more than a madcap frolic; in short, they were a parcel of wicked hoydens, bent on

mischief, who laughed in your face when you looked sentimental, and only tolerated your company when making
merry at your expense.

Something or other about us was perpetually awaking
their mirth. Attributing this to his own remarkable figure,
the doctor increased their enjoyment, by assuming the part
of a Merry Andrew. Yet his cap and bells never jingled but
to some tune; and while playing the Tom-fool, I more than
suspected that he was trying to play the rake. At home, it
is deemed auspicious to go a-wooing in epaulets; but among
the Polynesians, your best dress in courting is motley.

A fresh breeze springing up, we set our sail of matting,
and glided along as tranquilly as if floating upon an inland
stream; the white reef on one hand, and the green shore
on the other.

Soon, as we turned a headland, we encountered another
canoe, paddling with might and main in an opposite direction; the strangers shouting to each other, and a tall
fellow, in the bow, dancing up and down like a crazy man.
They shot by us like an arrow, though our fellow-voyagers
shouted again and again, for them to cease paddling.

According to the natives, this was a kind of royal mail-
canoe, carrying a message from the queen to her friends
in a distant part of the island.

Passing several shady bowers, which looked quite inviting, we proposed touching, and diversifying the monoto-
ny of a sea-voyage by a stroll ashore. So, forcing our canoe
among the bushes, behind a decayed palm, lying partly in
the water, we left the old folks to take a nap in the shade,
and gallanted the others among the trees, which were here
trellised with vines and creeping shrubs.

In the early part of the afternoon, we drew near the
place to which the party were going. It was a solitary house,
inhabited by four or five old women, who, when we
entered, were gathered in a circle about the mats, eating
poee from a cracked calabash. They seemed delighted at
seeing our companions, but rather drew up when introduced to ourselves. Eying us distrustfully, they whispered to
know who we were. The answers they received were not

satisfactory; for they treated us with marked coolness and reserve, and seemed desirous of breaking off our acquaintance with the girls. Unwilling, therefore, to stay where our company was disagreeable, we resolved to depart, without even eating a meal.

Informed of this, Marhar-Rarrar and her companions evinced the most lively concern; and equally unmindful of their former spirits, and the remonstrances of the old ladies, broke forth into sobs and lamentations, which were not to be withstood. We agreed, therefore, to tarry until they left for home; which would be at the " Aheharar," or Falling of the Sun; in other words, at sunset.

When the hour arrived, after much leave-taking, we saw them safely embarked. As the canoe turned a bluff, they seized the paddles from the hands of the old men, and waved them silently in the air. This was meant for a touching farewell, as the paddle is only waved thus, when the parties separating, never more expect to meet.

We now continued our journey; and following the beach, soon came to a level and lofty overhanging bank, which, planted here and there with trees, took a broad sweep round a considerable part of the island. A fine pathway skirted the edge of the bank; and often we paused to admire the scenery. The evening was still and fair, even for so heavenly a climate; and all round, far as the eye could reach, was the blending blue sky and ocean.

As we went on, the reef-belt still accompanied us; turning as we turned, and thundering its distant bass upon the ear, like the unbroken roar of a cataract. Dashing forever against their coral rampart, the breakers looked, in the distance, like a line of rearing white chargers, reined in, tossing their white manes, and bridling with foam.

These great natural breakwaters are admirably designed for the protection of the land. Nearly all the Society Islands are defended by them. Were the vast swells of the Pacific to break against the soft alluvial bottoms which in many places border the sea, the soil would soon be washed away, and the natives be thus deprived of their most productive lands. As it is, the banks of no rivulet are firmer.

But the coral barriers answer another purpose. They form all the harbors of this group, including the twenty-four round about the shores of Tahiti. Curiously enough, the openings in the reefs, by which alone vessels enter to their anchorage, are invariably opposite the mouths of running streams: an advantage fully appreciated by the mariner who touches for the purpose of watering his ship.

It is said, that the fresh water of the land, mixing with the salts held in solution by the sea, so acts upon the latter, as to resist the formation of the coral; and hence the breaks. Here and there, these openings are sentineled, as it were, by little fairy islets, green as emerald, and waving with palms. Strangely and beautifully diversifying the long line of breakers, no objects can strike the fancy more vividly. Pomaree II., with a taste in watering-places truly Tahitian, selected one of them as a royal retreat. We passed it on our journey.

Omitting several further adventures which befell us after leaving the party from Loohooloo, we must now hurry on, to relate what happened just before reaching the place of our destination.

CHAPTER LXXII.

A DEALER IN THE CONTRABAND.

It must have been at least the tenth day, reckoning from the Hegira, that we found ourselves the guests of Varvy, an old hermit of an islander, who kept house by himself, perhaps a couple of leagues from Taloo.

A stone's cast from the beach there was a fantastic rock, moss-grown, and deep in a dell. It was insulated by a shallow brook, which, dividing its waters, flowed on both sides, until united below. Twisting its roots round the rock, a gnarled " Aoa " spread itself overhead in a wilderness of foliage; the elastic branch-roots depending from the larger

boughs, insinuating themselves into every cleft, thus forming supports to the parent stem. In some places, these
pendulous branches, half-grown, had not yet reached the
rock; swinging their loose fibrous ends in the air like
whiplashes.

Varvy's hut, a mere coop of bamboos, was perched upon
a level part of the rock, the ridge-pole resting at one end
in a crotch of the "Aoa," and the other, propped by a
forked bough planted in a fissure.

Notwithstanding our cries as we drew near, the first hint
the old hermit received of our approach, was the doctor's
stepping up and touching his shoulder, as he was kneeling
over on a stone, cleaning fish in the brook. He leaped up,
and stared at us. But with a variety of uncouth gestures,
he soon made us welcome; informing us, by the same
means, that he was both deaf and dumb; he then motioned
us into his dwelling.

Going in, we threw ourselves upon an old mat, and
peered round. The soiled bamboos and calabashes looked
so uninviting, that the doctor was for pushing on to Taloo
that night, notwithstanding it was near sunset. But at length
we concluded to stay where we were.

After a good deal of bustling outside under a decrepit
shed, the old man made his appearance with our supper. In
one hand he held a flickering taper, and in the other, a
huge, flat calabash, scantily filled with viands. His eyes were
dancing in his head, and he looked from the calabash to
us, and from us to the calabash, as much as to say, "Ah,
my lads, what do ye think of this, eh? Pretty good cheer,
eh?" But the fish and Indian turnip being none of the
best, we made but a sorry meal. While discussing it, the
old man tried hard to make himself understood by signs;
most of which were so excessively ludicrous, that we made
no doubt he was perpetrating a series of pantomimic jokes.

The remnants of the feast removed, our host left us for
a moment, returning with a calabash of portly dimensions,
and furnished with a long, hooked neck, the mouth of which
was stopped with a wooden plug. It was covered with parti-

cles of earth, and looked as if just taken from some place under ground.

With sundry winks and horrible giggles peculiar to the dumb, the vegetable demijohn was now tapped; the old fellow looking round cautiously, and pointing at it; as much as to intimate, that it contained some thing which was " taboo," or forbidden.

Aware that intoxicating liquors were strictly prohibited to the natives, we now watched our entertainer with much interest. Charging a cocoa-nut shell, he tossed it off, and then filling up again, presented the goblet to me. Disliking the smell, I made faces at it; upon which he became highly excited; so much so, that a miracle was wrought upon the spot. Snatching the cup from my hands, he shouted out, " Ah, karhowree sabbee lee-lee, ena arva tee maitai! " in other words, what a blockhead of a white man! this is the real stuff!

We could not have been more startled, had a frog leaped from his mouth. For an instant, he looked confused enough himself; and then placing a finger mysteriously upon his mouth, he contrived to make us understand, that at times he was subject to a suspension of the powers of speech.

Deeming the phenomenon a remarkable one, every way, the doctor desired him to open his mouth, so that he might have a look down. But he refused.

This occurrence made us rather suspicious of our host; nor could we afterward account for his conduct, except by supposing that his feigning dumbness might in some way or other assist him in the nefarious pursuits, in which it afterward turned out that he was engaged. This conclusion, however, was not altogether satisfactory.

To oblige him, we at last took a sip of his " arva tee," and found it very crude, and strong as Lucifer. Curious to know whence it was obtained, we questioned him; when, lighting up with pleasure, he seized the taper, and led us outside the hut, bidding us follow.

After going some distance through the woods, we came to a dismantled old shed of boughs, apparently abandoned to decay. Underneath, nothing was to be seen but heaps of decaying leaves and an immense, clumsy jar, wide-mouthed, and, by some means, rudely hollowed out from a ponderous stone.

Here, for a while, we were left to ourselves; the old man placing the light in the jar, and then disappearing. He returned, carrying a long, large bamboo, and a crotched stick. Throwing these down, he poked under a pile of rubbish, and brought out a rough block of wood, pierced through and through with a hole, which was immediately clapped on top of the jar. Then planting the crotched stick upright about two yards distant, and making it sustain one end of the bamboo, he inserted the other end of the latter into the hole in the block; concluding these arrangements, by placing an old calabash under the farther end of the bamboo.

Coming up to us now with a sly, significant look, and pointing admiringly at his apparatus, he exclaimed, " Ah, karhowree, ena hannahanna arva tee! " as much as to say, " *This*, you see, is the way it's done."

His contrivance was nothing less than a native still, where he manufactured his island " poteen." The disarray in which we found it, was probably intentional, as a security against detection. Before we left the shed, the old fellow toppled the whole concern over, and dragged it away piecemeal.

His disclosing his secret to us thus, was characteristic of the " Tootai Owrees," or contemners of the missionaries among the natives; who, presuming that all foreigners are opposed to the ascendency of the missionaries, take pleasure in making them confidants, whenever the enactments of their rulers are secretly set at naught.

The substance from which the liquor is produced is called " Tee, " which is a large, fibrous root, something like a yam, but smaller. In its green state, it is exceedingly acrid; but boiled or baked, has the sweetness of the sugar-cane. After being subjected to the fire, macerated, and reduced to a certain stage of fermentation, the " Tee " is stirred up with water, and is then ready for distillation.

On returning to the hut, pipes were introduced; and, after a while, Long Ghost, who, at first, had relished the " Arva Tee " as little as myself, to my surprise, began to wax sociable over it, with Varvy; and, before long, absolutely got mellow, the old toper keeping him company.

It was a curious sight. Every one knows, that, so long as the occasion lasts, there is no stronger bond of sympathy and good-feeling among men, than getting tipsy together. And how earnestly, nay, movingly, a brace of worthies, thus employed, will endeavor to shed light upon, and elucidate their mystical ideas!

Fancy Varvy and the doctor, then; lovingly tippling, and brimming over with a desire to become better acquainted; the doctor politely bent upon carrying on the conversation in the language of his host, and the old hermit persisting in trying to talk English. The result was, that between the two, they made such a fricasee of vowels and consonants, that it was enough to turn one's brain.

The next morning, on waking, I heard a voice from the tombs. It was the doctor, solemnly pronouncing himself a dead man. He was sitting up, with both hands clasped over his forehead, and his pale face a thousand times paler than ever.

" That infernal stuff has murdered me! " he cried. " Heavens! my head's all wheels and springs, like the automaton chessplayer! What's to be done, Paul? I'm poisoned."

But, after drinking an herbal draught, concocted by our host, and eating a light meal, at noon, he felt much better; so much so, that he declared himself ready to continue our journey.

When we came to start, the Yankee's boots were missing; and, after a diligent search, were not to be found. Enraged beyond measure, their proprietor said that Varvy must have stolen them; but, considering his hospitality, I thought this extremely improbable; though, to whom else to impute the theft, I knew not. The doctor maintained, however, that one who was capable of drugging an innocent traveler with " Arva Tee, " was capable of any thing.

But it was in vain that he stormed, and Varvy and I searched; the boots were gone.

Were it not for this mysterious occurrence, and Varvy's detestable liquors, I would here recommend all travelers going round by the beach to Partoowye, to stop at the Rock, and patronize the old gentleman—the more especially as he entertains gratis.

CHAPTER LXXIII.

OUR RECEPTION IN PARTOOWYE.

UPON starting, at last, I flung away my sandals—by this time quite worn out—with the view of keeping company with the doctor, now forced to go barefooted. Recovering his spirits in good time, he protested that boots were a bore after all, and going without them decidedly manly.

This was said, be it observed, while strolling along over a soft carpet of grass; a little moist, even at midday, from the shade of the wood, through which we were passing.

Emerging from this, we entered upon a blank, sandy tract, upon which the sun's rays fairly flashed; making the loose gravel under foot well nigh as hot as the floor of an oven. Such yelling and leaping as there was in getting over this ground, would be hard to surpass. We could not have crossed at all,—until toward sunset,—had it not been for a few small, wiry bushes, growing here and there; into which we every now and then thrust our feet to cool. There was no little judgment necessary in selecting your bush; for if not chosen judiciously, the chances were, that on springing forward again, and finding the next bush so far off, that an intermediate cooling was indispensable, you would have to run back to your old place again.

Safely passing the Sahara, or Fiery Desert, we soothed our half-blistered feet by a pleasant walk through a meadow of long grass, which soon brought us in sight of a few straggling houses, sheltered by a grove on the outskirts of the village of Partoowye.

My comrade was for entering the first one we came to; but, on drawing near, they had so much of an air of pretension, at least for native dwellings, that I hesitated; thinking they might be the residences of the higher chiefs, from whom no very extravagant welcome was to be anticipated.

While standing irresolute, a voice from the nearest house hailed us: " Aramai! aramai, karhowree! " (" come in! come in, strangers! ")

We at once entered, and were warmly greeted. The master of the house was an aristocratic-looking islander; dressed in loose linen drawers, a fine white shirt, and a sash of red silk, tied about the waist, after the fashion of the Spaniards in Chili. He came up to us with a free, frank air, and, striking his chest with his hand, introduced himself as Ereemear Po-Po; or, to render the Christian name back again into English—Jeremiah Po-Po.

These curious combinations of names, among the people of the Society Islands, originate in the following way. When a native is baptized, his patronymic often gives offense to the missionaries, and they insist upon changing to something else whatever is objectionable therein. So, when Jeremiah came to the font, and gave his name as Narmo-Nana Po-Po (something equivalent to The-Darer-of-Devils-by-Night), the reverend gentleman officiating told him, that such a heathenish appellation would never do, and a substitute must be had; at least for the devil part of it. Some highly respectable Christian appellations were then submitted, from which the candidate for admission into the church was at liberty to choose. There was Adamo (Adam), Nooar (Noah), Daveedar (David), Earcobar (James), Eorna (John), Patoora (Peter), Ereemear (Jeremiah), &c. And thus did he come to be named Jeremiah Po-Po; or, Jeremiah-in-the-Dark —which he certainly was, I fancy, as to the ridiculousness of his new cognomen.

We gave our names in return; upon which he bade us be seated; and, sitting down himself, asked us a great many questions, in mixed English and Tahitian. After giving some directions to an old man, to prepare food, our host's wife, a large, benevolent-looking woman, upward of forty, also sat down by us. In our soiled and travel-stained appearance, the good lady seemed to find abundant matter for commiseration; and all the while kept looking at us piteously, and making mournful exclamations.

But Jeremiah and his spouse were not the only inmates of the mansion.

In one corner, upon a large native couch, elevated upon posts, reclined a nymph; who, half-veiled in her own long hair, had yet to make her toilet for the day. She was the only daughter of Po-Po; and a very beautiful little daughter she was; not more than fourteen; with the most delightful shape—like a bud just blown; and large hazel eyes. They called her Loo: a name rather pretty and genteel, and, therefore, quite appropriate; for a more genteel and lady-like little damsel there was not in all Imeeo.

She was a cold and haughty young beauty though, this same little Loo, and never deigned to notice us; further than now and then to let her eyes float over our persons, with an expression of indolent indifference. With the tears of the Loohooloo girls hardly dry from their sobbing upon our shoulders, this contemptuous treatment stung us not a little.

When we first entered, Po-Po was raking smooth the carpet of dried ferns which had that morning been newly laid; and now that our meal was ready, it was spread on a banana leaf, right upon this fragrant floor. Here, we lounged at our ease; eating baked pig and bread-fruit off earthen plates, and using, for the first time in many a long month, real knives and forks.

These, as well as other symptoms of refinement, somewhat abated our surprise at the reserve of the little Loo: her parents, doubtless, were magnates in Partoowye, and she herself was an heiress.

After being informed of our stay in the vale of Martair, they were very curious to know, on what errand we came to

Taloo. We merely hinted, that the ship lying in the harbor
was the reason of our coming.

Arfretee, Po-Po's wife, was a right motherly body. The
meal over, she recommended a nap; and upon our waking
much refreshed, she led us to the doorway, and pointed
down among the trees; through which we saw the gleam of
water. Taking the hint, we repaired thither; and finding a
deep shaded pool, bathed, and returned to the house. Our
hostess now sat down by us; and after looking with great
interest at the doctor's cloak, felt of my own soiled and
tattered garments for the hundredth time, and exclaimed
plaintively—"Ah nuee nuee olee manee! olee manee! "
(alas! they are very, very old! very old!)

When Arfretee, good soul, thus addressed us, she thought
she was talking very respectable English. The word "nuee"
is so familiar to foreigners, throughout Polynesia, and is so
often used by them in their intercourse with the natives,
that the latter suppose it to be common to all mankind.
" Olee manee " is the native pronunciation of " *old man*,"
which, by Society Islanders talking Saxon, is applied indiscriminately to all aged things and persons whatsoever.

Going to a chest filled with various European articles,
she took out two suits of new sailor frocks and trowsers;
and presenting them with a gracious smile, pushed us
behind a calico screen, and left us. Without any fastidious
scruples, we donned the garments; and what with the meal,
the nap, and the bath, we now came forth like a couple of
bridegrooms.

Evening drawing on, lamps were lighted. They were very
simple: the half of a green melon, about one third full of
cocoa-nut oil, and a wick of twisted tappa floating on the
surface. As a night lamp, this contrivance can not be excelled; a soft dreamy light being shed through the transparent rind.

As the evening advanced, other members of the household, whom as yet we had not seen, began to drop in. There
was a slender young dandy in a gay striped shirt, and whole
fathoms of bright figured calico tucked about his waist,
and falling to the ground. He wore a new straw hat also,

with three distinct ribbons tied about the crown; one black, one green, and one pink. Shoes or stockings, however, he had none.

There were a couple of delicate, olive-cheeked little girls —twins—with mild eyes and beautiful hair, who ran about the house, half-naked, like a couple of gazelles. They had a brother, somewhat younger—a fine dark boy, with an eye like a woman's. All these were the children of Po-Po, begotten in lawful wedlock.

Then, there were two or three queer-looking old ladies, who wore shabby mantles of soiled sheeting; which fitted so badly, and withal, had such a second-hand look, that I at once put their wearers down as domestic paupers—poor relations, supported by the bounty of My Lady Arfretee. They were sad, meek old bodies; said little and ate less; and either kept their eyes on the ground, or lifted them up deferentially. The semi-civilization of the island must have had something to do with making them what they were.

I had almost forgotten Monee, the grinning old man who prepared our meal. His head was a shining, bald globe. He had a round little paunch, and legs like a cat. He was Po-Po's factotum—cook, butler, and climber of the bread-fruit and cocoa-nut trees; and, added to all else, a mighty favorite with his mistress; with whom he would sit smoking and gossiping by the hour.

Often you saw the indefatigable Monee working away at a great rate; then dropping his employment all at once —never mind what—run off to a little distance, and after rolling himself away in a corner, and taking a nap, jump up again, and fall to with fresh vigor.

From a certain something in the behavior of Po-Po and his household, I was led to believe, that he was a pillar of the church; though, from what I had seen in Tahiti, I could hardly reconcile such a supposition with his frank, cordial, unembarrassed air. But I was not wrong in my conjecture: Po-Po turned out to be a sort of elder, or deacon; he was also accounted a man of wealth, and was nearly related to a high chief.

Before retiring, the entire household gathered upon the floor; and in their midst, he read aloud a chapter from a Tahitian Bible. Then kneeling with the rest of us, he offered up a prayer. Upon its conclusion, all separated without speaking. These devotions took place regularly, every night and morning. Grace too, was invariably said, by this family, both before and after eating.

After becoming familiarized with the almost utter destitution of any thing like practical piety, upon these islands, what I observed in our host's house astonished me much. But whatever others might have been, Po-Po was, in truth, a Christian: the only one, Arfretee excepted, whom I personally knew to be such, among all the natives of Polynesia.

CHAPTER LXXIV.

RETIRING FOR THE NIGHT.—THE DOCTOR GROWS DEVOUT.

THEY put us to bed very pleasantly.

Lying across the foot of Po-Po's nuptial couch, was a smaller one, made of Koar-wood; a thin, strong cord, twisted from the fibres of the husk of the cocoa-nut, and woven into an exceedingly light sort of net-work, forming its elastic body. Spread upon this, was a single, fine mat, with a roll of dried ferns for a pillow, and a strip of white tappa for a sheet. This couch was mine. The doctor was provided for in another corner.

Loo reposed alone on a little settee, with a taper burning by her side; the dandy, her brother, swinging overhead in a sailor's hammock. The two gazelles frisked upon a mat near by; and the indigent relations borrowed a scant corner of the old butler's pallet, who snored away by the open door. After all had retired, Po-Po placed the illuminated melon in the middle of the apartment; and so, we all slumbered till morning.

Upon awaking, the sun was streaming brightly through the open bamboos, but no one was stirring. After surveying the fine attitudes, into which forgetfulness had thrown at least one of the sleepers, my attention was called off to the general aspect of the dwelling, which was quite significant of the superior circumstances of our host.

The house itself was built in the simple, but tasteful native style. It was a long, regular oval, some fifty feet in length, with low sides of cane-work, and a roof thatched with palmetto-leaves. The ridge-pole was, perhaps, twenty feet from the ground. There was no foundation whatever; the bare earth being merely covered with ferns: a kind of carpeting which serves very well, if frequently renewed; otherwise, it becomes dusty, and the haunt of vermin, as in the huts of the poorer natives.

Beside the couches, the furniture consisted of three or four sailor chests; in which were stored the fine wearing-apparel of the household—the ruffled linen shirts of Po-Po, the calico dresses of his wife and children, and divers odds and ends of European articles—strings of beads, ribbons, Dutch looking-glasses, knives, coarse prints, bunches of keys, bits of crockery, and metal buttons. One of these chests—used as a bandbox by Arfretee—contained several of the native hats (coal-scuttles), all of the same pattern, but trimmed with variously colored ribbons. Of nothing was our good hostess more proud, than of these hats, and her dresses. On Sundays, she went abroad a dozen times; and every time, like Queen Elizabeth, in a different robe.

Po-Po, for some reason or other, always gave us our meals before the rest of the family were served; and the doctor, who was very discerning in such matters, declared that we fared much better than they. Certain it was, that had Eeemear's guests traveled with purses, portmanteaux, and letters of introduction to the queen, they could not have been better cared for.

The day after our arrival, Monee, the old butler, brought us in for dinner a small pig, baked in the ground. All savory, it lay in a wooden trencher, surrounded by roasted hemispheres of the bread-fruit. A large calabash, filled with taro pudding, or poee, followed; and the young dandy, over-coming his customary languor, threw down our cocoa-nuts from an adjoining tree.

When all was ready, and the household looking on, Long Ghost, devoutly clasping his hands over the fated pig, implored a blessing. Hereupon, every body present looked exceedingly pleased; Po-Po coming up, and addressing the doctor with much warmth; and Arfretee, regarding him with almost maternal affection, exclaimed delightedly, " Ah! mickonaree tata maitai! " in other words, " What a pious young man! "

It was just after this meal, that she brought me a roll of grass sinnate (of the kind which sailors sew into the frame of their tarpaulins), and then, handing me needle and thread, bade me begin at once, and make myself the hat which I so much needed. An accomplished hand at the business, I finished it that day—merely stitching the braid together; and Arfretee, by way of rewarding my industry, with her own olive hands ornamented the crown with a band of flame-colored ribbon; the two long ends of which streaming behind, sailor-fashion, still preserved for me the Eastern title bestowed by Long Ghost.

CHAPTER LXXV.

A RAMBLE THROUGH THE SETTLEMENT.

THE following morning, making our toilets carefully, we donned our sombreros, and sallied out on a tour. Without meaning to reveal our designs upon the court, our principal object was, to learn what chances there were for white men to obtain employment under the queen. On this head, it is true, we had questioned Po-Po; but his answers had been very discouraging; so we determined to obtain further information elsewhere.

But first, to give some little description of the village.

The settlement of Partoowye is nothing more than some eighty houses, scattered here and there, in the midst of an immense grove, where the trees have been thinned out, and the underbrush cleared away. Through the grove flows a stream; and the principal avenue crosses it, over an elastic bridge of cocoa-nut trunks, laid together side by side. The avenue is broad, and serpentine; well shaded, from one end to the other; and as pretty a place for a morning promenade, as any lounger could wish. The houses, constructed without the slightest regard to the road, peep into view from among the trees on either side; some looking you right in the face as you pass, and others, without any manners, turning their backs. Occasionally, you observe a rural retreat, inclosed by a picket of bamboos, or with a solitary pane of glass massively framed in the broadside of the dwelling, or with a rude, strange-looking door, swinging upon dislocated wooden hinges. Otherwise, the dwellings are built in the original style of the natives; and never mind how mean and filthy some of them may appear within, they all look picturesque enough without.

As we sauntered along, the people we met, saluted us pleasantly, and invited us into their houses; and in this way we made a good many brief morning calls. But the hour could not have been the fashionable one in Partoowye; since the ladies were invariably in dishabille. But they always gave us a cordial reception, and were particularly polite to the doctor; caressing him, and amorously hanging about his neck; wonderfully taken up, in short, with a gay handkerchief he wore there. Arfretee had that morning bestowed it upon the pious youth.

With some exceptions, the general appearance of the natives of Partoowye, was far better than that of the inhabitants of Papetee: a circumstance only to be imputed to their restricted intercourse with foreigners.

Strolling on, we turned a sweep of the road, when the doctor gave a start; and no wonder. Right before us, in the grove, was a block of houses: regular square frames, boarded over, furnished with windows and doorways, and two stories high. We ran up, and found them fast going to decay; very

dingy, and here and there covered with moss; no sashes
nor doors; and on one side, the entire block had settled
down nearly a foot. On going into the basement, we looked
clean up through the unboarded timbers to the roof; where
rays of light, glimmering through many a chink, illuminated the cobwebs which swung all round.

The whole interior was dark and close. Burrowing among
some old mats in one corner, like a parcel of Gipsys in a
ruin, were a few vagabond natives. They had their dwelling
here.

Curious to know, who on earth could have been thus
trying to improve the value of real estate in Partoowye, we
made inquiries; and learned that, some years previous, the
block had been thrown up by a veritable Yankee (one might
have known that), a house carpenter by trade, and a bold,
enterprising fellow by nature.

Put ashore from his ship, sick, he first went to work
and got well; then sallied out with chisel and plane, and
made himself generally useful. A sober, steady man, it
seems, he at last obtained the confidence of several chiefs,
and soon filled them with all sorts of ideas concerning the
alarming want of public spirit in the people of Imeeo.
More especially did he dwell upon the humiliating fact of
their living in paltry huts of bamboo, when magnificent
palaces of boards might so easily be morticed together.

In the end, these representations so far prevailed with
one old chief, that the carpenter was engaged to build a
batch of these wonderful palaces. Provided with plenty of
men, he at once set to work: built a saw-mill among the
mountains, felled trees, and sent over to Papeetee for
nails.

Presto! the castle rose; but alas, the roof was hardly on,
when the Yankee's patron, having speculated beyond his
means, broke all to pieces, and was absolutely unable to
pay one " plug " of tobacco in the pound. His failure involved the carpenter, who sailed away from his creditors
in the very next ship that touched at the harbor.

The natives despised the rickety palace of boards; and
often lounged by, wagging their heads, and jeering.

We were told that the queen's residence was at the extreme end of the village; so, without waiting for the doctor to procure a fiddle, we suddenly resolved upon going thither at once, and learning whether any privy counselorships were vacant.

Now, although there was a good deal of my waggish comrade's nonsense about what has been said concerning our expectations of court preferment, we, nevertheless, really thought, that something to our advantage might turn up in that quarter.

On approaching the palace grounds, we found them rather peculiar. A broad pier of hewn coral rocks was built right out into the water; and upon this, and extending into a grove adjoining, were some eight or ten very large native houses, constructed in the handsomest style, and inclosed together by a low picket of bamboos, which embraced a considerable area.

Throughout the Society Islands, the residences of the chiefs are mostly found in the immediate vicinity of the sea; a site which gives them the full benefit of a cooling breeze; nor are they so liable to the annoyance of insects; besides enjoying when they please, the fine shade afforded by the neighboring groves, always most luxuriant near the water.

Lounging about the grounds, were some sixty or eighty handsomely dressed natives, men and women; some reclining on the shady side of the houses, others under the trees, and a small group conversing close by the railing, facing us.

We went up to the latter; and giving the usual salutation, were on the point of vaulting over the bamboos, when they turned upon us angrily, and said we could not enter. We stated our earnest desire to see the queen; hinting that we were bearers of important dispatches. But it was to no purpose; and not a little vexed, we were obliged to return to Po-Po's without effecting any thing.

CHAPTER LXXVI.

UPON arriving home, we fully laid open to Po-Po our motives in visiting Taloo, and begged his friendly advice. In his broken English, he cheerfully gave us all the information we needed.

It was true, he said, that the queen entertained some idea of making a stand against the French; and it was currently reported, also, that several chiefs from Borabora, Huwyenee, Raiatair, and Tahar, the leeward islands of the group, were at that very time taking counsel with her, as to the expediency of organizing a general movement throughout the entire cluster, with a view of anticipating any further encroachments on the part of the invaders. Should warlike measures be actually decided upon, it was quite certain that Pomaree would be glad to enlist all the foreigners she could; but as to her making officers of either the doctor or me, that was out of the question; because, already, a number of Europeans, well known to her, had volunteered as such. Concerning our getting immediate access to the queen, Po-Po told us it was rather doubtful; she living at that time very retired, in poor health and spirits, and averse to receiving calls. Previous to her misfortunes, however, no one, however humble, was denied admittance to her presence; sailors, even, attended her levees.

Not at all disheartened by these things, we concluded to kill time in Partoowye, until some event turned up more favorable to our projects. So that very day we sallied out on an excursion to the ship, which, lying land-locked, far up the bay, yet remained to be visited.

Passing, on our route, a long, low shed, a voice, hailed us—" White men ahoy! " Turning round, who should we see but a rosy-cheeked Englishman (you could tell his country at a glance), up to his knees in shavings, and planing away at a bench. He turned out to be a runaway ship's carpenter, recently from Tahiti, and now doing a profitable business in Imeeo, by fitting up the dwellings of opulent chiefs with cupboards and other conveniences, and once in a while trying his hand at a lady's work-box. He had been in the settlement but a few months, and already possessed houses and lands.

But though blessed with prosperity and high health, there was one thing wanting—a wife. And when he came to speak of the matter, his countenance fell, and he leaned dejectedly upon his plane.

" It's too bad! " he sighed, " to wait three long years; and all the while, dear little Lullee living in the same house with that infernal chief from Tahar! "

Our curiosity was piqued; the poor carpenter, then, had been falling in love with some island coquet, who was going to jilt him.

But such was not the case. There was a law prohibiting, under a heavy penalty, the marriage of a native with a foreigner, unless the latter, after being three years a resident on the island, was willing to affirm his settled intention of remaining for life.

William was therefore in a sad way. He told us that he might have married the girl half-a-dozen times, had it not been for this odious law; but, latterly, she had become less loving and more giddy, particularly with the strangers from Tahar. Desperately smitten, and desirous of securing her at all hazards, he had proposed to the damsel's friends a nice little arrangement, introductory to marriage; but they would not hear of it; besides, if the pair were discovered living together upon such a footing, they would be liable to a degrading punishment:—sent to work making stone walls and opening roads for the queen.

Doctor Long Ghost was all sympathy. " Bill, my good fellow," said he, tremulously, " let *me* go and talk to her." But Bill, declining the offer, would not even inform us where his charmer lived.

Leaving the disconsolate Willie planing a plank of New Zealand pine (an importation from the Bay of Islands), and thinking the while of Lullee, we went on our way. How his suit prospered in the end, we never learned.

Going from Po-Po's house toward the anchorage of the harbor of Taloo, you catch no glimpse of the water, until coming out from deep groves, you all at once find yourself upon the beach. A bay, considered by many voyagers the most beautiful in the South Seas, then lies before you. You stand upon one side of what seems a deep, green river, flowing through mountain passes to the sea. Right opposite, a majestic promontory divides the inlet from another, called after its discoverer, Captain Cook. The face of this promontory toward Taloo is one verdant wall; and at its base the waters lie still, and fathomless. On the left hand, you just catch a peep of the widening mouth of the bay, the break in the reef by which ships enter, and beyond, the sea. To the right, the inlet, sweeping boldly round the promontory, runs far away into the land; where, save in one direction, the hills close in on every side, knee-deep in verdure, and shooting aloft in grotesque peaks. The open space lies at the head of the bay; in the distance it extends into a broad, hazy plain lying at the foot of an amphitheatre of hills. Here is the large sugar plantation previously alluded to. Beyond the first range of hills, you descry the sharp pinnacles of the interior; and among these, the same silent Marling-spike, which we so often admired from the other side of the island.

All alone in the harbor lay the good ship Leviathan. We jumped into the canoe, and paddled off to her. Though early in the afternoon, every thing was quiet; but upon mounting the side, we found four or five sailors lounging about the forecastle, under an awning. They gave us no very cordial reception; and though otherwise quite hearty in appearance, seemed to assume a look of ill-humor on purpose to honor our arrival. There was much eagerness to learn whether we wanted to " ship; " and by the unpleasant accounts they gave of the vessel, they seemed desirous to prevent such a thing, if possible.

We asked where the rest of the ship's company were; a gruff old fellow made answer, " One boat's crew of 'em is gone to Davy Jones's locker:—went off after a whale, last cruise, and never come back agin. All the starboard watch ran away last night, and the skipper's ashore kitching 'em."

" And it's *shipping* yer after, my jewels, is it? " cried a curly-pated little Belfast sailor, coming up to us, " thin arrah! my livelies, jist be after sailing ashore in a jiffy:— the divil of a skipper will carry yees both to sea, whether or no. Be off wid ye, thin, darlints, and steer clear of the likes of this ballyhoo of blazes as long as ye live. They murther us here every day, and starve us into the bargain. Here, Dick, lad, harl the poor divils' canow alongside; and paddle away wid yees for dear life."

But we loitered awhile, listening to more inducements to ship; and at last concluded to stay to supper. My sheath-knife never cut into better sea-beef than that which we found lying in the kid in the forecastle. The bread, too, was hard, dry, and brittle as glass; and there was plenty of both.

While we were below, the mate of the vessel called out for some one to come on deck. I liked his voice. Hearing it was as good as a look at his face. It betokened a true sailor, and no taskmaster.

The appearance of the Leviathan herself was quite pleasing. Like all large, comfortable old whalers, she had a sort of motherly look:—broad in the beam, flush decks, and four chubby boats hanging at the breast. Her sails were furled loosely upon the yards, as if they had been worn long, and fitted easy; her shrouds swung negligently slack; and as for the " running rigging," it never worked hard as it does in some of your " dandy ships," jamming in the sheaves of blocks, like Chinese slippers, too small to be useful; on the contrary, the ropes ran glibly through, as if they had many a time traveled the same road, and were used to it.

When evening came, we dropped into our canoe, and paddled ashore; fully convinced that the good ship never deserved the name which they gave her.

CHAPTER LXXVII.

WHILE in Partoowye, we fell in with a band of six veteran rovers, prowling about the village and harbor, who had just come overland from another part of the island.

A few weeks previous, they had been paid off, at Papeetee, from a whaling vessel, on board of which they had, six months before, shipped for a single cruise; that is to say, to be discharged at the next port. Their cruise was a famous one; and each man stepped upon the beach at Tahiti, jingling his dollars in a sock.

Weary at last of the shore, and having some money left, they clubbed, and purchased a sail-boat; proposing a visit to a certain uninhabited island, concerning which they had heard strange and golden stories. Of course, they never could think of going to sea without a medicine-chest filled with flasks of spirits, and a small cask of the same in the hold, in case the chest should give out.

Away they sailed; hoisted a flag of their own, and gave three times three, as they staggered out of the bay of Papeetee with a strong breeze, and under all the " muslin " they could carry.

Evening coming on, and feeling in high spirits, and no ways disposed to sleep, they concluded to make a night of it; which they did; all hands getting tipsy, and the two masts going over the side about midnight, to the tune of

> " Sailing down, sailing down,
> On the coast of *Barbaree*."

Fortunately, one worthy could stand, by holding on to the tiller; and the rest managed to crawl about, and hack away the lanyards of the rigging, so as to break clear from the fallen spars. While thus employed, two sailors got tranquilly over the side, and went plumb to the bottom; under the erroneous impression, that they were stepping upon an imaginary wharf, to get at their work better.

After this, it blew quite a gale; and the commodore, at the helm, instinctively kept the boat before the wind; and by so doing, ran over for the opposite island of Imeeo. Crossing the channel, by almost a miracle they went straight through an opening in the reef, and shot upon a ledge of coral, where the waters were tolerably smooth. Here, they lay until morning, when the natives came off to them in their canoes. By the help of the islanders, the schooner was hove over on her beam-ends; when, finding the bottom knocked to pieces, the adventurers sold the boat for a trifle to the chief of the district, and went ashore, rolling before them their precious cask of spirits. Its contents soon evaporated, and they came to Partoowye.

The day after encountering these fellows, we were strolling among the groves in the neighborhood, when we came across several parties of natives, armed with clumsy muskets, rusty cutlasses, and outlandish clubs. They were beating the bushes, shouting aloud, and apparently, trying to scare somebody. They were in pursuit of the strangers, who, having in a single night, set at naught all the laws of the place, had thought best to decamp.

In the daytime, Po-Po's house was as pleasant a lounge as one could wish. So, after strolling about, and seeing all there was to be seen, we spent the greater part of our mornings there; breakfasting late, and dining about two hours after noon. Sometimes we lounged on the floor of ferns, smoking, and telling stories; of which the doctor had as many as a half-pay captain in the army. Sometimes we chatted, as well as we could, with the natives; and, one day—joy to us!—Po-Po brought in three volumes of Smollett's novels, which had been found in the chest of a sailor, who some time previous had died on the island.

Amelia!—Peregrine!—you hero of rogues, Count Fathom!—what a debt do we owe you!

I know not, whether it was the reading of these romances, or the want of some sentimental pastime, which led the doctor, about this period, to lay siege to the heart of the little Loo.

Now, as I have said before, the daughter of Po-Po was most cruelly reserved, and never deigned to notice us. Frequently I addressed her with a long face, and an air of the profoundest and most distant respect—but in vain; she wouldn't even turn up her pretty olive nose. Ah! it's quite plain, thought I; she knows very well what graceless dogs sailors are, and won't have any thing to do with us.

But thus thought not my comrade. Bent he was upon firing the cold glitter of Loo's passionless eyes.

He opened the campaign with admirable tact: making cautious approaches, and content, for three days, with ogling the nymph, for about five minutes after every meal. On the fourth day, he asked her a question; on the fifth she dropped a nut of ointment, and he picked it up and gave it to her; on the sixth, he went over and sat down within three yards of the couch where she lay; and, on the memorable morn of the seventh, he proceeded to open his batteries in form.

The damsel was reclining on the ferns; one hand supporting her cheek, and the other listlessly turning over the leaves of a Tahitian Bible. The doctor approached.

Now the chief disadvantage under which he labored, was his almost complete ignorance of the love vocabulary of the island. But French counts, they say, make love delightfully in broken English; and what hindered the doctor from doing the same in dulcet Tahitian. So at it he went.

" Ah! " said he, smiling bewitchingly, " oee mickonaree? oee ready Biblee? "

No answer; not even a look.

" Ah! maitai! very goody ready Biblee mickonaree."

Loo, without stirring, began reading, in a low tone, to herself.

"Mickonaree Biblee ready goody maitai," once more observed the doctor, ingeniously transposing his words for the third time.

But all to no purpose; Loo gave no sign.

He paused, despairingly; but it would never do to give up; so he threw himself at full length beside her, and audaciously commenced turning over the leaves.

Loo gave a start, just one little start, barely perceptible, and then fumbling something in her hand, lay perfectly motionless; the doctor rather frightened at his own temerity, and knowing not what to do next. At last, he placed one arm cautiously about her waist; almost in the same instant he bounded to his feet, with a cry; the little witch had pierced him with a thorn. But there she lay, just as quietly as ever; turning over the leaves, and reading to herself.

My long friend raised the siege incontinently, and made a disorderly retreat to the place where I reclined, looking on.

I am pretty sure that Loo must have related this occurrence to her father, who came in shortly afterward; for he looked queerly at the doctor. But he said nothing; and, in ten minutes, was quite as affable as ever. As for Loo, there was not the slightest change in her; and the doctor, of course, forever afterward held his peace.

CHAPTER LXXVIII.

MRS. BELL.

One day, taking a pensive afternoon stroll along one of the many bridle-paths which wind among the shady groves in the neighborhood of Taloo, I was startled by a sunny apparition. It was that of a beautiful young Englishwoman, charmingly dressed, and mounted upon a spirited little white pony. Switching a green branch, she came cantering toward me.

I looked round to see whether I could possibly be in Polynesia. There were the palm-trees; but how to account for the lady?

Stepping to one side, as the apparition drew near, I made a polite obeisance. It gave me a bold, rosy look; and then, with a gay air, patted its palfrey, crying out, " Fly away, Willie! " and galloped among the trees.

I would have followed; but Willie's heels were making such a pattering among the dry leaves, that pursuit would have been useless.

So I went straight home to Po-Po's, and related my adventure to the doctor.

The next day, our inquiries resulted in finding out, that the stranger had been on the island about two years; that she came from Sydney; and was the wife of Mr. Bell (happy dog!), the proprietor of the sugar plantation, to which I have previously referred.

To the sugar plantation we went, the same day.

The country round about was very beautiful: a level basin of verdure, surrounded by sloping hillsides. The sugar-cane—of which there was about one hundred acres, in various stages of cultivation—looked thrifty. A considerable tract of land, however, which seemed to have been formerly tilled, was now abandoned.

The place where they extracted the saccharine matter, was under an immense shed of bamboos. Here we saw several clumsy pieces of machinery for breaking the cane; also great kettles for boiling the sugar. But, at present, nothing was going on. Two or three natives were lounging in one of the kettles, smoking; the other was occupied by three sailors from the Leviathan, playing cards.

While we were conversing with these worthies, a stranger approached. He was a sun-burnt, romantic-looking European, dressed in a loose suit of nankeen; his fine throat and chest were exposed, and he sported a Guayaquil hat, with a brim like a Chinese umbrella. This was Mr. Bell. He was very civil; showed us the grounds, and, taking us into a sort of arbor, to our surprise, offered to treat us to some wine. People often do the like; but Mr. Bell did more: he produced the bottle. It was spicy sherry; and we drank out of the halves of fresh citron melons. Delectable goblets!

The wine was a purchase from the French in Tahiti.

Now all this was extremely polite in Mr. Bell; still, we came to see *Mrs.* Bell. But she proved to be a phantom, indeed; having left the same morning for Papeetee, on a visit to one of the missionaries' wives there.

I went home, much chagrined.

To be frank, my curiosity had been wonderfully piqued concerning the lady. In the first place, she was the most beautiful white woman I ever saw in Polynesia. But this is saying nothing. She had such eyes, such moss-roses in her cheeks, such a divine air in the saddle, that, to my dying day, I shall never forget Mrs. Bell.

The sugar-planter himself was young, robust, and handsome. So, merrily may the little Bells increase, and multiply, and make music in the Land of Imeeo.

CHAPTER LXXIX.

TALOO CHAPEL.—HOLDING COURT IN POLYNESIA.

In Partoowye is to be seen one of the best constructed and handsomest chapels in the South Seas. Like the buildings of the palace, it stands upon an artificial pier, presenting a semicircular sweep to the bay. The chapel is built of hewn blocks of coral; a substance which, although extremely friable, is said to harden by exposure to the atmosphere. To a stranger, these blocks look extremely curious. Their surface is covered with strange fossil-like impressions, the seal of which must have been set before the flood. Very nearly white when hewn from the reefs, the coral darkens with age; so that several churches in Polynesia now look almost as sooty and venerable as famed St. Paul's.

In shape, the chapel is an octagon, with galleries all round. It will seat, perhaps, four hundred people. Every thing within is stained a tawny red; and there being but few windows, or rather embrasures, the dusky benches and galleries, and the tall spectre of a pulpit look any thing but cheerful.

On Sundays, we always went to worship here. Going in the family suite of Po-Po, we, of course, maintained a most decorous exterior; and hence, by all the elderly people of the village, were doubtless regarded as pattern young men.

Po-Po's seat was in a snug corner; and it being particularly snug, in the immediate vicinity of one of the Palm pillars supporting the gallery, I invariably leaned against it: Po-Po and his lady on one side, the doctor and the dandy on the other, and the children and poor relations seated behind.

As for Loo, instead of sitting (as she ought to have done) by her good father and mother, she must needs run up into the gallery, and sit with a parcel of giddy creatures of her own age; who, all through the sermon, did nothing but look down on the congregation; pointing out, and giggling at the queer-looking old ladies in dowdy bonnets and scant tunics. But Loo, herself, was never guilty of these improprieties.

Occasionally during the week, they have afternoon service in the chapel, when the natives themselves have something to say; although their auditors are but few. An introductory prayer being offered by the missionary, and a hymn sung, communicants rise in their places, and exhort in pure Tahitian, and with wonderful tone and gesture. And among them all, Deacon Po-Po, though he talked most, was the one whom you would have liked best to hear. Much would I have given to have understood some of his impassioned bursts; when he tossed his arms overhead, stamped, scowled, and glared, till he looked like the very Angel of Vengeance.

" Deluded man! " sighed the doctor, on one of these occasions, " I fear he takes the fanatical view of the subject." One thing was certain: when Po-Po spoke, all listened; a great deal more than could be said for the rest; for under the discipline of two or three I could mention, some of the audience napped; others fidgeted; a few yawned; and one irritable old gentleman, in a night-cap of cocoa-nut leaves, used to clutch his long staff in a state of excessive nervousness, and stride out of the church; making all the noise he could, to emphasize his disgust.

19

Right adjoining the chapel is an immense, rickety building, with windows and shutters, and a half-decayed board
flooring laid upon trunks of palm-trees. They called it a
school-house; but as such we never saw it occupied. It was
often used as a court-room, however; and here we attended
several trials; among others, that of a decayed naval officer,
and a young girl of fourteen; the latter, charged with
having been very naughty on a particular occasion, set forth in
the pleadings; and the former, with having aided and abetted
her in her naughtiness, and with other misdemeanors.

The foreigner was a tall, military-looking fellow, with a
dark cheek and black whiskers. According to his own account, he had lost a colonial armed brig on the coast of
New Zealand; and since then, had been leading the life
of a man about town, among the islands of the Pacific.

The doctor wanted to know why he did not go home and
report the loss of his brig; but Captain Crash, as they called
him, had some incomprehensible reasons for not doing
so, about which he could talk by the hour, and no one be
any the wiser. Probably, he was a discreet man, and thought
it best to waive an interview with the lords of the admiralty.

For some time past, this extremely suspicious character
had been carrying on the illicit trade in French wines and
brandies, smuggled over from the men-of-war lately touching at Tahiti. In a grove near the anchorage, he had a
rustic shanty and arbor; where, in quiet times, when no
ships were in Taloo, a stray native once in a while got
boozy, and staggered home, catching at the cocoa-nut trees
as he went. The captain himself lounged under a tree
during the warm afternoons; pipe in mouth; thinking
perhaps, over old times, and occasionally feeling his
shoulders for his lost epaulets.

But, sail ho! a ship is descried coming into the bay.
Soon, she drops her anchor in its waters; and the next day
Captain Crash entertains the sailors in his grove. And rare
times they have of it: —drinking and quarreling together,
as sociably as you please.

Upon one of these occasions, the crew of the Leviathan
made so prodigious a tumult, that the natives, indignant

at the insult offered their laws, plucked up a heart, and made a dash at the rioters, one hundred strong. The sailors fought like tigers; but were at last overcome, and carried before a native tribunal; which, after a mighty clamor, dismissed every body but Captain Crash, who was asserted to be the author of the disorders.

Upon this charge, then, he had been placed in confinement against the coming on of the assizes; the judge being expected to lounge along in the course of the afternoon. While waiting his Honor's arrival, numerous additional offenses were preferred against the culprit (mostly by the old women); among others was the bit of a slip in which he stood implicated along with the young lady. Thus, in Polynesia as elsewhere;—charge a man with one misdemeanor, and all his peccadilloes are raked up and assorted before him.

Going to the school-house for the purpose of witnessing the trial, the din of it assailed our ears a long ways off; and upon entering the building, we were almost stunned. About five hundred natives were present; each, apparently, having something to say, and determined to say it. His Honor— a handsome, benevolent-looking old man— sat cross-legged on a little platform; seemingly resigned with all Christian submission to the uproar. He was an hereditary chief in this quarter of the island, and judge for life in the district of Partoowye.

There were several cases coming on; but the captain and girl were first tried together. They were mixing freely with the crowd; and as it afterward turned out that every one— no matter who—had a right to address the court, for aught we knew they might have been arguing their own case. At what precise moment the trial began, it would be hard to say. There was no swearing of witnesses, and no regular jury.* Now and then somebody leaped up and shouted out something which might have been evidence; the rest,

* This anomaly exists, notwithstanding that, in other respects, the missionaries have endeavored to organize the native courts upon the English model.

meanwhile, keeping up an incessant jabbering. Presently, the old judge himself began to get excited; and springing to his feet, ran in among the crowd, wagging his tongue as hard as any body.

The tumult lasted about twenty minutes; and toward the end of it, Captain Crash might have been seen, tranquilly regarding, from his Honor's platform, the judicial uproar, in which his fate was about being decided.

The result of all this was, that both he and the girl were found guilty. The latter was adjudged to make six mats for the queen; and the former, in consideration of his manifold offenses, being deemed incorrigible, was sentenced to eternal banishment from the island. Both these decrees seemed to originate in the general hubbub. His Honor, however, appeared to have considerable authority, and it was quite plain that the decision received his approval.

The above penalties were by no means indiscriminately inflicted. The missionaries have prepared a sort of penal tariff to facilitate judicial proceedings. It costs so many days' labor on the Broom Road to indulge in the pleasures of the calabash; so many fathoms of stone wall to steal a musket; and so on to the end of the catalogue. The judge being provided with a book, in which all these matters are cunningly arranged, the thing is vastly convenient. For instance: a crime is proved,—say, bigamy; turn to letter B.—and there you have it. Bigamy:—forty days on the Broom Road, and twenty mats for the queen. Read the passage aloud, and sentence is pronounced.

After taking part in the first trial, the other delinquents present were put upon their own; in which, also, the convicted culprits seemed to have quite as much to say as the rest. A rather strange proceeding; but strictly in accordance with the glorious English principle, that every man should be tried by his peers.

They were all found guilty.

CHAPTER LXXX.

QUEEN POMAREE.

It is well to learn something about people before being introduced to them; and so, we will here give some account of Pomaree and her family.

Every reader of Cook's Voyages must remember " Otoo," who, in that navigator's time, was king of the larger peninsula of Tahiti. Subsequently, assisted by the muskets of the Bounty's men, he extended his rule over the entire island. This Otoo, before his death, had his name changed into Pomaree, which has ever since been the royal patronymic.

He was succeeded by his son, Pomaree II., the most famous prince in the annals of Tahiti. Though a sad debauchee and drunkard, and even charged with unnatural crimes, he was a great friend of the missionaries, and one of their very first proselytes. During the religious wars into which he was hurried, by his zeal for the new faith, he was defeated, and expelled from the island. After a short exile, he returned from Imeeo, with an army of eight hundred warriors; and, in the battle of Narii, routed the rebellious pagans with great slaughter, and reëstablished himself upon the throne. Thus, by force of arms, was Christianity finally triumphant in Tahiti.

Pomaree II. dying, in 1821, was succeeded by his infant son, under the title of Pomaree III. This young prince survived his father but six years; and the government then descended to his elder sister, Aimata, the present queen, who is commonly called Pomaree Vahinee I., or the first female Pomaree. Her majesty must be now upward of thirty years of age. She has been twice married. Her first husband was a son of the old King of Tahar, an island about one hundred miles from Tahiti. This proving an unhappy alliance, the pair were soon after divorced. The present husband of the queen is a chief of Imeeo.

The reputation of Pomaree is not what it ought to be. She, and also her mother, were, for a long time, excommunicated members of the Church; and the former, I believe, still is. Among other things, her conjugal fidelity is far from being unquestioned. Indeed, it was upon this ground, chiefly, that she was excluded from the communion of the Church.

Previous to her misfortunes, she spent the greater portion of her time sailing about from one island to another, attended by a licentious court; and wherever she went, all manner of games and festivities celebrated her arrival.

She was always given to display. For several years, the maintenance of a regiment of household troops drew largely upon the royal exchequer. They were trowserless fellows, in a uniform of calico shirts and pasteboard hats; armed with muskets of all shapes and calibres, and commanded by a great noisy chief, strutting it in a coat of fiery red. These heroes escorted their mistress whenever she went abroad.

Some time ago, the queen received from her English sister, Victoria, a very showy, though uneasy, headdress— a crown; probably made to order, at some tinman's in London. Having no idea of reserving so pretty a bauble for coronation days, which come so seldom, her majesty sported it whenever she appeared in public; and, to show her familiarity with European customs, politely touched it to all foreigners of distinction—whaling captains, and the like—whom she happened to meet in her evening walk on the Broom Road.

The arrival and departure of royalty were always announced at the palace by the court artilleryman—a fat old gentleman, who, in a prodigious hurry and perspiration, discharged minute fowling-pieces, as fast as he could load and fire the same.

The Tahitian princess leads her husband a hard life. Poor fellow! he not only caught a queen, but a Tartar, when he married her. The style by which he is addressed is rather significant—" Pomaree-Tanee " (Pomaree's man). All things considered, as appropriate a title for a king-consort as could be hit upon.

If ever there were a henpecked husband, that man is the prince. One day, his cara-sposa, giving audience to a deputation from the captains of the vessels lying in Papeetee, he ventured to make a suggestion which was very displeasing to her. She turned round, and, boxing his ears, told him to go over to his beggarly island of Imeeo, if he wanted to give himself airs.

Cuffed and contemned, poor Tanee flies to the bottle, or rather, to the calabash, for solace. Like his wife and mistress, he drinks more than he ought.

Six or seven years ago, when an American man-of-war was lying at Papeetee, the town was thrown into the greatest commotion by a conjugal assault and battery, made upon the sacred person of Pomaree by her intoxicated Tanee.

Captain Bob once told me the story. And by way of throwing more spirit into the description, as well as to make up for his oral deficiencies, the old man went through the accompanying action: myself being proxy for the Queen of Tahiti.

It seems, that on a Sunday morning, being dismissed contemptuously from the royal presence, Tanee was accosted by certain good fellows, friends and boon companions, who condoled with him on his misfortunes—railed against the queen, and finally dragged him away to an illicit vender of spirits, in whose house the party got gloriously mellow. In this state, Pomaree Vahinee I., was the topic upon which all dilated—"A vixen of a queen," probably suggested one. "It's infamous," said another; "and I'd have satisfaction," cried a third. "And so I will!"—Tanee must have hiccoughed; for off he went; and ascertaining that his royal half was out riding, he mounted his horse, and galloped after her.

Near the outskirts of the town, a cavalcade of women came cantering toward him, in the centre of which was the object of his fury. Smiting his beast right and left, he dashed in among them; completely overturning one of the party, leaving her on the field, and dispersing every body else except Pomaree. Backing her horse dextrously, the

incensed queen heaped upon him every scandalous epithet
she could think of; until at last, the enraged Tanee leaped
out of his saddle, caught Pomaree by her dress, and dragging her to the earth, struck her repeatedly in the face,
holding on meanwhile by the hair of her head. He was
proceeding to strangle her on the spot, when the cries of
the frightened attendants brought a crowd of natives to the
rescue, who bore the nearly insensible queen away.

But his frantic rage was not yet sated. He ran to the palace; and before it could be prevented, demolished a valuable
supply of crockery, a recent present from abroad. In the
act of perpetrating some other atrocity, he was seized from
behind, and carried off with rolling eyes and foaming at
the mouth.

This is a fair example of a Tahitian in a passion. Though
the mildest of mortals in general, and hard to be roused,
when once fairly up, he is possessed with a thousand devils.

The day following, Tanee was privately paddled over to
Imeeo, in a canoe; where, after remaining in banishment
for a couple of weeks, he was allowed to return, and once
more give in his domestic adhesion.

Though Pomaree Vahinee I. be something of a Jezebel
in private life, in her public rule, she is said to have been
quite lenient and forbearing. This was her true policy; for
an hereditary hostility to her family had always lurked in
the hearts of many powerful chiefs, the descendants of the
old Kings of Taiarboo, dethroned by her grandfather Otoo.
Chief among these, and in fact the leader of his party, was
Poofai; a bold, able man, who made no secret of his enmity
to the missionaries, and the government which they controlled. But while events were occurring calculated to favor
the hopes of the disaffected and turbulent, the arrival of
the French gave a most unexpected turn to affairs.

During my sojourn in Tahiti, a report was rife—which
I knew to originate with what is generally called the
" missionary party "—that Poofai and some other chiefs
of note, had actually agreed, for a stipulated bribe, to
acquiesce in the appropriation of their country. But sub-

sequent events have rebutted the calumny. Several of these very men have recently died in battle against the French.

Under the sovereignty of the Pomarees, the great chiefs of Tahiti were something like the barons of King John. Holding feudal sway over their patrimonial valleys, and on account of their descent, warmly beloved by the people, they frequently cut off the royal revenues by refusing to pay the customary tribute due from them as vassals.

The truth is, that with the ascendency of the missionaries, the regal office in Tahiti lost much of its dignity and influence. In the days of Paganism, it was supported by all the power of a numerous priesthood, and was solemnly connected with the entire superstitious idolatry of the land. The monarch claimed to be a sort of bye-blow of Tararroa, the Saturn of the Polynesian mythology, and cousin-german to inferior deities. His person was thrice holy; if he entered an ordinary dwelling, never mind for how short a time, it was demolished when he left; no common mortal being thought worthy to inhabit it afterward.

"I'm a greater man than King George," said the incorrigible young Otoo, to the first missionaries; "he rides on a horse, and I on a man." Such was the case. He traveled post through his dominions on the shoulders of his subjects; and relays of immortal beings were provided in all the valleys.

But alas! how times have changed; how transient human greatness. Some years since, Pomaree Vahinee I., the granddaughter of the proud Otoo, went into the laundry business; publicly soliciting, by her agents, the washing of the linen belonging to the officers of ships touching in her harbors.

It is a significant fact, and one worthy of record, that while the influence of the English missionaries at Tahiti has tended to so great a diminution of the regal dignity there, that of the American missionaries at the Sandwich Islands, has been purposely exerted to bring about a contrary result.

CHAPTER LXXXI.

WE VISIT THE COURT.

IT was about the middle of the second month of the Hegira, and therefore some five weeks after our arrival in Partoowye, that we at last obtained admittance to the residence of the queen.

It happened thus. There was a Marquesan in the train of Pomaree, who officiated as nurse to her children. According to the Tahitian custom, the royal youngsters are carried about until it requires no small degree of strength to stand up under them. But Marbonna was just the man for this —large and muscular, well made as a statue, and with an arm like a degenerate Tahitian's thigh.

Embarking at his native island, as a sailor, on board of a French whaler, he afterward ran away from the ship at Tahiti; where, being seen and admired by Pomaree, he had been prevailed upon to enlist in her service.

Often, when visiting the grounds, we saw him walking about in the shade, carrying two handsome boys, who encircled his neck with their arms. Marbonna's face, tattooed as it was in the ornate style of his tribe, was as good as a picture-book to these young Pomarees. They delighted to trace with their fingers, the outlines of the strange shapes there delineated.

The first time my eyes lighted upon the Marquesan, I knew his country in a moment; and hailing him in his own language, he turned round, surprised that a person so speaking should be a stranger. He proved to be a native of Tior, a glen of Nukuheva. I had visited the place more than once; and so, on the island of Imeeo, we met like old friends.

In my frequent conversations with him over the bamboo picket, I found this islander a philosopher of nature—a wild heathen, moralizing upon the vices and follies of the Christian court of Tahiti—a savage, scorning the degeneracy of the people among whom fortune had thrown him.

I was amazed at the national feelings of the man. No European, when abroad, could speak of his country with more pride than Marbonna. He assured me, again and again, that so soon as he had obtained sufficient money to purchase twenty muskets, and as many bags of powder, he was going to return to a place, with which Imeeo was not worthy to be compared.

It was Marbonna, who, after one or two unsuccessful attempts, at last brought about our admission into the queen's grounds. Through a considerable crowd, he conducted us along the pier to where an old man was sitting; to whom he introduced us as a couple of "karhowrees" of his acquaintance, anxious to see the sights of the palace. The venerable chamberlain stared at us, and shook his head: the doctor, thinking he wanted a fee, placed a plug of tobacco in his hand. This was ingratiating, and we were permitted to pass on. Upon the point of entering one of the houses, Marbonna's name was shouted in half-a-dozen different directions, and he was obliged to withdraw.

Thus left at the very threshold to shift for ourselves, my companion's assurance stood us in good stead. He stalked right in, and I followed. The place was full of women, who, instead of exhibiting the surprise we expected, accosted us as cordially as if we had called to take our Souchong with them, by express invitation. In the first place, nothing would do but we must each devour a calabash of "poee," and several roasted bananas. Pipes were then lighted, and a brisk conversation ensued.

These ladies of the court, if not very polished, were surprisingly free and easy in their manners; quite as much so as King Charles's Beauties. There was one of them—an arch little miss, who could converse with us pretty fluently —to whom we strove to make ourselves particularly agreeable, with the view of engaging her services as cicerone.

As such, she turned out to be every thing we could desire. No one disputing her will, every place was entered without ceremony, curtains brushed aside, mats lifted, and each nook and corner explored. Whether the little damsel carried her mistress' signet, that every thing opened to her thus, I know not; but Marbonna himself, the bearer of infants, could not have been half so serviceable.

Among other houses which we visited, was one of large size and fine exterior; the special residence of a European —formerly the mate of a merchant vessel,—who had done himself the honor of marrying into the Pomaree family. The lady he wedded being a near kinswoman of the queen, he became a permanent member of her majesty's household. This adventurer rose late, dressed theatrically in calico and trinkets, assumed a dictatorial tone in conversation, and was evidently upon excellent terms with himself.

We found him reclining on a mat, smoking a reed-pipe of tobacco, in the midst of an admiring circle of chiefs and ladies. He must have noticed our approach; but instead of rising and offering civilities, he went on talking and smoking, without even condescending to look at us.

" His Highness feels his ' poee,' " carelessly observed the doctor. The rest of the company gave us the ordinary salutation, our guide announcing us beforehand.

In answer to our earnest requests to see the queen, we were now conducted to an edifice, by far the most spacious, in the inclosure. It was at least one hundred and fifty feet in length, very wide, with low eaves, and an exceedingly steep roof of pandannas leaves. There were neither doors nor windows—nothing along the sides but the slight posts supporting the rafters. Between these posts, curtains of fine matting and tappa were rustling, all round; some of them were festooned, or partly withdrawn, so as to admit light and air, and afford a glimpse now and then of what was going on within.

Pushing aside one of the screens, we entered. The apartment was one immense hall; the long and lofty ridge-pole fluttering with fringed matting and tassels, full forty feet from the ground. Lounges of mats, piled one upon another, extended on either side; while here and there were slight screens, forming as many recesses, where groups of natives —all females—were reclining at their evening meal.

As we advanced, these various parties ceased their buzzing, and in explanation of our appearance among them, listened to a few cabalistic words from our guide.

The whole scene was a strange one; but what most excited our surprise, was the incongruous assemblage of the most costly objects from all quarters of the globe. Cheek by jowl, they lay beside the rudest native articles, without the slightest attempt at order. Superb writing-desks of rosewood, inlaid with silver and mother-of-pearl; decanters and goblets of cut glass; embossed volumes of plates; gilded candelabras; sets of globes and mathematical instruments; the finest porcelain; richly mounted sabres and fowling-pieces; laced hats and sumptuous garments of all sorts, with numerous other matters of European manufacture, were strewn about among greasy calabashes half-filled with " *poee*," rolls of old tappa and matting, paddles and fish-spears, and the ordinary furniture of a Tahitian dwelling.

All the articles first mentioned, were, doubtless, presents from foreign powers. They were more or less injured: the fowling-pieces and swords were rusted; the finest woods were scratched; and a folio volume of Hogarth lay open, with a cocoa-nut shell of some musty preparation capsized among the miscellaneous furniture of the Rake's apartment, where that inconsiderate young gentleman is being measured for a coat.

While we were amusing ourselves in this museum of curiosities, our conductor plucked us by the sleeve, and whispered, " Pomaree! Pomaree! aramai kow kow."

" She is coming to sup, then," said the doctor, staring in the direction indicated. " What say you, Paul, suppose we step up? " Just then a curtain near by, lifted; and from a private building a few yards distant, the queen entered, unattended.

She wore a loose gown of blue silk, with two rich shawls, one red and the other yellow, tied about her neck. Her royal majesty was barefooted.

She was about the ordinary size, rather matronly; her features not very handsome; her mouth, voluptuous; but there was a care-worn expression in her face, probably attributable to her late misfortunes. From her appearance, one would judge her about forty; but she is not so old.

As the queen approached one of the recesses, her attendants hurried up, escorted her in, and smoothed the mats on which she at last reclined. Two girls soon appeared, carrying their mistress' repast; and then, surrounded by cut-glass and porcelain, and jars of sweetmeats and confections, Pomaree Vahinee I., the titular Queen of Tahiti, ate fish and poee out of her native calabashes, disdaining either knife or spoon.

" Come on," whispered Long Ghost, " let's have an audience at once; " and he was on the point of introducing himself, when our guide, quite alarmed, held him back, and implored silence. The other natives also interfered; and as he was pressing forward, raised such an outcry, that Pomaree lifted her eyes, and saw us for the first.

She seemed surprised, and offended; and issuing an order in a commanding tone to several of her women, waved us out of the house. Summary as the dismissal was, court etiquet, no doubt, required our compliance. We withdrew; making a profound inclination as we disappeared behind the tappa arras.

We departed the grounds without seeing Marbonna; and previous to vaulting over the picket, feed our pretty guide, after a fashion of our own. Looking round a few moments after, we saw the damsel escorted back by two men, who seemed to have been sent after her. I trust she received nothing more than a reprimand.

The next day Po-Po informed us that strict orders had been issued, to admit no strangers within the palace precincts.

CHAPTER LXXXII.

WHICH ENDS THE BOOK.

DISAPPOINTED in going to court, we determined upon going to sea. It would never do, longer to trespass on Po-Po's hospitality; and then, weary somewhat of life in Imeeo, like all sailors ashore, I at last pined for the billows.

Now, if her crew were to be credited, the Leviathan was not the craft to our mind. But I had seen the captain, and liked him. He was an uncommonly tall, robust, fine-looking man, in the prime of life. There was a deep crimson spot in the middle of each sun-burnt cheek, doubtless the effect of his sea-potations. He was a Vinyarder, or native of the island of Martha's Vinyard (adjoining Nantucket), and—I would have sworn it—a sailor, and no tyrant.

Previous to this, we had rather avoided the Leviathan's men, when they came ashore; but now, we purposely threw ourselves in their way, in order to learn more of the vessel.

We became acquainted with the third mate, a Prussian, and an old merchant seaman—a right jolly fellow, with a face like a ruby. We took him to Po-Po's, and gave him a dinner of baked pig and bread-fruit; with pipes and tobacco for dessert. The account he gave us of the ship, agreed with my own surmises. A cosier old craft never floated; and the captain was the finest man in the world. There was plenty to eat, too; and, at sea, nothing to do but sit on the wind-lass and sail. The only bad trait about the vessel was this: she had been lanched under some baleful star; and so, was a luckless ship in the fishery. She dropped her boats into the brine often enough, and they frequently got fast to the whales; but lance and harpoon almost invariably " drew " when darted by the men of the Leviathan. But what of that? We would have all the sport of chasing the monsters, with none of the detestable work which follows their capture. So, hurrah for the coast of Japan! Thither the ship was bound.

A word now, about the hard stories we heard, the first time we visited the ship. They were nothing but idle fictions, got up by the sailors for the purpose of frightening us away, so as to oblige the captain, who was in want of more hands, to lie the longer in a pleasant harbor.

The next time the Vinyarder came ashore, we flung ourselves in his path. When informed of our desire to sail with him, he wanted to know our history; and, above all, what

countrymen we were. We said, that we had left a whaler in
Tahiti, some time previous; and, since then, had been—
in the most praiseworthy manner—employed upon a plantation. As for our country, sailors belong to no nation in
particular; we were, on this occasion, both Yankees. Upon
this he looked decidedly incredulous; and freely told us,
that he verily believed we were both from Sydney.

Be it known here, that American sea captains, in the
Pacific, are mortally afraid of these Sydney gentry; who, to
tell the truth, wherever known, are in excessively bad odor.
Is there a mutiny on board a ship in the South Seas, ten to
one a Sydney man is the ringleader. Ashore, these fellows
are equally riotous.

It was on this account, that we were anxious to conceal
the fact of our having belonged to the Julia; though it
annoyed me much, thus to deny the dashing little craft.
For the same reason, also, the doctor fibbed about his birth-
place.

Unfortunately, one part of our raiment—Arfretee's blue
frocks—was deemed a sort of collateral evidence against
us. For, curiously enough, an American sailor is generally
distinguished by his red frock; and an English tar, by his
blue one: thus reversing the national colors. The circumstance was pointed out by the captain; and we quickly explained the anomaly. But, in vain: he seemed inveterately
prejudiced against us; and, in particular, eyed the doctor
most distrustfully.

By way of propping the latter's pretensions, I was throwing out a hint concerning Kentucky, as a land of tall men,
when our Vinyarder turned away abruptly, and desired to
hear nothing more. It was evident that he took Long Ghost
for an exceedingly problematical character.

Perceiving this, I resolved to see what a private interview
would do. So, one afternoon, I found the captain smoking
a pipe in the dwelling of a portly old native—one Mai-
Mai—who, for a reasonable compensation, did the honors
of Partoowye, to illustrious strangers.

His guest had just risen from a sumptuous meal of baked
pig and taro pudding; and the remnants of the repast were

still visible. Two reeking bottles, also, with their necks wrenched off, lay upon the mat. All this was encouraging; for, after a good dinner, one feels affluent and amiable, and peculiarly open to conviction. So, at all events, I found the noble Vinyarder.

I began by saying, that I called for the purpose of setting him right, touching certain opinions of his concerning the place of my nativity:—I was an American—thank Heaven! —and wanted to convince him of the fact.

After looking me in the eye for some time, and, by so doing, revealing an obvious unsteadiness in his own visual organs, he begged me to reach forth my arm. I did so; wondering what upon earth that useful member had to do with the matter in hand.

He placed his fingers upon my wrist; and holding them there for a moment, sprang to his feet; and, with much enthusiasm, pronounced me a Yankee, every beat of my pulse!

" Here, Mai-Mai! " he cried, " another bottle! " And, when it came, with one stroke of a knife, he summarily beheaded it, and commanded me to drain it to the bottom. He then told me, that if I would come on board his vessel the following morning, I would find the ship's articles on the cabin transom.

This was getting along famously. But what was to become of the doctor?

I forthwith made an adroit allusion to my long friend. But it was worse than useless. The Vinyarder swore he would have nothing to do with him—he (my long friend) was a " bird " from Sydney, and nothing would make him (the man of little faith) believe otherwise.

I could not help loving the free-hearted captain; but indignant at this most unaccountable prejudice against my comrade, I abruptly took leave.

Upon informing the doctor of the result of the interview, he was greatly amused; and laughingly declared, that the Vinyarder must be a penetrating fellow. He then insisted upon my going to sea in the ship, since he well knew, how anxious I was to leave. As for himself, on second thoughts, he was no sailor; and although "landsmen" very often compose part of a whaler's crew, he did not quite relish the idea of occupying a position so humble. In short, he had made up his mind to tarry awhile in Imeeo.

I turned the matter over; and at last decided upon quitting the island. The impulse urging me to sea once more, and the prospect of eventually reaching home, were too much to be resisted; especially, as the Leviathan was so comfortable a craft, was now bound on her last whaling cruise, and, in little more than a year's time, would be going round Cape Horn.

I did not, however, covenant to remain in the vessel for the residue of the voyage; which would have been needlessly binding myself. I merely stipulated for the coming cruise, leaving my subsequent movements, unrestrained; for, there was no knowing that I might not change my mind, and prefer journeying home by short and easy stages.

The next day I paddled off to the ship, signed and sealed and stepped ashore with my "advance"—fifteen Spanish dollars, tasseling the ends of my neck-handkerchief.

I forced half of the silver on Long Ghost; and having little use for the remainder, would have given it to Po-Po as some small return for his kindness; but, although he well knew the value of the coin, not a dollar would he accept.

In three days time, the Prussian came to Po-Po's, and told us, that the captain, having made good the number of his crew, by shipping several islanders, had determined upon sailing with the land breeze, at dawn the following morning. These tidings were received in the afternoon. The doctor immediately disappeared, returning soon after with a couple of flasks of wine concealed in the folds of his frock. Through the agency of the Marquesan, he had purchased them from an understrapper of the court.

I prevailed upon Po-Po to drink a parting shell; and even little Loo, actually looking conscious that one of her hopeless admirers was about leaving Partoowye forever, sipped a few drops from a folded leaf. As for the warm-hearted Arfretee, her grief was unbounded. She even besought me to spend my last night under her own palm-thatch; and then, in the morning, she would herself paddle me off to the ship.

But this I would not consent to; and so, as something to remember her by, she presented me with a roll of fine matting, and another of tappa. These gifts placed in my hammock, I afterward found very agreeable in the warm latitudes to which we were bound; nor did they fail to awaken most grateful remembrances.

About nightfall, we broke away from this generous-hearted household, and hurried down to the water.

It was a mad, merry night among the sailors: they had on tap a small cask of wine, procured in the same way as the doctor's flasks.

An hour or two after midnight, every thing was noiseless; but when the first streak of the dawn showed itself over the mountains, a sharp voice hailed the forecastle, and ordered the ship unmoored. The anchors came up cheerily; the sails were soon set; and with the early breath of the tropical morning, fresh and fragrant from the hillsides, we slowly glided down the bay, and were swept through the opening in the reef. Presently, we " hove to," and the canoes came alongside to take off the islanders who had accompanied us thus far. As he stepped over the side, I shook the doctor long and heartily, by the hand. I have never seen or heard of him since.

Crowding all sail, we braced the yards square; and, the breeze freshening, bowled straight away from the land. Once more the sailor's cradle rocked under me, and I found myself rolling in my gait.

By noon, the island had gone down in the horizon; and all before us was the wide Pacific.

THE END.

APPENDIX.

DOCUMENTS ON THE *LUCY ANN* REVOLT.

The following are pertinent portions of notes and official records of the revolt kept by H.B.M. Acting Consul at Tahiti, Charles B. Wilson. They first came to light in 1936 when a portion of the British consular records was transferred from Tahiti to the Mitchell Library in Sydney, Australia. They were described and in part published by Ida Leeson in "The Mutiny on the *Lucy Ann*," *Philological Quarterly*, XIX [1940], 370-379. The Trustees of the Mitchell Library have kindly given permission for their inclusion in this volume.

[#1: Ship's Articles and Crew List of the *Lucy Ann*]

True copy. Charles B. Wilson, H.B.M. Acting Consul.

Articles of Agreement made this Twenty fifth day of January in the Year of Our Lord One Thousand Eight hundred and forty two Between Henry Ventom Master Mariner & commander of the Barque Lucy Ann belonging to the Port of Sydney New South Wales and now lying in Port Jackson, of the first part, and the several Officers, Seamen, and other persons whose names are hereunto subscribed and Seals affixed respectively of the second part; Whereas the said Henry Ventom being about to proceed from this Port with the said Vessel on a Whaling Voyage to the South Seas it has been mutually agreed by the parties hereto that the said persons and parties hereto of the second part shall receive the lay or proportion of the Cargo to be procured on board the said vessel hereinafter mentioned in lieu of all monthly wages. Now these presents witness that the several Officers & other persons signing this agreement parties hereto of the second part in consideration of the Lay or Share of the Cargo to be procured on board the

said Vessel set opposite to their respective names Do hereby
for themselves promise and agree to and with the said Henry
Ventom his executors administrators and assigns that they
the said persons shall and will obey and execute all the lawful
commands of the said Henry Ventom on board the said vessel
and on shore as the case may be as the Master thereof and the
commands of the Commanding Officer for the time being
during the said intended voyage and shall and will truly perform their duty in every respect as good and faithful Officers
and Seamen respectively and shall not absent themselves from
the said Ship day or night without leave from the Commanding
Officer during the continuance of this agreement and each and
every of them shall and will exert themselves to the utmost of
their power in taking and procuring Oil, Whalebone, and Head
Matter, or Seals or other animals or substances or articles
whatever that may be most for the benefit of the said Vessel or
the Owners thereof; And the said Henry Ventom in consideration of the services of the said several persons and parties
hereto of the Second part so to be done and performed as
aforesaid Doth hereby covenant Promise and Agree to and
with the said parties respectively that he the said Henry Ventom
shall and will well and truly pay or cause to be paid to them
respectively the estimated amount of Forty five Pounds Sterling
per imperial Ton for Sperm Oil and Head Matter and Twelve
pounds Sterling per Imperial Ton for Black Oil, and Fifty
pounds per ton for Whalebone which the said Vessel may bring
into and land or tranship in the Port of Sydney after such
whaling expedition aforesaid for such shares of Oil, head
matter and Whalebone as are set opposite to their respective
names subscribed at the foot of these presents and market price
for such other animal substances and articles as may be brought
into the Port of Sydney and landed or transhipped after such
voyage for such shares of these articles as are set opposite to
their respective names after deducting five shillings for Medicine
Chest for each individual and the parties to these presents
respectively to pay half the charge of a sworn Gauger for
gauging the Oil. Provided always and as hereby declared and
agreed that if any of the said Officers, Seamen or other persons
parties hereto of the second part shall desert and leave the said
vessel during the said voyage without leave of the Master or
Commanding Officer for the time being the party or parties so
offending shall forfeit the whole of such share of the said cargo

as would otherwise be due to him or them & it is also hereby agreed that an absence of Four and twenty hours is a desertion within the meaning of these presents; and it is hereby further declared & agreed by the persons parties hereto of the second part that in case of any of them being disorderly insubordinate or mutinous or not in every respect doing their duty as becometh good and faithful Officers and seamen respectively that the party or parties so offending shall not only be liable to all legal penalties for the same but also forfeit the whole lay or share of the cargo to be procured as would otherwise be due to him or them. And it is hereby further provided and agreed by the parties hereto of the second part that they shall not for their own use and emolument, Give, Sell, Barter, Exchange, or Secret any part of the Oil or other articles merchandize or substance whatever which may be obtained or taken or found in the aforesaid voyage. In witness whereof the said parties to these presents have hereunto set their hands and seals the day and year first above written.

Signed Sealed and Delivered in the presence of Witness this 25th day of Jany 1842.

Joseph Geo. Raphael   Henry Ventom

[Names italicized were cancelled on this list, which is Wilson's certified " True Copy." The list includes the original crew which sailed from Sydney (witnessed by Raphael, Latham, and German), those who signed on at various islands (witnessed by German), and those recruited at Tahiti (witnessed by Wilson).]

Name	Station	Lay or Share	Advances £ s d	Witness	Seals
James German	Mate	28th	20 » »	H. Ventom	
Gabriel King	2nd Mate	45th	10 » »	J. G. Raphael	
John Murray	Carpenter	90th & £ 2p.m.	7 » »	J. G. Raphael	
Edward Ewing X his mark	Cooper		10 » »	J. G. Raphael	
Jas. X Hall	Cook	120th lay	6 » »	J. German	
Willm B. Bell	Steward	110th	6 » »	J. G. Raphael	
John B. Troy	Steward	110th	6 » »		
Benbow X Byrne	Boatsteerer	100th	6 » »	J. German	
George X Anthony	Boatsteerer	100th	6 » »	J. G. Raphael	
Leaky X	Boatsteerer	100th	6 » »	J. G. Raphael	
William X Michidi	»	100th	6 » »	J. G. Raphael	HGL.
Walker	Able Seaman	120th	5 » »	J. G. Raphael	
Henry Smith	»	120th	5 » »	J. G. Raphael	
Manuel SeNore	»	120th	5 » »	J. G. Raphael	
Johnny X N Z	»	120th	5 » »	H. G. Latham	CWP
William X Brown	»	120th	6 » »	J. G. Raphael	
John Yeoman	»	120th	6 » »	J. G. Raphael	
George X Lefevre	» mutiny	120th	5 » »	J. German	
John H. Fish	2nd Offr.	45th	8 » »	Chas. B. Wilson	
Abm. Pierce	3 Offr.	80th	5 » »	Chas. B. Wilson	
David Fraser	Ordy. Seam.	140th	4 » »	J. G. Raphael	
John Nash	Do.	140th	4 » »	J. G. Raphael	
his Tommy X mark	Do.	140th	4 » »	J. G. Raphael	
Charles Stewart his	Able Sea.	120th	5 » »	J. G. Raphael	
James X Yeomans mark	Ordy. Sea.	140th	5 » »	J. G. Raphael	
Robert Davis	Do.	140th	4 » »	J. G. Raphael	
James Watts	Do.	140th	5 » »	J. G. Raphael	
James Smyth	Do.	140th	5 » »	J. G. Raphael	
William Mathews	Ordy. Seaman	140th Lay	5 » »	J. G. Raphael	
Charles F. P. Cross	»	140th	5 » »	J. G. Raphael	
James Watts	»	140th	5 » »	J. G. Raphael	
Henry Burke his	»	140th	5 » »	H. G. Latham	
Andrew X Blackburn mark	Cooper	90th & 2p mth	10 » »	T. Byrne	

Name	Station	Lay or Share	Advances £ s d	Witness	Seals
John Peter	Able Seaman	120th	6 J	J. G. Raphael	
James Bayley	»	120th		J. German	
John X Garretson	Boatsteerer	100th	the cruise	J. German	
Joseph Jackson	Carpenter	80th & ½ p mth		J. German	
Charles X Watts	Able Seaman	120th	the cruise	J. German	
Nicholas X Utley	Ordinary	140th	the cruise	J. German	
Herman Melville	Able Seaman	120th		J. German	
Friday X	Able Seaman	120th		J. German	
John X White	Able Seaman	120th		J. German	
William Bunnell	Able Seaman	120th		J. German	
Amado Silva	Able Seaman	120th	the cruise	J. German	
Tihemu X	Ordinary	140th		Chas. B. Wilson	
Maharo X	Ordinary	140th	2 » »	Chas. B. Wilson	
Peter Redpath Jr.	Ordinary	140th	2 » »	Chas. B. Wilson	
Joseph Louis his	Ordinary	140th	2 » »	Chas. B. Wilson	
Immanuel X Fanny mark his	Ordinary	140th	2 » »	Chas. B. Wilson	
Immanuel X Castille mark his	Ordinary	140th	2 » »	Chas. B. Wilson	
Henry X Chili mark	Ordinary	140th	2 » »	Chas. B. Wilson	
Henry Willoughby his	Ordinary	140th	2 » »	Chas. B. Wilson	
Francis X Lopez mark his	Boatsteerer	100th	2 » »	Chas. B. Wilson	
William X Place mark his	Able Seaman	120th	3 » »	Chas. B. Wilson	
George X Smith mark	Boatsteerer	100th	3 4 »	Chas. B. Wilson	
Thomas Silsbee his	Ordinary	140th	2 » »	Chas. B. Wilson	
Robert X Perry mark	Able Seaman	120th	3 » 12	Chas. B. Wilson	
Richard Jones	Able Seaman	120th	4 » »	Chas. B. Wilson	
Silvester Druitt	Able Seaman	120th	2 8 »	Chas. B. Wilson	

[# 2]

To C.B. Wilson Esq. H.B.M. Acting Consul
Sir According to order I have examined the following sick
seamen on Board the Barque Lucy Ann of Sydney and pronounce Nicholas S. Utley and Henery Smith unfit to proceed
to sea.

I have also Examined Wm. Matthews, John Troy, Herman
Melville, & James Smith. They are in my opinion fit to go on
the voyage and that in a week or two they with care will be
able to perform their duties as seamen.

Tahiti 22nd. Sept. 1842

Yours respectfy.
F. Johnstone Surgeon

[# 3]

To C. B. Wilson Esq. H.B.M. Acting Consul
Sir I hereby pronounce Captain Ventom of the Barque Lucy
Ann of Sydney unfit to proceed to Sea In consequence of a
deep Seated abcess having formed in the perineum accompanied
with Inflamation

Tahiti Sept. 24th 1842

Yours respectfully
F. Johnstone Surgeon

[# 4]

I do hereby certify on application of "Henry Ventom"
Master of the Barque "Lucy Ann" of Sydney who in evidence
of the truth thereof has unto me made solemn and sincere
declaration hereunto subscribing his name

That "Henry Smith" able Seaman as per articles signed
in Sydney on the 25th day of January 1842 — and "Nicholas
S. Utley" ordinary Seaman as per articles signed at the Island
of "Nukahiva," Marquesas on the 8th day of Augt. 1842 are
both incapacitated through sickness from doing their duty on
board of said vessel as certified by "Francis Johnstone" who
in evidence of the truth thereof hereunto subscribes his name.
And said barque being now about to proceed on her Whaling
Voyage the said "Henry Smith" and Nicholas S. Utley are
left behind for the cause above stated.

In testimony whereof I have hereunto delivered this my
certificate unto said Master at the British Consulate Tahiti

this twenty fourth day of September one thousand eight
hundred and forty two—

Chas. B. Wilson
H.B.M. Acting Consul
Master H. Ventom
Surgeon F. Johnstone

[#5]

24.9.42

Sir

I have to request that you will take the Bark "Lucy Ann"
into your hands *as* I am not able *through* sickness to do any
thing myself. A number of the people refused their duty while
lying off and on which forced the Chf Officer to bring her
into Port, which is contrary to my orders. It is running the
Ship to a great expence and sacrificing the owners property.
I therefore beg you will see every thing rectified—

H. Ventom
Master Lucy Ann

C.B. Wilson Esq
H B M Consul
—Tahiti—

[endorsed] Henry Ventom/ Sept. 24th. 42/ Complaint against
Crew

[addressed] C.B. Wilson Esq; H B M Consul

[#6: Pencilled note in Melville's handwriting]

On Board the Lucy Ann
September 25th 1842

Dear George

On arriving here the other day I was sorry to hear that you
were verry ill on board the French Frigate.—I should like
verry much to go and see you but I cannot possibly as I can
not be allowed to;—so I take the liberty to write you a few lines.
—You know we all agreed to hang out on your account when
we came aboard from the Corvette—but it so happened that
those who talked loudest were the first to return to their
duty. I was the last one that went forward, and would not have
turned to at all, but that I found it was of no use, so after
being in double irons some time I thought it best to go forward & do my duty as usual

You must remember me to Peter
I do not know that I have any thing further to say to you
   I often think of you & I & Young Smith have often talked
about you during the night watches at sea
                  —Good bye
                      My Dear George
                    Hoping you will be soon at liberty
                    I remain Yours &c
                      Henry Smyth
George Lefevre
On Board the French Frigate

[#7: Wilson's Notes]
1. James Watt ————
2. Henry Burke ————
3. Wm. Bunnel ————
4. Wm. Matthews ———— one day's allowance stopped—
5. John Garretson ———— Mr. German not fit to take charge
6. Amado Sylva ———— for continually drunkenness—
7. J. B. Troy ————
8. David Fraser ————
9. Charles Watt ————
10. James Smyth ————
11. Herman Melville ——

[#8: Wilson's Draft of a Letter, endorsed "No. 4 Letter to
Council respecting trial of Lucy Ann men. Oct 5/42".]

                                  B.C. Tahiti
                                  Oct. 5/42
Gentlemen: I have the honour to request the favour of your
assistance in deciding an exceedingly difficult case I have to
dispose of belong[ing] to the British Whaling Barque "Lucy
Ann."
   I have summoned all parties this day for a final examination, and have taken the necessary depositions respecting the
case. I shall therefore consider it a favour if you will attend
at the office of this Consulate at 2 P M this day if convenient,
and if it will not interfere with your official duties to render
me that assistance I require in making such final examination

and deciding and disposing of this Case according to the Evidence of such examination.

I have etc

C.B.W. HBMC

[#9: Reply of Provisional Council to #8]

4.10.42

Monsieur Le Consul

Depuis la lettre que vous venez de nous envoyer et par laquelle vous nous priez d'assister à l'interrogatoire que vous devez faire subir aux hommes du Baleinier anglais La Lucy-ann, nous vous annonçons avec regret que notre position ne nous permet pas de faire partie d'un conseil pour juger la conduite des marins à bord des Bâtiments étrangers.

Désirant çependant vous assister autant que faire se peut de notre part nous vous dirons, qu'après nous être consultés en commun; notre opinion sur la conduite à tenir dans cette circonstance ci est de contraindre les prisonniers, par tous les moyens que vous avez à vôtre disposition, à retourner a leur devoir.

Ceux auprès desquels échoueraient vos tentatives seraient condamnés à séjourner en prison jusqu'à l'arrivé d'un Bâtiment de guerre qui puisse en faire justice.

Croyez Monsieur à L'assurance de notre Parfaite considération

Les membres du conseil.

J.A. Moerenhout E. Reine De Carpegna

Taïti Le 5 8bre. 1842 ou Style véritable Le 4 8bre. 1842

Monsieur J. B. Wilson Consul de S.M. Britannique. Taiti

[Rough-note, translating the above]

Mr. Consul,

From the letter which you sent us and in which you beg us to be present at the examination which you are obliged to make the men from the English whaler the Lucy Ann to undergo we announce to you with regret that our position permits us not of forming a part of a council to judge the conduct of mariners on board of Foreign Vessels.

Desiring in the mean time to assist you, as much as possible on our part we have to tell you, that after consulting among ourselves our opinion upon the conduct to pursue in this affair it is to compel the prisoners by all the means which you have

at your command to return them to their duty. They with
whom your endeavours are unsuccessful ought to be condemned
to sojourn in prison till the arrival of a vessel of war which can
do justice in the case.

Believe Sir etc etc

[#10: Wilson's Notes]

Utley—at Nukahiva Augt. 8th
H. Melville at Do.   » 9th
Chas. Watts   Do.   » 8th
Troy Deserted at Nukahiva 7th Aug. apprehended on the 8th—
    with the medicines stolen same day
Arrived off Tahiti—Sept. 20th.
Capt. Ventom came ashore Sept. 22.
Lucy Ann Went aboard & exam crew on the 22nd.
Lucy Ann came in 24th. Saturday
On 24th. 10 men—put on board the Frigate
Monday 26th Prisoners landed from Frigate and given in
    charge of the native Authorities—
Thursday 29th Examined Prisoners, still refused & sent back to
    prison & Herman Melville joined the Ten—
Oct. 5 Finally examined the prisoners
Oct. 6—Shipped men in room of Prisoners—

[#11: "Tahiti Octr 5th 1842. Depositions against Eleven Seamen
    belonging to the Barque 'Lucy Ann' of Sydney for Revolt
    and refusing duty."]

British Consulate
Tahiti, October 5th 1842

I Charles Burnet Wilson, H.B.M. Acting Consul for the Society
and Friendly Islands by lawful authority duly appointed, Do
hereby certify that personally appeared before me; in my
presence and in the presence of the said "Richard Barff" at
the British Consulate, Tahiti, on the fifth day of October One
Thousand eight hundred and forty two, the within Named
"Henry Ventom"—"James German"—"Benbow Byrne"—
and "Joseph Jackson"—"Andrew Blackburn"—"William
Brown"—"George Antonio"—"James Hall"—"Charles F. P.
Cross" "Robert Davis"—and "Immanuel Senora"—all be-

longing to the Barque "Lucy Ann" of Sydney—and "Francis
Johnstone," Surgeon residing at Tahiti, Did all make oath to
the truth and correctness of the statements contained in the
Depositions herewith annexed made by them against the said
" John Garritson "—" William Bunnell "—" Amado Sylva "—
" Charles Watts "—James Smyth—Henry Burke—" James
Watts "—" William Matthews "—" David Fraser "—and " Herman Melville " also belonging to the said Barque — for committing a revolt and refusing to do their duty on board of the
said Barque "Lucy Ann"—and against the said "John B.
Troy" Steward of the said Barque for embezzling several
medicines from the medicine Chest belonging to the owners
of said Barque, and also for refusing to do his duty on board
of the said Barque "Lucy Ann"——

Given under my hand and Seal of Office at the British
Consulate of Tahiti this Fifth day of October, one thousand
eight hundred and forty two——

Chas. B. Wilson
H.B.M. Actg. Consul

No. 1

" Henry Ventom " master of the Barque "Lucy Ann " of
Sydney; sworn; deposeth,

I am master of the Barque "Lucy Ann " of Sydney, the
said Barque sailed from Sydney on a whaling voyage February
the eighteenth one Thousand Eight Hundred and Forty two.
Last June I took said Barque to the Marquesas Islands and on
the seventh of said month, anchored in Resolution Bay in the
island of " Sta. Christine," where I procured wood & water and
got refreshments for the ship's company. Eight of the crew and
the second officer deserted at said place and two more of the
crew for being mutinous I put in irons and delivered up to
the Commandant who delivered them up to the Rear Admiral
A. du Petit Thouars on board the French Frigate "Reine
Blanche" to be delivered up to the English Admiral commanding in chief at Valparaiso.

At the islands of " Nukuhiva " and " Dominica " I shipped
men in the room of the deserters and made up my complement
of crew. On the twentieth of August last I left the Marquesas
with the full complement of able & ordinary seamen but not
officers and made sail to the westward in the prosecution of
the voyage. I was then perfectly well in health & strength and
all on board with the exception of five of the crew who were

ailing & ill of the venereal. On the Twenty seventh of August last I was taken ill and on the fourth of September last I was confined to my cabin. My complaint increased and on the 8th of the same month I instructed Mr. German my Chief officer to proceed to Tahiti. We made Tahiti on the 20th of same month. I sent the Chief Officer on shore for a Doctor who brought one off (Doctor Johnstone) in the afternoon of the same day. After the Doctor examined me he said I must be removed on shore for the safety of my life. On the Twenty second day of the same month I was lowered down with the boat and taken on shore and put in a house engaged by Mr. Wilson the Acting Consul. When I came on shore I told the Chief officer to take charge of the vessel during my absence, to keep her off and on the port. I did not them make final arrangements for his prosecuting the voyage. I requested the Acting Consul to go on board to inform the crew of my being obliged (for the benefit of my health) to be left on shore & in the mean time to acquaint them that the Chief officer would take command and to respect him as such.

In the evening of the same day after returning from the vessel, the Acting Consul informed me that he had been on board and that the crew had no objection to prosecute the voyage during my sickness under my Chief officer, and had no complaint to make only that they wished the sick men taken out of the vessel and the full complement of seamen and officers, which the Acting Consul told them he had promised to make up and send on board the next day. The crew made no complaints before I left the vessel. I never told the Chief Officer to bring the vessel into port but gave him positive instructions to lay off & on the port only. Next day Mr. Wilson shipped two officers and two men for me who were to have gone on board in the afternoon of the same day, a boat being hired expressly to convey them on board.

On Saturday morning the Twenty fourth of the same month the vessel was brought into port. The Chief officer waited upon me and told me he was obliged to bring the vessel into port in consequence of Ten of the crew having refused to do any more duty, there not being left sufficient on duty to work the vessel, and to keep her at sea with safety. I again applied to the Acting Consul who went on board and had all who refused to do their duty who were the occasion of the vessel being brought into port taken out of the vessel and put into prison.

On Wednesday the Twenty Seventh of same month the

Acting Consul examined the Prisoners before me and in presence of Dr. Myrick, they all still positively refused to do their duty whether I again went on board or whether the Chief officer took command. They could assign no other reason than that " Mr. German the Chief Officer was not capable of taking charge of the vessel, that they signed under Captain ' Ventom ' and not under the mate, and that they would not do any more duty on board of her." They were all combined and would not return to their duty. The Acting Consul then sent them all back to prison and told them they should be kept there until they thought proper to return to their duty.

Having left the last port of the Marquesas only about six weeks since, there being plenty of provisions on board and everything else requisite for prosecuting the voyage, I did not consider it necessary for the vessel to be brought into port for the purpose of landing me and the others who were sick and to ship three or four men to make up the full complement of crew. If the men had behaved themselves as good seamen they would not have refused duty merely for the sake of going into port. The names of the men who refused to do duty are John B. Troy, " Henry Burk "—" James Smyth "—" William Matthews "—" David Frazer "—" Amado Sylva "—" John Garretson "—" William Bunnel "—" Charles Watts "—" James Watts "—and " Herman Melville ". The vessel coming into port has occasioned unnecessary expense & loss to the owners.

H. Ventom Master

Witnesses
Chas. B. Wilson

No. 2

Francis Johnstone Surgeon, sworn; deposeth, I reside at Tahiti; on the Twentieth of September I received a letter from Mr. Wilson the Acting Consul requesting me to proceed on board the Barque " Lucy Ann " then in the offing, to render Medical aid to the Master of said Barque. I went on board with the Chief Officer in the afternoon of the same day and examined the said master. I found him in a dangerous state. When I returned on shore, I reported to Mr. Wilson that the said Master was in such a state as to render it absolutely necessary for the recovery of his health to be left on shore and furnished the said Acting Consul with my certificate of the state of the said master. On the Twenty second same month the Captain was brought on shore. In the afternoon of the same day I was requested by said Acting Consul to accompany him on board the said Barque to examine some of the crew who complained of being sick. I examined them and furnished the said Acting Consul with my Certificate. "Utley" and "Henry Smyth" two of the six who complained of being sick were the only two necessary to be taken out of the vessel. I remember on the same afternoon the crew being called aft by Mr. Wilson. I heard them make no other complaint than that the vessel had not her complement of Seamen and officers. Mr. Wilson told them he would endeavour to make up the deficiency and send them on board the next day. I also heard Mr. Wilson tell them that there was no occasion for the vessel to be taken into port for that purpose.

I have rendered medicine and medical aid to the said master ever since and I now consider him out of danger and sufficiently well to conduct the vessel in the prosecution of her voyage.

                                        F. Johnstone, Surgeon
Witnesses
Chas. B. Wilson
Richard Barff

No. 3

James German, Chief officer, Sworn; deposeth,
I am Chief officer of the Barque "Lucy Ann" "Henry Ventom" Master. I shipped on board said Barque and signed articles in Sydney for a Whaling Voyage on the 25th January last, and sailed from Sydney in February last—We anchored in Resolution Bay at the Marquesas Islands in July last, and there procured wood, water, pigs and other refreshments for the crew. We laid at anchor in said Bay about three weeks— The second Mate, carpenter, and seven others of the crew deserted from the ship while laying in that Bay. I do not know the cause of their running away, they had good and plenty of provisions, good treatment and liberty time while in port —The carpenter run away with one of the boats. We got the boat back having been recovered by order of the French Commandant at said Island. After leaving Resolution Bay we went to the Islands of "Nukahiva" and "Dominica" and shipped men in the place of those who deserted. About a day or two after leaving the Marquesas the Captain complained of being

ill and soon after was confined to his cabin not able to walk —He instructed me to take the vessel to Tahiti for the purpose of getting medical advice. The Captain being in such a dangerous state I previously hauled up for Tahiti, without his knowledge—When we arrived off Tahiti on the 20th of September last I went on shore and brought Doctor Johnstone on board who examined the Captain and said that he would have to be left on shore to recover his health. On the 22nd of the same month I took the Captain on shore and brought on board Mr. Wilson the Acting Consul and Dr. Johnstone in the afternoon of the same day. The Doctor examined some of the crew who complained of being ill and not able to work—The Acting Consul had the men mustered aft—they all said in answer to Mr. Wilson's questions that they had good provisions on board and enough of them, that they had no fault to find with me, and had no objection to do their duty under me as commander for a short cruise while the Captain was left ashore for the benefit of his health, if they had the full complement of seamen and officers—Mr. Wilson said that if they had no other complaint he would endeavour to rectify it by shipping men and officers to make up the full complement of crew—that there should be sufficient to lower four boats. Soon after " Garretson "—" Sylva "— and " C. Watts " said that they would do no more duty on board of the vessel—they said "We signed under Captain 'Ventom' and not under the mate and our agreement is broken by the Captain's leaving and going on shore." Shortly after Mr. Wilson left the vessel several more of the crew refused to do their duty and during the night Twelve of the crew including those who said were ill were off duty—" Troy "—" Matthews "— " J. Smyth "—and " Melville " were reported by the Doctor well enough to do their duty " Utley "—and " Henry Smyth " were not well enough to do duty—and " Burk "—" Garretson " —" C. Watts "—" J. Watts "—" Sylva "—and " Fraser " refused because I was to take command of the vessel. Captain " Ventom " did not tell me to bring the vessel into port. I do not now remember him particularly telling me " *to lay off and on the port with the vessel.*" Next morning on the 24th those who refused to do duty last evening still remained so. When I told them to *turn to* they said they did not sign under me and would do no more duty on board; and would not proceed on the voyage, that the cruise was up and that I was not a fit person to command the ship. About seven o'clock of the same morning I bore up and took the vessel into the port of Papeete, because there were not sufficient men on board who did their duty to take care of the ship. After I brought the ship to an anchor, the Acting Consul came on board and asked me the reason I brought the ship into an anchor, contrary to the Captain's orders. I told him that I had not a sufficient number of men on duty to work the vessel. The Acting Consul then told me to muster the crew aft which I did & placed on one side of the deck all who refused to do duty. They then also said that they would do no more duty on board of the vessel.

In the afternoon of the same day the Acting Consul came on board again & soon afterwards an armed boat come alongside from the French Frigate " Reine Blanche " with an officer who took out of the ship all who refused to do their duty—" Garretson "—" Sylva "—" Bunnell "—and " Charles Watts "—were the first who refused their duty and I believe them to be the ringleaders in the affair—" Troy "—" Matthews " and " Henry Smyth " deserted at the island of Nukuheva in the Marquesas, were apprehended and returned on board—"Troy" had charge of the medicine chest and when he deserted stole several medicines which were afterwards found and returned to the Captain by the natives, the same now produced which I delivered to the Acting Consul at the Consulate on Tuesday last.

On Wednesday the 29th of the same month I was present when the said Acting Consul before the Captain & Doctor Myrick examined the prisoners who again requested of them to return to their duty, they refused & again gave the same reasons for refusing as they did the morning I took the ship in. " Herman Melville " also said that he would do no more duty and would share the same as the others who refused to do their duty. Their articles of agreement were then read to them and they all ordered to be taken back to prison till they would return to their duty.

I have never ill treated any of the crew during the voyage and they have never had any just reason to complain of their bad treatment on board the ship nor about the provisions.

On the night of the 23rd of the same month in the first watch I ordered " Benbow Burn " (who had charge of the watch) to set the Jib and Foresail; about an hour afterwards " James Watts " came to me and told me that said " Benbow " had struck him, because he the said " James Watts " wanted to set the Jib and said " Benbow " ordered him not. I then told said " Benbow " that he had no business to strike said " Watts "—I was not on deck when it happened—I did not see " Benbow " strike " Watts," neither did I sanction " Benbow's " striking said " Watts."

Wittnesses	James German
Chas. B. Wilson	Chief Officer
Richard Barff	Barque Lucy Ann

No. 4

Benbow Byrne, Boatsteerer, Acting third mate; sworn; deposeth,
    I am acting third mate on board of the Barque " Lucy Ann " of Sydney, Henry Ventom Master. I shipped and signed articles of agreement as Boatsteerer in Sydney to proceed on a whaling voyage. We were at the Marquesas Islands in July last. We anchored in Resolution Bay and laid there about three weeks, where we got wood, water, pigs and other refreshments. Several of the crew ran away there and others were shipped in their room at the Islands of Nukuhiva and " Dominica," Marquesas. Soon after we left the Marquesas Islands the Captain was taken sick and confined to his cabin. The Mate brought the vessel to Tahiti on account of the Captain's sickness to get medical advice for him. After the Captain was landed at Tahiti several of the crew refused to do their duty, " John Garretson "—" William Bunnell "—"Charles Watt " and " Armado Sylva " were the first who refused to do their duty because the Captain was to be left on shore and the Mate to have charge of the vessel for a short cruise while the Captain was recruiting his health. I remember the Acting Consul with the Doctor came on board in the afternoon of the same day the Captain was brought on shore. The Ship's company was mustered aft and the only complaint they made was that " there was not on board the full complement of seamen and officers ". They found no fault with the provisions nor with the treatment they had received on board of the said vessel. They also found no fault with the mate. The acting Consul then told them that he would make up the complement, of crew and officers and send them on board the next day. We were then two officers short and two ordinary seamen short of the full complement besides those who were sick. The Doctor examined the sick and said

there were only two "Utley" and "Henry Smith" required to be left on shore. After the Acting Consul left the Ship several others refused to do their duty. I had the first watch that night, the mate told me to set the Jib and Foresail. I ordered the watch to set those sails. "James Watts" said that he would not obey my orders and when I told him to haul down the fore tack, he replied saying "Ask my arse". I then struck him. "Troy" took his part. After the quarrel "Watts" said he would do no more duty and went below.

Next morning "Garretson"—"Bunnell" "Charles Watts" —"James Watts"—"Armado Sylva"—"James Smyth"— "Henry Burke"—"J. B. Troy"—"Matthews"—and "Fraser" were off duty and said they would do no more duty on board of the vessel. The mate said that he could not keep the ship out at sea if they still refused to do their duty to work the vessel. They still refused and the mate then bore up and brought the ship into Papeete harbour to an anchor. The night before the ship was brought in the mate was quite sober. I do not remember him saying that he would take the ship into the harbour at midnight. The crew appeared perfectly satisfied with their treatment on board after we left the Marquesas. I remember "Troy" having deserted at the Island of "Nukuhiva" and his having stolen several medicines. The natives apprehended him with the medicines and delivered them up to the Captain who sent them on board—They were rolled up in his (Troy) blanket. I opened the blanket on board when the medicines fell out. The medicines are those now produced.

I remember "Troy" saying in the presence of the Mate, just after supper one evening that he was drunk or else he never would have taken the medicines.

Witnesses	his
Chas. B. Wilson	Benbow X Byrne
Richard Barff	mark

No. 5

We the undersigned "Joseph Jackson", Carpenter— "Andrew Blackburn", Cooper—"William Brown", Able Sea-man—"George Antonio", Boatsteerer—"James Hall", Cook —"Charles F. P. Cross", ordinary Seaman—"Immanuel Se-nora", ordinary Seaman—and "Robert Davis", ordinary Seaman—belonging to the crew of the Barque " Lucy Ann " of Sydney—Henry Ventom, Master: Do Hereby Solemnly and sincerely declare on oath that " John Garetson " " William Bunnell "—" James Smyth "—"Charles Watts "—"Henry Burke " —" Amado Sylva "—" Herman Melville "—" John B. Troy "— " William Matthews "—and David Fraser—belonging to the crew of the said Barque " Lucy Ann ": did all on the Twenty seventh day of September last and on this day the fifth day of October in our presence, when requested by the said " Henry Ventom " and H.B.M. Acting Consul to return to their duty, positively refuse and declared that they would not do any more duty on board of said Barque " Lucy Ann ".

We hereby also do solemnly and sincerely declare on oath that we never have had cause nor did we refuse to do our duty on board of said Barque. Neither did we aid and abett the above named parties in refusing to do their duty and that we are perfectly satisfied with the provisions and treatment we have received from the same " Henry Ventom " and his Officers on board of the said Barque " Lucy Ann ".

Witnesses
Chas. B. Wilson
H.B.M. Acting Consul

Joseph Jackson

his
Andrew X Blackburn
mark

his
William X Brown
mark

his
George X Antonio
mark

his
James X Hall
mark

Charles F. P. Cross
Robert Davis

his
Immanuel X Senora
mark

[# 12]

British Consulate
Tahiti October 5th 1842

I, Charles Burnet Wilson H.B.M. Acting Consul for the Society and Friendly Islands by lawful authority duly appointed Do hereby certify that John Garretson William Bunnell—Amado Sylva—and Charles Watts did in my presence and in the presence of Francis Johnstone, Surgeon, on the evening of the twenty third day of September last refuse to do their duty on board of the said Barque " Lucy Ann " of Sydney——That on the morning of the Twenty fourth day of said month of September the said Barque " Lucy Ann " was brought into the Port of Papeete, Tahiti, by James German the Chief Officer of said Barque contrary to the orders of Henry Ventom the Master of said Barque, who was on shore incapacitated to do his duty through sickness and that the said James German was compelled to bring the said Barque into Port in consequence of the greater part of the crew having revolted in the offing and refused to do any more duty on board of said Barque——That before me on board of said Barque " Lucy Ann " on same said Twenty fourth day of September James Smyth—Henry Burke—James Watts—John B. Troy— William Matthews—and David Fraser did join the before said named Garritson—Bunnell—Sylva—and Charles Watts— and did all positively refuse to do their duty on board of said Barque—That on the afternoon of said day of said month I caused the above named said Garritson—Bunnell—Sylva— Charles Watts—James Smyth—Henry Burke—James Watts— John B. Troy—William Matthews—and David Fraser to be confined in prison for such revolt and refusal of duty—That on the Twenty seventh day of said month of September before me and in the presence of Doctor Myrick residing at Tahiti Herman Melville with the said Garretson—Bunnell—Sylva— Charles Watts—James Smyth—Henry Burke—James Watts— John B. Troy—William Matthews—and David Fraser did all refuse to return to their duty on board of said Barque " Lucy Ann " whether said Henry Ventom again went on board or not or whether the said " James German " then Commanding Officer was to take charge of said Barque for a short cruise while the said Henry Ventom remained on shore for the benefit of his health—That after such refusal I again caused the before named revolters to be again returned to prison there to remain until they the said revolters would return to their duty—That finally on this Fifth day of October the said revolters did all in the British Consulate Tahiti before me and in the presence of the said Richard Barff and in the presence of the said Master, Chief Officer and members of the crew of said Barque " Lucy Ann " positively refuse to return to their duty on board of said Barque without just cause or reason——

And I also do hereby certify that I the said Acting Consul on application of said Master caused the before named Garritson—Bunnell—Sylva—Charles Watts—James Smyth—Henry Burke—James Watts—John B. Troy—William Matthews—and David Fraser to be returned to prison and kept in confinement in charge of the Tahitian authorities for such *revolt* and *refusal of duty* as preferred against the before named Garritson—Bunnell—Sylva—Charles Watts—James Smyth—Henry Burke—James Watts—William Matthews—David Fraser—and for embezzlement and refusal of duty as preferred against the said " John B. Troy "——

In testimony whereof I have hereunto set my hand and seal of Office at the British Consulate Tahiti this Fifth day of October One Thousand Eight hundred and forty two——

Chas. B. Wilson
H.B.M. Actg. Consul

[# 13: Wilson's Memorandum, " Seamen belonging to Barque 'Lucy Ann ' of Sydney committed to the charge of Local Authorities for revolt and refusal of Duty, Tahiti, Oct. 5th 1842—"]

No.	Mens Names	Quality,	Situation When and where shipped	Lay
1.	John Garretson	Boatsteer	2nd Augt. Dominaca	100th
2.	William Bunnell	Able Seaman	26th Augt. Dominaca	120th
3.	James Smyth	ordy. Seaman	25th Jany. Sydney	140th
4.	Charles Watts	Able Seaman	8th Augt. Nukahiva	120th
5.	James Watts	Ordy. Seaman	25th Jany. Sydney	140th
6.	Henry Burke	Ordy. Seaman	25th Jany. Sydney	140th
7.	Amado Sylva	Able Seaman	26th Augt. Dominaca	120th
8.	Herman Melville	Able Seaman	9th Augt. Nukahiva	120th
9.	John B. Troy	Steward	25th Jany. Sydney	110th
10.	William Matthews	Ordy. Seaman	25th Jany. Sydney	140th
11.	David Fraser	Ordy. Seaman	25th Jany. Sydney	140th

[Columns for "Age," "Place, Quality, Birth, Situation," and "Balance Due" have been editorially omitted since no entries appeared in them. In a column for "Advance," advances of 5 pounds were listed for Smyth, J. Watts, Matthews, of 4 pounds for Burke and Fraser, and of 6 pounds for Troy.]

[#14: Draft of Wilson's report to the Governor of New South Wales]

B. C.
Tahiti Oct. 5, 1842

I have the honor to inform your Excellency that I have been necessitated to confine in charge of the local authorities of this Island & to be kept in confinement until the arrival of one of HBM's ships—Eleven seamen belonging to the Barque Lucy Ann of Sydney for a revolt refusing to do their duty, and forcing the Chief Offr in the absence of the Master thro sickness to take the said Barque into the Port of Papeete in this island.—

I have the honor to be Your Excellencys Most obdt. & humble CBW

[#15]

I do hereby certify on application of "Henry Ventom" Master of the Barque "Lucy Ann" of Sydney, who, in evidence of the truth thereof has unto me made solemn and sincere declaration and who with "James German" Chief Officer of said Barque hereunto subscribe their names, that "John Garretson" boatsteerer, as per Articles Signed at the Island of *Dominica*, Marquesas, on the 26th day of August, 1842— "William Bunnell" Able Seaman as per Articles Signed at the Island of *Dominica*, Marquesas, on the 26 th day of August 1842—"Charles Watts" Able Seaman as per Articles signed at the Island of "Nukahiva" Marquesas on the 8th day of August 1842—"Amado Sylva" Able Seaman, as per Articles Signed at the Island of *Dominica* Marquesas, on the 26th day of August, 1842.—"Herman Melville" Able Seaman, as per Articles Signed at the Island of "Nukahiva," Marquesas, on the 9th day of August, 1842. and "James Smyth"—Ordinary Seaman,—"James Watts" Ordinary Seaman,—Henry Burke Ordinary Seaman— "John B. Troy" Steward—"William Matthews" Ordinary Seaman,—

and " David Fraser " Ordinary Seaman, as per Articles signed at
Sydney on the 25th day of Jany. 1842.—
all having previously refused to do their
duty and which being the cause of the
said Barque " Lucy Ann " being brought
into the Port of Papeete, Tahiti, Did on
the fifth day of October, 1842, at the British
Consulate Tahiti in my presence, and in the
presence of Francis Johnstone and " Richard
Barff " all combine together and without
just cause positively refuse to return to
their duty on board the said Barque
" Lucy Ann "—
        And the said Barque " Lucy Ann " being now
about to proceed on her
Whaling Voyage the said " Garretson "—
" Bunnell "—" Charles Watts "—" James Watts "—
" Sylva "—" Melville "—Smyth "—Burke "—
" Troy "—" Matthews " and " Fraser " are left behind
as revolters, for the cause before stated—
and that on the Sixth day of October
with my privity others signed articles and
shipped on board said Barque Lucy Ann
in their room—
            In testimony whereof I have hereunto
        delivered this my certificate to said Master at the British
        Consulate Tahiti this sixth day of October, One thousand,
        eight hundred and forty two——
H. Ventom—Master—
        —Mate

                        Chas. B. Wilson
                        H.B.M. Actg. Consul

[#16]
Crew of Barque " Lucy Ann " at Tahiti—Oct. 6th/42

No.	Names	Situation	Advance
1.	Henry Ventom	Master	
2.	James German	1st Mate	
3.	John H. Fish	2nd Mate	40 p.
4.	Abraham Pierce	3d Mate	25 p.
5.	Andrew Blackburn	Cooper	

No.	Names	Situation	Advance	
6.	John Jackson	Carpenter		
7.	Benbow Byrne	Boatsteerer		
8.	George Antonio	Do.		
9.	Emmanuel Senore	Do.		
10.	Francis Lopez [cancelled]	Do.		
11.	James Hall	Cook		
12.	Charles F. P. Cross	Act. Steward		
13.	William Brown	Able seaman		
14.	William Place [cancelled]	Do.		
15.	Thomas ^{his} Brewer _{mark}	Ord S.	(14) 12 p.	
16.	Charles Bantom	Ordinary	(15) 12 p.	
17.	Robert Davis	Ordy. Seaman		
18.	Jacky Wai Marquesas	Do.		
19.	Peter Redpath	Do.	(1) 10 p.	
20.	Joseph Louis	Do.	(2) 10 p.	
21.	Immanuel Fanny	Do.	(3) 10 p.	
22.	Immanuel Castille	Do.	(4) 10 p.	
23.	Henry Chile	Do.	(5) 10 p.	
24.	Henry Willoughby	Do.	(6) 10 p.	16
25.	Francis Lopez	Boatsteerer	(7) 10 p.	3
26.	William Place	Able Seaman	(8) 15 p.	48
27.	George Smith	Boatsteerer	(9) 16 p.	40
28.	Thomas Silsbee	Ordy.	(10) 10 p.	18
29.	Robert Perry	Able Seam.	(11) 18 p.	
30.	Richard Jones	Able Seam.	(12) 20 p.	
31.	Silvester Druitt	Able Seam.	(13) 12 p.	

[# 17]

British Consulate
Tahiti. Oct. 12th 1842

No. 13

Provided that " Silvester Druitt " leaves Tahiti in the Barque
" Lucy Ann " of Sydney I promise to pay to his order the
sum of Twelve dollars—

$ 12

Chas. B. Wilson
H.B.M. Actg. Consul.

[There are similar numbered certificates for #2 Joseph Louis,
$10; #3 Immanuel Fanny, $10; #4 Immanuel Castille, $10;

#5 Henry Chile, $10; #6 Henry Willoughby, $10; #7 Francis
Lopez, $10; #8 William Place, $15; #9 George Smith, $16;
Thomas Silsbee, $10; #11 Robert Perry, $18; #12 Richard
Jones, $20.]

[#18: Wilson's Rough Notes on Captain Ventom's Expenses]

Advances 214
Hotel   20
House   54 2/4
           14

II

214 Advances
 20 Hotel
  5 House rent
 10 Cook cost [?]
 25 Harbour dues
 20 Private a/c (Drs)
 15 Ships   a/c (Doctor)
───
299

                              [upside down]
Consul a/c $

2 certificates   -2/ - 4- 0   Which compelled the said
12 men shipped   -- /2- 0   J. German in the absence
Espenses Genl   thro sickness
   to 6th from --   200   of the said master and
                        ───   contrary to the said masters
                          4   instructions to bring to
             ----17   192   the said Barque Lucy Ann
19   17   15   to anchor in the Port of
11   ───   Papeeti Tahiti
──   19
30   ───

          24th 5
                     ───
                     3
            27
           ───
            11

[# 19]

Duplicate
I do hereby certify on application of "Henry Ventom" Master
of the Barque Lucy Ann of Sydney, who, in evidence of the
truth thereof has unto me made solemn and sincere declaration
hereunto subscribes his name That Two hundred and Eighty
one Gallons imperial measure of Sperm Oil in Casks marked
No. 1 and 2 Sold unto William James Newton residing in
Papeete at Tahiti has been procured by crew of said Barque
"Lucy Ann"—

> In testimony whereof I have hereunto delivered this
> my Certificate at the British Consulate Tahiti this
> Twelfth day of October, One thousand and Eight
> hundred and forty two—

> > Chas. B. Wilson
> > H.B.M. Actg. Consul
> > Henry Ventom—Master—

[# 20]

> Consulate of the U S
> Society Islands
> October 27. 1842

C.B. Wilson Esq.
H.B.M. Acting Consul
   Sir—
   Application has this day been made to me by Capt Edwin
F. Cook, for the recovery of Manuel Silva a prisoner now in
charge of the Tahitian Authorities, taken from the British
Barque "Lucy Ann".
   Said Silva is alledged to have deserted from the Ship "Nile"
commanded by said Cook, during her present voyage, taking
with him a boat & other property belonging to said Ship—
   In accordance with the requisitions of the laws of the
U.S. in regard to the reclamation of deserters, I am obliged
to require that said Silva be delivered up to Capt. Cook—
> > Respectfully &c &c
> > Your Obedient Servant,
> > *S R Blackler*
> > > *Consul*

[#21: Wilson's Draft of a Complaint to the Provisional Council]

British Consulate
    Tahiti, Nov. 18, 1842.
Gentlemen:
    I have the honour of addressing you apprising you that yesterday morning between the hours of ten and eleven while sitting in my office writing a number of natives entered the premises of the Consulate and one who called himself an authority named Hinere [?] came into my office in a most abrupt manner demanding a girl who had been about an hour before seen in the office. I told him that she had left and after repetition of the demand in a most insulting manner I turned him out. He then with others demanded admission to search my office without warrant or any authority whatever. I refused and requested them to leave the premises. They persisted in demanding to search and furthermore grossly insulted me personally and as an official character. The mob consisted of about fifty. There were several of the authorities among them but I do not know their names. In defiance of me they remained on the premises about two hours surrounded the office and grossly ... [sic] and it was with greatest difficulty they left but not before they received orders from Mr. Moerenhout to whom I made a hasty application. As their proceedings are most unwarrantable I have most respectfully to request that you will aquaint the local authorities of the unwarrantable act committed and that if a reoccurrence of the act takes place I shall represent the same to H. B. Majesty's government, who will demand severe and just reparations for the insult offerred to her flag.
    I have further to inform you that I have this morning received a communication from Edwd. Lucett, Esq., a most respectable British ship owner and merchant now residing at Papeete, stating that about half past eight o'clock last evening while sitting in a native house he was seized by a number of natives and most violently handled and maltreated the marks of which I have myself this morning seen on his person and forcibly had both feet put into the stocks where the seamen for revolt were confined.
    I have written to the local authority respecting the case of Mr. Lucett and demanded from them commensurate reparation for such an unwarrantable and outrageous act of

violence committed upon the person of a respectable British subject and that in direct violation of the Proclamation issued under the Provisional Government in the name of Queen Pomare.

I have the honour
Gentlemen

[# 22 : Wilson's Draft of Another Complaint to the Provisional Council]

British Consulate
Tahiti
November 19th, 1842.

Gentlemen,

I have the honour of addressing you to inform you that through the repeated manifest and wilful neglect of the Local Authorities of this Island in suffering the Prisoners belonging to the British Barque " Lucy Ann " committed to their charge on the 26th September last for an act of revolt on board of said Barque, to go at large, in having taken them and allowing them to go to the other side of the Island on pleasure and on private business of natives of the Island, and in allowing four of them to make their escape from the Island I am bound to protest against said authorities for aiding and abetting said prisoners in their attempt to escape the ends of justice and for a violation of that right due to H.B.M. Government as that of the most Friendly Nation.

As the Provisional Protectorate of the Tahitian Government I feel it my duty to acquaint you of the above proceedings of said Authority that through your interference more effective measures may be taken for the treatment and confinement of the prisoners under their charge until the arrival of one of H.B.M. ships or until a proper opportunity offers of sending them to one of H.M. Colonies or to the Commr. in Chf. at Valpraiso.

The prisoners stand charged with having committed an act of revolt, in combining together and refusing to do their duty as articled seamen on board of the said Barque " Lucy Ann " without just cause or provocation which thereby distressed the said vessel, prevented her from prosecuting her voyage, and compelled the commanding officer to bring the vessel to anchor in the port of Papeete contrary to the Master's Orders.

Enclosed I send you for your perusal and further information the Documentary Evidence against the prisoners taken in this office, and request you will transmit me back the same. I have the honor to be, etc., etc.

[#23: Reply of Council to Wilson's Complaint]

Gouvernement Provisoire De Taiti

Monsieur Le Consul

En vous accusant reception de votre lettre du 19 courant relativement à l'évasion de quelques hommes du navire Anglais la Lucy-ann et après avoir pris connaissance des documents ci-joints que nous vous renvoyons.

Nous vous informons que nous avons fait prendre toutes les mesures nécessaires pour faire arrêter et détenir en prison, jusqu'à l'arrivée d'un bâtiment de guerre Anglais ou une nouvelle dècision de votre part, ceux de ces hommes qui se trouvent dans l'île.

Nous vous prévenons que les hommes détenus en prison resteront sans communication à moins d'une permission des autorités ou de leur Consul. Nous regrettons, dans l'intérêt de l'ordre ainsi que de la Discipline et de l'exemple, que vous ne nous ayez pas chargé plus tôt de ces hommes qui livrés à un trop grande liberté en ont profité pour s'évader et par ce moyen, se soustraire à une punition exemplaire.

Recevez Monsieur Le Consul l'assurance de notre parfaite Consideration.

Les Membres Du Conseil

J. A. Moerenhout   E. Reine   De Carpegna

Taiti Le 22 style véritable Le 21 9bre 1842

Monsieur J. B. Wilson Consul de S.M. Britannique à Papeiti

[Translation of above]

Provisional Government
    of Tahiti

    Mr. Consul

In acknowledging the receipt of your letter of the 19th current relating to the escape of some men of the English vessel Lucy Ann & after having taken knowledge of the documents inclosed we send them back to you.

We inform you that we have taken all the necessary measures to arrest & detain in prison till the arrival of an

English ship of war or to a new decision on your part, those
men who are still in the island.

We inform you that the men detained in prison shall
remain without communication unless by permission of the
Authorities or their Consul.

We regret for the interest of order as well as for discipline
& example that you did not charge us sooner in regard to
these men who were allowed too great liberty of which they
have taken advantage for their escape & by this means to
evade an exemplary punishment.

   Receive etc.

[#24]

Charles Burnett Wilson Esqre	Original [cancelled]
H. B. M. Acting Consul	Tahiti
for the Society and	Decr. 31st.
Friendly Islands	1842.
Duplicate	To Johnstone & Myrick, Surgeons.

Charles Burnett Wilson Esqre — Original [cancelled]
H. B. M. Acting Consul — Tahiti
for the Society and — Decr. 31st.
Friendly Islands — 1842.
Duplicate — To Johnstone & Myrick, Surgeons.

For Medicines & Medical

assistance for the following
distressed British Seamen
Men's Names — by your Order.

Men's Names		$	cts.
Thomas Seaton	from March 30 to June 20	104	75
John Johnson	from April 2 to May 2	38	50
Abraham Waugh	from April 10 to Dec 28	139	50
Richard Howard	from July 23 to Nov 7	34	25
Frederick Richardson	from Augt 12 to Dec 27	55	25
William Hunter	from Septr 12 to Oct 19	34	75
Henry Smith	from Septr 28 to Oct 23	28	25
Nicholas Utley	from Sep 28 to Novr 7	26	—
John Troy	from Octr to Novr 19	24	25
Henry Bourke	from Octr 13 to Novr 19	19	—
William Matthews	from Octr 13 to Nov 19	15	50
Herman Melville	from Octr 15 to Nov 19	19	50
John Garretson	from Octr 13 to Novr 19	18	25
William Higham	from Novr 20 to Decr 30	53	25
Donald Macqueen	from Decr 6 to Decr 30	26	37½
Daniel Miller	from March 26 to Apr 29	32	75
		$670	12½

  Received payment
  Johnstone & Myrick

[on other side of above bill]

This is to certify that we have received Medical Assistance and attendance as herein stated.

Thos Seaton

Daniel X Miller
  his
  mark
Witness William Ellenwood

John X Johnson
  his
  mark
Witness William Ellenwood

Abraham Waugh

Witnesses { R Hooton
{ H Hooton

Richard X Howard
  his
  mark

Witnesses { R Hooton
{ H Hooton

Henry Smith

Nicholas S. Utley

John Troy

H Bourke

Wm. Mathews

Herman Melville

John X Garritson
  his
  mark
Witness Amado Silva

William Higham

Fk. Richardson

Donald Mc Queen

We do hereby certify that "William Hunter" deceased received Medicine and Medical aid from Messrs Johnstone & Myrick from Sepr. 12th to Oct. 19th as within stated—

Witness our hands
John I. Jepson

Protestant Missionary

Chas. B. Wilson
H.B.M. Actg. Consul

EXPLANATORY NOTES.

*The passage in the text to which each note refers is indi-
cated by two numbers: the first gives the page and the second
gives the line on the page. The editors realize that there are
more notes than Omoo, in its own right, calls for. Their
justifications (if they have any) are: 1) that many notes are
necessary to show Melville's extensive and extraordinary use
of his source materials; 2) that many others will perhaps be of
use to students of the development of one of America's greatest
writers; and 3) that still other notes may assist readers using
the book as an anthropological or historical source-book.*

KEY
To works cited by short-title in the Notes.

Anderson: Charles R. Anderson, *Melville in the South Seas.*
New York, 1939.
Beechey: *Narrative of a Voyage to the Pacific and Beering's
Strait..., under the Command of Captain F. W. Beechey....*
London, 1831. 2 vols. A New Edition.
Circumnavigation: Circumnavigation of the Globe. New York,
1837 (Harpers' Family Library).
Davis: Merrell R. Davis, *Melville's 'Mardi': A Chartless
Voyage.* New Haven, 1952.
Ellis: William Ellis, *Polynesian Researches, during a Residence
of Nearly Eight Years in the Society and Sandwich Islands.*
New York, 1833 (Harper's Stereotype Edition). 4 vols.
Forsythe: Robert S. Forsythe, " More Upon Herman Melville

in Tahiti," *Philological Quarterly*. XVII [January, 1938], 1-17.

Foulque: Herman Melville, *Omoo: ou le Vagabond du Pacifique*. Traduit de l'anglais par Jacqueline Foulque. Gallimard, Paris, 1951.

Howard: Leon Howard, *Herman Melville: A Biography*. Berkeley & Los Angeles, 1951.

Log: Jay Leyda, *The Melville Log: A Documentary Life of Herman Melville*. New York, 1951. 2 vols.

Lucett: [Edward Lucett,] *Rovings in the Pacific....* London, 1851. 2 vols.

Perkins: Edward T. Perkins, *Na Motu: or, Reef-Rovings in the South Seas*. New York, 1854. [Sealts, # 399]

Revolt Documents: Documents on the *Lucy Ann* Revolt, presented in the Appendix.

Russell: *Polynesia: or an Historical Account of the Principal Islands in the South Sea....* by the Right Rev. M. Russell. New York, 1843. (Harpers' Family Library)

Sealts: Merton M. Sealts, Jr., *Melville's Reading: A Check-List of Books Owned and Borrowed*. Offprinted from *Harvard Library Bulletin*, II, III, IV [1948-1950].

Stewart: C. S. Stewart, *A Visit to the South Seas....* London, 1832. 2 vols.

Vancouver: Captain George Vancouver, *A Voyage of Discovery to the North Pacific Ocean....* London, 1798. 3 vols.

Wheeler: *Memoirs of the Life and Gospel Labours of the Late Daniel Wheeler....* London, 1842.

Wilkes: Charles Wilkes, *Narrative of the United States Exploring Expedition*. Philadelphia, 1845. 5 vols. [Sealts, # 532]

Wise: Henry Augustus Wise, *Los Gringos: or, An Inside View of Mexico and California, with Wanderings in Peru, Chili, and Polynesia*. New York, 1849. [Sealts, # 559a]

References to *Moby-Dick, Pierre, Piazza Tales, The Confidence-Man*, and *Collected Poems of Herman Melville* are to the Complete Works in process of publication by Hendricks House, the volumes already published, as follows: *Moby-Dick: Or, The Whale*. Edited by Luther S. Mansfield and Howard P. Vincent. New York, 1952; *Pierre: Or, The Ambiguities*. Edited by Henry A. Murray. New York, 1949; *Piazza Tales*. Edited by Egbert S. Oliver. New York, 1948; *The Confidence-Man*. Edited by Elizabeth S. Foster. New York, 1954; *Collected Poems of Herman Melville.* Edited by Howard P. Vincent. Chicago, 1947. To these as well as other works by Melville, citation is made, for convenience of reference to any edition, by chapter-number.

1.24. *about three months*: Actually about forty days, from the last week in September to the first week in November 1842. (*Log,* I, 146-156; Howard, pp. 58-59)

2.20. *No journal*: A contemporary contradiction appeared in "Voyages réels et fantastiques d'Hermann Melville," *Revue des deux Mondes,* II [1849], 545-546. The author, Philarète Chasles, met in Paris an American acquaintance of Melville who said he had discussed the books with Melville's cousin, who, in turn, claimed to have read Melville's "journal, ses *Rough-Notes,* actuellement entre les mains de son beau-père." Jay Leyda (*Log,* I, 300) has identified the acquaintance as Thomas Gold Appleton, Longfellow's brother-in-law, who was well acquainted with Melville's father-in-law, Lemuel Shaw, in Boston and with his cousin, Robert Melvill, in Pittsfield. (See also Davis, p. 6n.) The books themselves show no signs of having been written from a journal—indeed that is one of the marks of their originality, since most such travel-narratives were in journal form.

2.28. *Polynesian vocabularies*: Melville was mistaken in stating that no Tahitian vocabulary had been printed, for several had appeared, though he evidently did not use one. Many of the Tahitian words in *Omoo* he took from Ellis— proper names and names of specific objects and plants, as well as a number of phrases. Yet a few common Polynesian words he does seem to have remembered, and like Long Ghost courting Little Loo (Ch. 77) he managed to manipulate his few words into a surprising number of combinations. (Cf. his remarks in *Typee* [Ch. 30] on the way " one brisk, lively little word is obliged, like a servant in a poor family to perform all sorts of duties " in the Typee language.) His claim that he was "mostly governed by the bare recollection of sounds" has been too uncritically accepted; it is not true, of course, as to the many words he took from Ellis, but is is obviously true as to those common words he remembered from his Polynesian wanderings. In *Omoo* Melville used as Tahitian a fair number of the same words he had used in *Typee* as Marquesan: *arva* (a root), *ena* (*this*), *hanna* (*make*), *kanaka* (*native man*), *taboo kanaka*, *nuee* (*much*), *maro* (native garment), *moee* (*sleep*), *pehee* (*fish*), *pemi* (*come*), *poee-poee* (a food), *taboo, tamaree* (*boy*), *tappa* (*cloth*), *wai* (*water*), *whinhenies/wahenee* (*females*). Other common words in *Omoo* which he had not used in *Typee* were: *ita* (*no*), *maitai* (*good*), *oee* (*you*), *yar onor boyoee* (*hello*), and *karhowree* (for *white man*). Most conspicuous—a real " servant in a poor family " is the verb *haere* (*come*) which Melville spells so many ways it seems likely he had never recognized them all as forms of the same verb: *aramai* (*haere mai*) he uses repeatedly in various senses (*come, come in, come down, be off, get up*); other forms are *harree, heree,* and *hanree* (possibly a misprint).

Melville's spelling of Polynesian words has disturbed various readers. Best known of their complaints is that of Robert Louis Stevenson. When he visited Nukuheva and Tahiti with *Typee* and *Omoo* in hand, he " thought more than ever " of the picture given of them by that "howling cheese," "our admirable friend Herman Melville "; but at the same time he declared that Melville "had no ear for language whatever: his Hapar tribe should be Hapaa, etc." (*Letters,* [New York, 1918], II, 136, 217). He elaborated this comment in *In the South Seas*: "Or take the valley of Hapaa, known to readers of Herman Melville under the grotesque misspelling of Hapar. There are but two writers who have touched the South Seas with any genius, both Americans: Melville and Charles Warren Stoddard; and at the christening of the first and greatest, some influential fairy must have been neglected: ' He shall be able to see,' ' He shall be able to tell,' ' He shall be able to charm,' said the friendly godmothers; ' But he shall not be able to hear,' exclaimed the last." ([New York, 1918], p. 28). Later critics have echoed this remark on Melville's " poor ear," but have sought no more precise explanation of his spelling practises. Lewis Mumford quoted Stevenson's reproach and excused Melville on the ground that four years had passed between his four months among the Typees and the time he committed the names and words to paper. (*Herman Melville* [New York, 1929], p. 83) Actually, he declared, Melville had " a curiously accurate ear." (See note on 54.32.) Anderson (pp. 80, 451 note 24) refers to " Melville's usual phonetic inaccuracy " (apropos of his form " Tior " for " Taioa "); he quotes Stevenson; and he also quotes Max Radiguet's contemporary comment that the title of *Typee* is " bizarrement orthographié." The French translator of *Omoo*, Jacqueline Foulque, however, gives one explanation: " Les mots tahitiens sont orthographiés phonétiquement par Melville de façon assez fantaisiste, car l'auteur fut très influencé par d'autres dialectes maoris, en particulier par le marquisien et l'hawaïen." Teaching at L'Ecole des Languages Orientales, she had studied the various Oceanic languages and their inter-relationship; she had also visited the bays and valleys of the Marquesas. Thus she was able, says the publisher's note, "d'identifier certains mots indigènes, certains lieux géographiques que l'orthographe phonétique de Melville a déformés de façon souvent incompréhensible." ([p. 7]) In the ensuing notes, we have regularly and gratefully cited Jacqueline Foulque's versions of Melville's Polynesian words. Still, a further comment on his spelling needs to be made.

More than a " bad ear " and the intrusion of other Poly-nesian dialects is involved. The " bad ear " explanation (as well as that of Foulque) assumes that Melville had actually *heard* all the words, and, as he claimed, was " mostly governed by the bare recollection of sounds." But as stated above and as demonstrated in the notes, many of his words were borrowed from books, chiefly from Ellis; these words were *seen* on the page, not *heard*. His exceptionable spelling of some of these borrowed words may be due (a) to the " bad ear " or other phonetic shortcomings of his source-book, or (b) to Melville's careless transcription, or his misinterpretation, of the source. Obvious examples of both occur.

Granting these two non-aural sources of distortion, another point of explanation remains. A major source of the unfaith-ful spellings was Melville's attempt to render words into forms he supposed would make their pronunciation (or what he took to be such) more clear to readers accustomed to English spelling. The trouble arose over the vowels. As Ellis explained (I, 22 ff.; II, 22) the missionaries adopted a spelling system faithful to the Tahitian language, representing its vowels as follows: " *a* has the sound of a in father, *e* the sound of a in fate, *i* that of i in marine or e in me, *o* that of o in no, *u* that of oo in root. The diphthong *ai* is sounded as i in wine." This system (allowing that *e* and *o* are not diphthongs) approximates the usual continental rendition of vowels and so is close to the French spelling of Tahitian, for example that of Foulque, who, however, uses various diacritical marks. But what Mel-ville attempted, unsystematically and inconsistently, was to turn these "continental" spellings into customary English-American forms.

(1) *o* gave no trouble: *Imeeo, moee, tona*. (2) *u* was either retained by Melville (*nui, Lulee*), or represented as *oo* (*Roorootoo, Kooloo, toonee, Rartoo, tootai*). (3) *i* he rendered as *ee* (*nuee, tee, toonee*). (4) *e*, also, however, he often rendered by *ee* (*moee-moee, oee, poee, matee, harree, karhowree*); this confuses *i* and *e*; and anyway American readers would certainly take *ee* as indicating *i*. Here both Melville's "ear" and his conception of the sound were probably at fault. (5) *ai* was rendered by Melville in four ways: by *ai*, usually in words he simply kept as he found them written (*Matavai, Wai, maitai*); by *ay* (*tayo*); by *i* (*ita, Tior, Imeeo*); and by *y* (*Typee, Hytyhoo, Huwyenee*). (6) *ao*: as *ow* (*karhowree, Townor, now*); *oa*: as *or* or *oar* (*Townor, onor, Tior, Papoar, Teearnoar, Koar* wood); *ia*: as *yar* (*yar onor*); *au*: as *ow* (*owree, fow*). (7) *a*: this vowel causes the most trouble. Melville sometimes retained this as *a* (*taata, taboo, kannaka, Papeetee, tona*). But regularly he rendered it (and sometimes *aa* as well) as *ar* (*tararta* for *taata*; *Fararar* for *Faaa*; *Pararee* for *Paari*; *hevar* for *heiva*; *arva* for *ava*; *Tahar* for *Tahaa*; and so on—all deliberate changes of forms before him on the pages of Ellis). Stevenson cited the "grotesque misspelling" of *Hapar* (actually *Happar*) for *Hapaa*. Now why did Melville "hear" an *r* in all these words? The answer is simple enough: he didn't. The explanation is that in his Northeastern American dialect, the *r* in such positions is "silent," though the speaker considers that he is pronouncing it in making the preceding *a* long. So Melville wrote *ar* in these words to indicate long *a*, with no intention of indicating "pronounced" *r* (*e.g.*, Ellis's *a* as in *father*, which Melville evidently would have pronounced the same way he would have pronounced *farther*—with the sound often indicated by *ah*). Melville's *r* in his use of *or* or *oar* for final *oa* (*Townor, Tior, Koar* wood, *Papoar*) he would have pronounced "*ah*" (long *a*, in effect!), which is the way the name of the letter *r* itself is pronounced in his dialect; so what he "heard" and intended to indicate by his *Tior* spelling was correct for "Taioa." But he may indeed have pronounced final long *a* as *r*, New England fashion (*Martha* as *Marther, idea* as *idear*, etc.), as he obviously pronounced *kannaka* as he sometimes spelled it, "*kannaker*." In sum, given Melville's dialect and his notation, his "ear" and intention were sound enough. How in the world, though, was Stevenson, with his Scotch *r*'s, to realize the sig-

nificance of Melville's "silent" New England *r*'s? Or anyone else outside the Northeastern dialect area?

As to the consonants, Melville has two kinds of errors. (1) He employs consonants which do not occur in Tahitian, *c* (*k*), *l*, and *b*, their proper equivalents being *t*, *r*, and *p*. This error may be accounted for, as Foulque suggests, by his taking over the forms from Marquesan or Hawaiian; but his source-books share some of his errors in this respect. (2) He uses double consonants, which, according to both Ellis (I, 22) and Foulque, do not occur. Corrected forms, suggested by Foulque, are cited in ensuing notes, *passim*. (Examples: *tapu kanaka* for Melville's *taboo kannakers*; *tarahao ê* for *karhowree*; *Turu* for *Kooloo*; *tapu* for *taboo*.)

2.37. *Omoo*: We cannot find a word of similar sound and meaning in any Polynesian glossary. (The *omoo* tree is mentioned in *Typee*, Ch. 11, but even that does not appear in the glossaries.) To Murray, his publisher, Melville wrote, "I desire the title... to remain untouched—its oddity, or uniqueness... conveys some insight into the nature of the book. It gives a sort of Polynisian [*sic*] expression to its ' figure-head.'— At any rate, no one questions the right of a parent to dub his offspring as he pleases;—the same right should be accorded to an author." (Davis, p. 210) (Melville alluded to Murray's having changed the title of *Typee*.) Foulque (p. 12) accepts the title and explanation without comment.

3.2. "*Taboo kannakers*": "*Tapu kanaka*: littéralement « homme tabou, sacré »." (Foulque, p. 12, n. 3) In *Typee* (Ch. 10) Melville explains the term, and the usage of "kanaka." Cf. note on 170.1, also 128.3.

5.2. *INTRODUCTION*: Melville summarizes the events here as he reported them in *Typee*, his first book (1846), but his report was not autobiographically accurate in all respects. His sojourn among the Typees lasted at most one month, since he deserted the *Acushnet* on 9 July and signed aboard the *Lucy Ann* ("*Julia*") on 9 August 1842. (See Anderson, pp. 69 ff.; *Log*, I, 130-139; Howard, pp. 51-54.)

5.7. *Typee*: Taï-Pi. (Foulque, p. [15])

7.4. *Rio de Janeiro*: On the outward voyage, with Melville aboard, the *Acushnet* put in at Rio on 13 March and sailed on 15 March 1841. (*Log*, I, 116)

7.7. *four years previous... Liverpool*: Actually three years. Melville laid over in Liverpool from 2 July to 13 August 1839 with the crew of the *Saint Lawrence*, on his first voyage. (See William Gilman, "Melville's Liverpool Trip," *Modern Language Notes*, LXI [1946], 543-547; also Gilman, *Melville's Early Life and 'Redburn'* [New York, 1951], pp. 128-143.)

7.27. *My stipulation*: Melville's claim that he signed only for the cruise is not borne out by the copy of the crew-list preserved in the Revolt Documents. The notation "for the cruise" does appear after the names of four other men, ring-leaders in the revolt, who gave a version of this stipulation as their justification. Melville's claim may be based on fact (the copyist may have overlooked the notation after his name), or he may be simply seeking to justify his subsequent refusal of duty.

7.30. *not... that the captain felt any great compassion*: But at the end of *Typee*, where the literary context demanded that "rescue" be emphasized, Melville wrote, "Every attention was bestowed on me that humanity could suggest." Here the context calls for the captain to get no credit for humanity, since to the reader Melville's later behavior must not seem ungrateful (see end of Ch. 34). This is a fair sample, at the outset, of the way Melville let literary demands take precedence over fact in *Typee* and *Omoo*.

8.5. *tappa cloak*: tapa. (Foulque, p. 21) Ellis (I, 145) says that in Tahiti "the Sandwich Island word *tapa*" is never used in sense of *cloth*, the Tahitian word being *ahu*.

9.1. *Nebuchadnezzar fare*: " ... He was driven from men and did eat grass as oxen..." (*Daniel*, 4.33) The ordinary diet of the Typee valley was vegetarian. "I verily believe, that with a bushel of common Liverpool salt all the real estate in Typee might have been purchased." (*Typee*, Ch. 15)

10.7. *SOME ACCOUNT OF THE SHIP*: The "*Julia*" was the *Lucy Ann*, of Sydney, a barque of some 200 tons, built in New Brunswick in 1819, and brought to Sydney from London in 1827. She was bought for government service. In 1835 she was described as "a remarkably fast-sailing schooner." On the present cruise she sailed from Sydney on 14 or 18 February 1842, with a crew of about 30 (as Melville says), and returned on 20 May 1843 after "a remarkably unfortunate voyage,"

with only 250 barrels of sperm oil. She weathered another ten
years of active service. The "*Julia's*" identity as the *Lucy Ann*
was reported in 1849 by Wise (p. 399) and soon after by Lucett
(I, 294). See Anderson, pp. 199-202; Forsythe, p. 16. Mr. J. W.
Earnshaw generously loaned us his unpublished notes on the
Lucy Ann.

11.27. *The captain*: Captain Henry Ventom, described by
the ship's articles as a master mariner. It seems unlikely that
he was quite as nautically ignorant as Melville makes out;
still, the whole history of the cruise testifies to his incompetence.

11.37. *bore himself with becoming meekness*: The words
and idea occur prominently in connection with Wolsey and
Cranmer in *Henry VIII*: "You're meek and humble-mouth'd;/
You sign your place and calling, in full seeming,/ With meekness and humility; but your heart/ Is cramm'd with arrogancy,
spleen, and pride./ You have, by fortune and his highness'
favours,/ Gone slightly o'er low steps, and now are mounted/
Where powers are your retainers...." (II, iv, 106-113) See also
Cranmer's speech (V, iii, 62-63). In Ch. 46, below, Melville
uses the phrase "good easy man" from one of Wolsey's most
important speeches.

12.17. *John Jermin*: James German, according to the Revolt
Documents, in which everything goes to confirm the account
Melville gives of the mate. The English sea-novelist W. Clark
Russell (who admired and praised Melville's work toward the
end of the century and corresponded with him in his last years)
singled out this portrait of Jermin for special praise: "Neither
Smollett nor Marryat has given us a more remarkable picture."
("Editor's Preface" to *Omoo* [London, 1904], ix)

12.30. *he abhorred... and cleaved*: "Abhor that which is
evil; cleave to that which is good." (*Romans*, 12.9)

13.11. *the doctor*: The original of this character was John
B. Troy, who doubtless had unusual qualities that attracted
Melville. But he cannot have been just as Melville represents
him. He had shipped from Sydney, not in the gentlemanly
berth of ship's doctor, but as steward, for a 110th lay. His
doctorate, it appears, was bestowed only by his shipmates, from
his having charge, *ex officio*, of the ship's medicine-chest.
Still, the "doctor's" quarrel with the captain, his blow that

laid the captain flat, and his resignation and move from cabin to forecastle, very likely represent not sheer fiction but a fictionalized account of an actual quarrel between steward and captain. Stewards often bunked not in the forecastle but in quarters aft near the captain's cabin; they seem, according to many logbooks, to have been quarrelsome fellows; and Troy may well have had a row with Ventom, have knocked him down, been disrated and turned before the mast. Doctor Long Ghost's distinguished family in England, his learning, his travels, his air of a man-of-the-world, may have been real, or by vague hints and sheer effrontery Troy may have made Melville believe in them. Most likely, however, they were at least equally the product of Melville's own later invention. Though essentially a comic figure, Doctor Long Ghost shows a strong affinity with Melville's later characters who are partly imaginative creations—Redburn, Harry Bolton, Ishmael. Like them, Long Ghost throws out "hints of a patrimonial estate, a nabob uncle, and an unfortunate affair which set him a-roving." He is a gentleman and a reader of books. Now he has "fallen from high estate," and is an exile and a wanderer. Belonging in the cabin on terms of equality with the captain, he has been cast, partly by ill luck, partly by his own independent temper, down among the crew. He is not actually one of them, and they know it, but he sympathizes with them and they with him. So perhaps there is as much of Melville as of John Troy in the character of Doctor Long Ghost. See further long note on the doctor, below, 307.23.

From its first appearance, critics have praised *Omoo* more often for its rogues' gallery of comic portraits than for any other aspect. The full-length portrait of Doctor Long Ghost is the acclaimed masterpiece of the gallery. Among critics none has bestowed higher praise than D. H. Lawrence, who saw him as not a mere ne'er-do-well, but a "man of humorous desperation, throwing his life ironically away." He was Lawrence's favorite among Melville's characters. (*Studies in Classic American Literature* [New York, 1923] p. 208) Ronald Mason, on the other hand, finding advances in *Mardi* over *Omoo*, argues: "... Doctor Long Ghost, a character whom critics of Melville have praised very highly, seems on closer reading to be merely a static portrait of eccentricity, built up observantly, it is true, but lacking the informing vitality that distinguishes a character who can make a narrative stir with the quality of his individuality. Samoa and Annatoo, being primitives, are cruder than the depraved Westerner Long Ghost but are originally more alive than he...." (*The Spirit Above the Dust*: *A Study of Herman Melville* [London, 1951], pp. 43-44)

13.22. *he undertook... to leave the vessel clandestinely*: John B. Troy indeed jumped ship, at Nukuheva, on 7 August 1842, just a month after Melville and Toby Greene. He took along with him some "valuable medicines" belonging to ship. Captured by the natives next day and dragged back aboard, he excused his theft by pleading drunkenness. These were events of the two days before Melville came aboard, on 9 August. See Revolt Documents.

14.10. *his learning*: Long Ghost, that is, could quote the classics, philosophy, and poetry. Quoting Virgil, probably the *Aeneid*, in Latin showed an ordinary education. Melville himself used a Virgilian tag in the title of Ch. 8 of *Mardi*, "They Push Off, Velis et Remis," and alluded to Virgilian passages in later works. Thomas Hobbes of Malmsbury (1588-1679) was best known for his *Leviathan* (1651), which is quoted in the "Extracts" preceding *Moby-Dick*. In *Pierre* (Bk. XIX, i, p. 313) Melville speaks ironically of the Bohemian idealists whose "vacuity of... exchequers leads them to reject the coarse materialism of Hobbes." In *Israel Potter* (Ch. 8) he compares Franklin and Hobbes. *Hudibras*, the anti-Presbyterian, mock-heroic poem by Samuel Butler (1612-1680), would supply Long Ghost with plenty of ammunition against the Pacific Malvolios.

14.13. *seen the world*: Long Ghost had travelled in the Mediterranean, Africa, and Asia. *Palermo*: capital of Sicily. *Muscat*: seaport in southeast Arabia. *Caffres*: Kaffirs, South African Negroes in the region of the Cape of Good Hope. What Melville had read of their country echoed in his imagination. In *Mardi* (Ch. 1) he refers to "...zebra hunting in Caffraria, where the lively quarry bounds before you through leafy glades." In *Redburn* (Ch. 50) the image was still strong in his mind: "And indeed, in his striped Guernsey frock, dark glossy skin and hair, Harry Bolton, mingling with the Highlander's crew, looked not unlike the soft, silken quadruped-creole, that, pursued by wild Bushmen, bounds through Caffrarian woods. How they hunted you, Harry, my zebra!" Also, "...escorted as by a Caffre guard of honor...." ("Benito Cereno," *Piazza*

Tales, p. 85) And "...as the lion leaves the streaks of his nails on a Caffre." (*Confidence-Man*, Ch. 6, p. 36)

14.30. *as a young lion*: Frequent Old Testament figure (*e.g.*, *Psalms*, 17.12; *Isaiah*, 31.4). Possibly carried over by association from the Doctor's lion-hunting, above.

15.12. *thought of the morrow*: "Take therefore no thought for the morrow: for the morrow shall take thought for the things of itself." (*Matthew*, 6.34)

15.16. *The beef... a horse's hoof*: An example of the abundant folk-lore element in *Omoo* to which attention was called by Constance Rourke (*American Humor* [New York, 1931], p. 192) Sailors' customary name for salt beef was "salt-horse." (*Typee*, Ch. 1; *Redburn*, Ch. 8) In a sailor-song the idea occurs: "You [the horse] died from blows and sore abuse,/ And were salted down for the sailors' use./ The sailors they the meat despise,/ They turned you over and (ahem'd) your eyes,/ They ate the meat and picked the bones,/ And gave the rest to Davy Jones;/ And if you don't believe it's true,/ Go look in the harness cask, and find his shoes." (Laura Smith, *The Music of the Waters* [London, 1888], pp. 354 ff.) Joanna C. Colcord gives a version of this as the sailor's "grace before meat, when the beef-kids came in." (*Songs of American Sailormen* [New York, 1938], p. 206)

17.5. *Hytyhoo... St. Christina... Mendaña*: Vaitahu ("Whitihoo" in *Typee*, Ch. 1). Alvarado de Mendaña de Neyra (1541-1595) discovered the Marquesas (1595). He named the separate islands La Madelena (Fatuhiva), La Dominica (Hivaoa —Melville's "Hivarhoo"), San Pedro (Motane), and Santa Christina (Tauata), and gave the whole cluster the title of Las Marquesas de Mendoza in honor of his patron the Viceroy of Peru. In *Typee* (Ch. 2) Melville mentioned these discoveries and cited (Ch. 25) *Circumnavigation* (pp. 68-69). He long remembered the romantic circumstance that Mendaña's wife had also been on this voyage. "The picturesque, delightful stern-gallery... entered from the Captain's cabin, much as you might enter a lady's chamber; this charming balcony, where, sailing over summer seas in the days of the old Peruvian viceroys, the Spanish cavalier Mendanna, of Lima, made love to the Lady Isabella, as they voyaged in quest of the Solomon

Islands." (*White-Jacket*, Ch. 76) He fused two voyages and forgot that Isabella was Mendaña's wife. See also *Moby-Dick* (Ch. 57, p. 271); and the elaborate "Venetian-looking" ship's balcony on which "Lima viceroy's daughters had perhaps leaned." ("Benito Cereno," *Piazza Tales*, p. 88)

17.23. "*Beauty*" ... *the ship's carpenter*: The original carpenter of the *Lucy Ann*, John Murray, had deserted at the Marquesas and a replacement, Joseph (or John) Jackson, had been shipped there, both before Melville came aboard. Jackson may have looked like "Beauty," but he did not join the later revolt as "Beauty" does. He stayed clear of it, signed the deposition against the revolters, and sailed from Tahiti with the new crew. It seems doubtful, therefore, that he was, like "Beauty," at odds with the mate.

21.2. *WHAT HAPPENED AT HYTYHOO*: The happenings recounted in this chapter are based, with no great accuracy, on the desertions and revolt that had taken place here on the *Lucy Ann*, in July, 1842, during the weeks just before Melville came aboard. On 18 July six of the men ran off with a whaleboat and all the carpentry tools. The commander of a French corvette gave Ventom help in recovering the boat and capturing and disciplining some of the deserters; two of the ringleaders were imprisoned in irons aboard the corvette. Melville missed this exciting first phase of revolt on the *Lucy Ann*; but he makes literary use of it here, what his new shipmates told him about it being obviously too good to leave out. One shipmate, Henry Smith (or Smyth), after the ship reached Tahiti, got Melville to write a letter for him to one of the imprisoned ringleaders, George Lefevre, aboard the French frigate *La Reine Blanche*. See Revolt Document #6. Little is made of this prior fracas in the depositions, but details are supplied in letters of the French officers involved. (Wilson L. Heflin will publish these letters.)

As to the actual second visit of the *Lucy Ann* to the Southeastern Marquesas, when Melville was aboard, the captain's own official complaint makes no reference to further attempted desertions, and Melville is clearly not right in reporting that five of the former deserters were recaptured on this occasion. Four new able seamen were recruited, however, probably all at La Dominica on 26 August: John White, William Bunnell, and Amado Sylva—also a native, "Friday."

23

24.26. *La Dominica, or Hivarhoo*: Hivaoa. Gauguin was to die there.

26.22. *Wanton acts*: Since Melville's similar harangue in *Typee* (Ch. 4) was prompted by Stewart (I, 274-276; 293-294), the present passage, perhaps the whole episode of Ventom's foray on the natives — which seems unlikely in view of his character and present troubles — may stem from the same source. " Few who come among them deport themselves in a manner to secure their good will and respect. Regarding them as beings scarce above the brute in their nature and habits, as those alike ignorant and reckless of all distinction between that which is right and wrong, they treat them with utter contempt, except when views of immediate selfishness dictate the contrary. " (I, 293-294) Melville read of the Pomotu outrages in Wilkes's footnote: "... the poor natives have been fired upon by trading vessels engaged in the pearl-fishery, in mere wantonness, which will account for their hostile reception of us." (I, 314) Cf. *Gulliver's Travels*, Bk. IV, Ch. 12.

27.4. *Hannamanoo*: Hanamenu. Further echoes of Stewart (I, 201-202; 329) crop out in the description of the landscape and the narrowly-averted shipwreck. The source-books for *Typee* influenced these Marquesan chapters of *Omoo*, some materials in which were perhaps salvaged from *Typee* leftovers.

28.24. *embellishment of his countenance...worse than Cain's*: " And the Lord set a mark upon Cain, lest any finding him should kill him." (*Genesis*, 4.15) Always emotionally drawn to the outcast, Melville identified himself with the wronged (Ishmael), not with the merely wicked (Cain). In *Redburn* (Ch. 22) Jackson " seemed to run amuck at heaven and earth. He was a Cain afloat; branded on his yellow brow with some inscrutable curse; and going about corrupting and searing every heart that beat near him." In *Moby-Dick* (Ch. 32, p. 135), " The Fin-back [whale]... seems a whale-hater, as some men are man-haters..., the banished and unconquerable Cain of his race. bearing for his mark that style upon his back."

28.28. *Abana and Pharpar*: When Elisha told Naaman, captain of the host of the King of Syria, to wash in Jordan to cleanse his flesh of leprosy, Naaman scornfully exclaimed, " Are not Abana and Pharpar, rivers of Damascus, better than all the waters of Israel? " (*II Kings*, 5.12) Melville uses Damascus and these rivers in *Clarel* (Pt. IV, xxvi) as "shady haunts" of "grace and pleasure," and similarly in the closely related poem "L'Envoi." (*Collected Poems*, p. 310) See also "the delicious lands roundabout Damascus," in his letter to Sophia Hawthorne, 8 January 1852. (*Log*, I, 444)

28.30. *Lem Hardy*: A fictitious character, not mentioned in Max Radiguet's full account of a visit to Hanamenu two months earlier. (*Les Derniers Sauvages*... [Paris, 1929], 44-46. Cited by Anderson, p. 467 n.) Melville had an eye on Langsdorff's full-page engraving of the well-tattooed Frenchman Jean Baptiste Cabri who lived among the Marquesans and gave Langsdorff the information that Lem Hardy purportedly gave Melville (see note below, and Anderson, p. 154). Such renegades, however, swarm in the pages of South Seas voyagers, and a few put their adventures into print. Melville himself flirted with a renegade life among the Typees. John Coulter, an English ship's surgeon, spent three weeks on this island in 1833. He went ashore with "a gun and a good pouch of ammunition," became a chief and the *tayo* of the chief Toomoua, and had to undergo tattooing, don native clothing, turn his rifle against an enemy tribe, and then watch his cannibal comrades eat their slain enemies. Fifty pages of his *Adventures in the Pacific* [Dublin, 1845] come as close to *Typee* as any contemporary narrative, except possibly John F. O'Connell's *A Residence of Eleven Years in the New Holland and Caroline Islands* [Boston, 1841]. Another captive of the Marquesans was the author of *Torrey's Narrative: or, the Life and Adventures of William Torrey, Who for the Space of 25 Months, within the Years 1835, '36, and '37 was Held a Captive by the Cannibals of the Marquesas...* [Boston, 1848]. Melville, Coulter, O'Connell, and Torrey were temporary, partly unwilling sojourners among the natives, but many with Lem Hardy's history and motives were real renegades. Melville may have met a few; certainly he read about many. His reflections on Hardy's history parallel those of Captain Cook on a deserter at Tahiti (quoted in *Circumnavigation*, p. 270) in a passage from which Melville took other information.

30.27. *information obtained from Hardy*: Lem Hardy is the first of a string of fictitious South Sea informants in *Omoo*. The real source of the information here set down was G.H. von Langsdorff's *Voyages and Travels in Various Parts of the*

World,... *1803-1807*, 2 vols. [London, 1813], I, 117-121. Langsdorff was the naturalist on Krusenstern's expedition, and a close friend and travelling companion of Melville's uncle, Captain John De Wolf II. (See *Moby-Dick*, Ch. 45, pp. 206-207; *Redburn*, Ch. 7; and Anderson, pp. 15-16.) The account of tattooing here, as in *Typee*, Anderson points out, is not accurate, but it errs with Langsdorff's. (Anderson, pp. 149-156)

32.31. *Urim and Thummim*: "And thou shalt put in the breastplate of judgment the Urim and the Thummim [lights and perfections]; and they shall be upon Aaron's heart, when he goeth in before the Lord; and Aaron shall bear the judgment of the children of Israel upon his heart before the Lord continually." (*Exodus*, 28.30) Similar allusions in *Clarel* (Pt. II, xxii; Pt. III, xviii).

33.16. "*Lora Tattoo*"; Foulque (p. 47, n. 1) says the letter *L* does not exist in Marquesan: "Il doit s'agir plutôt des mots: « Oroà Tatau », ou « Fête du Tatouage », Melville n'ayant retenu qu'une phonétique approximative."

33.19. *a sort of colloquial chant*: This is modelled on a native chant translated for Langsdorff by Cabri (I, 164-168): "Where is that light?/ On Tauata./ Wherefore the light?/ To roast the enemy./ Let us make fire./ We have fire./ We shall roast him./ We have him./ He would fly./ Now he is dead./ The sister weeps./ His parents weep./..."

34.23. *Guy Fawkes's lantern*: The image of Guy Fawkes in the vaults of the Parliament House was one that stayed long in Melville's mind. In *White-Jacket* (Ch. 31) he says that as he watched an old gunner groping through the ship's vaults he "remembered Guy Fawkes and the Parliament-house, and made earnest inquiry whether this gunner was a Roman Catholic." Re-working materials of *White-Jacket* years later, Melville gave the image a moral significance: "The Pharisee is the Guy Fawkes prowling in the hid chambers underlying some natures like Claggart's." (*Billy Budd*)

34.28. *the formal baptism of Wymontoo:* A native was indeed shipped at La Dominica—he appears on the crew-list under the name "Friday" and the day was Friday, 26 August. Very likely he was the original of "Wymontoo," whom Melville says they thought of calling "Sunday" from the day they "caught"

him. " Friday," however, was an able seaman, not a raw landsman. So the account of Wymontoo would seem to be dressed
up from Melville's imagination and his memory of other such
native recruits, in the flesh and in such written accounts as
Captain Cook's passages on the Tahitian Tupia. Native sailors
were in fact common in the whale fishery. Three of them, Leaky
(a boatsteerer), Tommy (an ordinary seaman), and Johnny N. Z.
(that is, Johnny New Zealand—an able seaman), had sailed
from Sydney with the *Lucy Ann,* but were apparently among
the deserters in July, before Melville came aboard. Benbow
Byrne, boatsteerer and acting third mate, may have been
another, though nothing in the Revolt Documents indicates
that he was the semi-savage Maori that Melville makes
" Bembo " out. Polynesian sailors made a deep impression on
Melville, and from whatever actual acquaintance with them,
he created the pathetic Wymontoo, the savage Bembo, the
stoical Samoa (of *Mardi*), and the noble Queequeg.

35.14. *We were now fairly at sea*: This chapter is pretty
accurate in its account of the state of affairs aboard the *Lucy
Ann* as she left the Marquesas and turned west to get on with
the business of whaling. Five of the crew were " ailing and ill
of the venereal." And, as Melville states, " To crown all, the
captain again relapsed." This was on 27 August, the day after
signing the last recruits. Benbow Byrne—whether or not he
was a Maori, as Melville makes him—was acting third mate,
the original second mate, Gabriel King, having, as Melville
says, absconded. The reason that German, the first mate, never
revealed the ship's position was probably, as Leon Howard
suggests, that several days before Captain Ventom ordered him
to do so on 8 September, he had set course for Tahiti because
of his alarm at the captain's condition. (Howard, p. 56)

37.33. *Stubbs*: Files of the Sydney *Morning Herald* in the
early 1840's authenticate Melville's reference to Stubbs the real-
estate auctioneer and the rhetorical flourishes of his advertisements. The following is a fair specimen:
" It would require more than ordinary ability to pencil out in
true colours the diversified views and the beautiful scenery which
bursts upon the sight as you ramble on a fine day over the vine
clad hills and orchards at Kissing Point, elevated some hundred
feet above the level of the sea; the eye wanders over a vast
range of country which branches off into an immensity of the

most varied and finished forms—rich tints, splendid dyes, cultivated fields and streams (peaceful and sonorous as the Rhine) are amongst the most prominent materials that bloom around and beautify this delightful part of the country. Improve then the gentle hours, ye gentle cits of Sydney; attend the sale on Monday, 5th April 1841, and present your ' fair ones ' with one of the lillies of the allotments as catered for you by the proprietors of East and West Ryde. To be brief in the description hereof, Mr. Stubbs would respectfully observe that, looking to its present prospects there is everything to ensure the growth of a very populous town at Kissing Point; it would delight you to see its pretty little church on a Sunday in which the whole village meets together...." (From an unpublished paper, " Stubbs—Auctioneer: A Link With Herman Melville," by J. W. Earnshaw)

37.35. *Robins the Londoner*: George Henry Robins (1778-1847) contemporary English auctioneer who won wealth and fame by his unusual talents. He was " a *bon vivant*, a romancer in advertisements; a big gun among the cocknies, but he would have been a mere pop gun, compared with our knights of the hammer...." (New York *Weekly Mirror*, 17 April 1847)

41.16. *Trenck's mouse*: Baron Trenck (1726-1794) tamed an intelligent mouse during his ten years' imprisonment. See *The Life of Baron Frederick Trenck*, translated from the German by Thomas Holcroft, [Boston, 1793] II, 54-55.

41.31. *bread... eaten in secret... pleasant*: " Stolen waters are sweet, and bread eaten in secret is pleasant." (*Proverbs*, 9. 17) Considering the dead rat, Melville perhaps expected readers to recall the next verse: " But he knoweth not that the dead are there...."

41.38. *Clarence's*: Commissioned by Richard, the Murderer first stabs Clarence then drowns him " in the malmsey butt within." (*King Richard III*, I, iv)

42.14. *Baltimore's*: James Hall signed on as cook at Sydney, stayed clear of the revolt, deposed against the revolters, and sailed from Tahiti still as cook. His color is not mentioned. Black ship's-cooks, sometimes runaway slaves, were common. Writers usually presented them as clowns and butts. The cooks are black in *Typee*, *Redburn*, *White-Jacket*, and *Moby-Dick*.

"Old Fleece," the *Pequod's* black cook, gets baited by Stubb and delivers a bitterly humorous sermon to the sharks (*Moby-Dick*, Ch. 64., pp. 292 ff.)

44.18. *DEATH AND BURIAL*: Fictitious. On the frigate *United States*, however, Melville had witnessed burials at sea. (*White-Jacket*, Ch. 79-82; Anderson, p. 350) He always treated sea-burials with full pathos: *Mardi*, Ch. 99; *Clarel*, Pt. II, xxxix; *Billy Budd*. See also his *Meteor* Journal, *Log*, II, 623.

45.13. "*kentlege*": Pigs of iron used for ballast. "She is ballasted with utilities; not altogether with unusable pig-lead and kentledge." (*Moby-Dick*, Ch. 87, p. 378)

45.31. *disposal of his chest*: For a fuller explanation, see *Mardi*, Ch. 29.

46.12. *Antone, a Portuguese*: Possibly George Antonio, who appears on the crew-list. See "The 'Gees,'" Melville's ironic sketch about Portuguese sailors shipped by whaling captains at the Cape Verde islands.

47.4. *Finns*: This sailor-superstition was widespread, Finns being regarded most commonly as weather wizards with powers to raise or bind the winds. Dana so presents them in *Two Years Before the Mast* (Ch. 6), in a similar passage after the death of a shipmate. See also Wamibo the Finn in Conrad's *The Nigger of the Narcissus*. In *Mardi* (Ch. 20) there is an old bread-box "all over inscriptions and carving... [and] divers mystic diagrams in chalk, drawn by old Finnish mariners in casting horoscopes and prophecies." Also "Laplandish speculations" in *Moby-Dick* (Ch. 73, p. 327).

50.13. *the world of waters*: "The rising world of waters...." *Paradise Lost*, III, 11.

50.18. *Captain Guy... fast declining*: Actually it was not "some four weeks or more after leaving Hannamanoo" but about a week after, on 4 September, that Ventom's complaint had so increased that he was confined to his cabin, unable to walk. By 8 September he was so much worse that he at last ordered German to take the vessel to Tahiti for medical advice. German had already become alarmed, and a day or two earlier he had "hauled up for Tahiti without his knowledge."

52.12. *Rope Yarn*: Not identifiable from the crew-list; probably a largely fictitious portrait. Certainly his pathetic death and burial ashore at Tahiti are fictitious. In the associated items "Holborn Bars," "bakery," "rash embarkation in wedlock," and "bankruptcy," there is a curious connection between Ropey the steward's history and an important event in Israel Potter's career: "as stubborn fate would have it, being run over one day at Holborn Bars, and taken into a neighboring bakery, he was there treated with such kindliness by a Kentish lass, the shop-girl, that... the money saved up for his ocean voyage was lavished upon a rash embarkation in wedlock." (*Israel Potter*, Ch. 26) Since this is not in Potter's original narrative, Melville must either have recalled the details from *Omoo*, or have taken both passages from a common source. The same association of ideas seems to be present in *Moby-Dick* (Ch. 34, p. 149) where Dough-Boy, the *Pequod's* "bread-faced steward," is described as "the progeny of a bankrupt baker and a hospital nurse."

52.25. *bowels of compassion*: "But whoso hath this world's good, and seeth his brother have need, and shutteth up his bowels of compassion from him, how dwelleth the love of God in him?" (*I John*, 3. 17) Note the humorous use of Biblical and quasi-Biblical phrases in the ensuing account of Ropey: "... in an evil hour...," "... woe be unto him...," "... tribulations...," "veriest wretch...," "watery world...," "... furnace of affliction..." (*Isaiah*, 48.10), "... Land of Promise..." (*Hebrews*, 11.9), "... waxing snug...," "... took unto himself a wife...," "... worked him woe...," etc.

53.30. *Middle Ages... Jew*: Forbidden entrance to certain parts of the frigate *United States*, Melville says, "I was as a Roman Jew of the Middle Ages, confined to the Jew's quarter of the town." (*White-Jacket*, Ch. 31) Also "... ebon mud that stuck like Jews' pitch." (*Israel Potter*, Ch. 25) Because of some mental link, Melville alluded to Guy Fawkes and Medieval Jews close together in *Omoo*, *White-Jacket* (Ch. 31), and *Israel Potter* (Ch. 25).

54.32. *To give an instance*: Lewis Mumford quotes the ensuing scene, in which Flash Jack rags Ropey, to demonstrate that Melville's skill at character-drawing became more firm in *Omoo*, and also to disprove Robert Louis Stevenson's dictum (based on Melville's unsatisfactory rendering of Polynesian speech) that he had no "ear." "Melville had a curiously accurate ear," Mumford declares. "Here from an American writer, is perhaps the first clue to the existence of modern cockney. One will not discover that speech in the pages of Thomas Hood's Punch; one will not discover it in Pickwick Papers or Oliver Twist; what one finds there, as Mr. Bernard Shaw has pointed out, is an earlier urban dialect. In Omoo, on the contrary, Melville gives us the modern forms: the *ink* ending for *ing* and the dropped and added aitches. He was almost equally felicitous in rendering the difficult Belfast brogue: his transliteration of *haul* into *harl* is a test of it; and only an accurate ear will thus catch the living tongue." (*Herman Melville* [New York, 1929], pp. 83-84) The "Belfast brogue" to which Mumford refers is in the speech of the Belfast sailor in Ch. 76; and another speaker of Cockney is Shorty in Ch. 53 ff.

56.35. *Nelson... Copenhagen*: Horatio Nelson (1758-1805) lost his right eye in Corsica (1794) and his right arm at Santa Cruz de Tenerife (1797). In the battle of Copenhagen (1801) he brought the Danes to terms but was lucky to get his ships out of an untenable position; he by no means "flogged the whole shabby nation" there. Melville alludes frequently to Nelson; see especially the digression on him in *Billy Budd*.

60.14. *chronometer... true Greenwich time... quadrant*: The same instruments used comically here furnished major symbols for "The Quadrant," *Moby-Dick* (Ch. 118, pp. 493 ff.), and "Chronometricals and Horologicals," *Pierre* (Bk. XIV, iii, pp. 247 ff.).

61.12. *Pomotu or Low Group*: Melville took his details from Ellis (III, 225-229; II, 171-172); Wilkes (I, 307 ff.); and Russell (pp. 164-167).

61.27. *origin... ascribed to the coral insect*: For the geological theories Melville need not have gone beyond Russell (pp. 23-24), who presents this theory and the objections to it and states the reverse theory to which Melville's footnote refers. Neither theory is now held correct. The islands were piled up by submarine volcanoes, and the reefs were made by coral insects building upon the shoulders of these lava piles from a relatively shallow depth.

62.22. *pearl-shell fishermen*: From Wilkes (I, 345; II, 35). Wilkes learned at Tahiti that the pearl-shell fishery "was principally in the hands of the French consul" and that from 1832-1838 (not for one year as Melville says) its estimated value was $45,000 to $50,000. He names the French consul (II, 6) but not as a Dutchman by birth. Stewart (II, 11) mentions Mr. Marenhaut [*sic*] as a "Dutch gentleman." See Melville's fictional use of these islands in *Mardi* (Ch. 22) as the scene of the native seizure of a pearl-fishing vessel—a use perhaps suggested by Ellis's discussion, cited above.

62.26. *Moerenhout*: Jacques Antoine Moerenhout (1796 or 1797-1879). Born in Antwerp Province, under French occupation; educated in France; served in Napoleon's army; a merchant in Chile in 1826 ff.; became chief merchant engaged in Tahitian commerce, resident 1830-1843; friendly with Queen Pomare; was Pritchard's opponent in these years, developing French and Catholic interests in the islands; French consul at Monterey, 1845 ff.; resident of California 1846-1879. See his *Voyage Aux Iles du Grand Ocean*, 2 vols. [Paris, 1837]; also Abraham P. Nasatir, ed., a series of articles concerning Moerenhout's career, in *California Historical Society Quarterly* [1933, 1935, 1948]. At the time of Melville's visit, Moerenhout was head of the Provisional Council (see Documents Nos. 9, 23), but Melville seems to have known little of him personally.

Curiously enough, a reviewer of his *Voyage* had declared "... his whole work is a tissue of deliberate falsehoods. The truth is, that all he has told of the manners, customs, and history of Tahiti is stolen from Ellis's Polynesian Researches.... A little attention enables one to restore the pillaged property to its lawful owner...." (*Dublin University Magazine*, XXII [1843], 47).

64.4. *TAHITI*: Melville took details from Ellis (I, 28-29); Wilkes (II, 5). Of the peaks, it was Pirohitee (which Ellis, I, 296, mentions as Pito-hito) whose name stuck in Melville's memory: "... not greener the nine thousand feet of Pirohitee's tall peak, which, rising from out the warm bosom of Tahiti, carries all summer with in into the clouds...." (*Mardi*, Ch. 152) The Tahitian sailor on the *Pequod* hears in the squall "the roaring streams from Pirohitee's peak of spears, when they leap down the crags and drown the villages." (*Moby-Dick*,

Ch. 40, p. 172). This is the peak now known as Le Diadème. (Foulque, p. 79)

64.25. *Tempe*: A valley in the north of Thessaly, between Mount Olympus and Mount Ossa, a favorite haunt of Apollo; its scenery was often described by ancient poets. Melville probably had it in mind in referring to "the groves of our Thessalies." (*Redburn*, Ch. 50) In *Clarel* (Pt. II, v) Melville has a passage with an ironic point: "Fine shot was mine by Nazareth;/But birding's best in Tempe's vale." This was based on his 1856-1857 *Journal* entry: "Duckworth, the English resident... said he had been *a day's shooting in the Vale of Tempe*—Ye Gods! whortleberrying on Olympus, &c." (*Journal of a Visit to Europe and the Levant*, edited by Howard C. Horsford [Princeton, 1955], p. 72)

65.17. *Bougainville*: Louis Antoine de Bougainville (1729-1811), the first French circumnavigator, visited Tahiti for ten days in 1768, and named it La Nouvelle Cythère. Melville took the quotation from *Circumnavigation* (p. 186). In January, 1848, possibly for use in *Mardi*, he borrowed J. R. Forster's translation of Bougainville's *Voyage round the World* [London, 1772] from the New York Society Library. [Sealts, #85]. See Davis, pp. 63, 65.

65.21. *amiable dispositions*: Actually, their "amiability" emerged only after Wallis's cannon repulsed their war fleet and slaughtered a few of them—"toar to peces in such a manner as I am certain they neaver beheald before"—thus convincing them of his terrible superiority. See the wonderfully vivid and detailed journal of George Robertson, Master of Wallis's *Dolphin*, in *The Discovery of Tahiti* [London, Hakluyt Society, 1948]. Melville used *Circumnavigation* (pp. 155 ff.) which gave the same information. Robertson devotes many passages to "their very handsome Young girls."

65.25. *divine rights*: See Ellis (I, 248 ff.). Melville probably meant "divine rites."

65.28. *earlier and more full accounts*: In England the imagination of readers was greatly aroused by the publication in 1773 of John Hawkesworth's *An Account of the Voyages...in the Southern Hemisphere...by Commodore Byron, Captain Wallis, Captain Carteret, and Captain Cook....* Hawkesworth, a literary man of Romantic cast, did much by his editorial selection and comment to display the Tahitians in the glowing color of "noble savages," decidedly altering the effect of the realistic journals themselves. See Hoxie N. Fairchild, *The Noble Savage* [New York, 1928], pp. 104-112. Also Clara Rebecca Lesher, *The South Sea Islanders in English Literature, 1519-1798* [University of Chicago Dissertation, 1940].

65.35. *Omai*: A native not of Tahiti but of Ulietea, a neighboring island, he was taken to London by one of Captain Cook's officers in 1775. He was patronized by nobles, scholars, and ladies. He was painted by Reynolds, sung by Cowper, and, more to his taste, favored by celebrated beauties. He went home in 1777, on Cook's last voyage. Melville saw his story in *Circumnavigation* (pp. 259, 284-286, 306-309) and read about his life after his return in Ellis (II, 269). Miss Lesher, cited in the note above, recounts his impact on English poetry (pp. 80-105).

65.36. *Aotooroo*: Bougainville took Aoturu to Paris in 1769, where he stayed a year, arousing a good deal of interest, though some found him a stupid fellow. He died of smallpox on his way back to Tahiti. Melville read of him in the summary of Bougainville's *Voyage* in *Circumnavigation*.

65.38. *several eventful occurrences*: In 1846 Melville probably knew little more about these than he had gleaned from *Circumnavigation*, Russell (pp. 113-115), and Ellis. He was mistaken in supposing that Tahiti was visited by the Honourable John Byron (1765) or the ill-fated La Pérouse (1785-1788). He possibly derived the latter error from Russell (p. 115). Pedro Fernandes de Quirós, a Portuguese navigator in the service of the Spanish viceroy of Peru, discovered an island (1605) generally supposed by Melville's source-books to have been Tahiti, but now identified as Anaa or Chain Island (see *The Discovery of Tahiti*, xxx). Captain Samuel Wallis of the *Dolphin* is now usually credited with the discovery (1767). Captain James Cook visited Tahiti on each of his three voyages (1769, 1773-1774, 1777). His primary purpose on the first voyage was to observe the transit of Venus, for which Tahiti was chosen as the best station, upon Wallis's recent report. Bougainville's visit (1768) is noted above. Captain George Vancouver visited Tahiti with Cook in 1777 and on his own voyage in 1792. Melville later (Ch. 48) cites Vancouver. "The memorable mutiny of the

Bounty" (28 April 1789) had its origin at Tahiti, so Captain Bligh himself reported, because after twenty-three idyllic weeks there his men "had ideally assured themselves of a more happy life among the Otaheitans than they could possibly have in England, which joined to some female connections, has been the cause of the whole busyness." How far Bligh's own conduct was a cause is still disputed. (For selected documents and a bibliography, see *A Book of the Bounty*, Everyman's Library, 1938.) "The first regularly constituted Protestant missionaries" were sent to Tahiti by the London Missionary Society on the *Duff* in 1797.

66.23. *should the captain leave the ship, the crew were no longer bound by her articles*: As a matter of fact the articles of the *Lucy Ann* specifically stated: "...the several Officers & other persons signing this agreement...promise that they...will obey and execute all the lawful commands of the said Henry Ventom on board the said vessel and on shore as the case may be as the Master thereof and the commands of the Commanding Officer for the time being during the said intended voyage...." German's deposition states that at first the men made no objection to sailing under him but that on 24 September those who refused duty "said they did not sign under me and would do no more duty on board; and would not proceed on the voyage, that the cruise was up...." The two clauses here embody two separate claims: the first is that mentioned in the present passage; the second is the ground alleged by Melville himself and some others, that they signed "for the cruise" only and that the cruise was terminated when the ship was brought into port at Tahiti. Clearly, it was to forestall this claim that Ventom had ordered the mate to keep the ship off and on the port rather than to bring her in (See Revolt Documents, #1; #11, No. 3.)

66.25. *forecastle Cokes*: Equivalent for "sea-lawyers," referring to Sir Edward Coke (1552-1634), famous English jurist.

67.14. *Reine Blanche... Dupetit-Thouars*: Here and in *Typee* (Appendix) Melville set back the date of the *Lucy Ann's* arrival at Tahiti by eleven days (from 20 to 9 September); or else the frigate, which was indeed in the harbor, was firing a salute for some other occasion.

67.37. *the captain... intended to set himself ashore*: Melville alters the chronology of events here, perhaps through faulty memory, perhaps to make out a better case for the revolters. The *Lucy Ann* arrived off Tahiti on 20 September; that afternoon German went ashore and brought off Dr. Johnstone who examined the captain, discovered an abcess of the lung, and declared that Ventom must go ashore "for the safety of his life." Captain Ventom did so the next day (22 September by the Tahiti calendar)—not the day of their arrival as Melville declares, or before the doctor had examined him. It was on the second day (22 September), while German was taking the captain ashore, that Benbow Byrne ("Bembo") was left in command.

70.15. *Bay of Islands*: A harbor near the Northeast extremity of North Island, New Zealand. (See allusion in *Redburn*, Ch. 23.) Benbow Byrne, however, actually shipped at Sydney, so there is grave question whether he was a Maori at all. His "personal appearance" is very close to the description by Wilkes (II, 398). See also Ellis (III, 249).

73.15. "*Round Robin*": Evidently fictitious—no such document is preserved among all the scraps in Wilson's consular records. A variant manuscript version of the Round Robin has been preserved (reproduced, *Log*, I, 142). It lacks "Van"; has "Smut" for "Long Jim"; has "Blue Dick" cancelled, with "Black Dan" substituted; similarly "Chips" cancelled and replaced by "Beauty"; has "Bill Blunt alias" noted as an addition before "Liverpool." The evident significance of the variations is that Melville was concerned less with an accurate historical document than with a picturesque literary one.

74.22. *Pritchard*: George Pritchard came to Tahiti as a missionary in 1824, and resigned when appointed British consul in 1837. He was absent in England February, 1841, to February, 1843. Melville tells an apocryphal anecdote of Mrs. Pritchard's Barbara-Frietchie-like refusal to pull down the English colors flying before the consulate in defiance of a French order. (*Typee*, Ch. 3) Upon his return Pritchard became the backbone of opposition to the French, who imprisoned and deported him in 1844. The "Pritchard Affair" became an international incident, France eventually paying an indemnity to the British government. See the books by both Pritchard and his son, and Phyllis M. Brookes, *International Rivalry in the Pacific* (pp. 142-145).

74.24. *Wilson*: Charles B. Wilson, British Acting Consul at Tahiti from 1841 to 1843, son of the Rev. Charles Wilson. His part in the ensuing events was roughly as Melville represents it. Wilkes and Wise give reports that substantiate Melville's allegation that he was "unprincipled and dissipated." (Wilkes, III, 18-19; 39-40; 129) Lucett, however, was enraged by Wilkes's report and defended Wilson's "unimpeached veracity" and "high integrity." (I, 293-300)

75.8. *Doctor Johnson*: An actual person, Dr. Francis Johnstone. See Documents, *passim*, and later notes.

78.2. *PROCEEDINGS OF THE CONSUL*: Actually it was the second day off Tahiti, the same day that the captain went ashore (22 September by Tahiti calendar), that the consul and doctor came aboard; and they did so at Ventom's request, not because of a round robin. Once ashore, Ventom took up residence not at the consul's house but in one engaged for him by Wilson. In his deposition he declares that the crew made no complaint before his departure. His actions however, betray that he had sharp enough ears to hear their "whispered maledictions." For no sooner had he got ashore than he requested the consul to go off to his vessel and inform his crew that their captain must remain at Tahiti. His orders were that they should proceed with the ship on a three months' cruise, under German's command. Accordingly, that same afternoon (22 September), Wilson went aboard, taking along Dr. Johnstone. What ensued was more like what Melville reports than the amicable events both the consul and the doctor swore to in their depositions. The doctor at once examined those who complained of being sick. There were only six (despite the impression Melville gives), and, just as Melville reports, Johnstone found two (Nicholas Utley and Henry Smith) sick enough to need shore treatment and four (William Mathews, John Troy, Herman Melville, and James Smith) "fit to go on the voyage." Meanwhile Wilson summoned the others aft and delivered the captain's orders. According to his deposition, he "heard no complaints" except that the sick should be taken off and the full complement of men and officers made up."

He agreed to these points. Neither he nor Johnstone, they later declared, heard so much as a word against German or against continuing the cruise under him, or against the food. Nevertheless, complaints were indeed made, and made probably as Melville states, after the consul had flung the captain's orders at the crew, browbeaten them into silence, and then declared the matter officially settled and his ears officially closed. In their depositions German and Byrne both betray that there was really trouble: before the consul left, John Garretson, William Bunnell, Amado Sylva, and Charles Watts had all refused further duty, because, they said, "we signed under Captain Ventom and not under the mate and our agreement is broken by the Captain's leaving and going on shore." Three of these were men Ventom had recruited in the Marquesas "for the cruise only," and the basis of their revolt evidently was that the cruise for which they signed was over or at least the agreement broken by Ventom's going ashore. One further complaint was voiced: a later scribbled note of Wilson's, opposite Garretson's and Sylva's names on a list of revolters, indicates that they assigned a reason for not sailing under the mate, "Mr. German not fit to take charge for continually drunkenness." Strangely enough, the revolt was spearheaded by these recruits of the previous month, who did not claim sickness, and who had not been aboard to be involved in the earlier, July, revolt at St. Christina. One of them was very likely Melville's "Salem," who thrusts aside the cooper, speaks up to the consul, flourishes a knife and proclaims himself "a bloody beachcomber who shipped at the Islands four months ago." In his whole account of the affair thus far, though he doubtless exaggerates and dramatizes, Melville's chief invention is the round robin, and his chief distortion, perhaps, is the way he puts himself with Long Ghost in the center of things.

85.19. *THE SECOND NIGHT OFF PAPEETEE*: Though Melville is not accurate as to chronology and invents a certain amount of going and coming and comic drunken business for the mate, the events he reports in this chapter are much of the sort that evidently took place aboard the *Lucy Ann* after the departure of consul and doctor on 22 September and during the following day and night. What with the sick-list men (including Melville) off duty and some six men now refusing duty, few were left to man the watches. The quarrel reported

here between Bembo and Sydney Ben is a heightened version
of the one reported in the depositions, between Benbow Byrne
and James Watts—Watts rejected an order of Byrne's with a
high retort and Byrne struck him; Watts went below to
complain to German, who, drunk or sober, reprimanded Byrne.
Things were out of hand and next morning the mate concluded,
orders notwithstanding, that all he could do was bring the
vessel into port.

89.34. *the fell purpose of Bembo*: A wholly fictitious episode, doubtless shaped out of similar instances Melville had
heard and read about. For example, in 1809 a New Zealander
" having been punished for neglect of duty, resolved to have
his revenge when the vessel should come to anchor in the neighborhood of his tribe." So the savages murdered the captain,
crew, and women and children aboard, then grounded and
burned the ship. (Russell, p. 286) See Melville's account of
savages seizing the *Parki* in *Mardi* (Ch. 22,28).

96.12. *not long after midnight*: German's deposition declares that "about seven o'clock" he bore up and took the vessel
into port; Benbow Byrne testifies, " I do not remember him
saying that he would take the ship into the harbour at
midnight " —which implies that somebody charged that German did say so, and suggests that Melville had some basis for
connecting midnight with German's decision to put into port.

97.24. *Papeetee Bay... ticklish*: Cf. Wilkes (II, 40) for similar
information in a passage which Melville used at the end of
Ch. 23.

97.24, 29. *Papeetee... Matavai*: Papeete, Mata-vaï. (Foulque,
p. 112) Ellis used the forms Papeete and Matavai (*e.g.*, I, 23).

98.28, 30. pemi.... ita maitai: pé' é maï.... aïta maïtaï. (Foulque, p. 113) Ellis (II, 18) gives *maitai* as *good*; so does Stewart
(II, 42). *Typee*, Ch. 18, 28, 33.

99.8. sabee: Foulque adds to Melville's footnote, " Ce terme,
généralement orthographié *sabbee* fait partie du jargon poly-
glotte dit « Bichlamar » ou Bêche de Mer ." (p. 114, n. 1)

99.9. *Jim*: Though Jim the pilot was quite real, a personage
reported by various visitors, this episode is probably fiction,

based on passages in Wilkes (II, 4,39) where all the necessary details are to be found. See Anderson (pp. 211-212).

99.14. ita maitai nuee: *aïta maïtaï nui.* (Foulque, p. 114)

101.3. *the tides*: Straight from Ellis (I, 37), including the footnote reference to Newton and (I, 80) the native term ("tui-ra-po") for midnight. The behavior of the tide at Tahiti, although disputed by scientific visitors for years, actually follows the usual pattern, the apparent anomaly being due to the inadequate size of the little island as a measuring stick. In *Clarel* (Pt. IV, xviii) Melville had a confused memory of something unusual in the tides: " [Tahiti] That vine-wreathed urn of Ver, in sea/ Of halcyons, where no tides do flow/ Or ebb, but waves bide peacefully/ At brim...."

101.11. *a large ship...bilged upon the beach*: This was the *Alexander Mansfield* of Hudson, New York, 320 tons, which sailed in 1839 and was condemned at Tahiti in 1840. Olmsted saw her there in September, 1840, and his passages may be Melville's prompting source, though the hulk had actually been there for him to see. (Francis A. Olmsted, *Incidents of a Whaling Voyage* [New York, 1841], p. 275. Cited by Anderson, p. 218)

102.1. *more than forty days after leaving the Marquesas*: Actually about twenty-nine days.

102.3. *a boat came alongside with our esteemed friend Wilson*: Melville's account, in this and the next chapter, of Wilson's way of handling the revolt is accurate enough, as measured by Wilson's own records in the Revolt Documents, except in particulars and in the grand fact that Melville took no part in the revolt at this stage and was not one of the ten men removed from the *Lucy Ann* and imprisoned on *La Reine Blanche*. From the depositions it is not quite clear whether Wilson came aboard at once, as Melville reports here, or only after German had waited upon Ventom with the bad news and Ventom had written a complaint to Wilson requesting him to take the vessel in charge. In any case, Wilson did come aboard, muster the sheep and the goats apart, leave to arrange matters with the French, and return in the afternoon to supervise removal of the ten revolters to imprisonment aboard the French ship. Melville remained aboard the *Lucy Ann*, whence, the next day, he wrote at Henry Smyth's dictation, a letter to George Lefevre " aboard the French frigate." (See Revolt Document #6.) The frigate's logbook confirms the arrest. (Anderson, p. 206)

103.4. *Flash-Gorger*: *Flash*, " showy "; in Australia, " vainglorious or swaggering." *Gorger*, " a well-dressed man " or " a gentleman." See John S. Farmer, *Slang and Its Analogues* [London, 1890], III, 10, 186.

104.24. *as we swept under the bows*: This scene of the removal of the revolters in the frigate's cutter, especially Navy Bob's farewell to the " Little Jule," Salem's leaping to his feet and waving his hat to the shipmates looking over at them, and the lieutenant's command —is strikingly similar to that of Billy Budd's removal from the ship *Rights of Man* at the end of the first chapter of *Billy Budd*.

105.9. *Old Gamboge*: Since gamboge is a gum-resin used as a bright yellow pigment, the lieutenant's " yellow face " suggested the nickname. Melville uses the word thus several times. The malevolent Jackson is " yellow as gamboge." (*Redburn*, Ch. 12) Stubb calls Fedallah a " gamboge ghost." (*Moby-Dick*, Ch. 73, p. 323)

107.29. *As long... as navies are needed... no substitute for it*: A curious statement, considering Melville's attitude toward flogging in *White-Jacket*. It perhaps indicates the literary exaggeration in which he indulged there.

108.13. *the Reine Blanche*: The chances are that Melville wrote this detailed description from a printed source, though we have been unable to find it. He had certainly seen the ship several times; but—especially since he was not actually among the revolting sailors confined on her—we may well wonder with the sceptical reviewer for *Blackwood's* (LXI [1847], 760) at his familiarity with her internal arrangements and architecture: " the minute details..., the disposition of her guns and decks, the complicated machinery..., even the rich hangings, mirrors, and mahogany of the Captain's cabin."

108.25. *French flummery*: Similarly in *Moby-Dick* (Ch. 91, pp. 401-402) Stubb notes " the fanciful French taste " in the carving of the upper part of the stem-piece of the *Rose-Bud*.

109.28. *asked for meat*: From Melville's favorite Biblical passage, the Sermon on the Mount. " Or what man is there of you, whom if his son ask bread, will he give him a stone? Or if he ask a fish, will he give him a serpent? " (*Matthew*, 7. 9-10; *Luke*, 11.11)

110.30. *Five days and nights... we were aboard the frigate*: As usual Melville expands the time (and, as stated above, he himself was not imprisoned on the French frigate at all). The prisoners were taken aboard *La Reine Blanche* on Saturday afternoon, 24 September, and set ashore in custody of the native authorities on Monday, 26 September. The French frigate sailed for Valparaiso early in the morning. Doubtless, as Howard conjectures, the imprisonment aboard the warship had been a bluff on the part of Wilson and Ventom, " for Captain Ventom could hardly have afforded to send the British authorities in Valparaiso two sets of mutineers along with reports of desertions that, all together, accounted for more than four-fifths of his original crew." (Howard, p. 58)

111.7. *Accosted by Wilson*: According to the Revolt Documents, Wilson held two sessions with the revolters after they came ashore: the first, not on Monday as soon as they landed, as Melville reports here, but later in the week (either Wednesday or Thursday —the records are confused and contradictory). In the presence of Ventom, German, Johnstone's partner Dr. Myrick, and the loyal members of the crew, Wilson, as here, asked the revolters whether they would return to their duty, and all refused. It was on this occasion—after the French warship had sailed and all serious consequences gone—that " Herman Melville also said that he would do no more duty and would share the same as the others who refused to do their duty." (See German's deposition.) The ship's articles were read to them, to no effect, and they were all, now including Melville, sent back to the native " prison."

113.20. *Broom Road*: Details seem to be culled from Wilkes, (II, 33-34) and Stewart (II, 13-14). Bennett explains the name: " ...the task of sweeping it, and keeping it in repair, being the more common punishment inflicted upon offenders against the laws." (Frederick Debell Bennett, *A Whaling Voyage Round the Globe*... [London, 1840], I, 65) In 1852 Perkins saw some jolly convict girls sweeping it with brooms. (p. 298) Even today it retains the name. Foulque (p. 128, n. 1) gives the Tahitian form as *Purumu*.

113.25. *Taiarboo*: Taiarapu (Ellis: Taiarabu). Melville is short one syllable.

113.36. *Whaiherea*: Vaihiria. See Wilkes (II, 25 ff.).

114.9. *Pawnee-Loups*: One of the great groups of plains Indians. " The Loups are famous for their horses, and it is often that you see a warrior on the prairies far better mounted than a congressman in the settlements." (Cooper, *The Prairie*, Ch. 18)

115.1. *Calabooza Beretanee*: Lucett describes it as "a calliboose," with a "massive pair of wooden stocks" in which he was confined by the ankles, along with six or seven of the mutineers. (I, 288-289) Foulque (p. 130, n. 1) gives the Tahitian form as *tarapu*, "la langue maorie ignorant le *c*, le *l*, le *b* et l's." In 1845-1846 Lt. Walpole saw "the *carabouse*, or State-prison of former times, where Omo [*sic*] passed, according to his own account, a most disagreeable captivity." (*Four Years in the Pacific* [London, 1849], II, 111) See Anderson, pp. 213 ff.

115.36. "*hannapar*": Cf. Stewart (I, 239) who gives *hana paa* as "make fast." Foulque (p. 131) makes this *haa na pô*.

116.9. "*moee-moee*"... "*maitai*": moè-moè... maïtaï. Foulque (p. 131); *Typee*, Ch. 12,16,33.

118.9. *Capin Tootee*: Cook's last visit was in 1777. He reported that the natives called him "Tute." Visitors in the twenty years before and even a decade after Melville ran into natives who "remembered" him. Here, by innuendo, Melville has Bob claiming that Cook was his *tayo* and shared his wife.

119.2. "*kow-kow*": Foulque (p. 134) gives the form *Kai-kai*, explaining in a footnote: "Le mot serait correct en marquisien et donnerait en tahitien: *aï-aï*. Melville demeure influencé par son séjour à Typee lorsqu'il reproduit des mots maoris." In *Typee* (Ch. 12, 13) Melville does use *ki-ki* for *eat* (the form *kie-kie* occurs in one of his source-books, David Porter's *Journal*... [Philadelphia, 1815], II, 50). Cf. note on 301.28.

120.27. *PROCEEDINGS OF THE FRENCH*: Melville's sources, as he states, were what he heard at the time of his first visit (September-November, 1842) and his "subsequent visit" (12-19 October 1843—as a crew-member of the frigate *United States*), and "reliable accounts" which he had seen since reaching home. Of the numerous printed accounts we have examined, only that of Wilkes (II, 19), pointed out by Anderson (p. 275), seems clearly to have been used by Melville, but Melville gives many details not reported by Wilkes. As Anderson concluded, Melville's chapter is substantially correct but biased against the French. For a recent history of the proceedings see Phyllis M. Brookes, *International Rivalry in the Pacific*, Ch. 5. The priests Laval and Caret were expelled in November, 1836, the technical ground being that they had landed clandestinely, without the Queen's permission. The Protectorate was established by Dupetit-Thouars in September, 1842, Pomare having under duress signed the necessary document on 9 September. Melville gives an even more bitter account of this "outrage" in *Typee* (Ch. 3). The battles Melville mentions were fought in the first half of 1844, and the "gallant though useless" warfare of resistance kept up until 1847. The "great feast" given by Kitoti, in 1845, is similarly described by Lucett (II, 95) and by Lt. Walpole (*Four Years in the Pacific*, II, 317). Apparently echoing Melville's report of the aged warrior's speech, Walpole declares, " The natives often said ' Frenchmen very bad, but French wine *nui, nui mité*— very, very good. ' "

122.25. *Louis Philippe*: Louis-Philippe, King of the French, 1830-1848.

123-124, *passim*: Foulque gives the following equivalents for Melville's forms of the proper names on these pages: Aitoa for Adeea; Hitoti, Tâti, and Utami for Kitoti, Tati, Utamai; Mahaena for Mahanar; Taiarapu for Taraiboo; Haapape for Hararparpi; Faaa for Fararar; Pari for Paree. (pp. 138-139) She identifies Fergus as " aide de camp de Charles Thierry, aventurier qui se proclama, en 1835, roi de Nuka-Hiva; il mourut à Papeete."

124.22. *Aeorai Society*: Misspelling of Areoi (*Typee*, Ch. 26, " Arreory "). Ellis (I, 182 ff.) devotes an entire chapter to it. " They were a sort of strolling players, and privileged libertines," an élite fraternity claiming divine origin and observing "abominable practices," including infanticide.

125.28. "*Karhowrees*" (*white men*): Foulque (p. 141) gives the form *Tarahao ê*, and in translating Melville's parenthetical gloss "(white men)" alters it to "(les étrangers)"—which is, in fact, the meaning Melville himself gives the word later (144.36), translating "karhowree toonee" as "crazy stranger." Cf. 152.12.

125.31. *a fine opportunity of making observations*: But Melville made them in the pages of Ellis (I, 73-77).

125.33. *sickly or deformed persons*: Directly from Ellis (I, 73-74): "Among the many models of perfection..., instances of deformity are now frequently seen, arising from a loathsome disease, of foreign origin, affecting the features of the face, and muscular parts of the body. There is another disease, which forms such a curvature of the upper part of the spine, as to produce what is termed a humped or broken back. The disease which produces this distortion of shape, and deformity of appearance, is declared by the natives to have been unknown to their ancestors; and, according to the account some of them give of it, was the result of a disease left by the crew of Vancouver's ship. It does not prevail in any of the other groups; and although such numbers are now affected with it, there is reason to believe that formerly, except the many disfigurements produced by the elephantiasis, which appears to have prevailed from their earliest antiquity, a deformed person was seldom seen."

126.8. *Fa-Fa, or Elephantiasis*: Fefe, described by Ellis and other voyagers. We find no direct source.

126.26. *Roorootoo*: Rurutu. (Ellis, I, 25; Foulque, p. 141)

127.20. *Notwithstanding the physical degeneracy*: Melville returns to Ellis's account (I, 75): "...the chiefs... are, almost without exception, as much superior to the peasantry or common people, in stateliness, dignified deportment, and physical strength, as they are in rank and circumstances...."

127.23. *diminutive women*: Ellis (I, 75) notes "a considerable difference between the stature of the male and female

sex... yet not so great as that which often prevails in Europe. "
The females are "stronger and larger than the females of
England... sometimes remarkably tall and stout. A roundness
and fullness of figure... distinguishes the people in general,
particularly the females. "

127.24. *the nymphs who... swam round the ship of Wallis*:
They didn't so swim, according to Robertson (cited above) who
has much to say about them in his downright manner. (*The
Discovery of Tahiti*, p. 148)

127.25. *Tahitian beauty... seducing as it proved to the crew
of the Bounty*: Testimony on this point varied astonishingly.
Robertson (p. 167) says, "...all the sailors swore they neaver
saw handsomer made women in their lives. " Vancouver,
however, could not perceive their beauty, and remarked sourly
upon his surprise at the *Bounty's* crew being so seduced. The
Duff missionary brethren in 1797 vere "disappointed." ([William Wilson, ed.], *A Missionary Voyage to the Southern Pacific
Ocean... In the Ship Duff....* [London, 1799], p. 327) Later
visitors so disagreed that one can only conclude that at Tahiti
as elsewhere beauty is in the eye of the beholder.

127.29. *natural complexion of both sexes*: Still Ellis: "...In
one of their songs, the following sentiments are inculcated;—
'If black be the complexion of the mother, the son will sound
the conch-shell; if vigorous and strong the mother, the son will
be a governor '.... The prevailing colour of the natives is an
olive, a bronze, or a reddish brown.... At the time of their birth,
the complexion of Tahitian infants is but little if any darker
than that of European children; and the skin only assumes the
bronze or brown hue as they grow up under repeated or
constant exposure to the sun.... The females, who are much
employed in beating cloth, or other occupations followed under
shelter, are usually fairer than the rest; while the fishermen,
who are most exposed to the sun, are invariably the darkest
portion of the population.... Darkness of colour was generally
considered an indication of strength; and fairness of complexion, the contrary. Hence the men were not solicitous
either to cover their persons or avoid the sun's rays, from any
apprehension of the effect it would produce on the skin. When
they searched the field of battle for the bones of the slain, to
use them in the manufacture of chisels, gimlets, or fish-hooks,

they always selected those whose skins were dark, as they
supposed their bones were strongest. When I have seen the
natives looking at a very dark man, I have sometimes heard
them say *Taata ra e, te ereere! ivi maitai tona*; 'The man,
how dark! good bones are his.' A fair complexion was not an
object of admiration or desire. They never considered the
fairest European countenance seen among them, handsomer
than their own; and sometimes, when a fine, tall, wellformed,
and personable man has landed from a ship, they have remarked as he passed along, 'A fine man that, if he were but
a native.' " (I, 76-77)

128.3. *"taata tona,"* or *man of bones*: Taken from Ellis
(see note above). Foulque appends a note to the phrase: " Melville écrit *tona*, mais il s'agirait plutôt de *to'a*, dur, fort,
indomptable, courageux." (p. 143)

128.5. *fish-hooks and gimblets... cups and saucers*: Melville
was fascinated by such utilitarian use of bones, partly (like
Hamlet considering Caesar's dust stopping a bunghole) because
of the ironic contrast of trivial utility with the vastness of
Death, and of living pretension with dead insignificance; partly (like Byron drinking from a skull) because of the bravado
displayed. In *Mardi* occur the avengers' threats to quaff Taji's
blood from his own skull (Ch. 100), a skull used as a canoe-
bailer (Ch. 114), " a quaint little Fish-hook (made from the
Finger-bones of Kravi the Cunning) " (Ch. 122), militant kings
merrily shaking ivory coins in a skull (Ch. 139), cannikins
made from the skulls of baboons (Ch. 174). In *Moby-Dick*
the utilitarian Jeremy Bentham's skeleton "hangs for cande-
labra " (Ch. 55, p. 265), a foreign friend of Ishmael's uses an
enemy's vertebrae to inlay the beaked prow of his canoe (Ch. 80,
p. 347), a bower in the Arsacides is made of a whale's skeleton
(also in *Mardi*, Ch. 45), the cannibal urchins using the whale's
smallest vertebrae to play marbles with (Ch. 102-103, pp. 445
ff.). In " Benito Cereno " a murdered Spaniard's skeleton is
used for the ship's figurehead. In *Clarel* (Pt. I, xxii) " Hard
by, as chanced, he once beheld/ Bones like sea corals; one
bleached skull/ A vase vined round and beautiful/ With flowers; felt, with bated breath/ The floral revelry over death."

128.14. *"Ita maitai nuee,"* or *very bad exceedingly*: See
notes on 98.28, 30 and 99.14. (Foulque, p. 143) *Typee*, Ch. 13,
and *passim*.

130.17. *scarcity of edibles*: See Wilkes (IV, 219) on the same subject. Ellis (III, 36) implies that the class differential in diet was one of long standing, but Melville would have damaged his case by admitting that the scarcity antedated " the distressing consequences of civilization."

131.17. *seeking what they might devour*: "... The devil. as a roaring lion, walketh about, seeking whom he may devour." (*I Peter*, 5.8) Melville applies this to the Tiger shark in *Mardi*, Ch. 13.

131.31. *Doctor Johnson*: Dr. Johnstone paid several calls on the crew, and though Melville's account is exaggerated for comic effect, there is little doubt that he described Dr. Johnstone recognizably. In 1848 Wise wrote in his journal: " His friend Dr. Johnstone is not to be pacified — intends shortly to prosecute the English publishers — he politely permitted me to copy the following items from his dose book—evidence by the way that the ' embrocation ' so relished by ' Long Ghost' (John Troy) was a villanous preparation having the least taste of gin in the world and made up of laudanum—turpentine and soap liniment!—here it is—

"Ship Lucy Ann—Captain Venton [*sic*]
Octr 15. 1842 —Melville Herman   —Stocks
» 16 »   Embrocation —— .75
» 19 »   Do   — .75
————————
1.50

I felt no inclination to taste it, since I found the Doctor's other potions unexceptionable—Mr Long Ghost must have been seriously indisposed—he had a large quantity...." (See the published version in *Los Gringos*, p. 399; manuscript version transcribed by Jay Leyda.) Lucett, a friend of the Doctor, reported similarly: " I had the curiosity to search Dr. Johnstone's medical diary: the names of all the mutineers were enrolled there, and amongst them stands Herman Melville's. The whole of the doctor's charges for medicine and medical attendance amounts to but a few dollars; and the only item charged against Herman Melville is a bottle of embrocation, as the man complained of pains in his limbs: but the doctor believing him to be an imposter, which by the way I think he has clearly shown himself to have been, paid no further heed to his complaints." (I, 295-296) Lucett declares Melville "grossly scandalized" and "grievously misrepresented" Dr. Johnstone; but his own report above is our means of authenticating Melville's hunch that the bill was padded. For the bill which Johnstone rendered the British consul included $19.50 for Melville! Another acquaintance, Robert Elwes, reported that in 1849 the doctor "was excessively angry at the description, and always threatened an action against Mr. Murray." (*A Sketcher's Tour Round the World*, [London, 1854], p. 222) See Forsythe, pp. 8-12; Anderson, pp. 227-228.

136.26. *WE ARE CARRIED BEFORE THE CONSUL AND CAPTAIN*: This is evidently a pretty accurate description of Wilson's final session with the revolters, on 5 October. Included among the Revolt Documents are the depositions referred to here, of German, Ventom (longer than Melville implies), the loyal "seamen remaining aboard the vessel," as well as that of Benbow Byrne, and the ship's articles (Wilson's copy). Upon conclusion of this examination, at which none of the revolters relented, Wilson consigned all eleven, including Melville, to the native authorities, and drew up all the necessary papers for any subsequent trial and for clearing his own and Captain Ventom's hands of them. The next day a new crew was shipped.

137.7. *the "Kihee"*: See Ellis (I, 151): "They frequently manufacture a sort of girdle, called tiheri, six inches in width, and sometimes twenty yards in length...." Melville evidently confused this with the tehei, or Hawaiian kehei, described by Ellis (II, 288) and Stewart (I, 231) as a mantle, but by Melville (Ch. 47) as a petticoat. Foulque (p. 152), *tihi*.

139.29. *THE FRENCH PRIESTS*: Fathers François d'Assisi Caret, Armand Chausson, and Columba Murphy. Father Murphy had been trying since 1833 to propagate the Catholic faith in the Gambier, Sandwich, and Marquesas Islands, as well as in Tahiti. Having got into Tahiti disguised as a carpenter, he was twice expelled from there, in 1835 and 1836, but he returned in 1841. Robert S. Forsythe concluded that Melville's picture of him (his personal morality aside) is "fairly accurate." ("Herman Melville's Father Murphy," *Notes and Queries*, CLXXII [1937], 254-258, 272-276)

141.35. *"Hytee Belteezers"*... *land beavers*: A teasing epithet, indeed (high-tea, or hoity, bell-toppers?). Foulque translates it "grands Balthazar." (p. 157)

143.28. *LITTLE JULE SAILS WITHOUT US*: Melville reports three sessions with the consul, where the Revolt Documents report only two. It was on 6 October, the day following their last interview with Wilson on 5 October, that Captain Ventom signed aboard a new crew. As Melville states, advances were necessary, ranging actually from $10 for the ordinary seamen, through $12 to $20 for the able seamen, to $25 for the new third mate and $40 for the new second mate. To cover this and other accumulated expenses, Captain Ventom, as Melville states, sold some of the little whale-oil they had managed to accumulate. As for the " Mowree " being carried to sea in irons and poor Ropey being left ashore to die at Townor (Taonoa)— both of these matters are fictitious. The *Lucy Ann* sailed on 15 October, twenty-five days after arriving off Tahiti, just " about three weeks " after entering the harbor, as Melville reports.

144.36. *"Karhowree toonee,"* or *crazy stranger*: " Tarahao tuni..., l'étranger fou..." (Foulque, p. 160) See note on 125.28, also 152.12.

147.25. *Townor*: Ellis gives Taonoa; Foulque (p. 163), Taunoa.

148.11. *harree*: *haere*. (Foulque, p. 164) Cf. note on 239.1.

149.18. *to give no thought as to wherewithal we should be clothed and fed*: "Therefore take no thought, saying, 'What shall we eat? or, What shall we drink? or Wherewithal shall we be clothed?'" (*Matthew*, 6.31) This light paraphrase from the Sermon on the Mount was the only passage the English editors found offensive enough to require change—thus, "telling him to be quite at ease on the score of our food and clothing."

149.28. *Mahinee*: Mahine, a chief of Eimeo and Huahine, is mentioned a number of times by Ellis (II, 113 ff., 202 ff.).

150.17. *" Beretanee, Fenooa Pararee "*: From Ellis (II, 170): "*Beri-ta-ni-e! fenua paari*: O Britain! land of skill, or knowledge." The exclamation of the natives who saw the first printing press in operation (1817). Foulque (p. 166): Paretane, Fenua Paroere.

150.37. " *tayos* ": A custom remarked by various early visitors (see Anderson, p. 231). Melville's friends Poky and Kooloo have not yet been used to substantiate amateur diagnoses of latent homosexuality, as has his bosom friendship with Queequeg, which Melville is, of course, deliberately representing as one between tayos. Foulque (p. 166) gives the form taió.

151.10. *Damon and Pythias*: In classical legend each of these devoted friends sought execution in the other's stead. See *Israel Potter* (Ch. 22).

152.12. " *tayo karhowree nuee* "... *particular white friend*: taió tarahao nui. (Foulque, p. 168) Cf. 125.28.

152.15. *damsel...fair to look upon*: " And the damsel was very fair to look upon...." (*Genesis*, 24.16).

152.19. *Tamatoy, King of Raiatair*: Tamatoa (died 1831— eleven years before Melville's visit) is mentioned several times by Ellis. See John Williams, *A Narrative of Missionary Enterprises* [London, 1837], pp. 373 ff. The name of his " heir " Tooboi, Melville probably took from Tubuai, an island. Foulque (p. 168) gives *Tapoa*, also mentioned by Ellis, and Raiatea.

153.9. *Kooloo*: Foulque (p. 171) corrects this to Turu, since Tahitian has neither *k* nor *l*.

153.20. " *nuee, nuee, nuee* ": nui, nui, nui, (Foulque, p. 171)

153.27. *sounding brass*: " Though I speak with the tongues of men and of angels, and have not charity, I am become as sounding brass, or a tinkling cymbal." (*I Corinthians*, 13.1) In *The Confidence-Man*, Melville used the whole epistle as a major thematic reference. See Miss Foster's Introduction, pp. lvi ff.

154.19. " *Yar onor, boyoee* "... *how d'ye do*: Ia ora na, boy oé, in the rendition of Foulque (p. 172), who adds the note: " Littéralement: « Que tu vives! » (salut)." Ellis (II, 19): *Ia ora na oe i.*

154.28. *European chapel*: Built by foreign residents at Papeete for their own use. Various visitors mention it.

154.35. *high seat in the synagogue*: " Beware of the scribes which love to go in long clothing, and love salutations in the marketplaces, and the chief seats in the synagogues...." (*Mark*, 12. 38-39)

155.20. *about this time, that the whaling-ships... began to arrive*: Wilson L. Heflin finds eight American ships listed as arriving in port from 5 to 23 October.

155.27. *tobacco...as a solace*: No author has paid more frequent or heartfelt homage to tobacco than Melville. Scarcely a one of his books is without at least a sentence in its honor. See, for examples, *Mardi* (Ch. 121); *Redburn* (Ch. 54); *White-Jacket* (Ch. 91); *Moby-Dick* (Ch. 10-11, 30); " I and My Chimney "; " The Paradise of Bachelors "; *The Confidence-Man* (Ch. 30); " Herba Santa," *Collected Poems* (pp. 236-238). Tobacco is an agent of " lenitive and calm," and the shared smoke is Melville's repeated ritual of sociality. Ahab's pitching overboard his pipe is a major gesture.

156.18. *a word about the canoes*: Captain Cook's estimate is from Ellis (I, 219). Melville read a general account of Tahitian canoes in Ellis (I, 126-139), and perhaps found a hint for his mishap with Captain Bob's sulky (I, 135). Allusions occur in the enormous catalogues of canoes in *Mardi* (Ch. 149) and *White-Jacket* (Ch. 50).

158.11. *MOTOO-OTOO*: Motu uta, " the islet near the shore." (See F. D. Bennett, *Narrative of a Whaling Voyage*, I, 67; Wheeler, pp. 250-251; both parallel Melville's account). Friedrich Gerstäcker, the German translator of *Omoo*, noted it in 1851: " The next day, the 11th of February, I intended to visit the little island of Motuuta, a most beautiful spot in the bay of Papeete, and formerly the summer residence of the Pomares, consequently a sacred spot, not to be profaned by other feet. This also was the reason why H. Melville...was not allowed, by the funny old sentry, to land from his canoe there...." (*Narrative of a Journey Round the World* [New York, 1853], p. 364)

158.19. *Down in these waters*: Similar submarine scenes occur in Ellis (II, 161-162) and Russell (p. 27). See the descrip-

tion of Ruth in *Clarel* (Pt. I, xvi): " But as in haven fringed
with palm,/ Which Indian reefs embay from harm,/ Belulled
as in the vase the wine—/ Red-budded corals in remove,/Peep
coy through quietudes above;/ So through clear olive of the
skin,/ And features finely Hagarene;/ Its way a tell-tale flush
did win...."

159.17. *" dogs of war "*: " Cry ' Havoc,' and let slip the dogs
of war." (*Julius Caesar*, III, 1, 273)

160.9. *Arheetoo*: Arahitu. (Foulque. p. 178)

160.10. *learned Theban*: " I'll talk a word with this same
learned Theban." (*King Lear*, III, iv, 154)

160.11. *whether it was... lawful... Sabbath*: Cf. *Mattew*, 12;
Mark, 2; *Luke*, 6; *John*, 5.

162.13. *other side of the road*: Alludes to the parable of the
Good Samaritan, in which the priest and the Levite " passed by
on the other side." (*Luke*, 10.29-37) Also used in *Clarel* (Pt.
II, ix).

162.29. *Wilson, the father*: The Reverend Charles Wilson
(1770-1857), not one of the first missionaries on the *Duff* (1797),
came in 1801, retired in 1842, the year of Melville's visit. See
Forsythe, p. 15.

164.3. *no less than thirty-six... mere barns*: From Ellis (II,
282-283), but Melville subtracts thirty from the sixty-six Ellis
stated there were by 1818, and makes " mere barns " of what
he described as places that " differed little from common native
houses."

164.16. *Royal Mission Chapel of Papoar*: Rewritten from
Ellis. " Pomare [II] had been... erecting a chapel at Papaoa...
called the Royal Mission Chapel... an astonishing structure. It
is seven hundred and twelve feet in length, and fifty-four wide.
Thirty-six massy cylindrical pillars of the breadfruit tree sustain
the centre of the roof, and two hundred and eighty smaller ones,
of the same material, support the wall-plate along the sides,
and around the circular ends, of the building. The sides or
walls around are composed of planks of the bread-fruit tree,
fixed perpendicularly in square sleepers. The whole, either
smoothed with a carpenter's plane, or polished, according to

the practice of the natives, by rubbing the timber with smooth coral and sand.... The most singular circumstance, however, connected with the interior of the Royal Mission Chapel, is the number of pulpits. There are no fewer than three.... This immense building was opened... on the 11th of May, 1819.... Three distinct sermons, from different texts, were preached at the same time, to three distinct congregations.... The whole number of hearers... was about seven thousand.... I was surprised to see a watercourse five or six feet wide, crossing, in an oblique direction, the floor of the chapel. On inquiry of the people who accompanied our party, they said it was a natural water-course from the mountains to the sea; and that, as they could not divert its channel so as to avoid the building without great additional labour, and constant apprehension of its returning, they had judged it best to make a grating at each side under the wall, and allow it to pass in its accustomed course.... In the rainy season, when the water is constantly flowing through, its effect must be rather singular.... The king, determined in his purpose, levied a requisition for materials and labour on the chiefs and people of Tahiti and Eimeo—by whose combined efforts it was ultimately finished. The Missionaries were far from approving the scale on which Pomare was proceeding.... But the king was not thus to be diverted.... It is probable... he had some desire to emulate the conduct of Solomon in building a temple...." (Ellis, II, 278-282) Melville made some changes: he says there were no walls; he invents the three weeks' construction time; he ignores the " carpenter's planes " in order to make the Biblical allusion " neither hammer nor axe," etc., (I *Kings*, 6. 7); and he has shifted Ellis's label " the most singular circumstance " from the number of pulpits to the flowing brook. Although Ellis remarks that in 1822 the chapel had already begun to decay, Stewart (II, 16) observed in 1829 a section still standing in good repair; members of the Wilkes expedition saw it in 1839; and Lieut. Walpole noted it was " now falling to ruins " in 1845 (II, 119).

165.10. *The present metropolitan church of Tahiti*: This church was described by Wilkes (II, 9) as a " large frame building much like a New England meeting-house," and by Captain Fitzroy (cited by Anderson, p. 242) as " a large wooden structure capable of holding six hundred people, covered by a partly Otaheitan roof, in lieu of one formed completely in their own style." Melville boldly transfers to this church the native interior of the chapel at Huahine described by Ellis a few pages before the account of the Royal Mission Chapel. *blinds, but no sashes... rustic thatch*: "The roof was covered with pandanus leaves, the windows closed with sliding shutters...." (Ellis, II, 265) *Within, its aspect is unique*: "The interior of the roof was remarkable for the neatness of its appearance, and the ingenuity of its structure. The long rafters, formed with slender cocoanut, casuarina, or hibiscus trees, were perfectly straight, and polished at the upper end. The lower extremities were ornamented with finely-woven variegated matting, or curiously braided cord, stained with brilliant red, or black and yellow native colours, ingeniously wound round the polished wood, exhibiting a singularly neat and checkered appearance. The ornament on the rafter terminated in a graceful fringe or bunch of tassels. (II, 265) *floor... of rude planks*: "The floor was boarded with thick, sawn planks, or split trees...." (II, 266, *the pulpit*: "The pulpit, situated a short distance from the northern end, was hexagonal, and supported by six pillars of the beautiful wood of the pua, which resembles in its grain and colour the finest satin-wood. The panels were of rich yellow bread-fruit, and the frame of mero, a fine-grained, dark, chestnut-coloured wood." (II, 265-266) *gallery*: There wasn't one in the Huahine chapel whose interior Melville was working from, but Wilkes (II, 9) noted "a large gallery" in the Papeete church Melville is describing. *Its facings... daubed... without uniformity*: "Uniformity was as deficient in the seats of the chapel as in the houses of the town, each family fitting up their own.... For a considerable extent around the pulpit, the seats were in the form of low boarded pews neatly finished. Behind them appeared a kind of open, or trellis-work, line of pews, which were followed by several rows of benches with backs.... The colour and the kind of wood used in the interior was as diversified as the forms in which it was employed; it was, nevertheless, only when empty that its irregularity and grotesque variety appeared. (Ellis, II, 266).

166.26. *sacrifices... Oro*: To Oro, chief god of the Society Islands, human sacrifices had indeed been offered in pagan days. (Ellis, I, 274 ff.) In *Mardi*, Taji rescues Yillah from this fate. In "The Piazza" (*Piazza Tales*, p. 10) memory of the custom still lingered in Melville's mind: "She shyly started, like some Tahiti girl, secreted for a sacrifice, first catching sight, through palms, of Captain Cook."

166.28. *a bell... struck with a bar of iron*: This image, and the paragraph were suggested by Ellis's long discussion (II, 283 ff.) of the substitutes for bells.

167.14. *Sabbath School... gallery*: See Ellis (II, 302).

168.2. *A MISSIONARY'S SERMON*: For the order of service, Melville kept an eye on Ellis (II, 302). For the sermon itself, he pieced together several missionary attitudes. The allusions to England seem to be from Ellis's catalogue (II, 307 ff.) of topics discussed at Monday conversational meetings: "Their inquiries referred not only to historical, biographical, and other facts connected with the sacred volume, but to those relating to other nations of the earth.... The cities, towns, houses, carriages, dress, and manners of the English, the royal state of King George, the numbers in his army, the evolutions of his troops, the laws of the kingdom, the punishment of crimes, the principles of commerce, and the extent and variety of manufactures, were... brought forward." (II, 317-318) The reference, in sermon and footnote, to Pomare's coach, a gift from Queen Victoria, is a damning anachronism—she did not have it yet at the time of Melville's visit, since it did not arrive in Tahiti until January, 1843, on the *Vindictive*, with Pritchard. Other visitors varied in their impressions of the church services, a number agreeing in general with Melville.

168.8. *Old Hundred... The singers*: Echoed from Ellis (II, 238-239).

168.14. *they sang right joyously*: "Make a joyful noise unto the Lord...." (*Psalms*, 100.1) A few paragraphs above, with the phrase "praises and thanksgivings" Melville had already echoed the fourth verse of this Psalm; "Enter into his gates with thanksgiving and into his courts with praise."

170.1. *kannaka*: Foulque gives the form *kanaka* and adds to Melville's footnote, "Le mot *taàta* s'emploie à Tahiti." (p. 188) Cf. note on 3.2.

170.27. *Great Revival*: No specific source located. See Russell, (p. 276).

171.5. *those very traits*: See Russell (pp. 90, 115).

171.24. *knocked out their teeth*: Mentioned by various writers; see Ellis (I, 311-313). In *Mardi* Melville refers to this custom three times with a similar point. (Ch. 68, 99, 122)

171.27. *Vancouver relates*: Vancouver's only account of such an occasion refers to one which occurred at Tahiti, and the assumption of light-heartedness was not caused by any gifts. (I, 117 ff.)

172.17. *"hevar"... jolly heathen dance*: Heïva. (Foulque, p. 190) Ellis (I, 164) also uses the form *heiva*, noting it was the general name for all their games, though voyagers have restricted it to their dances.

172.20. *Sabbath... "Taboo Day"*: From Ellis (II, 304) and Wilkes (II, 13).

172.32. *KANNAKIPPERS*: Foulque gives the form *tanatipé*, adding the note: "Melville orthographie ce nom ... tel qu'il crut l'entendre...." (p. 191) Melville explains its derivation, 175.13.

173.2. *"maroo boro," or bread-fruit shade*: "Maru *uru*, bread-fruit shade." (Ellis, III, 11) *Maru*: shade; *uru*, a variety of bread-fruit. Foulque (p. 191), maru ùru.

173.17-18. *"Oee tootai owree..., itai maitai"*: Oé tutae uri! Aita maïtaï! (Foulque, p. 192) Cf. note on 176.33; also 128.14. Cf. *Typee*, Ch. 13, *owle*.

173.29. *Farnow*: Foulque makes this *Faanoa* (p. 192) Cf. 269.18.

174.3. *the game of "Now"*: na ó. (Foulque, p. 192)

174.10. *Miss Ideea*: Idia, mother of Pomare I, is mentioned frequently by Ellis (II, 13 ff.) and her name is on his list illustrating the pronunciation of native names. Foulque (p. 192): "Ah! *Aitéa, mitinaré oé*," And she adds. "Mitinaré *ÉNA*."

174.37. *Epistle to a lady*: Pope, *Moral Essay II*: "To a Lady. Of the Characters of Women." "A very heathen in the carnal part, / Yet still a sad, good Christian at her heart." / Melville reversed the order of the lines to make them coincide with the order of the girl's speech and to emphasize his point.

175.8. *spying out the wickedness thereof*: "Wickedness is in the midst thereof.... Wickedness is in their dwellings, and among them." (*Psalms*, 55, 9-15) "...to spy out the land...." (*Numbers*, 13.17)

175.37. *Daniel Wheeler*: The allusion to the whippers-in occurs in an Appendix to the *Memoirs* (pp. 763-764), written not by Daniel Wheeler but by his son Charles. See Anderson (p. 474 n.) for further references.

176.3. "*good easy man*": "... And when he thinks, good easy man...." (*Henry VIII*, III, ii, 356)

176.22. "*love in a cottage*": Years later the image of this couple recurred in *Clarel*, (Pt. IV,xxvi): "... Rich, tumbled, chestnut hood of curls, / Like to a Polynesian girl's, / Who, inland eloping with her lover, / The deacon-magistrates recover—/ With sermon and black bread reprove / Who fed on berries and on love./" The quotation itself stems from "The Clandestine Marriage," by George Colman the younger (1732-1794): "Love and a cottage! Eh, Fanny! Ah, give me indifference and a coach and six!" (I, ii)

176.33. "*Tootai Owree*": From Beechey, cited by Melville below (Ch. 48): "... many of the inhabitants are still tooti-ouris or bad characters, an old expression signifying literally rusty iron, and now indiscriminately used for a dissenter from the Christian religion and a low character." (I, 306) *Tutaé uri.* (Foulque, p. 195)

176.35. *Titus Oates*: Notorious professional anti-Catholic in the reign of Charles II. In *Billy Budd*, Melville described Claggart's chin as having "something of strange protuberant broadness in its make that recalled the prints of the Rev. Dr. Titus Oates, the historic deponent with the clerical drawl in the time of Charles II and the fraud of the alleged Popish Plot."

176.38. *pharisaical prayer-meeting*: "Woe unto you, scribes and Pharisees, hypocrites! for ye devour widows' houses, and for a pretence make long prayer...." (*Matthew*, 23.14)

176.39. "*Boora-Artuas*": From Ellis's account of the first native converts, in 1813: "... A term of reproach from their enemies, the designation of *Bure Atua*, literally, prayers to God...." (II, 92) *Puré Atua.* (Foulque, p. 195)

177.2. *HOW THEY DRESS IN TAHITI*: Melville took all his facts about Tahitian dress, old and new, from the chapter of Ellis right after those from which he had just finished appropriating the two native churches. (II, 287 ff.) In Wilkes (II, 15) he found the charge that European dress discouraged work and encouraged idleness. Ellis says he and his brethren promoted the change not because they found the native costume indecent but to encourage work and discourage idleness.

177.9. *ladies of the mission... teaching them to sew*: No scandalous report, but Ellis's complacent history. (II, 287 ff.)

177.12. *" kihee whihenee"*: Ellis (II, 288) and others describe the *tehei* or *kehei* (Hawaiian) as a mantle worn over the shoulder, rather than a skirt or petticoat. *Whihenee*: *vahine*, woman, (*Typee*, Ch. 1, *whinhenies*; Ch. 33, *whihenee.*) Foulque (p. 196): *tihi vahiné*.

177.20. *horrid hats*: From Ellis (II, 294-297). Melville slyly goes the missionary one better by taking seriously the charge Ellis dismisses, that these new fashions only " minister to the silliest vanity." Wilkes (II, 7) and many others say the hats are horribly unbecoming but do not give the reassurance that the young girls eschew them.

177.34. *men... who aspire to European garments*: Melville dramatizes the antics of " Kooloo " and Captain Bob's bachelor friend from Ellis's passage (II, 291), and follows Ellis's generalization that the native men paid little attention to propriety in wearing European garments and combining them with native garb. "... It was often amusing to see a native *sans culotte*, without waistcoat or shirt, with a maro or pareu round his waist, and a fashionably made black coat on his back. The men are generally above the middle stature, and proportionably stout, so that few of the coats, &c. belonging to the captains or officers of vessels touching at the islands were large enough. If, however, they could by any means thrust their large muscular arms through the sleeves, it was thought to fit very well. Notwithstanding the warmth of the climate, they are fond of wearing the coat buttoned; and although when thus fastened it appeared less repulsive to our opinions of propriety, than when, standing open, it exposed the naked breast of the wearer, it was often quite distressing to see the

imprisoned and pinioned arms occasionally struggling for
liberty, and the perspiration oozing from the pores of the
skin, indicating the laborious confinement of the body it
enclosed." Visitors even after Melville's time regularly comment on similar scenes.

178.31. *original national costume*: In the same context
Ellis describes and praises it (II, 290-291), but finds nothing
about it to blush at and does not object to its gayness. He
describes the natives' old practise of braiding wreaths and
garlands of flowers in their hair, and says it was given up
partly because of its connection with old evil practises and
partly because of the introduction of European caps and
bonnets. (I, 113-114) Melville probably also took a cue from
Wilkes (II, 23), who regrets that the custom "has been
discouraged by their teachers, who have taught them that such
vanities are unbecoming to Christians."

179.1. *sports and pastimes*: Melville found all these
described by Ellis (I, 155-182), who testifies that many were
brutal and few innocent. Nearly all were "intimately blended
with the ancient idolatry." Melville recalled these sports in
Clarel (Pt. III, xvi): "Sports such as might the mound con-
front,/ The funeral mound, by Hellespont,/ Of slain Patroclus.
Linger still / Such games beneath some groves of bloom / In
mid Pacific, where life's thrill / Is primal—pagan; and fauns
deck/ Green theatres for that tattooed Greek / The Polynesian...."

179.11. "*Opio,*": From Ellis (I, 46-47), who tells about an
old community custom "almost entirely discontinued" of baking
large quantities of breadfruit in an immense oven. The product,
not the festivity, was called *opio*. The district ovens, he says,
were not so injurious as the public stills, but were "usually
attended with debauchery and excess, highly injurious to the
health, and debasing to the morals of the people, who frequently relinquished their ordinary employment, and devoted
their nights and days to mere animal existence of the lowest
kind—rioting, feasting, and sleeping, until the *opio* was
consumed."

179.14. *Against tattooing... a severe law*: The code of laws
adopted at Tahiti in 1819 outlawed tattooing because it
belonged "to ancient evil customs." Penalties, varying for the

first and second offense, were specified in numbers of fathoms of road or wall to be built, or for women, in numbers of mats or fathoms of cloth to be woven. (Ellis, III, 142)

179.19. " hevars," or dances: Heïva. (Foulque, p. 198). Cf. note on 172.17.

179.23. effect... lamentable: Cf. Wilkes (II, 14-15), who, however, concedes that " it was indispensable to put down those amusements which were the means or incentives to debauchery." Also Beechey, (I, 307).

179.28. Temple of Tanee: Tane was a principal deity, tutelary idol of Huahine. The large national temple of Tane was near Ellis's house there. (III, 13 ff.) Games were not celebrated in the temples, but the players went there before and after the games.

179.30. TAHITI AS IT IS: Despite his disclaimer, Melville is not objective. He minimizes the good accomplished by the missionaries and confuses their failures with the evils brought by Europeans in general. His bias shows in his triple qualification here [editors' italics]: " Although it may be urged that the labors of the latter have at times been more or less obstructed by unprincipled foreigners...." Most observers stated this as a fact; and many reviewers of Omoo pointed out that on his own testimony Melville and Long Ghost were themselves such foreigners. Melville concludes fairly: "... Although their circumstances, upon the whole, are bettered by the presence of the missionaries, the benefits conferred by the latter become utterly insignificant when confronted with the vast preponderance of evil brought about by other means." But such a judicious conclusion is not the total effect of his discussion.

Whether Melville's unfavorable opinions were right is a complex question. The answer, now as then, depends upon one's assumptions. The cultural relativist would agree with Melville. So would the romantic. The evangelical Christian would and did disagree. So, less sharply, would the simply practical man (such as Wilkes) who assumes that the inroads of Western civilization, for better or worse, on such cultures are inevitable, and who therefore respects the ameliorative value of missionary efforts. (A history of the Polynesian missions is badly needed.)

In 1858 Melville was to feel about the missions he observed in Palestine as he had felt about those in Polynesia. " Might as well attempt to convert bricks into bride-cake as the Orientals into Christians. It is against the will of God that the East should be Christianized...." " The whole thing is half melancholy, half farcical — like all the rest of the world." (*Journal of a Visit to Europe and the Levant...*, edited by Howard C. Horsford [Princeton, 1955], pp. 130, 159)

180.23. *Nearly sixty years*: Somewhat unfair—for from 1797 to 1812 no converts were made, and the nation did not become Christian until after 1817, only twenty-five years before Melville's visit.

180.28. *the earlier laborers*: In accordance with a deliberate policy of selection, of the first band, on the *Duff*, only four were ordained ministers. Among the others were a linen draper, a butcher, a weaver, a hatter, a shopkeeper, a tailor, a cabinet maker, a harness maker, a bricklayer, a carpenter. Russell (p. 110) commented that " An illiterate artisan, if animated with zeal, and not ignorant of the first truths of his religion, is, for breaking up the ground of pagan superstition, an instrument better fitted than the brightest ornament of a university...."

181.5. *Sandwich Islands*: Kamehameha II (reigned 1819-1824) abolished the national idolatry in 1819, before the first missionaries arrived (1820). See Russell (pp. 255-259); Ellis (IV, 30).

182.14. *Russell*: In this chapter and the next, Melville borrowed in several ways from Russell. (His bibliographical citation is correct.) In his first draft he apparently wrote Ch. 49 as a continuation of Ch. 47, using Ellis only; later he seems to have inserted Ch. 48 and the first two paragraphs of Ch. 49, based primarily on Russell, supplemented by Ellis and Wilkes, and fortified by the other quotations. He took up the topics discussed by Russell, often reversing Russell's conclusions but in several respects adopting Russell's views, which were not uncritical of the missionary reports. In this passage he quotes Russell's summary of Turnbull's and Kotzebue's unfavorable remarks: " ... It is not without pain that we advert to less favourable opinions entertained by writers whose sentiments can not fail to have much weight with the public." Melville makes it appear that Russell also refers here to Beechey, although in fact his first quotation from Beechey is not in Russell's book at all and the second appears in another context- (pp. 324-325). Melville found the quotation from Kotzebue and his second quotation from Beechey in Russell, but in each case he went also to the passage in the original volume to take something not quoted by Russell, and to get the full-title for his footnote. From Beechey's own work he also lifted his first quotation. Since he made little further use of Kotzebue and Beechey, two reporters whose views were close to his own, it seems likely that he did not have their works to draw upon while he was writing his first draft, but looked them up later for amplification of what he had found quoted by Russell. It seems significant that Kotzebue's volumes were charged to Lemuel Shaw's membership at the Boston Athenaeum, 3 December 1846, while Melville was paying a short visit to the Shaws (28 November-7 December). [Sealts, #313] The manuscript of *Omoo* had just been " completed " but he was to make revisions on his return to New York.

182.22. *Kotzebue*: Otto von Kotzebue (1787-1846). The quotation except for a brief omission and the substitution of " ignorance " for " bigotry " is accurate, and the citation is correct (" Service " is substituted for " Navy " in the title). Russell paraphrases part of the same passage, and his refutation of Kotzebue's extreme charges may have led Melville to admit that the Russian navigator was "somewhat too severely denouncing the undeniable errors of the missions."

182.32. *Captain Beechey*: Melville's citation is accurate, though his quotation is, as usual, somewhat garbled. Beechey (I, 284-287).

183.2. *Turnbull*: Melville took over the footnote citation accurately from Russell (p. 96). Nothing shows that he used Turnbull's *Voyage*.

183.5. *Daniel Wheeler*: Melville cites the source correctly, but the quotation is from Daniel's son Charles. As Anderson noted (p. 268), the quotation misrepresents the context in which it occurred. Insofar as Charles Wheeler was " bewailing their social condition "—specifically the " predominance of the principle of gain "—he was blaming it upon unprincipled foreigners.

"It is nearly impossible for a visitor, who cannot even speak the language to pronounce with much certainty on a subject of such moment, as the religious state of the community. Certainly appearances are unpromising; and however unwilling to adopt such a conclusion, there is reason to apprehend that Christian principle is a great rarity. Far, however, be it from me to depreciate the labours of those who have been instruments of the change produced in this island. So far from considering the beneficient results of their efforts as unimportant and insignificant, I regard them as of the highest moment, and as fully equal to what could in reason have been anticipated." He listed several good results which Melville chose to ignore. (p. 757)

183.19. *instead of estimating the result*: This paragraph and the next were probably suggested by Russell's discussion (pp. 89 ff., 317 ff.) of the general problem of converting heathen, and by the similar distinction Russell draws between true and nominal conversion. Russell (p. 95) sees that " It is almost inseparable from the duties of an uninspired missionary to exaggerate the amount of his success by contemplating the increased number of his proselytes." He also sees (pp. 90, 318 ff.) that the conversions throughout Polynesia came about through the authority of the chiefs and in the hope of material gain.

184.1. *Even in one or two instances*: This paragraph, including the instance of apostasy told by Williams, is based on Russell (pp. 321-322).

184.5. *Williams*: The Reverend John Williams (1796-1839) was martyred by the natives of Erromanga, in the New Hebrides. Nothing shows that Melville used his *Narrative of Missionary Enterprises* [London, 1837]. Thomas Trood (*Island Reminiscences*, [Sydney, 1912], p. 32) says that Melville's Dr. Long Ghost, whom he ran across in Conception, Chile, in 1856, was one of the companions who got away from the natives when Williams was killed. See note on the doctor, 307.23.

184.14. *a seminary*: From Ellis (III, 199-206). Ellis explains that the South Sea Academy was set up to educate the children of missionaries, but also " native children of piety and talent." With frank distress he writes several pages about the " trials... of bringing up a family in the midst of a heathen population." " So strongly did we feel this in the Sandwich Islands, that the only playground to which our children were allowed access was one strictly interdicted to the natives...." (III, 201) Melville borrows also from Wilkes (II, 57) who visited the academy in 1839 and frowned upon its policy of segregation.

184.32. *Captain Wilson*: Melville plucked this statement from the midst of contradictory evidence in the very frank appendix on the " Natural and Civil State of Otaheite " in *A Missionary Voyage...in the Ship Duff* [London, 1799] p. 332 (not 336). The appendix was written not by " the excellent Captain Wilson " but by " A Committee Appointed for the Purpose by the Directors of the Missionary Society."

184.35. *Vancouver*: Melville's citation is accurate.

185.8. *Captain Beechey*: Accurately paraphrased, not quoted, from Beechey (I, 269). Russell (pp. 324.325) quotes the part of this included in Melville's garbled quotation, but Melville at least consulted Beechey's original passage, for Russell does not name Ellis or his *Polynesian Researches*, referring only to " a distinguished missionary."

185.26. *It has been said*: From Russell (p. 98) who is paraphrasing an unfavorable criticism of the South Sea Missions in the *Edinburgh Review* (LIII, 217): " It is justly remarked, that the first step toward civilizing a people is to form them to habits of industry, and if possible to create in their minds a desire to better their condition."

186.16. *recently from a primitive valley*: Dr. John Coulter had just the opposite reaction when he got to Tahiti (1833) after his similar experience in a primitive valley of the Marquesas (see note on Lem Hardy above, Ch. 7). " In the places I lately came from, there was war, devouring each other, and savage confusion everywhere. Here all was peace—man and nature were in harmony with each other. The power of religion had completely altered the naturally uncontrolled character of the native, and effectually subdued barbarism." (*Adventures in the Pacific*, p. 268) Coulter was much impressed by the missionaries and their works, and found that while Papeete was a wicked place, most natives were "far more decided Christians than the chief part of their civilized visitors." (p. 269)

186.23. *good old Quaker Wheeler*: Again it is Charles, not Daniel, speaking: " There is nothing, perhaps, in the Tahitian habits more striking or pitiable than their aimless, nerveless mode of spending life." (p. 753) Again Melville shuts his eyes to Wheeler's further generalization: " Their outward circumstances, there can be no doubt, have derived material benefit from the introduction of Christianity."

186.25. *Attempts*: Melville based the next three paragraphs on Ellis's pages about the missionaries' attempts to get the natives used to work. He ignored Ellis's report that the failures were not altogether due to their indolence. (II, 209-226) Cultivation of cotton (1819) was given up partly because of low prices. Cultivation and milling of sugar cane were successfully introduced (1818) but were given up because interested white traders frightened Pomare II by malicious reports that English planters were going to seize the islands and make slaves of the natives as they had in the West Indies, and because the chiefs would not stand for making rum, without which making sugar would not pay. The cotton mill from England ran briefly at Papetoi (1824) and again (1829) at Afareaitu (" Afrehitoo "), but failed, mostly because the natives were indolent and impatient, but partly because white traders discouraged it in order to choke off competition. The mill's failure, less sudden than Melville makes it, is mentioned by Wilkes (II, 15, 59), Beechey (I, 291), and others, but none of them says it was "packed off to Sydney." Indeed Coulter (*Adventures in the Pacific*, p. 285) saw what was left (1834) after the natives had made off with all the iron parts they could carry.

187.1. *Bligh*: From Ellis (II, 217).

187.13. *at Honolulu*: His three months at Honolulu (18 May to 17 August 1843) gave Melville a better chance to observe its " civilization " than his four weeks in the Typee valley or his circumscribed six weeks in Tahiti and Imeeo. His remarks about Honolulu are always more bitter. (See *Typee*, Ch. 25. 26) He was probably put on the topic here by Russell's opposite conclusions (p. 105) and his reference to a billiard room at Honolulu, " the best that can be seen in any part of the world," and by the American editor's tart footnote, " We can hardly suppose the reverend author seriously intends to adduce this as an evidence of *real* ' social improvement '." (pp. 336-337)

187.26. *the population of Tahiti*: From here to the end of the chapter Melville borrowed the materials, but not the attitudes largely from Ellis's long discussion of the depopulation

(I, 89-95). He borrowed also, probably for later insertions, from Russell (pp. 337-340) and Wilkes (II, 48-49), who were them-selves indebted to Ellis; and probably from an unidentified source containing his quotations from Ruschenberger and perhaps Cook. More in the debater's than the historian's spirit he appropriated from these writers whatever bolstered his thesis, and skipped over whatever contradicted it. So he seized their statement of the enormous depopulation and their willing assignment of blame to the drunkenness and diseases brought by foreigners. But he ignored their unanimous warning that the early estimates of the population were far too high, and preferred Cook's estimate of 200,000 to Captain Wilson's cal-culation of 16,000 twenty years later (1797) when the first mis-sionaries arrived. (All in Ellis, I, 89.) Likewise he dismissed the large share they blamed on the *alleged* " wars, child murders, and other depopulating causes" of former times, and passed over Ellis's contention that much of the decline came from these causes before the European invasion. To develop his thesis, Melville had to hold that effective evils were " solely of foreign origin." Finally, he rejected Ellis's statement that since 1820 the population had been " rapidly increasing," and of Wilkes that it had been " nearly stationary." He preferred the gloomy poetry in the conclusion of Russell, who forsakes Ellis here, that the natives were doomed to extinction.

In an interesting appendix to an edition of *Omoo* [John Lane, New Pocket Library, London, 1904], titled " Tahiti in 1842: as Melville Saw It...," M. C. Balfour, after praising *Omoo* highly for its " truth," and declaring that Melville paints " pictures few with pen alone have been able to surpass " though "he sacrifices nothing merely to picturesque effect," remarks all the same that Melville " does not perhaps sufficiently account for what Tahiti was, by justly explaining what it had been." Basing his own account mostly on Ellis's pages, with no inkling that Melville had used them at all, Balfour goes on to give a fair explanation of the disrupted social conditions Melville saw, to correct his mis-statements about the population changes, and to assert that " Melville does not do justice to the energy and devotion of the early missionaries, judging them (as he evidently did) by the results, by no means all of their making." (pp. 452-462)

187.34. *U. S. Exploring Expedition*: Wilkes (II, 48-49). Mel-ville's treatment of this passage is a good instance of his highhanded way of using his source-books: " A census recently taken gives for the population of Tahiti nine thousand, and for that of Eimeo one thousand. When this is compared with the estimates of the navigators who first visited these islands, an enormous decrease would appear to have taken place. The first estimates were, however, based on erroneous data, and were unquestionably far too high; yet there is no doubt that the population has fallen off considerably in the interval. The decrease may be ascribed in part to the remains of the old custom of infanticide, in part to the new diseases introduced from abroad, and the evils entailed upon them by foreigners, and in part to the transition now going on from a savage to a civilized life. Whatever may have been the case, during the first years after it was visited by Europeans the population for the last thirty years has been nearly stationary; the births and deaths are now almost in equal numbers." The depopulation of certain districts in the Sandwich Islands is recorded by Wilkes (IV, Ch. 2-7).

187.38. *Ruschenberger*: From the statistics for five districts of Hawaii (1832, 1836) Melville chose those for the largest, with the greatest decrease. W.S.W. Ruschenberger gave totals for the Sandwich Islands: 129,814 in 1832; 108,383 in 1836; a decrease of 21,421, or 6%. He blamed the depopulation on such causes as infanticide and intemperance, and—Melville chose to ignore this—*perhaps* on the effects of civilization, though he found no verifying data. He devoted four chapters to " Sketches in the Sandwich Islands." Melville's accurate quoting of the statistics, without a page reference, and his not using Ruschenberger's *Voyage* elsewhere, suggest that he found the statistics quoted in another source. (II, 364-367)

188.8. *a virulent disease*: Melville exaggerated the incidence of venereal disease. Wheeler, in the passage Melville quoted below, reported hearing that one-fourth of the population was " miserably affected "; the *Duff* missionaries heard the same estimate in 1798. But Wilkes (II, 49) blamed its prevalence on improper medical care, and the surgeon of his expedition " saw less evidence of the disease among them than can be seen among the lower orders of any American city or port." (Quoted from the surgeon's journal, Anderson, p. 281) Nevertheless, Ellis made clear that several diseases of European origin had been as devastating as plagues. (I, 93) In *Typee* (Ch. 26) where his literary purpose was different, Melville was willing to follow Ellis (I, 200 ff.) in blaming the devastation partly on the natives' own ways—the laxity of marriage ties and the "universal licentiousness" spread by the "Arreory Society."

188.16. *Distracted with their sufferings*: Dramatized from Ellis (II, 63-64): "The ravages of diseases originating in licentiousness, or nurtured by the vicious habits of the people, and those first brought among them by European vessels, appeared [1807] to be fast hastening the total desolation of Tahiti. The survivors of such as were carried off by these means, feeling the incipient effects of disease themselves, and beholding their relatives languishing under the maladies of foreign origin, inflicted, as they supposed, by the God of the foreigners, were led to view the missionaries as in some degree the cause of their suffering; and frequently, not only rejected their message, but charged them with being the authors of their misery, by praying against them to their God. When the missionaries spoke to them on the subject of religion, the deformed and diseased were sometimes brought out and ranged before them, as evidences of the efficacy of their prayers, and the destructive power of their God. The feelings of the people on this subject were frequently so strong, and their language so violent, that the missionaries have been obliged to hasten from places where they had intended to have addressed the people. Instead of listening with attention, the natives seemed only irritated by being, as they said, mocked with promises of advantage from a God, by whom, as they imagined, so much suffering had been inflicted." In the pages just before, Ellis had told about similar conditions in 1803, and also about the death of Pomare I, which did not result from venereal infection. (II, 56 ff.)

188.26. *old Wheeler*: Really old Daniel this time, not his son Charles, breaking forth, mostly about the liquor trade. The quotation is accurate, though Melville omits the estimate that one-fourth of the population are affected with venereal disease— since he had enlarged it to "at least two-thirds of the common people." (p. 317)

189.5. *Their prospects are hopeless*: From Russell (pp. 337-339), who could not share Ellis's assurance that the downward trend had been halted: "But amid these tokens of improvement, painful proofs are everywhere making themselves manifest that the natives are doomed to extinction, from the operation of causes more or less connected with the arrival of the white men.... In all parts of the world where Europeans have been permitted to establish colonies, the natives have gradually disappeared, losing at once their name and their inheritance.... There seems to be a certain incompatibility between the tastes of the savage and the pursuits of civilized man, which, by a process more easily marked than explained, leads in the end to the extinction of the former.... In all parts of the globe, indeed, where the exotic takes root, the indigenous plants wither and decay; and we fear that, notwithstanding the favourable symptoms just recorded [by Ellis], Polynesia will not prove an exception." An earlier passage, from Russell's summary of Kotzebue's remarks, provided one clause of Melville's paragraph: " ... They are worse than barbarians, having borrowed from civilization nothing but the vices by which it is dishonoured, and exhibiting in their character a deplorable union of all that is most corrupt and profligate in the two opposite states of society which are thus brought into juxtaposition." (p. 98)

In *Mardi* (Ch. 167) Melville returns poetically to the theme of the Eden-like fascination of the South-Sea islands for Europe, and of the blight Europe breathes on them. Says Babbalanja, "If here, Yillah will not stay our coming, but fly before us through the groves. Whenever a canoe is beached, see you not the palm-trees pine? Not so where never keel yet smote the strand. In mercy let us fly from hence. I know not why, but our breath here must prove a blight." See also *Clarel* (Pt. IV, ix) on the Anglo-Saxons, " Who in the name of Christ and Trade /... Deflower the world's last sylvan glade! "

According to the best authorities of today, the decline in population had already begun before the white invasion. which hastened a decadence already under way in Polynesian societies. It appears that the "native" population of Tahiti, however, has remained stationary at around 8,000 since the first missionary census in 1808. Elsewhere in the Pacific, there was conspicuous decline both before and after the arrival of Europeans, up to about 1890. In the twentieth century the decline has been halted, and in most islands there has been some increase. In Hawaii, the native population declined steadily from an estimated 142,000 in 1823 to 39,000 in 1896, and to 14,000 in 1940. But today the native and part-native population is slowly increasing; the total in 1940 was 65,000.

In Melville's beloved Marquesas, almost alone, did his gloomy
forecast of hopeless extinction come to pass—ironically and,
in his terms, inexplicably, since they were the most vigorous
and independent, and most successful of all in resisting
European inroads. (See Stephen H. Roberts, *Population Problems in the Pacific* [London, 1927], pp. 17-102; the *Pacific
Islands Yearbook*, 1944; and Warren S. Thompson, *Population
and Peace in the Pacific* [Chicago, 1946].)

189.14. *Pomaree II... prediction of Teearmoar*: Melville
wrenches Pomare's speech and " Teearmoar's" prediction from
the midst of Ellis's discussion of the decline in population,
and makes both speakers seem to blame it on European civilization, when actually they were doing precisely the contrary:
" Their priests formerly denounced the destruction of the
nation, as the greatest punishment the gods could inflict, and
the following was one of the predictions: *E tupu te fau, e
toro te farero, e mou te taata*: 'The fau (hibiscus) shall grow,
the *farero* (coral) shall spread or stretch out its branches, but
man shall cease.'... This was denounced as the punishment that
would follow disobedience to the injunctions or requisitions of
the priest, delivered in the name and under the authority of
the gods. Tati, however, remarked to Mr. Davies, that it was
the observing, not the neglecting, of the directions of the priest
that had nearly produced its actual accomplishment. At the time
when the nation renounced idolatry, the population was so
much reduced, that many of the more observant natives thought
the denunciation of the prophet was about to be literally ful-
filled. Tati, the chief of Papara, talking with Mr. Davies on
this subject, in 1815, said, with great emphasis, that ' if God
had not sent his Word at the time he did, wars, infant-murder,
human sacrifices, &c. would have made an end of the small
remnant of the nation.' A similar declaration was pathetically
made by Pomare soon after, when some visitors from England,
I think the deputation from the Missionary Society, waited
upon him at his residence. He addressed them to the following
effect: 'You have come to see us under circumstances very
different from those under which your countrymen formerly
visited our ancestors. They came in the era of men, when the
islands were inhabited, but you are come to behold just the
remnant of the people.' I have often heard the chiefs speak
of themselves as only a small *toea*, remainder, left after the
extermination of Satani, or the evil spirit; comparing them-

selves to a firebrand unconsumed among the mouldering embers of a recent conflagration. These figures, and others equally affecting and impressive, were but too appropriate, as emblems of the actual state to which they were reduced." (I, 90-92)

189.19. *Teearmoar*: From Ellis (III, 86), Melville culled the name of "Tairimoa, one of the priests," and assigned to him the prediction quoted by Ellis, above. Thus Melville made the prediction personal and dramatic, and even claimed to have heard it chanted by aged Tahitians. He changed the spelling to suit himself, as usual. He wanted to substitute the palmtree for the hibiscus, as more emblematic of the islands; so he hunted up *haari*, cocoa-nut tree, elsewhere in Ellis (I, 53). But he was misled by the word-order of the original line, and substituted *haari* for the verb, *tupu*, grow, instead of for the noun, *fau*, hibiscus—so that the first line of his chant has both cocoa-nut and hibiscus but no verb ("shall cocoa-nut the hibiscus")! The spelling *now* for *mow* (Ellis, *mou*) in the third line was possibly a typesetter's error. Pierre Loti's use of *Omoo* is betrayed by his placing Melville's impossible version, with corrected spelling, on the title-page of *Le Mariage de Loti*, as a "Vieux dicton de la Polynésie." Foulque (p. 207) renders the priest's name as Tiamoa, of Paré, but does not notice the curious changes of "harree" for *tupu* or *now* for *mou*, though altering the spellings *fow* to *fau*, *now* to *nau*, *harree* to *haari*.

189.32. *Dr. Johnson paid his last call*: This episode is based on fact, but, contrary to Melville's statement here, both he and John Troy (Doctor Long Ghost) signed the paper "to certify that we have received Medical Assistance and attendance as herein stated." Their signatures, together with those of six of the other revolters, appear on the verso of the bill for medical services to "distressed British Seamen" from April through December 1842, submitted by Johnstone & Myrick to Wilson as British consul. Evidently Dr. Johnstone collected the signatures on a single sheet as the services were performed, then at the year's end (the bill is dated 31 December 1842) made out his itemized bill on the reverse side of that sheet—so that in effect the patients had signed a blank receipt. The itemized charge for services to Melville "from Octr 15 to Nov 19" (though he had left the islands some days before November 19) was $19.50; for John Troy for the same period it was $24.25. Since these charges were for both "Medicines & Medical assistance" the bill may be honest enough despite its discrepancy with Dr. Johnstone's "dose-book" entry of $1.50 for "embrocations" for Melville on 16 and 19 October; but the record pretty much favors Long Ghost's idea that Johnstone had "made money out of the transaction." See earlier note on "Doctor Johnson" (131.31), and Document # 24.

191.2. "*Potata*": *potéhétéhé*. (Foulque, p. 209)

193.17. *WILSON GIVES US THE CUT*: "About three weeks after the *Julia's* sailing" [on 15 October] would be about 5 November, by which date Melville had finished the wanderings about which the rest of *Omoo* tells, and had signed or was about to sign aboard the *Charles and Henry* and to leave the islands. Actually, he must have "escaped" from the Calabooza and departed for Imeeo within a few days after the *Lucy Ann* sailed. As to Wilson's attitude toward the revolters whom he had consigned to the custody of the native authorities to await the arrival of a British warship and the justice it would dispense, Melville's hunch that "he wished to get rid of us altogether but without being suspected of encouraging our escape" may be correct. Not until a month had passed did he address, on 19 November, a letter to the French Provisional Government complaining that the laxity of the local officials had allowed the prisoners to go at large and four of them to escape from the islands. In their reply the French officials expressed their regret at his delay in calling the situation to their attention and promised that the revolters still at hand would be confined without communication until the arrival of a British warship. See Documents # 22, # 23.

193.5. 'Ita! ita! — oee mattee—mattee nuee': *Aïta! Aïta! Oé maté! Maté nui*. (Foulque, p. 211) Stewart (I, 246, 249) gives *mate* as *sick*.

195.22. *Fanning's Island*: "Near Christmas Island, midway between the Society and Sandwich Islands..., now desolate...." (Ellis, I, 106) This island kept an aura of desolation in Melville's mind, associating itself in *Moby-Dick* (Ch. 53, p. 237) with the inhospitable wild of the Pine Barrens in New York, or the equally desolate Salisbury Plain in England—"at the ends of the earth— off lone Fanning's Island, or the far away King's Mills...."

196.10. *we never saw them again*: Melville's really exciting experiences in and around Tahiti were now over, and from here on in writing the book he had to piece out his relatively meagre memories of Imeeo with liberal borrowings from Ellis. So it is too bad he lost another rich episode by deserting his fellow mutineers some weeks before the over-zealous " kannakippers " dragged a resident English merchant, Edward Lucett, into the calaboose, where he fell afoul of the mutineers—and later assailed Melville in print as the " dastardly dog " among them who attacked him with oaths and a sheath-knife. (See Lucett, I, 287-290; 293-297; also Daniel Aaron, " An English Enemy of Melville," *New England Quarterly*, VIII [1935], 561-567; Forsythe, pp. 2-8; Anderson, pp. 232-236; *Log*, I, 156-157.) Lucett was freed the same night with apologies from the kannakippers, who had mistaken him for a sailor or beachcomber violating the eight o'clock curfew law. Early the next morning, however, he ran and complained to Wilson, the Acting-consul, and showed him his bruises. See Document #21.

196.24. *Marling-spike*: Probably the mountain whose peak was pierced by a hole supposed by the natives to have been made by the weapon of a god. Melville exploited this legend in *Mardi* (Ch. 69). (Ellis, I, 256) Foulque (p. 214) notes that the peak is now called " la Dent de Requin "—the Shark's Tooth—which should please Melville.

197.14. *Martair*: Maatea, of which Ellis speaks several times as a valley neighboring his first mission station at Afareaitu. (II, 165 ff., 185) Daniel Wheeler preached to a sleepy congregation there in 1835. (p. 304) Foulque (p. 215), Maatéa.

200.10. *FARMING IN POLYNESIA*: Three later travellers picked up reports about Shorty and Zeke. In October, 1848, Lieut. Wise asked about Melville's acquaintances and wrote in his journal (p. 326) " Shorty still devotes himself to potatoes at Aimeo—this is all the information I was able to gather." In *Los Gringos* (p. 399) he added that Shorty was " strongly suspected of shooting his neighbor's cattle." In February, 1851, Friedrich Gerstäcker visited Martair: " I heard also here of a couple of white men who had lived in the neighborhood, and ' raised potatoes.' And where were they now? Gone to the diggings, of course, and whites no longer existed at Emao." (*Narrative of a Journey Round the World* [New York, 1853], p. 341)

In the spring of 1853, Edward T. Perkins ran into a carpenter at Imeeo who claimed to be the one Melville wrote about at Partoowye, and a Yankee (possibly Zeke, though he did not claim to be) who knew about *Omoo* and remarked, " I don't know what the devil *has* become of Shorty." (pp. 321-323) See note on the carpenter, below (Ch. 76).

200.16. *the Monument*: In Fish Street Hill, London, commemorating the great fire. To Melville, as to most literate Americans of his day, the landmarks of London were familiar before seen. References to the Monument as a kind of symbol of London occur in *Redburn* (Ch. 30), *Israel Potter* (Ch. 26), and Melville's letter to John Murray, 2 September 1846 (Davis, p. 207).

203.2. " *Were you ever in Dumbarton?* ": There is nothing particularly indecorous (though one can see possibilities) in the Scottish folk song with this title collected by William Main Doerflinger from an elderly man in New York City who learned it as a boy in the woods of Ontario. (See Doerflinger, *Shantymen and Shantyboys...* [New York, 1951], p. 307.) Possible analogues are " Highland Laddie," which has the lines " Were you ever in Quebec?... Dundee?... Mobile Bay?... etc." (*ibid.*, p. 51); " Were you ever in Quebec? " (Thomas Wood, *The Oxford Song Book* [London, 1927]); and " Oh, say, was you ever in Rio Grande?" (Joanna C. Colcord, *Songs of American Sailormen* [Revised Edition, New York, 1938]), pp. 85-86. Miss Colcord remarks that " several distinct sets of words " are sung to the tune she gives.

203.27. *'ot enough to melt the nose h'off a brass monkey*: Castrated version of a folk hyperbole still widely current.

204.20. *aramai! (get up)*: *Haere maï!* (Foulque, p. 223) Cf. 148.11, 209.21, 239.1.

205.2. *SOME ACCOUNT OF THE WILD CATTLE IN POLYNESIA*: This curious chapter was developed mostly out of hints culled from Wilkes's account of Hawaii (IV, 99-231). Its origin is betrayed by the digression to the subject of Hawaii, its volcanoes and wild cattle, and by the citation of Wilkes. There are few references to such bullocks in the Society Islands, and possibly the whole bullock-hunting episode is a bubble blown up from Wilkes.

205.5. *Vancouver*: Melville is mistaken. On this third voyage, in 1777, Captain Cook left animals among the Society Islands; but Vancouver, who was there with Cook in 1777, remarked on his only later visit, in 1792, that most of these had " fallen a sacrifice to the ravages of war." The black cattle had been carried to Imeeo, and at that time numbered four cows and one bull, which " has very unfortunately received a hurt in his loins, which renders him an entire cripple." Vancouver feared for their further propagation. (I, 137)

205.14. *a black, misanthropic ram, nibbling the scant herbage of some height inaccessible to man, in preference to the sweet grasses of the valley*: Here, briefly, in passing, Melville associates the contrast of mountain and valley with the contrasting values of misanthropy and domesticity, independence and conformity, individual and herd, darkness and light, difficulty and ease, etc. Later he was to feel deeply the tension between these opposed values, and to develop it at length by using similar symbols—for example, the Enceladus myth, and the general contrast of Isabel and Lucy in *Pierre*. Mr. Bernard Mosher once suggested to the editors that critics interested in myth in Melville's writings should be able to make something out of this whole chapter on wild cattle in Polynesia, for here are assembled materials adumbrating the myth of Profanation. The mountainous inland is sacred, forbidden, dangerous; wrath, mutilation, death, fall on those who violate it. The cattle belong to the Queen, or the King, or the Goddess Pelee; they are *sacred* cattle, slain impiously by alien " hunters " or recusant natives. (Homer and Joyce of course employ this mythology.) In wider reference the invasion of these regions and slaughter of these cattle may suggest the myth underlying *Omoo: the desecration of a culture*. (The attack on Moby Dick is not unrelated.) The narrator's ambiguous attitude, Mr. Mosher hinted to us, is portentous of Melville's whole psychological and spiritual complex — but we leave that for him to elucidate in his own way. (Surely he would cite the " misanthropic hill-scaling goat " of *Pierre*, Ch. XXV, iv, p. 404.)

205.30. *Tonoi abounded in bullock stories... a spice of the marvellous*: Again Melville invents a native narrator to dramatize material from a printed source. In Hawaii, says Wilkes, " Bullock hunting seems to partake somewhat of the chase of wild beasts, and has much of its attraction. Many stories are related of natives having been tossed, gored, and carried on the animal's horns for hours, and from these reports the natives are easily alarmed with the appearance even of a half-tamed animal... Many rencontres, partaking too much of the marvelous to be repeated here, were told me." (IV, 205) It is possible, of course, that Melville too had been told such stories in Hawaii.

206.15. *his success upon Hawaii*: In 1793 Vancouver took from California to the island of Hawaii two ewes and a ram, five cows, and a bull too sick to stand (" I flattered myself the bull would recover."). (II, 99 ff.) From them the wild cattle observed by Wilkes were descended. Tamehameha had tabooed them for the first ten years. Melville's source for this reference was probably Wilkes (IV, 200).

206.18. *Lord Sandwich*: On his third voyage (1777) Cook discovered the Hawaiian group and named it for the 4th Earl of Sandwich, who was First Lord of the Admiralty and sponsor of Cook's second and third voyages. Melville found this information, together with that about the area of Hawaii, the names of the three volcanoes, and the estimated height of 17,000 feet, in Ellis (IV, 9-26).

206.24. *Pelee*: The volcanoes and the goddess Pele are discussed in each of the volumes cited in Melville's footnote; but he borrowed directly only from Wilkes and Ellis. The works referred to are: *Voyage of H.M.S. Blonde to the Sandwich Islands in the Years 1824-1825..., Captain the Right Hon. Lord Byron, Commander* [London, 1826], pp. 174-191; and William Ellis, *A Journal of a Tour Around Hawaii* [Boston, 1825]. In the edition of *Polynesian Researches* that Melville used as his major source in *Omoo*, this work was the fourth volume.

207.9. *Spanish hunters*: Described by Wilkes, also by Olmsted (pp. 233 ff.). Melville may have had another source for the details that follow.

207.26. *Tammahammaha III*: Kamehameha III (reigned 1834-1854). See note on him below (Ch. 65).

209.21. *Aramai! come down*: *Haere mai!* (Foulque, p. 228) Cf. 148.11, 204.20, 224.11, 239.1. Cf. *Mardi*, Ch. 52: *aramai* (" come ashore ").

210.8. *canoe-tree*: Misappropriated from Ellis's account of the native chestnut tree, which the natives used mostly for firewood and not for canoes. "Like other chestnut-trees, the ma-pe is of stately growth and splendid foliage.... From the top of a mountain I have often been able to mark the course of a river from the winding and almost unbroken line of chestnuts, that have towered in majesty above the trees of humbler growth. The ma-pe is branching, but the trunk, which is the most singular part of it, usually rises ten or twelve feet without a branch, after which the arms are large and spreading. During the first seven or eight years of its growth, the stem is tolerably round, but after that period, as it enlarges, instead of continuing cylindrical, it assumes a different shape. In four or five places round the trunk, small projections appear, extending in nearly straight lines from the root to the branches. The centre of the tree seems to remain stationary; while these projections increasing, at length seem like so many planks covered with bark, forming a number of natural buttresses round the tree.... I have observed buttresses, not more than two inches in thickness, projecting four feet from the tree, and forming between each natural recesses, in which I have often taken shelter during a shower.... The wood... being remarkably perishable, is seldom used, excepting for firewood. Occasionally, however, they cut off one of the buttresses, and thus obtain a good natural plank, with which they make the long paddles for their canoes, or axe-handles. The leaf is large and beautiful, six or eight inches in length, oblong in shape, of a dark green colour...." (I, 61-62) Melville confused the ma-pe with the ati or tamanu, of which Ellis says, "It is one of the most valuable kinds of timber, and is used... as the keels for their largest canoes, as it is a kind of wood which the insects never perforate." (I, 39) A private form of humor in which Melville habitually indulged, in using source-books, is illustrated here by his changing Ellis's statement that *he* had often taken shelter behind the buttresses to "there were signs of the wild cattle having sheltered themselves behind them." See his similar concealed jibes at Scoresby in *Moby-Dick* (Howard P. Vincent, *The Trying-Out of Moby-Dick* [Boston, 1949], p. 134).

210.19. *burial-place..., site of a village*: Melville took suggestion or reminder from Ellis (II, 162).

210.32-33: tamaree (*boy*) ... kannaker (*men*) ... pehe kannaka (*fishermen*): *tamaiti* (enfant) ... *taàta* (hommes) ... *péhi taàta* (pêcheurs). (Foulque, p. 229) Cf. *Typee*, Ch. 22: *Tamaree, boy*.

210.38. *Ati..., Hotoo*: Both from Ellis (I, 39).

211.20. *MUSQUITOES..., Nathan Coleman*: The topic was probably suggested by Ellis, who relates that near Maatea (Melville's Martair) in 1817 he was kept awake by the "exceedingly numerous and annoying" mosquitoes, and was forced to leave the house soon after midnight and spend the night sitting on the beach. Tyerman and Bennet were tormented by mosquitoes at Imeeo in 1821, and likewise at Tahiti, though Melville says (Ch. 52) the insects were unknown there. Olmsted (p. 296) was terribly tormented by them at Papeetee, and the *Duff* missionaries report mosquitoes there in 1798 (p. 344). "Captain Nathan Coleman" and his mean deed are apocryphal. No such Coleman is listed in *Vital Records of Nantucket, American Whaling Masters*, or Starbuck's *History of the American Whale Fishery*. Melville may have borrowed the name from Captain Jonathan Coleman in Joseph C. Hart's *Miriam Coffin* [New York, 1834], which he was later to use as a source for *Moby-Dick*. Or he may have been thinking of Captain John B. Coleman, Jr. Some sort of native legend, however, lies behind this piece of lore. In *Typee* (Ch. 29), Melville observes that "Among the numerous afflictions which the Europeans have entailed upon some of the natives of the South Seas, is the accidental introduction among them of that enemy of all repose and ruffler of even tempers—the Mosquito." Lieutenant Walpole says that at Tahiti the natives had a legend that a whaler sent a boat ashore for water and "out of her water-casks came fleas which courted the musquitoes, and so they were married, and lived long and happily ever afterwards." (*Four Years in the Pacific*, II, 89) Wilson L. Heflin has pointed out to us an item in the *Sandwich Islands Gazette*, 3 September 1836. "It is asserted that mosquitos were introduced at Oahu, by a gentleman from New England, who being much attached to his native country, and its peculiarities—could not sleep without the ' bizz, bizz,'... so to regain the lost charms of home, the gentleman imported a pair of mosquitos from 'Yankeechusetts' and—ergo, we have them now in abundant perfection." In any case, Melville saw the mosquitoes as just one more affliction introduced by Europeans.

212.13. *an old war-canoe*: The details of this description are drawn, with some inaccuracy, from Ellis (I, 126 ff.).

213.30. *Fair dawned... the jocund morning*: Possibly an echo of "...jocund day stands tiptoe on the misty mountain tops." (*Romeo and Juliet*, III, v, 9)

218.10. *bearers of burdens*: Cf. " bear ye one another's burdens...." (*Galatians*, 6.2) Also " hewers of wood and drawers of water." (*Joshua*, 9.21, 23, 27)

219.20. *Afrehitoo*: Afareaitu. Ellis had his first missionary station there in 1817 and did the first printing in Tahitian there. (II, 163 ff.) The dilapidated schoolhouse had formerly been occupied by the South Sea Academy, later at Papetoi.

219.37. *eighth commandment*: "Thou shalt not steal." (*Exodus*, 20.15)

224.11. *"Aramai! (come here)*: Haére mai! (Foulque p. 242) Cf. 209.21.

224.20. *Callao to Lima*: About 1 January 1844, Melville with his shipmate Oliver Russ (the "Nord" of *White-Jacket*), while on shore-leave from the *United States* in the harbor of Callao, went to and from Lima over this road. Images scattered throughout his writings mark the lasting impressions of what Melville saw in Peru.

225.31. *beach-de-mer*: Biche-de-mer: sea slugs usually caught on the reefs, below water, by native divers. The prepared article found a ready sale in China as an ingredient for rich soups. Wilkes devotes several pages to the various types and the ways of processing them. (III, 218-222) Melville perhaps got the idea of their sailing a trading schooner from Ellis's discussion, in the pages Melville was following (II, 170-180), of the schooner *Haweis*, built for this purpose by the missionaries.

228.12. *Tamai*: The whole visit to Tamai is certainly fictitious, since the account of the native dance, its chief episode, was written for *Typee* (see note below on the Dance). Melville found the location and description of the village in Ellis (II, 183; also I, 30). But his description mislocates it badly. Foulque (p. 246), *Témaé.*

228.21. *"Ve,"*... *"Arheea"*: From Ellis (I, 61): "The *vi*, or Brazilian plum...is an abundant and excellent fruit, of an oval or oblong shape, and bright yellow colour.... The *ahia*... resembles, in shape, a small oblong apple, is of a bright beautiful red colour, and has a white, juicy, but rather insipid pulp."

229.1. *Taloo*: Ellis (I, 30) describes Taloo Harbour and says Opunohu is its proper name, Cook having taken the native name (Tareu) of a rock near its mouth for the name of the harbour. Foulque (p. 247) gives the form *Talou*, and notes that the bay is now called Opunohu or Papetoai.

229.16. *"Roora"*: From Ellis (II, 291; also I, 147). Ellis calls it *tiputa*; Melville's word "roora" may come from *ruru vehe*, the name Ellis (I, 147) gives for a bale of cloth. Foulque (p. 247), *rura*.

230.32. *Bashaw*: This image, with various others in *Omoo*, reflects Melville's reading in the popular Eastern romances. These were models for his travel romances, especially *Mardi*, which Easternizes Polynesian life.

231.36. "poee": *poé*. (Foulque, p. 250) In *Typee* (Ch. 10 and *passim*) Melville uses the form *poee-poee* and describes it: "This staple article of food among the Marquese islanders is manufactured from the produce of the bread-fruit tree. It somewhat resembles in its plastic nature our bookbinders' paste, is of a yellow colour, and somewhat tart to the taste." Cf. Ellis, I, 45 ff.

232.22. *"karhowries"*: Tarahao ê. (Foulque, p. 251) Cf. note on 125.28, 150.37.

233.11. *"hevar"*: See note on 172.17.

233.13. *Rartoo*: Foulque (p. 251) renders this as Raatu.

233.22. *A DANCE IN THE VALLEY*: Melville wrote on 29 January 1847 to John Murray: "You will perceive that there is a chapter in the book which describes a dance in the valley of Tamai. This discription [*sic*] has been modified & adapted from a certain chapter which it was thought best to exclude from Typee. In their dances the Tahitians much resembled the Marquesans (the two groups of islands are not

far apart) & thus is the discription faithful in both instances."
(Davis, p. 210) No source for the description has been found.

234.8. "tappa herree": *tapa faré.* (Foulque, p. 253)

234.36. *"Ahloo! ahloo!"* Foulque (pp. 253-254) renders this,
each time, as *Aué! Aué!*

235.28. *the Lory-Lory:* Foulque (p. 254) renders this as *òri-
òri.* Ellis (I, 172) says, " Ori is the native word for dance, but
each kind of dance had a distinct name." He describes the
hura as the least objectionable and says many others were
" too indelicate or obscene to be noticed." Cf. note on 233. 22.

236.14. *" hanree perrar! "* (*be off...*): *haére péra.* (Foulque,
p. 255) Cf. 148.11, 204.20, 209.21, 224.11, 239.1. (*hanree* is
possibly a misprint for *harree.*)

239.1. heree! heree! (*make our escape*): *haére! haére.* (Foulque,
p. 258)

239.18. *setting our faces:* Cf. *Luke,* 9.51.

239.29. *Partoowye:* Papetoi. Foulque (p. 258), Papétoaï.

240.30. *At Amboi... a vagabond Welshman:* Melville is
remembering two picturesque passages in Wilkes's account of
the Feejee and Tonga Islands. One concerns a state reception
at Rewa, near Abau: " They are very particular to see that no
one touches the king's cup except the king's cupbearer. On the
present occasion, a worthless Englishman by the name of James
Housman, called Jim or Jimmy, officiated. Few would have
distinguished him from a native, so closely was he assimilated
to them in ideas and feelings, as well as in his crouching before
the chiefs, his mode of sitting, and slovenly walk...." (III,
115) The other passage describes Feejee tonsorial customs:
"The chiefs... pay great attention to the dressing of their heads,
and for this purpose all of them have barbers, whose sole occupation is the care of their masters' heads.... To dress the head
of a chief occupies several hours, and the hair is made to spread
out from the head, on every side, to a distance that is often
eight inches.... In the process of dressing the hair, it is well
anointed with oil, mixed with a carbonaceous black, until it
is completely saturated. The barber then takes the hairpin... and

proceeds to twitch almost every separate hair. This causes it to frizzle and stand erect. The bush of hair is then trimmed smooth, by singeing it, until it has the appearance of an immense wig." (III, 74-76) Melville bestows this job on an old man-of-war's man, along with that of stirring up the fleas with a skewer—an operation not mentioned here by Wilkes though other voyagers are horrified by similar habits. The frizzed-hair image stuck in Melville's mind and he gave the dandies of Pimminee "enormous heads of hair, combed out all round variously dyed, and evened by being singed with a lighted wisp of straw." (*Mardi*, Ch. 128) See also the colored steward in *Redburn* (Ch. 17) who "sported an uncommon head of frizzled hair, just like the large, round brush, used for washing windows, called a *Pope's Head*."

240.33. *morning cup of "arva"*: àva. (Foulque, p. 259) In *Typee* (Ch. 23) Melville describes "*arva*" as a root generally dispersed over the South Seas from which a medicinal and intoxicating beverage is made. His description seems to correspond with Ellis's account of the ti-plant (IV, 201; II, 102 ff.) Cf. note on 263.23; also that on 265.15, and the explanation, 266.32-38.

241.5. *a low rabble of foreigners... about... Tammahammaha*: No one else mentions this crew, and in 1848 Charles E. Hitchcock writing at Honolulu in the *Polynesian* (IV, 174), denied their existence: "The whole of his *genuine* information is about on a par with his assertion that 'the Monarch of the Sandwich Islands has three foreigners about his Court—a negro to beat the drum—a wooden-legged Portuguese to play the fiddle, and Mordecau, a juggler, to amuse his Majesty with cups and balls and slight of hand.' Mr. Melville does very well as a romancer, but tarnishes all by his attempts to ape the historian." Melville, who did not take to the Hawaiian king, remarked in *Typee* (Ch. 26), "His 'gracious majesty' is a fat, lazy, negro-looking blockhead, with as little character as power. He has lost the noble traits of the barbarian, without acquiring the redeeming graces of a civilized being; and although a member of the Hawaiian Temperance Society, is a most inveterate dram-drinker." Note, by the way, the wooden-legged Portuguese who, like Ahab, has "lost his leg by a whale." (See Anderson, pp. 340-342.)

241.20. *auctioneer to his majesty*: Probably Isaac Montgomery for whom Melville contracted to work for one year as book-keeper and general clerk, at Honolulu, (*Log*, I, 167-168.)

241.25. *to leave all and follow him*: " ...Go and sell that thou hast..., and come and follow me." (*Matthew*, 19.21) "... Lo, we have left all, and have followed thee." (*Mark*, 10.28; *Luke*, 18.28)

242.23. *Rizzio*: David Rizzio (1533?-1566), an Italian musician and bass singer, a favorite of Mary Queen of Scots.

245.18. *The doctor... swimming*: Either Melville nods, or the doctor made haste and learned how to swim after his narrow escape from drowning in Ch. 41, where he was " unable."

247.32. *to a degree... altogether superfluous*: An innuendo that her sexual services were offered, the guests being regarded as tayos. Such " superfluous" hospitality was regularly offered to distinguished guests, from Wallis and Cook on down. That Wilkes's companion, Captain Hudson, was greatly badgered thereby at Amboi, was related in the pages from which Melville borrowed the king's cupbearer.

247.36. *hospitality to an amazing extent*: From Ellis (I, 85): "Their hospitality has, ever since their discovery, been proverbial, and cannot be exceeded. It is practised alike by all ranks, and is regulated only by the means of the individual by whom it is exercised. A poor man feels himself called upon, when a friend from a distance visits his dwelling, to provide an entertainment for him, though he should thereby expend every article of food he possessed; and he would generally divide his fish or his bread-fruit with any one, even a stranger, who should be in need, or who should ask him for it.... For every such entertainment, the individual expects to be reimbursed in kind, whenever he may visit the abode of his guest."

247.37. *Waiurar*: Wai-ura, on Ellis's map. Foulque (p. 267), Vaïrao.

248.25. *marrying into a family*: From Wilkes (IV, 257): " In the opinion of a native, the most distant relationship or connexion, justifies him in calling on and receiving entertainment. They not only consider that they have a right to partake of the hospitality but speak of it as a great convenience; so that in choosing a wife or husband, one who has many relations is a more desirable match on this account than one who has few." This idea is dramatized in an episode in *Mardi* (Ch. 128). A servant turns the wayworn travellers from the door and Babbalanja remarks, "... These varlets take after their masters; who feed none but the well-fed, and house none but the well-housed."

248.5. *"ah, ena maitai"* (*this one will do...*): Ah! éna maïtaï! (Foulque, p. 267). Cf. note on 128.14. Cf. *Typee*, Ch. 34: *ena: here*.

248.13. *" karhowrees"*: taraho ê. (Foulque, p. 267) Cf. note on 125.28.

248.30. *Darby and Joan*: Humorous literary tag for a devoted old rustic couple. See *Mardi* (Ch. 23): " This husband and wife were no Darby and Joan. Their married life was one long campaign, whereof the truces were only by night."

249.19. *Loohooloo*: Foulque (p. 268) renders this as Lou-houlou, but adds a note: " L'orthographe phonétique, parfois fantaisiste de Melville, ne permet pas de situer avec exactitude ce hameau. Mais, d'après la description et l'itinéraire de l'auteur, il s'agit probablement de l'une des deux baies voisines: Vaïanahé (Tétoatoa) ou Haapiti (Hataùaù), sur la côte occidentale."

249.24. *The names of these three damsels*: The names are lifted directly out of Ellis (III, 28); the damsels probably out of imagination. See note below on Ereemear Po-Po, 269.18.

249.37. *"Keekee (Zeke) maitai... nuee nuee hanna hanna portarto"*: Tété maïtaï... nui nui haà haà putete. (Foulque, p. 269) Cf. note on 115.36; also 153.20.

250.17. *they ushered us to dinner*: Melville took the cuisine directly from Ellis's description (II, 159) of the first native meal he ever sat down to. But, finding the fare of that meal too meagre, Melville, whose heart always was warmed by a groaning board, drew from Ellis's catalogue elsewhere (I, 38 ff.) of the native food. " This was the first native meal I had sat down to, and it was served up in true Tahitian style. When the food was ready, we were requested to seat ourselves on the dry grass that covered the floor of the house. A number of the broad leaves of the purau, *hibiscus tileaceus*, having the stalks plucked off close to the leaf, were then spread on the ground, in two or three successive layers, with the downy or under side upwards, and two or three were handed by a servant to each individual, instead of a plate. By the side of these vegetable plates a small cocoanut-shell of salt-water was placed for each person. Quantities of fine large bread-fruit, roasted on hot stones, were now peeled and brought in, and a number of fish that had been wrapped in plantain leaves, and broiled on the embers, were placed beside them. A bread-fruit and a fish was handed to each individual, and, having implored a blessing, we began to eat, dipping every mouthful of bread-fruit, or fish into the small vessel of salt-water,—without which, to the natives, it would have been unsavoury and tasteless. I opened the leaves, and found the fish nicely broiled; and, imitating the practice of those around me, dipped several of the first pieces I took into the dish by my side; but there was a bitterness in the sea-water which rendered it rather unpalatable; I therefore dispensed with the further use of it, and finished my meal with the bread-fruit and fish." Foulque (pp. 270-272) gives the native names as follows: for " pooroo," *purau*; for " poee," *poé*; for " Indian turnip," *taro*; for " avees," pommes-Cythère; for " Pehee Lee Lees," (small fish), *péhi iti iti*; for "Lownee," *lownee* (with note " Il s'agit... du *Miti Hué* "). *Typee*, Ch. 28: *pehee*: fish.

250.20. *ferns—called " nahee "*: Nahe. Ellis (I, 52).

251.37. *" Yar onor boyoee"*: Foulque (p. 271), *Ia ora na boy oé*. Cf. note on 154.19.

253.11. *nicknames*: Melville profited from Beechey's comment: " It is very desirable to secure a favourable impression by liberality on your first arrival at this island; it being a constant custom with the natives to mark those who have any peculiarity of person or manner by a nickname, by which alone the person will be known as long as any recollection of his visit may remain." (I, 273, 278) Beechey instances an English captain dubbed " Tapane Matapo "—Captain Blind-Eye, and a few pages later refers to the Queen's first husband " who in consequence of his marriage was allowed to bear the royal name of Pomarree, to which, however, in allusion to his figure, and in conformity with their usual custom, they had added the appropriate but not very elegant surname of 'Aboo-rai,' or big-belly." Foulque (p. 272) gives *Mata Poé* for "Atee Poee."

253.21. *George IV*: King of England 1820-1830; as Prince Regent known as the "First Gentleman of Europe." In the sketch "Poor Man's Pudding and Rich Man's Crumbs" Melville alludes to him ironically.

253.23. "*Pomaree*": Ellis tells how the father of Otu (Pomare I) got the name: "He was travelling, with a number of his followers, in a mountainous part of Tahiti, where it was necessary to spend the night in a temporary encampment. The chief's tent was pitched in an exposed situation; a heavy dew fell among the mountains; he took cold, and the next morning was affected with a cough; this led some of his companions to designate the preceding night by the appellation of *po-mare*, night of cough, from *po*, night, and *mare*, cough. The chief was pleased with the sound of the words thus associated, adopted them as his name, and was ever afterwards called Po-ma-re." (II, 59) Melville as usual twists this to adorn his tale, fastening the epithet on the king rather than the night, and translating *po-mare*, for ridiculous effect, as "one talking through his nose."

254.2. *THE COCOA-PALM*: Melville re-wrote Ellis's six pages on the same subject (I, 53-59) introducing a few items from other passages of Ellis. See Anderson (pp. 145-147), who quotes the passage from Ellis *in extenso* because it offers "a most instructive example of how Melville almost habitually leaned upon his authorities even in matters with which he certainly must have had a first-hand acquaintance."

254.21. *overgrown with... guava-bush*: Melville's observations on native neglect of the trees were suggested by Ellis (II, 159) and Wilkes (II, 50).

255.5. *Tree of Life*: "...To him that overcometh will I give to eat of the tree of life, which is in the midst of the paradise of God." (*Revelation,* 2. 7)

255.36. *Oro*: Actually, Oro, the principal deity, was "a rude, uncarved log of aito wood, *casuarina equisatifolia*, about six feet long," not a cocoa-nut log. (Ellis, I, 273; II, 121) The tree revered as a deity on one of the Tonga Islands is mentioned by Wilkes.

259.1. *Often we went fishing*: Rather spectacularly, Melville is again dramatizing the facts of Ellis (I, 115-124): "... the smoothness and transparency of the sea within the reefs was favorable to aquatic sports; and a chief and his men, furnished with their spears, &c. often set out on their fishing excursions with an exhilaration of spirits equal to that with which a European nobleman pursues the adventures of the chase.... Next to the net the spear was most frequently used.... Since their intercourse with foreigners, the best spears have been made with iron, barbed only on one side.... I have often, when passing across the bay, stopped to gaze on a group of fishermen, standing on a coral reef, or rock, amid the roar of the billows, and the dashing surf and foam, that broke in magnificent splendour around them.... These and a variety of other methods of fishing are pursued by day-light; but many fish are taken by night; sometimes the fishery is carried on by moon-light, occasionally in the dark, but fishing by torch-light is the most picturesque. The torches are bunches of dried reeds firmly tied together. Sometimes they pursue their nocturnal sport on the reef, and hunt the *totara* or hedgehog fish. Large parties often go out to the reef; and it is a beautiful sight to behold a long line of rocks illuminated by the flaring torches. These the fishermen hold in one hand, and stand with poised spear in the other, ready to strike as soon as the fish appears.... Few scenes present a more striking and singular effect than a band of natives walking along the shallow parts of the rocky sides of a river, elevating a torch with one hand, and a spear in the other; while the glare of their torches is thrown upon the overhanging boughs, and reflected from the agitated surface of the stream. Their own bronze-coloured and lightly clothed forms, partially illuminated, standing like figures in relief; while the whole scene appears in bright contrast with the dark and almost midnight gloom that envelops every other object." A vignette on the title-page of Ellis's first volume illustrates this scene.

260.1. *a Tahitian swing*: Probably suggested by a picture in Wilkes (II, 8). A native boy is " swinging with a single rope from a tall cocoa-nut tree " which leans far out over the water. Ellis (I, 181) also describes the sport. George Washington Peck, the hostile reviewer of *Omoo* for the *American Whig Review* (July, 1847) took this as one passage at which to direct his sarcasm. Refusing to believe that "those poor savage maids could possibly have been... half so attractive" as Melville reported, he declared, "*Omoo* may titillate the appetites of many of his readers by describing how he swung in a basket for hours at Tahiti with 'some particular friends of his', but he touches us not a jot.... The next stout boatsteerer that came along, with a rusty nail or a shred of an old bandana handkerchief, would disturb, we fear, our domestic felicity—knock us out of the basket, and go to swinging himself." (VI, 43)

262.11. "*Aheharar*,"... *sunset*: "Sun-setting—Ahiaha." (Ellis, I, 81) *Ahià-Râ*. (Foulque, p. 281)

262.27. *the reef-belt still accompanied us*: Melville re-wrote the next four paragraphs from Ellis's description of coral reefs (I, 32-33). Ellis also describes the "little islets... clothed with shrubs and verdure, and adorned with a number of lofty cocoanut trees" inside the reefs; they "appear like emerald gems in the ocean...," and their tall cocoa-nut trees serve to guide the native mariner "to the spot where he knows he shall find a passage to the shore."

263.2. *twenty-four round about... Tahiti*: From Wilkes (II, 4).

263.15. *Pomaree II... selected one*: From Ellis, who refers to a "favourite retreat" of Pomare II on two reef-islands "a few miles south of Papetoai [Partoowye]." (I, 29) This is reminiscent of the island to which Taji retires with Yillah. (*Mardi*, Ch. 62)

263.23. *A DEALER IN THE CONTRABAND*: Another fictitious episode, suggested by Ellis's mention of distillation (II, 102-103) and dramatized around his description of a native still. "By the Sandwich islanders... the natives had been taught to distil ardent spirits from the saccharine *ti* root.... Whole districts frequently united, to erect what might be termed a public still. It was a rude, unsightly machine, yet it answered but too well the purpose for which it was made. It generally consisted of a large fragment of rock, hollowed in a rough manner, and fixed firmly upon a solid pile of stones, leaving a space underneath for a fire-place. The but-end of a tree was then hollowed out, and placed upon the rough stone boiler for a cap. The baked *ti* root, *Dracanae terminalis*, macerated in water, and already in a state of fermentation, was then put into the hollow stone, and covered with the unwieldy cap. The fire was kindled underneath; a hole was made in the wooden cap of the still, into which a long, small bamboo-cane, placed in a trough of cold water, was inserted at one end, and when the process of distillation was commenced, the spirit flowed from the other into a calabash, cocoanut shell, or other vessel placed underneath to receive it.... Travellers among the natives experienced greater inconvenience from these district stills than from any other cause.... Sometimes in a deserted still-house might be seen the fragments of the rude boiler, and the other appendages of the still, scattered in confusion on the ground...." A line drawing shows the still in operation with all the parts itemized by Melville, including a "crotched stick" not mentioned in Ellis's text. But Melville left the condenser out of Varvy's outfit!

263.25. *Varvy*: Melville probably borrowed his name from Vahaivi, one of the principal followers of Mahine, the King of Huahine, who is mentioned several times by Ellis.

263.32. "*Aoa*": Varvy's tree likewise grew in the pages of Ellis (I, 41). Melville used Ellis's same account of the aoa more fully for Donjalolo's retreat in *Mardi* (Ch. 74).

265.15. "*Ah, karhowree sabbee lee-lee, ena arva tee maitai!*": *Ah! Tarahao ê sabbee iti iti, ena àva te maitaï!* (Foulque, p. 284) For "arva tee" (Foulque: *ava tî*), cf. note on 240.33, also 99.8.

266.18. "*Ah, karhowree, ena hannahanna arva tee!*": *Ah! Tarahao ê, éna hana-hana ava tî!* (Foulque, p. 285) Cf. note on 265.15.

266.27. "*Tootai Owrees*": *Tutae Auri* (Foulque, p. 286). But cf. note on 176.33 for Melville's source; also note on 173. 17-18.

267.19. *a voice from the tombs*: Cf. *Mark*, 5: Watts, Hymn 63. In *Pierre* (III, i, p. 54) there is reference to "... a voice that seems to come from under your great-grandfather's tomb." And in *Clarel* (Pt. I, xxviii), "A call... strange in hollowed tone/ As 'twere a voice from out the tomb."

267.25. *automaton chessplayer*: Edgar Allan Poe, in his essay, " Maelzel's Chess-Player," traces the history of the chess-player invented by Baron Kempelen in 1769 and afterwards exhibited in various cities of Europe and the United States. See *Complete Works of Edgar Allan Poe*, ed. James A. Harrison [New York, 1902], XIV, 6-37. Melville alludes to it again in *Israel Potter* (Ch. 19 *Continued*).

268.9. *OUR RECEPTION IN PARTOOWYE*: There are two interesting facts about the chapters dealing with Partoowye (Papetoi): they are based on Ellis's account of a different set-tlement, at Fa-re, on another island, some twenty years before Melville's visit; and they curiously reduplicate topics that had come up as Melville had written about Captain Bob's neigh-borhood (Ch. 31 ff.). (Melville was to use the same pages of Ellis in writing his description of Media's isle of Odo, in *Mardi*, Ch. 63.) The picture of Ereemear's old-style native household is idealized from Ellis's paragraphs about the bestial huts at Fa-re.

" When we landed at Fa-re in Huahine, I do not think there were more than ten or twelve houses in the whole district. Four, besides those we occupied, were of considerable size, belonging to the chiefs; the others were mere huts. In the latter, the inmates took their food, and rested on their mats spread upon the floor, which, had it been simply of earth, would have been comparatively clean and comfortable. The temporary roof of thatch was often pervious to the rays of the sun, and the drops of the frequently descending shower. In these cabins, parents, children, dogs, and frequently pigs and fowls, passed the night, and the greater part of the day. The houses of the chiefs were better built, and more capacious. The roofs generally impervious, and the sides frequently enclosed with straight white poles of the hibiscus-tree. Their interior, however, was but little adapted to promote domestic comfort. The earthen floor was usually covered with long grass. This, by being repeatedly trodden under foot, became dry, broken, and filled with dust, furnishing also a resort for vermin, which generally swarmed the floors in such numbers, as to become intolerable. In these houses the people took their meals, sitting in circles on the grass-spread floor. Here the fresh water used in washing their hands, the cocoanut-water, which was their frequent beverage, and the sea-water in which they dipped their food, was often spilt. Moisture induced decay: and although over these parts of the floor they often spread a little fresh grass, yet many places in the native houses frequently resembled a stable, or a stable-yard, more than a suitable dwelling-place for human beings.

"In the drier parts of the house, along each side, the inmates slept at night. However large the building might be, there were no partitions or screens. Some of their houses were two hundred feet long; and on the floor hundreds have at times lain down promiscuously to sleep. They slept on mats manufactured with palmleaves spread on the ground. These mats were generally rolled up like a sailor's hammock in the morning, and spread out at night. The chief and his wife usually slept at one end of the house, without the least partition between them and the other inmates of their dwelling. Instead of a single mat, three or four, or even ten, were sometimes spread one upon the other, to give elevation and softness; and this, with the finer texture of the mats, was the only difference between the bed of the chief, and that on which the meanest of his dependents slept. Instead of being spread on the floor, the mats were sometimes spread on a low bedstead, raised nine or twelve inches above the floor. The sides and bottom of this bedstead were made with the boards of the breadfruit tree. Next to the chiefs, the members of his own family spread their mats on the floor, and then the friends and attendants—the females nearest the chief, the men towards the opposite end of the building.... There was no division or screen between the sleeping-places, but the whole ranged along in parallel lines from one end of the house to the other. What the state of morals must necessarily have been among such a community it is unnecessary to show; yet such were the modes of life that prevailed among many, even after they had renounced idolatry." (II, 251-253)

269.10. *"Aramai! aramai, karhowree!"*: Haéré maï! Haéré maï! Tarahao ê! (Foulque, p. 288)

269.18. *Eereemear Po-Po*: His name and all the others, along with those of the native damsels Melville has just left, come straight out of Ellis's discussion of baptism and native names: "...Every blasphemous, idolatrous, or impure name...we recommended should be discontinued.... A few of the adults chose foreign, and in general scriptural names.... Formerly, all names were descriptive of some event or quality—as Fanauao, day-born, Fanaupo, night-born, Mataara, wakeful or bright-eyed,

Matamoe, sleepful or heavy-eyed, Paari, wise, or Matauore, fearless, &c. A number of terms were now introduced as Adamu Adam, Noa Noah, Davida David, Ieremia Jeremiah, Hezekia Hezekiah, Iacoba James, Ioane John, Petero Peter, &c...." (III, 27-28) In *A Missionary Voyage... in the Ship DUFF,* " Dr. Gilham's tayo, named Popo," is mentioned (p. 341—Melville earlier cites pp. 342). Foulque (pp. 269, 289), has slightly different renditions of the names.

270.12. *the only daughter of Po-Po*: Melville is writing literarily rather than historically: as always in song, romance, and travelling-salesman jokes, Loo is the " only daughter," but two pages later her twin sisters appear!

271.3. *Arfretee, Po-Po's wife:* Foulque gives us Afaïti, Pô-Pô, Lou, Moni, for the family names. (pp. 288 ff.)

271.19. *" Olee manee"*: From Ellis: " 'Oli mani,' a corruption of the English words 'old man,' is the common term for any thing old; hence, a blunt, broken knife, and a threadbare or ragged dress, are called 'oli mani.' A captain of a ship at anchor in one of the harbours was once inquiring of a native something about his wife, who was sitting by. The man readily answered his question, and concluded by saying, 'Oli mani hoi,' she is 'also an old man '." (II, 19) The *Duff* missionaries noted the same locution. (*Missionary Voyage,* p. 348) Foulque (p. 290) gives *oré mané.*

271.27. *like... bridegrooms*: " ... the sun, which is as a bridegroom coming out of his chamber...." (*Psalms,* 19. 4-5) See *Moby-Dick*: " ... fresh and all aglow: as bridegrooms new-leaped from out the daintiest Holland." (Ch. 98, p. 425)

271.29. *lamps*: From Ellis (II, 189; 268).

272.33. *a pillar of the church*: Originally from *Revelation,* 3.12.

273.16. *bed*: A family sleeping scene touched off by that of Ellis, quoted above. The dandy's " sailor's hammock " is perhaps from Ellis's " sleeping mats... rolled up like a sailor's hammock."

274.7. *The house itself... vermin*: From Ellis (II, 251-252), pieced out.

274.28. *every time, like Queen Elizabeth, in a different robe*: Olmsted (p. 286) reports Queen Pomare's similar habit, but with no allusion to Elizabeth. See *Pierre* (Bk. I, iv, p. 13): " the country, like any Queen... sometimes... changes her dress twenty-four times in the twenty-four hours...."

275.10. "*Ah! mickonaree tata maitai!*": *Ah! Mitinaré taàta maïtai!* (Foulque, p. 294)

275.24. *A RAMBLE THROUGH THE SETTLEMENT*: Melville pieced out his hazy memory of the village with details from Ellis's village of Fa-re. The passage (II, 253-265) is too long to be quoted entire here. Its topics run: horrid native huts; the missionaries urge chiefs to build frame and plaster cottages; they go to work; construction of the houses; problem of windows and doors; natives move into half-finished houses; Captain Gambier's surprise at seeing the semi-European village; its general appearance; buildings of coral blocks; irregular placement of houses; chief's houses on piers; construction of a chapel.

275.33. *description of the village*: " We sometimes advised them to build their houses and form their public roads in straight lines.... They could perceive nothing... advantageous in a straight road, or regularity in the site, and uniformity in the size or shape, of their habitations.... The public road, from six to twelve feet wide, which led through the district, extending in a line parallel with the coast, presented all its curvatures. Some of the natives built their houses facing the sea; others, turning their fronts towards the mountain, reared them within five or six feet of the road; while several, of a more retiring disposition, built in the centre of their plantations, or under the embowering shade of a grove of bread-fruit trees, enclosing them within the fence that surrounded their dwelling." (Ellis, II, 263-264)

276.15. *solitary pane of glass*: " ...Some of the windows glazed." (Ellis, II, 262)

276.16. *rude... door..., wooden hinges*: " ... They constructed their doors by fastening together three upright boards, about six feet long, by means of three narrow pieces... fastened by... strong wooden pegs.... Only a few... were able to procure iron hinges.... Many... set to work to make wooden hinges. They were generally large, and when attached to a light thin door, looked remarkably clumsy...." (Ellis, II, 257-258)

276.18. *in the original style... mean and filthy*: A concession to Ellis's native huts (II, 252).

276.31. *appearance of the natives*: Confirmed by Wilkes (II, 58).

276.37. *a block of houses... thrown up by a veritable Yankee*: It is impossible not to suspect that Melville adapted these two-story frame houses from Ellis's frame and plaster cottages, some of which were of two stories. " We were amused at the state in which we found the houses occupied by their proprietors. Some appeared with only the walls on the outside plastered, others with both sides plastered; some having their doors and window-shutters fixed, others with a low fence only across the door-way; some with grass spread over the whole floor, while others had a portion boarded sufficiently large to contain their sleeping-mats at night." (II, 258) We fear Melville laughed in his sleeve and made a Yankee carpenter out of poor Ellis. Consider the parallel to the missionary: "... a sober, steady, man," who sold the chiefs the idea of forsaking their "paltry huts of bamboo," and embarking upon the construction of magnificent palaces of boards— just as Ellis did at Fa-re.

278.1. *the queen's residence*: From Ellis's description of the chief's houses at Fa-re: " Those who were frequently upon the waters, and enjoyed the gentle sea-breezes, or wished to excel their neighbors, built a massy pier or causeway in the sea, and, raising it four or five feet above high-water mark, covered it with smooth flat stones, and then erected their houses upon the spot.... The labour required... prevented any but chiefs from building in such stuations." (Ellis, II, 263-264) The bamboo picket is mentioned a few sentences later.

280.13. *Lullee... Tahar*: Foulque's forms are *Louli, Tahaa*. (p. 299)

280.18. *a law prohibiting... the marriage of a native with a foreigner*: Wilkes (II, 57) and Wheeler (p. 567) refer to this law, but in less specific terms. The French translation of the Code of 1842 indicates that earlier regulation had been supplanted by a law absolutely prohibiting marriage between foreigners and the women of Tahiti: " Que dans aucun cas les étrangers ne soient unis en mariage aux femmes de Tahiti—telle est actuellement la véritable loi." (*Livre des Lois Pour La Conduite du Gouvernement de Pomare-Vahine* [Papeete, 1842] pp. 24-25)

280.38. *disconsolate Willie*: Perkins says he met this carpenter at Imeeo in 1853, having a convivial revelry with a down-East Yankee and three native girls, one of them his hard-won little Lullee (" minus the left visual organ " and ten years the worse for wear). The man knew he had been mentioned in Melville's book—" I don't thank Mr. Omoo for saying I was up to my——knees in New-Zealand pine-shavings, making a work-box; nor insinuating that that scamp of a Long Ghost offered to do my courting for me." The Yankee may have been Zeke; he didn't know " what the devil *has* become of Shorty." His suspecting Perkins might be Herman Melville " come to spy us out " throws doubt on that possibility, however. (pp. 321-323) See Anderson (pp. 305-309) and *Log*, (I, 474-475).

281.4. *harbor of Taloo*: Melville refreshed his memory of this harbor by reading Ellis's description (I, 30), and perhaps those of Wilkes (II, 56) and Stewart (II, 22-23).

281.27. *the good ship* Leviathan: The *Charles and Henry*, of Nantucket. See notes below.

283.27. " *Sailing down... On the coast of* Barbaree ": " High Barbaree " was one of the most popular traditional sea songs. It is recorded in various versions. See Colcord, *Songs of American Sailormen*, pp. 152-153.

284.31. *Smollett*: The three volumes were apparently parts of *Peregrine Pickle* and *Ferdinand Count Fathom*. " Amelia " is probably Emilia Gauntlet, Peregrine's beloved. *Omoo* owes some of its picaresque qualities to the general tradition of Le Sage and Smollett, but direct influence crops out more obviously in *White-Jacket*, where Melville uses Smollett-like names, borrows heavily from *Roderick Random* for Cadwallader Cuticle (Ch. 61-63), mentions Ferdinand as " suckled at a puncheon," and praises *Peregrine Pickle* as a book the mere sight of whose title will drive off the spleen of a sour-tempered man. (Ch. 8, 12) In *Redburn* (Ch. 29) Melville alludes to the "exaggerated sailors of Smollett."

286.18. *MRS. BELL*: One of Melville's real encounters. In 1847 Walpole noted that Mr. Bell, a young Englishman, had a large sugar manufactory. (*Four Years in the Pacific*, II, 156-157) In 1848 Lieut. Wise found that "Charming Mrs. Bell had taken to hard drink, *before* Mr. Melville's rencontre, and may have been slightly elevated on that occasion." (p. 399) Finally, in 1853 Perkins learned that she had been drowned in the Navigator Islands. (p. 323) See Anderson (pp. 303-304, 307-308).

288.9. *increase, and multiply*: "Be fruitful and multiply." (*Genesis*, 1.22). See also *Typee* (Ch. 26).

288.12. *TALOO CHAPEL*: More from Ellis and Stewart. "The coral rock is also more durable than the plaster; and although soft, and easily hewn when first taken out of the sea, it afterwards assumes a degree of hardness which resists the weather for a long series of years. A chapel has been built with this material in the island of Eimeo, and will probably last longer than any other yet erected." (Ellis, II, 262) "In the island of Eimeo... a neat and substantial chapel has been built with white hewn coral." (II, 283) "The chapel is very superior, and more substantial than any other building yet erected in the South Seas, being of hewn coral, not dissimilar in its appearance to a light free-stone or marble. It is an octagon, sixty or seventy feet in diameter, well plastered and whitewashed within, and furnished with convenient seats constructed of the timber of the bread-fruit tree. The gallery, and a handsome pulpit, are of the same material." (Stewart, II, 23) Melville was not describing it from accurate memory, for he is wrong in placing it on a pier, as Lucett's lithograph of it demonstrates. (II, frontispiece)

288.21. *before the flood*: Genesis, 6-8.

288.24. *famed St. Paul's*: Old St. Paul's Cathedral, dating from the 11th century, was destroyed by the great fire of 1666, and was replaced by the present cathedral, designed by Wren. Melville's allusions to St. Paul's are frequent.

288.32. *On Sundays, we always went to worship here*: Without red-handed borrowings, these scenes of Sunday and weekday services betray the use of Ellis, particularly in the association of topics. It looks as if Melville, having used up the native huts (II, 251-253) for Po-Po's menage, and the new houses (II, 254 ff.) for the village and the Queen's residence, now takes up Ellis's allusion to the Eimeo coral chapel (II, 262). Encountering Ellis's description of the Huahine chapel (II, 265) which he had already plundered for his Church-of-the-Cocoanuts, he sends Po-Po and family off to church. He reduplicates from his earlier church scene the palm pillars, youngsters in the gallery, and a queer old native—perhaps from his real memory of a single service. He leafs along past the material he had already used in his first church sequence: the Royal Mission Chapel (II, 278-282); small native chapels (II, 282); various substitutes for bells (II, 283-286); personal adornment and dress (II, 286-299); Sabbath and taboo-day (II, 299-301); church services (II, 301-307). Next he comes to Ellis's account of week-day assemblies (II, 307-321) and the topics discussed at them. From these he had built up his travesty of a full-scale missionary sermon. Now he takes Po-Po to such a service and lets him sound forth. Perhaps Melville also looked at the third chapter of the next volume (III, 46-74) where such services are again described by Ellis, and an election of deacons is reported.

290.5. *court-room*: Various visitors described similar court scenes. (Wilkes, II, 50; Beechey, I, 294.) Melville as usual plays up the comic aspects. He probably took his hint from Ellis's discussion of legal customs and the new Code of Laws. (III, 133 ff.)

291.33. *no swearing of witnesses... no regular jury*: Ellis says there were no oaths (III, 150), but there was a six-man jury "excepting in minor offenses, quarrels, &c." (III, 144)

292.17. *penalties*: Melville was looking with amusement at the Code adopted at Huahine in 1822, which differed only a little from that of Tahiti. (Ellis, III, 133 ff.) It laid down laws about such matters as murder, theft, damage done by dogs or hogs, lost property, buying and selling, disregard of Sabbath, stirring up war, bigamy, marital desertion, adultery, divorce, marriage, false accusations, unnatural crimes, seduction, rape, fornication, drunkenness, conspiracy, unauthorized climbing for food, taxes, tattooing, voyaging in large companies, appointment of judges and magistrates, judges, juries, marooned or runaway seamen, harbor regulations. It affixed specific penalties to each crime, but did not list them alphabetically—that is Melville's humorous flourish. Its most severe penalty was banishment; it specified others, as Melville says, in terms of roadbuilding or matmaking and cloth-pounding.

293.5. *Pomaree and her family*: Melville took the Pomare family history from Ellis, making errors or deliberately changing it to show the career of Pomare II less favorably to the missionary cause. The following summary indicates the information he found in Ellis and the changes he made. (Later historians differ from Ellis, as noted after this summary.) " Pomare [II] originally called Otoo, was the son of Pomare and Idia: the father was sovereign of the larger peninsula when it was first visited by Cook, and was then called Otoo; subsequently, being aided by the mutineers of the Bounty, he became king of the whole island, and adopted the name of Pomare, which at his death was assumed by his son, and has since been the hereditary name of the reigning family." (III, 188; also II, 57) Pomare II (c. 1774-1821) became "king" at birth, in accordance with Tahitian custom. (III, 79) He had grave faults but was always friendly to the missionaries. (III, 193) He waged his wars (1802) for political not religious motives (not moved as Melville says by " his zeal for the new faith "), and during them he was faithful to Oro. Because of defeat and exile (1808-1812) he lost faith in Oro and opened his heart to Christianity. (II, 72) In 1811 he welcomed the return to Eimeo of the missionaries, whom his civil wars had driven out of the islands, and announced his acceptance of Christianity. According to Ellis, he undertook to convert his people (1812-1815) peacefully and did not seek the battle of Narii (1815), but was forced into it by his pagan enemies while he and his 800 " followers " (not " warriors ") were at Sabbath worship. In the fierce battle " several [*sic*] were killed on both sides." Unexpectedly victorious, Pomare amazed and converted his foes by sparing them and restoring their possessions. (II, 113 ff.) Ellis records his death in 1821, the brief reign (1824-1827) of his infant son Pomare III, and the accession (1827) of his sixteen-year-old daughter Aimata as Pomare IV. (Pomare IV reigned until her death in 1877, though restricted by French control after 1843. Her son and successor, Pomare V, reigned only until 1880, when he abdicated under French pressure, and died in 1891, bringing the dynasty to a close. His wife survived until 1934.)

Later historians have shown the Pomare dynasty in a different perspective than Ellis afforded Melville. In pre-European days, they tell us, no single chief had supreme authority over the whole island, which was divided into a few main districts in turn subdivided into numerous lesser districts, with corresponding great chiefs and lesser chiefs, allied or separated by complicated clan relationships. From the first, Europeans automatically saw Tahiti as a European monarchy and thought it must have a monarch. This mistake, and a geographical accident, gave rise to the Pomare dynasty. When Wallis discovered the island in 1767, the Teva clan, belonging to the Southern districts, had been dominant for over a century, and Wallis supposed that " Oberea " (Purea), its most powerful chiefess, was " Queen." By the time of Cook's first visit (1769), Purea's attempts to extend her domination had brought about her defeat by other chiefs, among them Tu (later Pomare I). Tu was actually chief only over the districts bordering Matavai Bay, which happened to be the best anchorage for European ships, but on all three visits (1769, 1773, 1777) Cook honored him as " King " of all Tahiti, thus unwittingly encouraging his ambitions and uniting other neglected chiefs to destroy him. In 1789 Bligh looked on him as a monarch beset by rebellious subjects, and the Bounty's muskets rescued him from a hopeless position and set him up in domination over almost the whole of Tahiti and Eimeo. From this time on, the Europeans, including the missionaries, consistently supported him and then his son, Pomare II, in their fluctuating efforts to exterminate rival ("rebel") chiefs. It was as much the muskets as the new faith supplied by the missionaries that converted Pomare II and enabled him in 1815 to defeat his rivals and establish his supremacy over the islands. This version of Tahitian history stems from the Memoirs of Arii Taimai, edited by Henry Adams [Paris, 1901]. It is accepted by Robert W. Williamson in Social and Political Systems of Central Polynesia [Cambridge, 1924], I, 170-249; and Bolton G. Corney in Quest and Occupation of Tahiti, II, [London, 1915], xxiv ff. John La Farge, Adams's companion on his voyage to Tahiti, records some of Arii Taimai's legends and also mentions Melville's Typee and Omoo several times as contributing to his own romantic view of the South Seas. (Reminiscences of the South Seas [New York, 1916], pp. 288-387)

293.6. " Otoo ": Tu. Melville follows Ellis who followed Cook's original error, that by which O, the verb " it is," was

mistaken as part of the Polynesian nouns, as in Otaheite for
Tahiti, and Otoo for Tu. Cf. Ellis's explanation, I, 21.

293.29. *Her majesty*: She was titled Pomare IV, but Melville is following Stewart who calls her " Pomare Vahine I...,
or the female Pomare I. of Tahiti." (II, 14) As to her age, Melville's sources varied by a year or two, all making it from
thirty-two to thirty-five years in 1846. Teuira Henry, *Ancient
Hawaii* (Berenice P. Bishop Museum Bulletin 48 [1928], p. 249)
gives her birthdate as 28 February 1813. In Stewart (II, 14) and
Ellis (III, 197), Melville learned of her first marriage to a young
chief, of Huahine not Imeoo. In Stewart he found a report
(1829) of her low morals, and misread a mention of the excom-
munication of her mother and aunt, to refer to herself. Here
he also read about her bodyguard and her love of royal pomp.
(II, 36, 43) In Wilkes he read a blow-by-blow account of her
husband's assault on her (7 May 1840) and evidently thought it
happened while an American man-of-war attached to Wilkes's
expedition was in the harbor. (IV, 272) He probably saw some
other report, since he has details not from Wilkes. Sir Edward
Belcher reported the episode in *Narrative of a Voyage Round
the World... 1836-1842* [London, 1843], II, 5 ff.; the *Edinburgh
Review*, LXXIX [1844], 33, summarized his report. Although
Melville need scarcely have gone beyond Wilkes (II, 17-20)
for the rivalry between the queen and the chiefs around Poofi
(Paofai), he had probably read about it in his sources for Ch.
32. In Wilkes (II, 4) he saw that the laundry business of visiting
ships was "among the prerogatives of the queen and chiefs."
See Anderson, pp. 312 ff.

294.19. *uneasy headdress*: " Uneasy lies the head that wears
a crown." (*Henry* IV, Pt, ii, III, i, 31)

294.34. *a Tartar*: Melville found the shrewish wife a funny
subject, at least in his early works. See his account in *Mardi*
(Ch. 23-35) of Samoa and his wife Annatoo, whom Melville
calls " a Tartar, a regular Calmuc," and compares to Antonina
of Belisarius. See also in *Mardi*: " Spiders, vixens, and tigers
all war with a relish; and on every side are heard the howls of
hyenas, the throttlings of mastiffs, the din of belligerent beetles,
the buzzing warfare of the insect battalions, and the shrill cry
of lady Tartars rending their lords.... Come on then, plague,
war, famine, and viragos! " (Ch. 138) And: " But if the sea

was King Bello's bride, an Adriatic Tartar he wedded; who, in her mad gales of passions, often boxed about his canoes, and led his navies a very boisterous life indeed." (Ch. 149) Again, Babbalanja suggests that "Without imagination... an armless man, born blind, could not be made to believe, that he had a head of hair, since he could neither see it, nor feel it, nor has hair any feeling of itself "; and Mohi retorts, " Methinks, though... if the cripple had a Tartar for a wife, he would not remain sceptical long." (Ch. 151)

294.36. "*Pomaree-Tanee*": *Tane* is the regular Tahitian word for *husband*, and so the name was not as ignominious as Melville makes it out. It corresponds to Pomare *Vahine* and signifies *king-consort*. Melville may have taken this item from Olmsted (p. 282), who also translates the name as " Pomare's man." Certainly Melville humorously violates the language by calling him " Tanee."

295.2. *cara-sposa*: "Dear wife," a colloquial Italian epithet similar to the French *chère amie*. In Ch. 67 above, Melville uses the same epithet in English—"dear spouse."

296.17. *possessed with a thousand devils*: Cf. *Mark*, 5.

296.22. *Jezebel*: Wife of Ahab, King of Israel. Archetypal wicked, unruly female. (I Kings, 16-21) In *Typee* (Ch. 25) Melville calls Kaahumanu, the gigantic dowager queen of Hawaii a " monstrous Jezebel "—in a rage she snapped a man's backbone across her knee. Some captains, he says in *White-Jacket* (Ch. 24), " regard the genius of the Cape as a willful, capricious jade, that must be courted and coaxed into complaisance.... They woo the Jezebel...."

296.29. *Poofai*: Paofai. See Wilkes (II, 11, 50). Melville probably read of his death in newspaper accounts.

297.4. *King John*: King of England (1199-1216) whom the Barons forced to sign the Magna Carta at Runnymede, 15 June 1215.

297.10. *the regal office... lost... dignity*: Later historians, cited above, tell us that on the contrary the "regal office" was the creation of Europeans, not least the missionaries. But it is true that the missionaries soon limited the " king's " powers, by promoting the adoption of a constitution. And the conversion to Christianity of course did destroy the ancient religious sanctions hedging all the great chiefs, including this monarch. Melville took these from Ellis (III, 78 ff.): " ... Their persons were regarded as scarcely less sacred than the personifications of their deities.... The ground on which they even accidentally trod became sacred; and the dwelling under which they might enter must for ever after be vacated by its proprietors.... The sovereign and his consort always appeared in public on men's shoulders.... A number of attendants ran by the side of the bearers..., and when the men who carried the royal personages grew weary, they were relieved by others.... It is said that Pomare II once remarked that he thought himself a greater man than King George, who only rode a horse, while he rode on a man." In *Mardi* (Ch. 55) Melville weaves in this custom; the natives throw down the house walls for the King and Taji.

297.14. *bye-blow*: A relationship to which Melville refers often. In *White-Jacket* (Ch. 4) he explains Jack Chase's noble qualities by saying, " Jack must have been a by-blow of some British Admiral of the Blue." The same thought occurred to him when he described Billy Budd's background.

297.14. *Tararroa*: Taaroa was the father of the gods, Oro his first son. (Ellis, I, 249)

298.11. *Marbonna*: Melville read about the Tahitian custom of carrying royal youngsters, in the same passage by Ellis from which he had just drawn Otoo's remark about riding on a man. Probably, therefore, Marbonna was invented according to this hint, to take the job. Foulque (p. 317) gives his name as *Mahona*.

298.29. *Tior*: Taioa. In *Typee* (Ch. 4) Melville described this glen, modelling his account directly on Stewart s and recounting a picturesque meeting between the French admiral and an old chief, likewise suggested by Stewart's scene. (I, 254, 297) Wilson L. Heflin, however, warns us that Melville may indeed have witnessed such a meeting there. (Cf. Anderson, pp. 79 ff.)

300.6. *a European... marrying into the Pomaree family*: Probably Alexander Salmon, an Englishman, who married the Queen's niece, 28 May 1842. She was Arii Taimai, whose memoirs Henry Adams edited. (See note, above, on Queen Pomare.)

301.21. *Hogarth... Rake*: William Hogarth (1697-1764). Melville had more likely seen his series of engravings, *The Rake's Progress*, recently in America, than in Pomare's apartment. Melville often put into the manuscripts he was working on some sort of predated references to books that were currently interesting him. He was evidently fond of Hogarth: "I will sell my Shakespeare, and even sacrifice my old quarto Hogarth, before I will part with [the old Picture of Liverpool]." (*Redburn*, Ch. 30) "Among all the wondrous prints of Hogarth...." (*White-Jacket*, Ch. 90) He criticizes Hogarth's "Perseus Descending" in *Moby-Dick* (Ch. 55, p. 262).

301.28. *aramai kow kow*: *Haére maï ai ai.* (Foulque, p. 320) Cf. note on 119.2, also 204.20.

301.32. *the queen entered*: Melville's description corresponds with that of other visitors.

302.21. *behind the tappa arras*: An echo of Polonius's going "behind the arras." (*Hamlet*, III, iv) See also Falstaff "fast asleep behind the arras." (*Henry IV, Pt. i*, II, iv)

303.3. *the Leviathan*: Melville jumped his first whaler the *Acushnet*, after 18 months, and refused duty on his second the *Lucy Ann*, after one and a half months. On his third whaler his experience, reflected here and presumably in the opening chapters of *Mardi*, was a happier one. This ship, on which he left the Society Islands for his last whaling cruise, has been identified by Wilson L. Heflin as the *Charles and Henry*, of Nantucket, commanded by Captain John B. Coleman, Jr., and belonging to Charles and Henry Coffin. Melville probably signed aboard between 2 and 7 November 1842. The *Charles and Henry* was reported at Imeeo, in November 1842, with only 350 barrels of sperm oil—"a luckless ship in the fishery," as Melville reports the *Leviathan* was. On 7 November she was reported at Tahiti. After a cruise of six months, she touched at Lahaina, Island of Maui, in the Sandwich group, and discharged Melville about 3 May 1843. In two weeks Melville got passage to Oahu, where he lived at Honolulu for three months, from about 18 May to 17 August 1843. Here he signed aboard the U.S. Frigate *United States*. See Wilson L. Heflin, "Melville's Third Whaler," *Modern Language Notes*, LXIV [1949], 241-245.

303.4. *the captain*: The captain of the *Charles and Henry* was John Brown Coleman, Jr. According to information supplied by Wilson L. Heflin from his forthcoming study of Melville's whaling years, Captain Coleman was born 12 November 1800 at Halifax, Nova Scotia, the son of John Brown and Elizabeth Coffin Coleman, members of a Quaker colony which left Nantucket and went to Nova Scotia in 1786. He was considered an American citizen, however, and was serving in American whalers by 1825. Shortly before Mr. Heflin's identification of Melville's third whaler (see note above), Jay Leyda found among the miscellaneous documents in the whaling collection of M. M. Armstrong, of Mystic, Connecticut, a letter from Captain Coleman to Charles and Henry Coffin, owners of his ship, dated from Imeeo, 2 November 1842, reporting in forthright whaleman's English upon the unsatisfactory progress of the voyage. The likelihood, suspected by Leyda, that Melville was the boatsteerer whom Coleman expected to ship the next day, was enormously increased by Heflin's positive identification of the ship. In any case the letter reveals how much Melville's account of the *Leviathan's* cruise is like the actual cruise of the *Charles and Henry*. (*Log*, I, 155; Davis, p. 47)

This captain, Coleman, is the only one Melville has a good word for among the fictional representatives of his actual commanders.

303.39. *what countrymen*: Probably an echo of Shakespearean diction, in a similar situation: "I had a sister/Whom the blind waves and surges have devour'd./Of charity, what kin are you to me? What countryman? What name? What parentage?" (*Twelfth Night*, V, i, 238) The question also occurs twice in *The Taming of the Shrew*. Melville uses the phrase again in *Clarel* (Pt. I, xli).

304.9. *Sydney gentry*: The population of Sydney, of course, had a large element of convict origin. See Melville's explanation of Ticket-of-Leave men, above, Ch. 23. In "The Town Ho's Story" Melville declares of the Erie Canallers, "scarce any race of mankind, except Sydney men, are so much distrusted by our whaling captains." (*Moby-Dick*, Ch. 54, p. 249)

305.31. *of little faith*: "O ye of little faith." (*Matthew*, 6.30; 8.26; 14.31; 16.8; *Luke*, 12.28)

28*

307.23. *the doctor... I have never seen or heard of him since*:
"John B. Troy" is still little more than a ghost. His trail before
he became steward of the *Lucy Ann* has not been struck, but
a few tracks after his farewell to Melville have been scented.
In 1848 Lieut. Wise heard that "The Ghost is supposed to
be in Sydney or gold digging in California—diversity of opinion about his present residence." (*Los Gringos*, p. 399; Cf. his
Ms. "Journal" entry, *Log*, I, 281) In 1853 the carpenter's
native wife could remember "Long Ghost, who lived upon
Mr. Bell's plantation," and it was reported that "Long Ghost
led a free-and-easy life for some time, and afterwards took his
departure." (Perkins, p. 323) Meanwhile, Melville had heard
from him, so George Duyckinck wrote to a friend in September,
1850, "Do you remember 'Long Ghost' in one of his books?
He had a letter from him the other day dated from California—that mesh net of humanity." (*Log*, I, 395) In 1852,
E. H. Lamont sailed from San Francisco in his clipper brig
Chatham. "Some time previous to this concerted voyage, I
had met in San Francisco a gentleman who professed an
intimate knowledge of the islands. Dr. R——(I need not give
the name by which he was introduced to me) proposed to par-
ticipate in our expedition; and, from his presumed knowledge
of the island trade, I most gladly availed myself of his services."
(E. H. Lamont, *Wild Life among the Pacific Islanders* [London,
1867], p. 1) Years later Capt. H. B. Sterndale of New Zealand
declared that Lamont's "Dr. Rouke was none other than the
Dr. Long Ghost immortalized by Herman Melville in his story
'Omoo'." (Wellington *Monthly Review*, II, [1890]) Certainly
Dr. R——'s appearance and his behavior on the *Chatham's*
voyage would fit Long Ghost. "An educated and really intelligent man" he was, says Lamont, by turns amiable, quarrelsome,
dictatorial, "brave as a lion," amorous. He knocked down
the cabin boy and when the Captain interposed, "the Doctor
replied he ...would strike any man on board, from the captain
to the cook, and was insolent to him." He entertained "schemes
for rapidly amassing great fortunes." At Manke he resolved to
settle, turn sugar planter, raise tobacco, coffee, cotton, indigo,
and all the spices of the East. When the brig was wrecked on
the Penrhyn Islands in January, 1853, he assumed authority
amongts the sailors, "his personal strength and intelligence
both being beyond the ordinary range." When the natives
threatened to sacrifice him, he "seemed more annoyed and
angry than frightened.... Stretching out his long bony hand

over to me, he said, ' I think we may bid farewell to each
other, Lamont; we are selected first to be cooked. '' Later he
took charge of the house they built. " His temper, not the
most amiable at best, was soured by what he had now to endure; being a man incapable of philosophically putting up
with trifling inconveniences. The food, the uncomfortable
lodging, and the habits of the natives so irritated him, that
it was far from pleasant to be much in his company. '' Later,
" suddenly to the surprise of those who had been acquainted
with his amorous character in the other islands, he issued a
ukase to the effect that whoever harboured a regard for the
nut-brown maids of Te Pitaka would fall under his displeasure and forfeit his esteem. I was, like the rest, astonished
at the doctor's conduct, believing that he entertained tender
feelings towards the fair Tokarora, then in the bloom of
youthfull womanhood. I learned, however, afterwards, that he
had made proposals (how honourable I don't know) to the
young lady, by whom they were scornfully rejected, and that
this was the cause of his becoming suddenly a misogynist. ''
At last, one morning Lamont was awakened by the natives
crying, " The boat is gone, the Long Man is gone! '' Dr.
Rouke, the Captain, and two more had made off for Chile
with the boat, leaving behind Lamont, who never saw him
again.

A final witness, however, places Long Ghost in Chile.
"John C. Williams... is the son of the celebrated Missionary
John Williams, who was murdered with Mr. Harris at Er-
romanga, their companions escaping. One of them a surgeon,
whose name appears fictitiously as ' Dr. Long Ghost ' in one
of Herman Melville's island novels, I saw at Conception,
Chile, in 1856, where he had married and settled." (Thomas
Trood, *Island Reminiscences* [Sydney, 1912], p. 32) Here Long
Ghost's trail disappears. Mr. J. W. Earnshaw, of Sydney, who
has long tracked him, and who discovered the allusions by
Sterndale, Lamont, and Trood, has attempted inconclusively
to identify him with W. C. Cunningham who accompanied
Williams at Erromanga and who was left as Vice Consul in
charge at Tahiti in February, 1841, when Pritchard went to
England. This last circumstance argues against the identifica-
tion. See Earnshaw's researches as presented by Jean Simon,
" Recherches australiennes sur Hermann Melville," *Revue
Anglo-Americaine*, XIII [1935], 114-129. Mr. Earnshaw has also
generously placed unpublished materials at our disposal.

307.31. *all before us was the wide Pacific*: Appropriately, Melville takes leave of the island Paradise, though voluntarily, with an echo of Adam and Eve's leaving Eden: "The world was all before them, where to choose/Their place of rest...." (*Paradise Lost*, XII, 646) See also *Mardi* (Ch. 9), "The Watery World is All Before Them." Although in *Omoo* Melville contrasts corrupted Tahiti with the "unspoiled valley" of the Typees, his later allusions to Tahiti habitually evoke the emotional associations of its pristine state, as Eden. "For as this appalling ocean surrounds the verdant land, so in the soul of man there lies one insular Tahiti, full of peace and joy, but encompassed by all the horrors of the half known life. God keep thee! Push not off from that isle, thou canst never return!" (*Moby-Dick*, Ch. 58, p. 274) "She shyly started, like some Tahiti girl, secreted for a sacrifice, first catching sight, through palms, of Captain Cook." ("The Piazza," *Piazza Tales*, p. 10) "...But to me/ That vine-wreathed urn of Ver, in sea/ Of halcyons, where no tides do flow/ Or ebb, but waves bide peacefully/ At brim, by beach where palm-trees grow/ That sheltered Omai's olive race —/ Tahiti should have been the place/ For Christ in advent." (*Clarel*, Pt. IV, xviii; see also *Journal of a Visit to Europe and the Levant*, edited by Howard C. Horsford, p. 263) In retrospect he seems to have included Tahiti with the Typee valley, as in his nostalgic poem "To Ned" [Toby]: "...glenned isles that be/ Authentic Edens in a Pagan sea." And finally, in *Billy Budd*, he wrote: "And this sailor way of taking clerical discourse is not wholly unlike the way in which the primer of Christianity full of transcendent miracles was received long ago on tropic isles by any superior *savage* so called—a Tahitian say of Captain Cook's time or shortly after that time. Out of natural courtesy he received but did not appropriate."

TEXTUAL NOTES.

Omoo offers no textual complexities because Melville never revised it. He sent John Murray proof-sheets of the first American edition (New York: Harper & Brothers, 1847) as the basis of the first English edition (London: John Murray, 1847), with no changes of his own that can be identified. In Murray's edition numerous changes were made in spelling and punctuation to suit English usage; a few minor errors were corrected, and a few crept in. The present text follows that of the first American edition, emending only typographical errors and obvious misspellings of Occidental proper names. These emendations are listed below. The numbers represent page and line numbers in the text of the book. The first number stands for the page, the second for the line. Readings of the American edition are labelled A; those of the English edition, B; those of the present edition are given first.

Emendations

2.14.   B observer.] A observer
17.6.   Mendaña] AB Mendanna
18.4.   B missing.] A missing
22.18. B flask] A flash
38.3.   B jokes.] A jokes
49.30. B oldest seaman] A oldest seamen
62.26. Moerenhout] AB Merenhout
65.17. Bougainville] AB De Bourgainville (also 66.3)
66.3.   La Pérouse] A Le Perouse B La Perouse
67.16. Dupetit-Thouars] A Du Petit Thouras] B Du Petit Thouars

81.14.   B practicable.] A practicable
121.9.   Caret] AB Caset
121.32.   Dupetit-] AB Du Petit
121.35.   Moerenhout] AB Merenhout (also 122.16)
122.9.   Dupetit-Thouars' frigate] AB Du Petit Thouar's frigate
122.15.   Carpègne] AB Carpegne (also 122.19)
122.25.   B. Philippe] A Phillippe
124.7.   Lefèvre] AB Lefevre
124.31.   Dupetit-Thouars] AB Du Petit Thouars
182.32.   Beechey: AB Beechy
183.34.   Beechey] AB Beechy
185.9.   Beechey] AB Beechy
185.19.   B habits."] A habits.
185.32.   Beechy's: AB Beechy's
189.14.   Tyerman] AB Tyreman
191.19.   B propounded;] A propounded
206.37.   Wilkes'] A Wilke's] B Wilkie's
256.20.   B to lift] A to lifts
260.10.   B by the hour.] A by the hour
284.31.   B Smollett's] A Smollet's
295.28.   B It's infamous] A Its infamous

Listed below are a number of variations between the first American edition and the first English edition. These do not include the wholesale changes made in the English edition to suit British spelling and punctuation. In all the cases listed below the reading of the American edition is adopted in the present text.

Variations

3.6.   A [no date] B New York, January 28. 1847.
9.27.   A you!] you?
11.8.   A bottom.] B bottom?
24.7.   A King] B king
31.20.   A hands of a tattooer] B hands of the tatooer
32.25.   A by the gentlemen] B by gentlemen
36.14.   A there is doubt] B there is no doubt
58.9.   A sail streamed] B sails streamed
59.19.   A flying-jib-boom] B flying-gib-boom
64.2.   A twigs!] B twigs.
65.25.   A divine rights] B divine rites
70.17.   A frequently enter] B frequently entered